A TANGLED LEGACY

Legacy, Book One

Mickie B. Ashling

A NineStar Press Publication

Published by NineStar Press
P.O. Box 91792,
Albuquerque, New Mexico, 87199 USA.
www.ninestarpress.com

A Tangled Legacy

Printed in the USA
First Edition
August, 2018

Print ISBN: 978-1-949340-46-4

Also available in eBook, ISBN: 978-1-949340-36-5

Warning: This book contains sexually explicit content, which may only be suitable for mature readers.

Prince Colin of Sendorra would have been the spare instead of the heir if fate hadn't intervened. Like his father and forefathers, Colin is expected to marry and father a child or his principality reverts to Spain at the time of his death. Filling the royal nursery with healthy babies seems easy enough until Princess Charlotte—his childhood friend and intended bride—breaks off their engagement.

Nobel Prize winner—and powerful gray witch—Alain de Gris isn't looking for love. Science and research have taken center stage for years until he walks into a club and lays eyes on Colin, thirteen years his junior.

Bisexual by nature, Colin seeks to avoid another engagement repeat by shying away from a same-sex relationship. There are no acceptable alternatives to provide legitimate offspring if he follows his heart.

But Colin can't stay away from Alain and the witch finds him irresistible. Ignoring the absolutes isn't easy when a legacy is in jeopardy. And while magic may offer a solution, it could also create more problems.

Table of Contents

Prologue

IT STARTED WITH a mild headache and rapidly progressed to blinding pain. The attending physician, on standby for days in anticipation of any eventuality, wrapped Errol's arm with the blood pressure cuff and frowned in alarm. A shot of medication did nothing to bring down the numbers. Hypertensive disorder had plagued this pregnancy from the start. The ambulance was dispatched a phone call later.

Sebastian let out a bloodcurdling scream while Errol's eyes rolled back and he seized. It lasted about a minute, and when it was over, the spark of recognition in his striking green eyes had disappeared. Another seizure struck as they were loading him onto the gurney, and the interminable ride to the hospital turned into a race against time.

External fetal monitors indicated lowered heart rates, another alarming symptom that the twins were in as much danger as their father.

An emergency cesarean was proposed, and Errol shook his head in protest. He'd regained enough of his senses to know it was too soon. A grimace of agony forestalled further argument.

"Cut them out," Sebastian ordered the doctors crowding around the room. "I don't care if they're four weeks early."

"Help the lads first," Errol muttered.

Sebastian pulled the attending out of earshot and commanded him to save Errol before anyone else.

"Your Highness—"

"That's not a request," Sebastian whispered fiercely. "The duke is not expendable."

Imperial Palace, Principality of Sendorra

His Royal Highness, Prince Sebastian, is pleased to announce that Errol, the Duke of Maitland, was safely delivered of a son today at 11:30 A.M. Both father and child are doing well.

The reigning monarchs, Prince Emile and Princess Alexandra, are delighted to welcome their first grandson, now third in line to the throne. A naming ceremony will be announced at a later time.

The royal couple request donations to the Intersex Society of Northern Europe in lieu of gifts.

Part I

Genesis

Chapter One

COLIN

I slipped through a break in the eight-foot hedge that separated my granny's rose garden from our garage. It was the same gap I used whenever I snuck out of the palace. Familiar with the prickly branches, I knew how to get through without a tear or a scratch. My bodyguards would be frantic the minute they realized I was missing, but the chance to sample nightlife as an ordinary man instead of a prince was too tempting.

Saddled at birth by a title I didn't deserve, I'd spent all my life trying to convince everyone, myself included, that I had a right to exist. It wasn't my fault that my twin, older by five minutes and thus the legitimate heir apparent, had been stillborn. Survivor's guilt weighed heavily on my psyche, although it was pure chance that he died and I didn't.

More than likely, the problem had lain with my method of conception. That story was glorified in the annals of our nation's history. Male pregnancy had been risky from the word go, and no one knew this better than the man who gave me life, my father's consort, Errol, the Duke of Maitland. He was a commoner who'd received the title after he married my other father, Prince Sebastian, who was heir apparent at the time. They'd been delighted to welcome me into the world, but it had been bittersweet after they were informed that my brother hadn't made it.

Nonetheless, I was loved and pampered from the moment I first opened my eyes. Everyone doted on me, and I had a wonderful, albeit lonely, childhood. Once in a rare while, someone heartless would point out that I was the spare who'd usurped his brother's title, but the incidents were few and far enough apart to be ignored.

Of course, no one bothered to ask me how I felt about having two dads and no mother. Not that they were bad parents—far better than most, or so I'd been told—and my granny, the Dowager Princess Alexandra, and her ladies-in-waiting provided all the feminine influence I could possibly need, but that didn't stop me from wondering if I'd be a different person had I been created conventionally.

As things stood, I was determined to cram as many life experiences as possible before assuming the throne. Hopefully, my father, the current ruler, would live well into his seventies so I could achieve my goals. Since my twin was watching me from somewhere beyond these earthly boundaries, I wanted him to take comfort knowing I was doing a fine job with the role I'd unintentionally usurped.

My red Beemer purred to life, and I inched my way out of the garage, hoping no one would hear the engine. Most of the staff had already gone for the day. It was late, way past dinner, and the odds of being stopped were slim. Thankfully, my exit was uneventful.

I drove slowly until I hit the open road and gassed the engine when the palace faded from view. Dancing was on my mind, and the songs blaring from my radio helped to put me in the right mood. Since I had succeeded in a clean getaway, I decided on something different tonight. There was a new club in town—one that catered to a sexually fluid crowd—and this would be the perfect opportunity to check it out.

My interest in exploring my gay side wasn't something new. I'd been attracted to both sexes growing up but had chosen my childhood friend, Princess Charlotte of Navarre, for my future bride. My fathers had been delighted, but they warned me things might change. A first crush seldom worked out, they'd cautioned, but I was determined to make it work, and thus avoid the complications that might arise from a same-sex union. Rather than risk another man's life, or that of my unborn child, I would go the conventional route and marry a woman. Charlotte was the perfect choice, until she wasn't.

My best friend, the sweet girl who'd promised to be my forever love, no longer held my interest, nor I hers. Our recent breakup—remarkably amicable thanks to multiple shots of vodka—signaled the end of childhood dreams and aspirations. And now, I was single again, trying to figure out what to do with the rest of my life. Until I turned twenty-one. Then the invisible clock would start ticking, and pressure to marry and begin a family would escalate.

At the club entrance, I scanned my surroundings. Across the mass of heaving bodies, someone caught my eye. The stranger's dark hair was combed back, probably tied in a low tail, but I couldn't say for sure. He was surrounded by people but ignored the crowd after our eyes locked. Even from a distance, the tingling in my groin led me to believe we'd be a good fit.

My royal status precluded random pairings as the inevitable fallout would be disastrous in more ways than I could count; however, the intensity in the brunet's gaze was pushing me to break a few of my own rules tonight.

I was wearing a tight navy-blue sweater to complement my eyes, and a pair of skinny jeans. The sweater's fabric stuck to me like a second skin, the perfect showcase for hard-earned shoulder and arm muscles. My blond hair was chin length, and I normally tucked it behind my ears. Even though I'd been told many times that it needed to be at least two inches shorter, I resisted because it was one of the few things in my regimented life I could control.

As next in line to the throne, I'd been brought up with a strict code of conduct, and I did my best to adhere to tradition. But with my formative years behind me, there was less room for mistakes. Eyes were on me twenty-four seven, and slipping through the proverbial cracks was always a thrill. My energy was on high alert tonight.

Although I had Prince Sebastian's fair coloring, I was built more like my other father, Errol. My wide shoulders, narrow waist, and muscular thighs combined with my height—six two on bare feet—were imposing, especially in formal attire. My facial hair was more a heavy scruff than a beard, but it was a disguise I'd adopted after my sixteenth birthday. Some know-it-all mentioned I was too young to be in such a position of power. The beard seemed to have the desired effect, adding the necessary years and a certain flair that drew men and women in equal measure.

My stranger disappeared from the dance floor, and I headed toward the rear of the club. There was a room, where one could presumably get more intimate, and I glanced around, hoping to spot him. He seemed to have vanished. Irritated that he'd eluded me, I went back to the main area and ordered a beer and a shot. Killing time until someone else caught my eye, I ordered another one-and-one after inhaling the first, and one more after that. The sudden buzz didn't do much to improve my mood. I'd been looking forward to a few hours of mindless fun, and sex had been high on my list.

I cleared my tab with cash to stay incognito and decided to make one more attempt to find the brunet. As soon as I entered the dark room, I felt the man's presence. He was leaning against a wall, staring at me with purpose. We met halfway, and I was hypnotized by catlike eyes, an interesting mix of browns and greens. The chemistry between us was sending shock waves directly to my groin. I didn't want to appear inexperienced, but I hadn't been with a guy in a long time, and I was nervous. It took a boatload of willpower to keep up my cool façade.

Finally, the stranger broke the silence. "Are you alone?"

"Yes."

Circling my waist with strong arms, he dragged me against his body. We were the same height, and as our mouths got closer, so did our hips, but I avoided his kiss. I wasn't ready for that yet and hoped he'd get the message. Without faltering, my hookup deftly moved to my neck and slowly licked his way up to the outer shell of my ear, whispering dirty nothings along the way. I could feel the barriers crumbling as my need took over, and the next time he tried to kiss me, I let him.

His lips were surprisingly soft, but stubble against stubble was a sensation I'd never felt before. Gradually, I responded to his questing tongue and let his strong hands clutch my ass cheeks and drag me against his growing erection. The jolt of desire made him reckless.

"Can we get out of here?" I asked hopefully.

"You bet," my mystery man answered. He held my hand and led me toward the exit. A few seconds before we'd made a clean getaway, I felt a heavy hand on my shoulder. David, the royal event planner, and his partner, Sam, stood in our way.

"What are you doing here?" David asked, ignoring the guy beside me.

I was surprised to see him and went on the defensive. "None of your damn business."

David was visibly shocked by my combative attitude but stood his ground. "You'll be sorry in the morning."

"Take your hands off him," the stranger snarled. "He's with me."

"Look," David said, trying a more amicable approach. "You don't know who you're dealing with, and he's obviously had too much to drink."

"He gave me a clear message, and I'm acting on it."

"Think again."

Sam and David sandwiched me and headed toward the exit. My hookup was probably fuming, but our connection had been broken, and I couldn't find the energy to put up a fight. David got behind the wheel of the car, and Sam sat in the back seat beside me.

After a few mild protests, I slumped against Sam and drifted off…

UNFAMILIAR SOUNDS WERE coming from somewhere in this strange place. Voices murmured in the background while pots clanked, a tea kettle whistled, and the smell of frying bacon made my stomach heave. I seemed to have swallowed the entire ocean somewhere along the way, judging by the taste in my mouth and an urgent need to piss. The room spun when I sat up, and the marching band in my head made me rethink my next move, but I forced myself to find a toilet before I wet the bed.

Holding on to the wall for support, I shuffled down the hallway, relieved to spot an open door, which led to the sought-after bathroom. It took far longer than usual to empty my bladder while I swayed dangerously. Fortunately, my aim was true, so one less thing to worry about. At the sink, I washed up and spied a bottle of mouthwash. I chugged a capful, swished it around, and spat out the minty liquid. Feeling marginally better, I risked a peek in the mirror to assess the damage.

The eyes that stared back at me were bloodshot, not a good look on anyone, especially the heir apparent. I knew I should go outside and find out where the hell I was, or who in fuck had rescued me the previous night. Hopefully, it was a good guy and not a scammer intent on milking this situation for all its worth. My fathers would raise holy hell if they learned I'd made a spectacle of myself at the club. Or had I? I remembered drinking and dancing, enjoying the press of half-naked men, and having a great time. Everything after that was sort of fuzzy.

Dude, you look like shit.

I narrowed my eyes. "Shut the fuck up."

Just saying.

Ignoring the pesky voice in my head and bracing for the worst, I opened the door and followed the noise down the hallway and into the kitchen. There, the palace chef, Sam, stood over the kitchen counter beating something in a green bowl, and his partner, David, sipped coffee and read the paper.

"Thank god," I said, pulling out a chair. "It's you guys."

Wordlessly, Sam grabbed a cup off the mug tree, filled it with brew, and placed it close to my right hand. "Cream and sugar are at your fingertips," he said, pointing to the matching set of ceramic containers.

"Thank you," I replied.

"No problem."

"You must be cold," David remarked.

Bare-chested and only clad in boxer briefs, I grimaced. "About last night—"

"Hold that thought," David said. He stood and disappeared for a minute. He returned with a terrycloth robe and draped it around my shoulders. "Better?"

"Much," I acknowledged with a nod. "Some aspirin and another cup of coffee to chase it down will be much appreciated."

"Let me get you the bottle," Sam said.

He was back in an instant and shook out two pills.

I popped them in my mouth, and after swallowing, I asked David, "How'd I get here?"

"Don't you remember?"

"Not much."

"You were pretty out of it at the club, and we thought it best if you crashed here," David said diplomatically.

Sam had no such qualms. "What on earth were you thinking?"

Insulted by his tone of voice and the implications, I pulled the royal card. "Have you forgotten who you're dealing with?"

Shame made him flush, but he didn't back down. "I mean no disrespect, Your Royal Highness. If we hadn't been there last night, there's no telling what might have happened."

"Clarify," I demanded, looking from one to the other.

"You were on your way out the door with some guy you'd picked up in the back room," David informed me in a steady voice.

David had joined my granny Alexandra's staff when I was a newborn and had a fatherly interest in my well-being. Nonetheless, he looked uncomfortable with our current situation.

"What was I doing in the back room?"

"Dear lord," David murmured.

"Probably having some form of sex," Sam deadpanned.

"You're kidding," I said dubiously.

"I'm serious," Sam replied.

"Nothing happened," I said adamantly. "I would remember."

"I don't know," David said gently. "You looked shitfaced."

"I didn't drink enough to blackout."

"Maybe someone slipped you a roofie?"

The idea was chilling. Did that happen, or was David trying to scare me? Should I report the club to the local cops so they could investigate? Sam interrupted my train of thought with another question.

"What were you doing at a gay club in the first place?"

I shrugged. "Checking it out."

"Did I miss the memo about you being gay?" David asked.

"I'm bi."

"Since when?" Sam queried.

"Since forever."

Sam and David exchanged worried glances.

I pushed back from the table and stood to go. "You all assumed I was straight because I was engaged to Princess Charlotte. And don't get me wrong, I cared for her a lot and have no regrets, but I've always been fluid with regards to my orientation. As far as last night is concerned, you should keep this to yourself."

Sam cocked his head. "May I ask you something, Your Royal Highness?"

"Seeing as how I'm half-naked in your kitchen, you can drop the honorific."

"A lifetime of training won't allow it," Sam said deferentially.

"Ask your damn question."

"Do men and women get you off equally, or do you feel stronger about one sex?"

"Sam!" David said, looking horrified by his partner's impertinence.

"What?" Sam asked. "I'm trying to understand."

"That's enough," I said, feeling frustrated and vulnerable, "I'm going home. Is my car outside?"

Sam reached out and stopped me. "We're on your side, Your Highness. Not judging."

"The fuck you're not!" I spat out.

David sighed. "Your car is still at the club. We'll drive you there once you get dressed."

"Thanks." I stalked out of the room, but I could still hear the heated conversation going on in the kitchen.

"Hell," Sam huffed. "That didn't go well at all."

"You were too hard on him," David admonished.

"Someone had to be. If any of the royals get wind of this, it'll be a lot worse."

"Well, they're not going to find out from me," David said. "The prince needs guidance from people he can trust. Not finger wagging."

"I wasn't doing that," Sam rounded.

"It felt like it."

"Stop being so sensitive on his behalf," Sam said. "I know you have a soft spot for the prince, but he needs a firm hand, not a couple of enablers."

"Let's talk about this later. I want to get him back to his car, so he can get home before anyone raises the alarm, okay?"

"Do you want me to come with you?" Sam asked.

"No," David replied. "I'd like to be alone with him if you don't mind."

In the car, I was silent for most of the way. David attempted to make small talk, but I replied in monosyllables. He pulled into the parking lot and slid his sedan beside my Beemer. Before I got out of the car, David reached for me.

"Your Highness, please don't be upset with us. We care about you."

"I understand your concerns, but my sex life is off-limits."

"Perhaps," David admitted, "but we couldn't let you walk out of the club with a stranger while intoxicated. I had no idea if it was his idea or yours to find privacy. Furthermore, this is the first time you've shown an interest in a man. Excuse me for being overly protective."

"This isn't my first rodeo, David."

"Your Highness," David continued. "I'm the last person who'll judge if you choose to spend your life with another man, but you should be more circumspect. There's no telling what might have happened if you fell into the hands of a predator."

"Agreed. This was a spur-of-the-moment thing, and I wasn't thinking. In the future, I'll try not to make a fool of myself."

"If you're still attracted to this guy the next time you run into him, then maybe we should look into his particulars."

I embraced David. "Thanks for taking care of me last night. Tell Sam too. And for heaven's sake, not a word to my fathers or Granny. Let me figure this out before we do any vetting."

"You can count on us, Your Highness."

I waved goodbye to David before noticing the business card stuck underneath my wiper. I pulled it out gingerly.

"Call me if you want another go at this" was scribbled in bold strokes and signed Alain. The other side of the gray card was blank except for a blood-red logo I didn't recognize and a phone number.

My pulse quickened and I shook my head in amazement. What was it about this guy that caught my interest? Wanting answers, I decided to give him a call later. If a few words on a business card could set me off so easily, there was no telling what would happen if we laid eyes on each other again. And the next time, I planned to be stone-cold sober.

Chapter Two

ERROL

The balcony of our summer palace overlooked the sparkling waters of the Bay of Biscay. Biarritz always drew huge crowds during the month of May until the first week of September. Sun worshippers on colorful blankets spread out like starfish, while children and their parents frolicked on the shoreline. Surfers, hoping to catch the next big wave, waited patiently on their boards. Past the breakwater, sailboats bobbed, sharing space with fishing boats heading back to the ancient stone pier to unload the daily catch.

It was another beautiful morning, and yet, it wasn't. Today was the thirty-first of May, my forty-ninth birthday, and I'd promised Bash to quit smoking, a nasty habit I'd picked up shortly after the birth of our son, Colin. My pregnancy had been difficult, to put it mildly, and I hadn't been able to keep any food down the first trimester. Things had changed for the better in the fourth month, and I made up for lost time. The weight started to pile on. After my delivery, and deep depression over the loss of our firstborn, I looked to food for solace. The pounds kept adding up, and even as my mental state improved, I couldn't stem the food cravings despite my best efforts—until I discovered cigars. Bash had objected stridently, calling the habit disgusting and off-putting. He threw in the health card as well, making sure I read all the material on lung and tongue cancer, but I'd endured a lot to bring Colin into the world, and I reminded Bash that I was entitled to this one concession.

He'd given in reluctantly; however, that had been two decades ago. Whenever Bash had mentioned quitting, I'd come up with another good reason why I shouldn't. To stop the infernal nagging, we had picked a date in the future, and I swore to give up the odious habit as soon the day arrived. It was a promise I'd made under duress, but one I would honor regardless. It would be difficult, but I'd never broken a promise or shied away from a challenge and wasn't about to start at this late date.

I drew one last puff on my Cuban cigar, crushed it out on the concrete railing I was leaning on, and tossed it over the side.

"That's that," I said wistfully, and Snow, my second-generation Pyrenean, named after her beloved mother who we had lost a while back, must have heard the note of sadness in my voice since she howled mournfully. I stepped back into the room and gazed at my husband who was reading the daily news on his iPad.

"All done?" he asked without taking his eyes off the page.

"Aye."

"That's the last we'll see of those cancer sticks, right?"

"Or what?"

Although I intended to comply, his assumption set my teeth on edge, and I wasn't going down without a fight. Arguing with my husband had become one of my favorite pastimes. Not because I was aggressive by nature, but Bash was too used to getting his way. People crawled over each other to do his bidding and the power exchange between us became a part of our routine; my way of reminding Bash who was in charge behind closed doors.

"You're sleeping in the guest room until you comply."

"I don't think so."

"You were supposed to quit years ago but insisted on continuing to pollute your lungs and the air around us, so I'm putting my foot down. Either quit smoking or..."

"What?"

Bash peered at me over his reading glasses and gave a half smile.

"Are you threatening me?"

Bash heaved a dramatic sigh, removed his glasses, and put his iPad aside.

"Errol," he said quietly. "I hold my breath after you have a physical, waiting with a lump in my throat for the bad news, convinced they'll find some form of cancer. You exercise like a fiend, eat the right food, and take vitamins by the handful, and yet you continue to poison your body with the fucking smokes. I don't understand how someone so brilliant can be so incredibly dumb."

"And you're saying that if I don't quit, you'll withhold sex? Now who's being a dumbass?"

Bash was bare-chested and had the duvet pulled up over his lap. He still had a full head of golden hair and had filled out in all the right places.

There was an aura about him that was ridiculously entitled but, in my opinion, immensely appealing. The willful twenty-five-year-old I'd married nineteen years ago was gone, and in his place, was a man in his prime dedicated to the small principality he'd inherited after his father's untimely death six years ago. Despite his busy schedule, Bash was a devoted husband and father.

I was also at the top of my game, having perfected my craft as a sculptor. I'd garnered awards, was admired and envied by many, and there was no bigger fan than my husband. We'd been good for each other, despite all the naysayers, and the emotional stability added another layer to the multidimensional personality that was Crown Prince Sebastian of Sendorra.

I removed my robe and noted the spark of interest in Bash's clear blue eyes. Say what you want about smoking, but it had served a purpose—keeping me lean—and the sexual chemistry that existed between us from the first hadn't faded through time. Naked, I sank down beside Bash and rolled on my side, propped my head on one hand, and pushed the duvet aside so I could explore the enticing curves of Bash's body.

"Blackmail has never worked with me," I reminded him, skimming lightly over the planes of his chest. "You will not win this battle, so don't even try."

Bash's breathing kicked up a notch.

I leaned in and tickled Bash's ear with my tongue and then sucked gently on the lobe while loving the sigh of contentment that slipped out of his throat. Goose bumps appeared on his arms, raising the golden hair. I changed position, licking a wet swath down Bash's neck, and stopped at one nipple. It pebbled after a few seconds, and I continued my journey southward. My full beard scraped the tender landscape, brushing over Bash's firm abdomen, and continued past the light layer of fur ending in a point above his cock.

I glanced up at Bash, noting the color rising slowly up his neck. "How long do you think you'd be able to resist this?" I asked in a low rumble, listening with satisfaction to his frustrated whimpers. "You presume you have control over this body, which has been completely mine for nineteen years."

Bash gripped my wrist, trying to move me in the right direction, but I shook him off and laughed.

"Oh, no, you don't. Picture yourself lying beside me, yearning for the slightest bit of pressure on your straining cock."

I caressed him in ever-widening circles, then pushed his thighs apart. "Please..."

"Surrendering already?"

"You're a monster."

I chuckled. "Tell me again how you're going to resist this."

"Damn you!"

"Do you really want to deprive yourself?" I asked, barely holding on to my own desires.

Bash keened.

"Tell me again how you're going to stay away from me if I don't quit my cigars," I taunted. "How you'll spend night after night alone in our great bed with nothing to hug except your pillow."

Bash's pupils were blown and tiny drops of moisture dotted his forehead. His hair lay in lanky strands against his cheek, but he'd never looked more beautiful.

"What's it going to be, Your Highness?"

"I want you," Bash said.

"And the cigars?"

"I don't care, Errol, please...get on with it."

"Tell me what you're not going to do."

"I will not withhold sex," Bash replied and kissed me deeply.

OUR MAKEUP SEX had been glorious, but getting my point across was even better. My victory was short-lived because the infernal promise was brought up once I reached over his head to pull a cigar out of the leather case I kept on the nightstand.

"Give it up for me...please," Bash implored. "I want you around for a long, long time. It'll kill me if you get sick."

"You know how much I enjoy a good smoke after making love to you."

"Do I have to get on my knees and beg?"

"That's not necessary, but you have to accept I'm going to die eventually."

"I know we're not immortal, but there's probably nothing worse than trying to catch a breath because your lungs are black with disease. Or watching all your hair fall out because of the chemicals they'll pump into your body. And if cancer doesn't get you, emphysema surely will. Even Armani can't dress up an oxygen tank."

"Jaysus, Bash. Stop being so morbid. And just so you know—" I paused for dramatic effect. "—you'll get better results if you ask nicely. Don't ever threaten me again."

Bash nodded.

"Good. Now I have to figure out how to quit without gaining twenty pounds. What am I going to use to satisfy my oral fixation?"

Bash cracked a smile. "Do you need to ask?"

"Your courtiers are understanding, but they're not voyeurs," I reminded him. "They'll have better things to do than wait on the sidelines while I suck on your cock."

"What could be more important?"

Statements like this reminded me how much he cared. Despite his rank and multiple engagements, Bash always put me first. Even with increasing amounts of gray overtaking my dark strands—a by-product of living with a drama king—he still found me attractive. After two decades and a clean track record, the odds that we'd go to our graves without cheating were clearly in our favor.

"I could have a plaster cast made of my royal dick," Bash mentioned, getting back to the problem at hand.

"Walking around with your cock in my pocket is counterproductive. I'd get nothing accomplished."

"Why not?"

"I'll have a cockstand all day, and pulling you out of meetings to satisfy my urges will send your ministers into a tailspin."

"My mother would roll over in a dead faint," Bash remarked.

"No she won't. The Dowager Princess is far more resilient than people realize. Putting up with you and your father all these years has made her a master negotiator; plus, she's the only one among us who seems to handle Colin with alacrity. Ye ken that takes talent."

"I'd rather not discuss Colin at the moment."

"He's headstrong. I'll grant you that, but he's a good lad, and his heart is in the right place."

"I hate to break this to you, my sweet husband, but Colin is a man, not a lad. Now that he's broken up with Charlie—I hate that nickname by the way—he'll have to start looking for his future bride. The last time I mentioned it, the brat actually growled and told me to bugger off."

"He's disappointed."

"No shit."

"He'll come around, and when he does, we'll throw him a big party. Take a page from our playbook and see if it works as well."

Bash sighed. "I hope you're right. Do you mind if I take a nap?"

"Not at all. We'll catch up later."

After dressing, I headed downstairs for breakfast. It would do Bash good to stay in bed after what transpired. Bouncing back from sex games wasn't that easy at our age. Thoughts of my prince were pushed aside by the sound of a car engine I'd recognize anywhere. Colin's BMW was pulling into the driveway. Had he stayed out all night, and if so, who was he with?

As I continued down the long flight of stairs, I met up with Colin as he was taking the marble steps two at a time. Instead of berating him, I greeted him warmly. "Good morning."

"Da! You should be having breakfast in bed on your birthday."

Colin's shock at seeing me wasn't reassuring. Had he been up to no good, or was I reading too much into this?

"Thank you kindly, but I'd rather have breakfast with you."

"I'm not hungry."

"Join me anyway."

"All right," Colin said. "Where's Papa?"

"Still in bed."

Colin raised an eyebrow. "Did you wear him out last night?"

"This morning," I said with a satisfied smile. "Don't ask any more questions, you impudent pup."

Colin laughed. "How can you guys still be sexually active after being married so long?"

"You'll find out after you meet your match."

"Don't hold your breath," Colin said bitterly.

Chapter Three

ALAIN

After my stud was rescued by his meddling friends, I'd made inquiries, trying to find out more about this mystery man. No one had ever seen him before. Not surprising since Biarritz was primarily a vacation destination. Hooking up with total strangers wasn't uncommon, but someone had to have seen this guy around town before now. He was too hot to be invisible. Unless he was straight or in the closet.

That might explain his reaction in the back room. The aversion to kissing, a case in point. If he was experimenting, locking lips with a guy for the first time might be a bit daunting. Still, there were undeniable sparks coming from both sides. The bastard who cockblocked us had insinuated the guy was drunk. He seemed more out of place than inebriated, like he'd just fallen out of the sky and landed in a gay bar by accident.

I left my business card under the windshield wiper of a BMW that supposedly belonged to him. The valet wasn't certain, but I left the card regardless. The personalized license plate—HRH2—would be listed in some database. I had enough contacts in the area to help me uncover the owner, but I wasn't sure I cared enough to go through all the trouble. I'd known the guy for what...five minutes? Not enough time to get invested. Maybe if he showed up again and actually followed through, I might rethink my need to know.

Taking my frustration out on my Porsche, I stomped on the gas. The drive up to my cliffside home consisted of a series of hairpin curves that were challenging at normal speeds, but I was gunning the engine, taking the turns like a Le Mans driver and loving each hair-raising second. My need for speed was inconsistent with my methodical personality, but there were some things even I couldn't explain.

The wrought-iron gate guarding my property swung open with a thumb tap on my steering wheel. It was all preprogrammed and convenient as hell. The steep driveway was lined with bushes of pink and blue hydrangeas that were in full bloom. My home, a nineteenth-century Italian-style villa, overlooked the city. It was my sanctuary, the one place I could be myself. Not that I was a vampire or werewolf, but I *was* my mother's son. Isabelle was the high priestess of the Simon Coven, and I had inherited her gift. I'd been told that my powerful aura could be daunting at times, a problem if you were looking to get laid.

Unlike my mother, I preferred to go it alone, steering clear of the politics and drama that went hand in hand with being a member of her coven. My mother scoffed at my views and warned me that I'd need her help someday, but thirty-three was a little late for an epiphany. I was an acknowledged loner, avoiding the witches and warlocks that existed in and around the Pyrenees. They called me a gray witch, one who strove for balance but recognized the existence of white and black magic. That was the main reason I legally changed my surname to de Gris. If I was going to keep my distance, it was better to drop the ancient, and more recognizable, Simon.

My goal was to only use my supernatural gifts to bring positive changes to the world. I was driven in my pursuit of answers that had intrigued me since I attended college in Edinburgh. Starting out as a medical student, I realized my thirst for knowledge lay in the world of herbs and pharmacology, in large part because of my ancestors. Back in the day, witches were known as healers, and people flocked to their cottages, hoping to find a cure. From skin rashes to more difficult cases of brain fever or pleurisy, they came from all over the countryside. Why not continue the family trade but with modern techniques? I switched my major, earning a degree in science, and eventually got my doctorate of pharmacology, a fascinating field with endless possibilities.

There were cures for most diseases, and it was my job to find them. I had the edge on my classmates as I was more than familiar with the composition and efficacy of existing herbs, but there was much more to learn, and I applied myself with single-minded purpose. My biggest accomplishment to date had been a preventive for Alzheimer's disease, a discovery that had changed the world and earned me a Nobel Prize. It had been rewarding in the extreme and justified long hours holed up in my laboratory buried in research. The personal toll had been inevitable, and I couldn't begin to count the number of relationships laid to waste getting to this point. The fact that people now had a pill to forestall a disease from turning one into an empty husk made the sacrifices worthwhile.

This was what I told myself as I spent evening after evening with Merlin and a glass of good wine for company. Rarely did I think about what might have been if I'd chosen a different kind of life. As things stood, I'd gained a reputation as a confirmed bachelor—a myth I perpetuated to avoid entanglements. There was no time for a committed relationship, and to be honest, I hadn't met anyone interesting enough to make me reevaluate my choices. Most of my hookups were too dim to realize there was more to me than fucking.

I wasn't a monk and enjoyed sex whenever the opportunity arose. Bisexual by nature, I was open to any and all possibilities, and never too embarrassed to admit it. But my self-imposed walls became impenetrable the minute my date du jour started asking questions. Intensely private for obvious reasons, I showed them the door the moment they overstepped. Opportunities were plentiful, and I didn't have to look far to get someone new in my bed. College was a series of first dates that ended up with one of us being disappointed. Normally, it was me who drifted away. As much as I admired the soft curves of a female and the hard planes of a male's chest, I was more drawn to one's intellect than anything else. I could not tolerate stupidity in any form.

Because I'd disappointed my mother by stepping out of the preordained box, she was pressing me to marry and create a grandchild who might actually meet her expectations. I was no more interested in marriage than I was in taking up black magic. Each time I rejected one of her candidates, icicles formed around our tight bond, and the look in her eyes spoke volumes. I was two for two in her opinion, and even the meteoric rise in my chosen field couldn't tip the scales in my favor.

My inherited abilities did come with some nice perks, and I didn't hesitate to use my knowledge to accomplish mundane domestic tasks that were time-consuming and utterly tedious. Especially in an elegant home with too many flat surfaces accumulating dust. Why hire outside help when a few choice spells could get the same results? I knew I was considered high maintenance, but I liked beautiful things and took great pride in my home.

My front door swung open the moment I approached. As soon as I walked into the foyer, lights began to flicker, and one by one, they burned bright. Although it was summer, my granite home was always cool, and the fireplace routinely stacked with wood. With a snap of my fingers, the logs burst into flames, warming the cavernous space within minutes. My Norwegian Forest cat, Merlin, hissed in response to the pyrotechnics. After pouring a glass of wine, I toed off my shoes, and sat on my comfortable sofa to enjoy the warmth and the excellent vintage. Merlin hopped up beside me and nudged my arm, intent on finding a spot on my lap. His loud purrs set me at ease for the first time since I'd left town.

There was a possibility I would end up back at the club tomorrow. I tried to analyze my feelings. Why was I so intrigued by the one who got away? Yes, he was good-looking, with a body to match his face, but perhaps it was the vulnerability in his eyes that kept me interested. Our brief kiss had given me a hint of what was to come if I pursued the connection. Some unknown force—one I'd never experienced before—had swirled between us, and I couldn't get him out of my head. Who was he, and why was I hooked?

As I stared into the bright flames, I conjured up the image of my missed opportunity. His mouth was made for kissing, among other things, and imagining what I could do with that plump lower lip made me squirm. Merlin's indignant meow and hasty retreat to his favored spot on top of a bookshelf didn't break my concentration. I continued to stare into the flames and attempted to get a clearer picture of this guy, but he quickly faded away. I tried again, employing another spell, but nothing worked. He seemed to have some sort of protective shield I couldn't penetrate, adding another element of intrigue to the mystery.

I spent most of the next day in my home office answering emails and looking over the numerous invitations to speak at conventions for a sizable fee. Ever since the big win in Sweden, I was inundated with requests. It was flattering, as well as financially rewarding, but it involved crowds and schmoozing, and I had no use for either. However, I had to make a few appearances, or people would assume I was a mad scientist, in the Frankenstein tradition, locked in my dungeon torturing small animals and growing humans out of potato spuds. The thought was so ludicrous it made me laugh because I could easily become that guy. In truth, anyone famous who shied away from the spotlight was like catnip to the paparazzi, especially if said person was accomplished, attractive, and single—qualities I possessed according to the press.

Around five in the afternoon, my cell phone buzzed. I didn't recognize the number, but the caller ID was the same as the personalized license plate HRH2.

I accepted and answered with a curt, "Alain here."

"How's it going?"

The person on the other end sounded young. Far too young for me, but his voice had a sexy gravel that drew me like a magnet. "Who is this?"

"The guy you almost took home last night."

"Does this guy have a name?" I asked, unable to keep the smile off my face.

"Colin."

"What's Colin's last name?"

There was a long pause, and finally Colin replied, "I'll tell you another time."

Interesting. "What can I do for you?"

"You asked me to call if I wanted another go."

"And do you?" I asked.

Colin laughed softly into the phone. "Yeah."

The satisfaction I felt upon hearing his answer was surprising, but I refused to dwell on the reasons. I did, however, jump on the opportunity to get a second chance. "When?"

"How about tonight?"

"Will your overprotective friends be around?"

"About that—"

"No explanation needed."

"Maybe not, but I want to assure you that I'm not a minor," Colin explained. "Seeing me at a gay bar was a bit of a shock for my friends, and I was obviously tipsy. They decided I needed to sober up before making any rash decisions."

"You're not out?"

"No."

Disappointment quickly snuffed out my enthusiasm. "That's too bad."

"I have my reasons," Colin argued, "and I'll be happy to share them with you the next time we meet."

"I'm too old for this scenario, kiddo."

"Please don't call me that," Colin said.

"My apologies. In any case, I think you should be with someone your own age. I'm terrible at subterfuge, and furthermore, I don't give a fuck what other people think."

"How old are you anyway?"

"Thirty-three."

"Wow." He seemed shocked by my revelation.

"How about you?"

"Twenty."

Alain sighed. "Call me in about five years."

"You'd still be thirteen years older."

"I can count."

"Give me one night," Colin insisted.

"I'm sorry, Colin. You'll end up getting hurt."

"Don't presume to know me," Colin said imperiously.

There was something about his tone that made me rethink my decision. He was either a spoiled brat or used to being in charge. I could do without the attitude, but I liked men who were in control and spoke their minds.

"One night," I said. "Meet me outside the club at nine."

"I'll be there," Colin said and disconnected.

Chapter Four

COLIN

After the call ended, I panicked. All my life I've been shielded from danger, real and imagined, and I'd just agreed to meet up with a guy I barely knew. By myself. David and Sam wouldn't be at the club two nights in a row, and I sure as hell couldn't show up with bodyguards. Alain would take one look at them and realize I was not only too young, I was a fucking liability. His age and barely disguised contempt for my closeted status gave me reasons to believe I'd made a terrible mistake. Or not.

Alain's reticence was actually a good sign. If he were a true predator, he'd have agreed to meet me no matter the obstacles. My logic might be colored by pride and desire, but I wasn't going to back out after twisting his arm. The endgame remained a mystery. Wanting to avoid a male pregnancy at all cost had cast a shadow over my sexual experiences. Attracted to other men, I'd messed around with guys at boarding school, but I always ended up going back to Charlotte, determined she would carry my heir. We'd agreed to date others, in part because we were too young to be tied down, but also because we were naturally curious. Ultimately, the experiment had broken us apart. She knew I was torn between my duty and my natural inclination.

Our breakup had gutted me, and I had vowed to do better the next time I got engaged. So why was I jumping headfirst into a possible disaster? Once the summer was over, I'd have to return to my old routine and sit down with my parents to work out a plan to find a bride. The rules of our principality hadn't changed since I was born. Like my forefathers, I was expected to sire a legitimate heir before I passed or Sendorra would revert to Spain.

Throwing caution aside, I decided to trust my gut instinct—hook up with Alain regardless. What harm could one night do in the grand scheme of things? Deciding what to wear presented another challenge. Should I try to look older or parlay my youth? I settled on a tight black button-down and white jeans. The black would highlight my blond hair, and the white would draw Alain's attention to the right place. I was well-endowed and wouldn't hesitate to use all the weapons in my arsenal—a thirteen-year age gap was difficult to ignore. I couldn't possibly compete, experience-wise, but unspoiled looks could work to my advantage. If I'd managed to hold his interest the first time, I could do it again. My recently shampooed hair gleamed, falling in shiny waves around my face. The image staring back at me was as good as it could get. I picked up my car keys and snuck out of the villa.

As I drove into town, I wondered again if I had the nerve to go through with this. I was clutching the steering wheel in a death grip. I forced myself to relax. What was the worst that could happen? Alain would say thanks but no thanks.

Are you certain this is wise?

That pesky voice again. "Stay out of my business."

Someone's got to keep you in check.

"It's not going to be you."

I'll stick around just in case.

"Like hell you will."

At the club, I parked in the corner spot, which was vacant again, and paid the entrance fee. It was packed, and I scanned the crowd but couldn't spot Alain. My initial anxiety reared its ugly head, and I wondered if he'd had a change of heart. At the bar, I asked for a club soda with a twist, deliberately keeping alcohol out of the equation. No one could possibly accuse me of being too drunk tonight.

The bartender stared at me. Unless he was a celebrity stalker, there was no way he'd recognize me. There had been a lot of media coverage on my twentieth birthday party, but that had been almost a year ago. Unlike many celebrities, I was camera shy and preferred to keep the photo ops to a minimum. Nevertheless, I wasn't going to give the bartender the opportunity to figure out if he'd ever seen my mug.

I found a spot on a raised walkway, where I could keep an eye on the entrance. This strategic position would allow me to get a second look to make sure I'd made the right decision. Memories of our encounter had plagued me for the last twenty-four hours, and in my dreams, he got better and better looking.

My pulse quickened when he finally stood at the front door. As I soaked up the vision of Alain in a tight T-shirt and ripped jeans—unexpected given his age—anticipation thrummed in my veins, obliterating the fear and indecision. My feet moved of their own accord. Finally, we were standing eye to eye, and I felt this crazy energy swirling between us.

"You're here," I said lamely.

His tiger eyes crinkled with amusement. "I'm true to my word."

"Good to know."

"May I buy you a drink?" Alain asked, never taking his attention off my face.

Holding the stare, I said, "Sure."

With his hand on my lower back, Alain guided us to the bar. I was hyperaware of his touch, and although there was one layer of fabric between his hand and my skin, the heat transferred between us. At the bar, I asked for a refill on the tonic water, and he ordered a vodka martini, extra dirty.

"You're not drinking alcohol tonight?"

"No."

"Do you want to dance?" Alain asked after he finished his drink.

"Okay."

We moved toward the dance floor. Alain was in the lead, and it gave me a chance to admire his gorgeous ass. He reached for me, and I moved in willingly and wrapped my arms around his waist. Alain's smile set me at ease, and we swayed to the beat.

"You're even better in person than in my dreams," I murmured.

"I was just thinking the same thing," Alain said, bending forward and kissing me lightly on the lips. "Thoughts of you have been distracting me all day."

"Why?"

"I'm not sure," Alain admitted. "You're not my type."

"It appears I am."

Alain grinned. "Cheeky. I like that."

"Let's see if I can't do something more to convince you." I pulled Alain closer and claimed his smile. The chemistry between us flared brightly, and I could tell he was surprised by my aggression, but he followed through, matching my moves with several more of his own. We were both short of breath after the kiss.

Alain raised both eyebrows. "You've made your point."

"No shit," I replied. "Can we move to the back room?"

"I don't do back rooms," Alain informed me. "Last night was a fluke."

"If you don't come up with a good alternative, I'll get down on my knees and make a fool of myself."

"What makes you think I'll object?" Alain asked.

"Are you an exhibitionist?"

"No," Alain said firmly.

"Then perhaps we should take this elsewhere."

"Do you always get what you want?" Alain asked, amusement tugging at the corner of his mouth.

"More often than not."

Alain smiled widely, revealing gleaming white teeth. It completely changed his look from untouchable to approachable.

"I'll let you have your way tonight. Do you want to go to my place?"

"Is it close?"

"About thirty minutes."

"I'll follow you in my car," I said. There's was no way in hell I was going anywhere without some method of escape.

Alain nodded and we moved toward the exit.

In the parking lot, I asked, "Where's your car?"

"Over there." Alain pointed to a black Porsche.

"Nice. Drive at your normal pace," I said. "I'll keep up."

Alain raised an eyebrow but didn't comment. At the wheel of my car, I kept telling myself I was insane, and I hoped to live long enough to regret this. Then again, the urgency of the situation was pressing against my zipper, and I had no more fucks left to give.

I gunned the engine.

Alain's home in the hills overlooking the city wasn't too far from our summer palace. For one second, I thought he was leading me back home. Except he veered left instead of right at a fork in the road, and then I knew I'd been mistaken.

His place was a little smaller than ours, but not by much, and I was impressed. If I was going off the rails, at least I was doing it in style. We didn't even bother with the garage but left our cars parked in the circular driveway at the foot of the stone steps leading up to his intricately carved front door. It swung open as we approached, and I looked at his hand to see if he had some kind of remote to activate a signal, but all he had were his car keys. I suppose that should have made me hesitate, but I was driven forward by my cock and nothing else mattered except the man in front of me.

I trailed behind Alain who was taking the stairs to the second floor two at a time. He seemed just as eager to get naked, judging by the way he tore off his jacket and shirt inside the palatial bedroom. A fire was already burning invitingly, and I wondered how he'd manage it without a servant in sight.

I stopped thinking after he threw his clothes on the sofa and pulled a bottle of water from a tiny refrigerator hidden inside an armoire.

"You want some?" he asked, holding up the bottle.

"No, thanks. You have a beautiful home," I said.

Alain was shirtless and had just taken a huge gulp of water. "Thank you."

"Have you had it long?"

"About three years."

"Where did you live before this?"

"Can we do the Q&A afterward?" he asked, stepping closer.

"Sure, except we haven't been properly introduced," I maintained. "I only know your first name."

"Alain de Gris."

"Cool name. So you're French?"

"Half."

"And the other half?"

Ignoring my question, Alain asked, "Does Colin have a surname?"

"Maitland," I said automatically. Using Da's name was safer than tossing out my title. I didn't have a proper surname like most people. In school, I was called HRH, or H for short, and didn't give it much thought. Until now.

"Are your parents Irish?"

I shook my head. "My father is Scottish."

"And your mother?" Alain asked.

"Will you shut up and kiss me before I die of boredom?"

Instead of doing my bidding, Alain laughed at my audacity. The wide smile I'd previously admired made another appearance.

"I like it when you look at me like that."

"Why?"

"Makes me feel less like a child and more your equal."

"And your lips, Colin Maitland, were made for kissing," Alain stated, removing my jacket as he spoke.

"Among other things."

My breath caught in my throat as Alain moved forward and lifted my chin with his forefinger.

"You've been taunting me for the last hour, dear boy. It's time you make good on your brash statements."

Before I could say another word, his mouth was on mine, and the push of his tongue shot electrical currents straight to my groin. He unbuttoned my fly and released my cock in one slick move while he continued to explore my mouth. It was too much, and I was afraid I would come in his hand.

"Hold on," I begged, breaking our connection. "I can't breathe."

"You've never done this before, have you?" Alain asked, thumbing my lower lip.

"Not with a complete stranger."

"But you have been with other men?"

"Of course. I'm bisexual...or at least I think I am."

I was light-headed with apprehension. From the moment I first laid eyes on Alain, I wanted him, but things were moving faster than I'd anticipated, and I needed some reassurance.

"Don't be afraid," Alain said gently. "We can stop anytime you're uncomfortable."

"You must think I'm the worst cock tease," I muttered, leaving his side and walking toward a window. My erect cock jutting through the gap in my pants was obscene. I tried to get it back in place, but it was impossible in this state.

Alain was behind me within seconds, and his soothing voice was warm at the back of my neck. "Talk to me," he urged gently.

"Bending your ear wasn't part of my seduction plan."

With his arm across my chest, Alain pulled me closer. Even though I couldn't see his face, I could sense the concern in his reply. "Let's forget about your cock and have a conversation instead. Your circumstances are probably different than mine, but fear and confusion is universal. No one said this meeting has to be a sterile one-off. I'm a good listener, Colin."

Sighing, I explained, "I'm weighed down by expectations I can't possibly meet."

"Now *that* I understand. For years, I've tried to please my mother and do the expected. It took a long time for me to gather up the courage to go my own way."

"What about your father?"

"He died a long time ago," Alain said.

"That must have been hard on you."

"I was too young to feel the loss."

"Still, it must have been difficult to grow up without a father."

"Are you close to yours?"

"Yes." For obvious reasons, I didn't add that I had two loving fathers.

"What's troubling you at the moment?"

"I was engaged to my childhood sweetheart," Colin said. "We broke up recently and now I'm questioning a lot of my decisions."

"Aren't you a little young to be getting married?"

"It's complicated," I replied.

"Was she pregnant?"

"What? No!"

Seeing my reaction, Alain changed his tactic altogether. "Colin, we're here because there's an attraction, but I don't want you feel any pressure. The next move is yours."

"I was looking for some mindless fun the other night and found you instead."

"Some people would say you got lucky," Alain teased.

"I'm not blind. You're clearly more than I had any right to expect, but I'm afraid our encounter can't be more than a one-night stand. I think it's only fair to tell you that we have no future."

Alain's breathy chuckle tickled my ear. "Rest assured, Colin. You're a complication I don't need. Stay if you want to have sex or go. I'll respect your wishes."

"I'd like to stay, but no more questions, okay? Let's pretend we're just two horny guys who met on a dating app."

"Oh, please. Could you be a little more creative?"

"Whatever," I said, turning around and facing him. "Why don't you start by kissing me again?"

Alain looked at me and I was relieved to see desire flaring in his studied gaze. After my presumptuous warning, I expected him to lose interest, but that didn't appear to be the case. He still wanted me, and despite all the voices in my head telling me to run, I wanted this one night more than anything in my recent past.

Alain caressed my face, scratching my scruff gently, and then outlining my lips with infernal patience. My flagging cock was rallying, and I hoped he'd speed up, but I let him take the lead. Alain reached for my hand and licked my palm, a move that sent my lust into overdrive. He followed through by sucking on each of my fingers while staring into my eyes. I could feel the heat of arousal staining my cheeks, and my erection was out of my control.

"I'm not going to last," I confessed.

"This isn't a contest," he assured me. "Do what feels right."

"What about you?"

"Watching you come apart is my guilty pleasure."

I was caught in a swirl of emotions that were turning my insides into complete mush. In all the time I'd been with my mates at school, I'd never felt this way. Alain's touch was taking me to a whole new level. Was this the kind of attraction between my fathers? If it was anything close, I could finally understand their unquenchable need.

"Alain," I warned, feeling myself on the brink.

He crushed my mouth, tongue fucking aggressively, the way I hoped he'd take me on the bed. But that wasn't happening. The unrelenting kisses didn't stop until we had to catch our breaths, and then he moved his mouth close to my ear, telling me how he wanted to suck me off and taste my cum.

I was no match for this aggressive assault, and to my everlasting embarrassment, I came with his thigh pressed between my legs.

"Shit, look what you made me do," I muttered, completely humiliated.

"Don't be embarrassed. I'm flattered as hell. The only reason I haven't come all over myself is because I jerked off before our meeting."

"God." I slumped against him.

"Let me get a washcloth," he said thoughtfully.

"No, I can do it," I insisted. "Where's the bathroom?"

He pointed at a door and I took off in that direction. I needed some private time to unscramble my brains. If this is what happened after a kiss, I would probably burst into flames if he ever fucked me for real.

"Hey," Alain called before I disappeared behind the door.

I looked back at him. "What?"

"Come right back. I'm not done with you yet."

"Oh my god."

Chapter Five

ALAIN

I poured myself a drink while I waited. Something unexpected was happening tonight, and my reaction—to shield Colin rather than lay waste—was puzzling. What was it about this cheeky boy that called up such a protective streak? Was it our age difference that concerned me or his mild case of jitters? The latter was surprising after his posturing. Colin Maitland was entitled and accustomed to issuing orders. Most significant of all was his assumption that I was expected to do his bidding. There was a key element to this Gordian knot that was infuriating.

Once again, I tried getting more information from the flames that rose up from the iron grate. Murmuring familiar incantations, I waited for a vision. The fire gradually changed from gold to purple. There was a castle in the mist, and the image of another boy who looked like Colin but opposite in coloring. The ghostly figure was decked out in full Scottish regalia, complete with sword and cap, but the yards of forest-green and black tartan wool were too much for his slight figure. He looked like a child playing dress up. The eerie apparition left more questions than answers.

Colin fumbled with the bathroom door, and I snapped my fingers, sending the amethyst vapors back where they came from. He was wearing one of my robes, the maroon brocade, and any trepidation I'd felt a moment ago vanished the moment our eyes locked. Colin was stunning, and the invisible thread between us tugged hard, enough for me to unbutton my fly and step out of my pants while he watched. I was already shirtless, and as I walked naked toward him, the color rose in his cheeks. The stirring of fabric at his groin was another good sign that he was emerging from his recent meltdown, the resilience of youth working in my favor.

"Alain," Colin whispered.

"At your service," I replied, my voice gone husky with need.

Colin licked his lips and joy flooded my veins. I wasn't sure what I would have done if he'd resisted, but that didn't seem to be an issue as he soaked up the sight of my body.

"You're fucking gorgeous," Colin said, transfixed.

"For an old man," I replied.

Colin waved away the joke and stepped closer, eyes bright with anticipation. He stopped in front of me and took what he needed, savoring my taste like a guest at a banquet. I tugged off the robe and silk pooled at his feet. Colin was stunning, by any standards, and my mouth watered as I envisioned his impressive cock stuffed down my throat.

But the boy slowly sank to his knees and buried his face in my pubes. He seemed intent on pleasuring me, and I sure as hell wasn't going to stop him. To be fair, I'd had better blowjobs, but Colin's inexperience was trumped by his unrestrained enthusiasm. He feasted on my organ, taking my length in a gluttonous move that made him gag, but he quickly adjusted. Sound effects—whimpers, moans, sloppy sucking—added an erotic component that heightened my pleasure. I was too close and clutched his head to control the tempo. He relinquished the lead, and his compliance acted like a spark to my parched libido. I drove in deep, and since he didn't object, I picked up speed and began fucking his mouth in earnest. Colin curled his hands around my thighs, but he didn't pull away, allowing me to use him. Lights flickered and colorful sparks of energy flared around us as I came with a shout, pumping hot spend down his throat in a steady stream. He swallowed convulsively while warm cum splashed my calves and feet as Colin crested and shuddered through his own orgasm.

I helped him off his knees, and we staggered toward the bed. Colin looked drugged, high on success and mind-numbing pleasure while I was wiped. This experience had been more than I hoped, but still not enough. I wanted to possess him, and I vowed he would be mine before the night was over. We fell asleep in each other's arms.

He was gone in the morning.

Panic hit hard and fast. I tried to recall if there was anything I'd said or done to scare him off, but I drew a blank. He had seemed blissfully content as he lay in my arms before we drifted off. I threw the covers aside and padded to the bathroom. The maroon robe was folded neatly on a stool, and Colin's clothes were gone. Snatching the same robe, I wrapped it around myself and hurried downstairs.

As I expected, the front door was locked as were all the windows. My home was normally impenetrable, a challenge to the most experienced burglar, and Colin didn't fit the image. Only an extraordinary hacker could bypass my system. Maybe his abilities extended beyond sex, and I'd been too blinded by lust to delve a little further into his background. Well, enough was enough. I hated mysteries, and this one was about to be solved.

I willed the coffee to start brewing so the twelve-cup pot was already half full by the time I reached for a mug. Determined to get answers sooner rather than later, I headed toward my home office and powered on my computer. Merlin padded into the room and I scooped him up and placed him on my lap while we waited for the system to boot up. His familiar purr was as comforting as the strong brew. The soft ding and colorful image on the computer screen prompted me to get rid of my cup and get down to business. If my magic couldn't find answers, then maybe technology would solve this riddle.

I typed Colin Maitland into the search bar and waited. There were several hits, but none of them were my guy. What in the ever-loving...?

Frustrated, I hacked into the Department of Motor Vehicles site and typed HRH2 in the customized plates section. Voila! The car belonged to the royal family of Sendorra, a tiny principality tucked away between France and Spain. It was also home to a clan of witches who'd been at odds with my family for centuries. Great. I left the site and typed Sendorra into the search bar. Useless trivia about the country popped up, but I clicked on the royal family to see what it revealed.

My elusive boy was the fucking heir apparent.

Holy, crap. This mystery had just evolved into a Shakespearean tragedy.

Even if I was remotely interested in pursuing Colin, there was no way on earth I could step into his realm without being summarily dismissed by the people who ran his life. I zoomed in on the photo of the royal family and took a hard look. There was no mother in the picture. Only two serious men decked out in royal finery bracketing Colin. His resemblance to the reigning monarch was only in coloring. Most of Colin's features were a mirror image of the royal consort.

I dug a little deeper and learned my boy was one of a set of twins born to his intersex father, Errol *Maitland.* There lay the surname Colin had unhesitatingly thrown out so freely. Too bad he didn't fill in the other blanks before I fell under his spell. Dammit to hell!

Trying to push Colin out of my mind was pointless since I could still smell him on my skin. The orderly world I'd structured to prevent this sort of thing from happening had been rudely flipped by a mere boy. Colin would be insulted if I ever called him that to his face, but there was a vulnerability about him that belied his confident posturing. It was this quality that set off a possessive streak I didn't even know I possessed.

I'd never wasted time on a hopeless cause, especially a romance. There were too many men out there who would better suit my needs, but I knew the laws of attraction had nothing to do with rational thinking. Perhaps Colin had inherited more than good looks. Mother had warned me for years that magic always trumped science, and if he'd cast a spell over me without my knowledge, it was noteworthy.

I powered off my laptop and went to shower and change. There was a long list of minutiae awaiting my attention at the office, and I'd already wasted too much time. Thoughts of Colin would have to go on the back burner for now.

In the car, I had more time to dwell on my predicament. I was irritated that Colin had omitted the truth. I wouldn't have touched him if I'd known he was a royal. In fairness, he did warn me that we had no future, but I'd been too intent on jumping his bones to let the words sink in. If anyone had predicted I'd be caught up in such a tangled web with someone thirteen years my junior, I would have laughed in their face. And taking it a step further, if the attraction was more than physical, I would have told them they were crazy.

But that's exactly what was happening. The vivid memory of Colin servicing me on his knees with such unguarded enthusiasm was something I would treasure for a long time. If he had any idea how stunning he looked when his eyes burned with passion, he could ask for the world and might actually get it. I had to resist the urge to call. Our situation was beyond complicated. Inundating him with the outward trappings of a jilted lover—phone calls, flowers, and cards—would only scare him off. In truth, I was scaring myself. It would be better to bide my time until I could process my feelings.

There was a good possibility that Colin left in a hurry because he was fighting his own personal demons—whatever those might be. I could only guess that he was being pressured to produce an heir, sooner rather than later. What about his brother? Where had he run off to? Had he abdicated in favor of Colin? Was he damaged and hidden away in some moldy attic?

Perhaps I should give in and call him. I had far too many questions and hardly any answers. There wasn't a reasonable way around this dilemma as too many variables were involved. Mother might offer some insight. Then again, she might muddy the waters or cast a more powerful spell and turn Colin into a gargoyle just to spite me. She could be dangerous if crossed.

No. Confiding in her was out of the question. I would have to be patient and let things unfold naturally. Cold logic obliterated the fanciful notion that I would be happy with a guy I barely knew. Beyond the attraction was some powerful magic brewing between us. I intended to root out the source before I put my proverbial foot into a romantic bog. Princes were not made to be one-night stands. They were keepers, and I knew this reality would play heavily in my decisions going forward.

Chapter Six

COLIN

Slipping away in the dead of night would only confirm Alain's initial misgivings. I was too young to be with a man of his caliber. In truth, I planned on staying until morning, but I was way out of my league, falling too fast, and already emotionally invested in the guy before we'd even fucked. Once that happened, there would be no turning back.

I'd managed to dress and sneak out of the room without disturbing Alain, but there was a moment of blind panic after I tried the front door and it didn't give. Locks were meant to keep out intruders, not imprison those already inside. I willed myself to calm down and concentrate on the problem at hand. I knew I was capable of getting out of a tight spot, but my powers had been dormant for a while, and it would take some concentration to make this happen. Calling upon secrets I'd learned at Granny's knee, I plucked energy from sources around me and used it to my advantage. At the moment, the closest thing was Merlin, Alain's cat. The persnickety mound of fur wasn't too thrilled by my presence, and he radiated anger like a live wire. All I had to do was snatch his energy away for a few seconds and send it hurling toward the lock. Which I did. The tumbler reacted to the forceful blast, and the door swung open.

I ran down the stairs, started my car, and sped away. Trying to explain my powers to Alain posed another problem. After my granny discovered I had magic in my blood, she'd sworn me to secrecy. My grandda, Prince Emile, despised witchcraft in all its forms. He'd ordered Granny to put away her grimoire and give up the family business if she wanted to remain by his side. It was for this reason she'd made me pinky swear not to tell anyone— especially the three men in my life—that I was gifted. It was one more thing I couldn't possibly share with Alain.

I had to seek advice from a trusted source, and the only one who might understand would be Granny. Fortunately, she always accompanied us on our summer holiday. I had to find a way to discuss this in private because her ladies-in-waiting were prone to gossip, and my hijinks, always a favorite topic, were too juicy to keep under wraps.

I showered and slipped on comfortable lounging pants hoping for a few more hours of sleep, but I was too wired. Now that I had Alain's full name, I could get more info off a search engine. Nothing I uncovered could be worse than the parts of myself I'd conveniently left out of my narrative, but I had to learn more, so I could answer Granny's questions with some semblance of knowledge.

I was shocked to discover Alain was a respected member of the scientific community, but learning he'd recently won a Nobel Prize was intimidating as hell. Despite my rank, I'd never be able to compete with Alain's many accomplishments.

Imagining him at my side as a ruler was inconceivable. Not because he wasn't capable, but he had so much more to offer the world than becoming my consort. And even if he was mad enough to take me on, I would be breaking my self-imposed rule. No male pregnancies. Ever. Except Alain had cast his net, and I was caught, as surely as the fresh flounder Da insisted on eating at least once a week.

It was past five by the time I fell asleep. Papa's familiar ringtone woke me around nine thirty. I hit accept, knowing it was pointless to ignore the call. He'd send a footman to find out what the devil was going on. I picked up, and before I could say a word—

"Colin, are you there?"

I rolled my eyes. Who else would pick up my fucking phone? "What's up?"

"I haven't seen you in days. Come and have breakfast with your da and me."

"Not hungry."

"This isn't a request."

"God, are you pulling rank so early in the morning?"

"Yes, I am. Get your butt down here immediately."

Fuck...did he know? It was an unreasonable worry and one I had to shrug off. There was no way in hell his network of spies would be on to me, but I lay on my bed feeling like a thirteen-year-old caught masturbating. My father was our ruler and well-versed on a majority of things, but he didn't have an intuitive gene in his body so I had to assume this was just standard fatherly meddling.

"I'll be down in ten minutes."

"Are you okay, Colin?"

Alarmed by his concern, I deflected. "Why are you asking?"

"Your broken engagement must be upsetting. I want to make sure you're all right."

My eyes got blurry at his kindness. I wished desperately that I had the nerve to tell him what was going on, but decided not to say anything until I consulted with Granny.

"I'm fine."

"Are you sure?"

"Yes, but thanks for asking."

"See you in a few."

"Okay."

I put down the phone and wiped a stray tear, wishing I had someone my age to talk to.

What do you want to talk about?

I pinched the bridge of my nose, hoping to ward off the headache that often accompanied these internal monologues. "Nothing you'll understand."

Try me.

The phone buzzed, and Alain's name showed up on caller ID. I held my breath, trying to decide the best course of action. Should I continue to act like an adolescent or man up?

Don't answer!

"Fuck off!"

You said it would be a one-time thing.

"This is Colin," I said, ignoring my conscience.

"I missed you this morning."

His casual tone was unexpected, and I felt doubly guilty for running off. "Sorry about that. I have a standing breakfast meeting with my father and didn't want to wake you."

"It wouldn't have been a problem," Alain assured me. "What are your plans for the rest of the day?"

"Nothing important."

"You want to meet at my club for a game of tennis?"

"Um, sure." I was surprised by his request, and despite my earlier intention to keep my distance, I couldn't bring myself to say no. "Where and when?"

He gave me directions, and then asked, "How does four thirty sound?"

"Perfect."

"I'll see you later."

Alain disconnected and I stared at my phone. Was I being foolish? I could have sworn I'd vowed to keep away, and here I was jumping at another chance to meet up with the guy. Now, more than ever, I needed to consult with Granny.

Except it would have to wait. At breakfast, I was informed she was on her way to Paris for a few days of shopping. My grandmother disliked mobile phones and never carried hers. If there was an emergency, one could always reach her security guards, but to try to have an actual conversation with her, one as important as this, wouldn't work.

My fathers were pleasant and inquired about my whereabouts the last few nights. I mentioned I'd been out dancing to try to take my mind off Charlie. It was a shitty lie, but I wasn't prepared to deal with harsh realities since I hadn't figured anything out for myself.

I HAD TO circle several times to get a parking spot at Alain's club. The tennis courts were easy to spot, and I wandered over to see if he'd arrived. I couldn't see him, so I inquired about changing and was directed to the men's locker room. It didn't take long to get into my shorts and T-shirt. By the time I'd finished tying my shoes, Alain walked in.

"Hey," he greeted. "Glad you could make it."

"Me too."

He was wearing a conservative light-gray suit and navy-blue shirt, but the lemon-yellow tie was the perfect accessory to change his look to fashionable and attractive as hell. Even the harsh neon lights couldn't take away his appeal. His dark hair gleamed, and he broke into an easy smile after he caught me checking out his ass. Alain removed his jacket and hung it up while we continued to chat.

"Do you work out a lot?" I asked.

"I try to get down here at least three times a week."

Alain unbuttoned his fly and stepped out of his pants, folding them with absolute precision before hanging them away. I couldn't take my eyes off him, noting how tanned he was and how his endless legs were perfectly shaped with clearly defined calf and thigh muscles. After he shrugged on a Lacoste T-shirt and pulled up tennis shorts, he sat beside me on the bench to tie his athletic shoes.

"Ready?" he asked, grabbing his racket.

I nodded and followed him out the door with my equipment bag in hand.

We were a good match and played three sets, winning one apiece with Alain claiming victory in the end. Afterward, we sat on a bench and rehydrated with bottled water.

"That was fun," I exclaimed.

"Yeah, we should do this more often," Alain replied. "How long will you be in the area?"

"All summer."

"That should give us plenty of time for a rematch."

I didn't have a good answer so I didn't reply.

"Do you want to sit in the sauna for a bit?" Alain asked.

"Sure."

In the locker room, we separated to take a quick shower and met up again in the large steam sauna thick with fog. There was a group of three on the far end of the room. I followed Alain to the opposite corner, and we sat on the warm wooden benches with fresh water bottles in hand.

I couldn't prevent my gaze from straying to the dark hair covering Alain's upper body, then tapering into a tantalizing love trail that disappeared under the white towel he'd wrapped around his waist. Sweat dotted his forehead, and his dark hair curled around his neck. His eyes were closed, and his mouth slightly open. He looked like a fantasy in the dim light, a gorgeous apparition strategically placed there for my pleasure.

Before I could analyze my feelings or change my mind, I kissed him gently on the lips.

His eyes flew open and pinned me with a predatory stare. "What are you doing, Colin?"

I looked around the room to see if anyone was watching. The three guys who were sitting in the corner earlier had disappeared, and there was no one else to stand in my way.

"You're irresistible," I offered, "and unless you tell me otherwise, I plan to have my way with you."

His breathing shifted, and my name gusted out in a soft exhale.

I reached under the towel and my hand slowly traveled up his furry thigh. His cock expanded beneath my touch. Encouraged, I scooted closer and sucked on the tender flesh behind his ear. Alain moaned, and I shifted attention, possessing his mouth frantically. His tongue met mine with the same urgency while I continued the unrelenting strokes on his rigid shaft. The silence and cloying heat in the atmosphere lent a surreal feel to this encounter, as if we were alone in the world and free of all responsibilities except our own pleasure.

"Suck me off," Alain ordered after he broke the kiss.

Incapable of refusing, I pulled his towel aside and got down on my knees between his spread thighs. Alain's cock was a work of art, fully engorged with clear drops of fluid sliding tantalizingly down his length. I gazed into his tiger eyes and saw a combination of lust and admiration, which made my pulse speed up.

"You're beautiful on your knees," Alain said, holding my stare. "I need to come down your throat."

I nodded and bent to capture the prize.

Intent on doing my best to give Alain what he wanted, I was unaware that someone had walked in the room. Even through the thick fog, my performance was no longer a solitary event.

My recklessness would have repercussions, but it would be a while before I realized the magnitude of our indiscretion. At the moment, all I could think of was Alain and his impending orgasm.

Chapter Seven

ERROL

"You must be mistaken," I repeated.

Bash looked uncomfortable but resolute. "I'm afraid not. Security insists Colin was at the Biarritz Tennis Club."

"Blowing some guy in a sauna? That's impossible!"

"He's obviously been leading a secret life."

I scrubbed my face in frustration.

"This is disappointing, Errol, but we need to move on and figure out how to handle him going forward."

I shook my head, still in denial. "It can't be true."

"Sweetheart," Bash said gently. "Hasn't it occurred to you that our son might be bisexual?"

"Don't lecture me, Bash! I don't give a donkey's arse if the lad is gay or bisexual. What's bothering me about this is that he hasn't confided in us."

"Maybe this is just damage control after the breakup."

"And I have no problem with that, but to do it in public is foolish, not to mention dangerous as hell. The lad was born with a bull's-eye on his forehead. This is why he has round- the-clock security—"

"Who have obviously failed at their job," Bash snapped. "I'm firing the entire team and starting over."

"Don't be impulsive," I cautioned. "Colin has always been an elusive weasel. At least this current team of bodyguards knows what they're dealing with."

"Unacceptable," Bash argued. "We pay top dollar for their services and to admit they lost sight of him is grounds for dismissal. I want fresh eyes on our boy."

"Did you get a name?"

"Excuse me?"

Errol sighed. "Who's the object of his desire, and where have they been hanging out?"

"I don't know his name, but I can find out easily enough," Bash said testily.

"All right. Gather as much information as possible before we confront Colin. I don't want to stir up any trouble unless we're certain this isn't more than a random event."

"The nature of the relationship is irrelevant," Bash said. "What matters the most are safety and discretion. He can't be handing out blowjobs like some common rent boy."

"I agree, but you know how angry he gets when we try to impose restrictions."

Bash quivered with impatience. "He has an obligation he can't shirk because it's inconvenient."

"Give him some leeway, Bash. The lad is only twenty."

"You know there's no fudging on this," Bash argued. "It's our business to keep an eye on our son."

"If Colin needs our help, then he'll get it," I replied, "but let's get the details before we go in guns blazing."

"You're a fool when it comes to that boy," Bash conceded.

"Maybe I'm a little softer than you, but I know what it's like to be estranged from my parents. I swore I'd never be that kind of father."

"I'm sure Colin is aware of your feelings."

"He's never verbally acknowledged it, but I ken he appreciates me."

"We both love and appreciate you," Bash said gently. He kissed me on the lips and walked out. I picked up the piece I'd been sculpting before he stormed into my studio. Coincidentally, it was a bust of Colin, commissioned to celebrate his upcoming twenty-first birthday in July. I was working off some photos I'd shot before we left home. He looked happier in the stills, nothing like the woebegone lad who had sat with us at breakfast earlier. That alone should have set off a few parental alarms, but I was too focused on my porridge to pay any attention to him. Which was a missed opportunity and a damn shame.

Bash and I had always assumed our lad would be gay, and it had come as somewhat of a surprise when he announced his feelings for Princess Charlotte. I'd been prepared to teach him everything I knew about growing up homosexual, but we'd never had that conversation. If Colin had ever been attracted to men, he'd chosen not to share this with us.

Which was surprising in and of itself. We would have greeted the news with alacrity, but since there had been no big reveal, we'd become complacent. Worrying about the line of succession was no longer necessary. This had been a secret fear of mine. After losing our first born, Andrew, I didn't like the idea of another man being put in such an untenable position. Marrying into a royal family was difficult enough. Despite the advances in the last two decades, male pregnancies were still dangerous. I wouldn't wish that fate on anyone, especially our son, but my fears had proven groundless.

Until now.

With this new development, Colin or his loved one would be at risk. I'd have to adjust my mindset and get back to being a nervous wreck.

Several hours later, Bash appeared with a folder in his hand. "I had him investigated."

"That was quick."

"It's amazing what you can find once you know what to look for. Security got the man's name from the club."

I reached for the folder and skimmed the contents. After staring at the photo of a man who was clearly too old to be involved with Colin, I read the text and absorbed every informative sentence. I was stunned by the facts.

Looking up at Bash in horror, I exclaimed, "This man is thirty-three years old."

"Correct," Bash said. "I don't care how many Nobel Prizes he has under his belt or how good-looking he is. Alain de Gris has no business sniffing around our boy."

Blood rushed to my head, but I tamped down the urge to overreact. If I lost my composure, there was no telling what Bash would do. Once the paparazzi got wind of a scandal, it would be all over social media. "Let's be canny rather than impulsive."

"What did you have in mind?" Bash asked.

"Find out where he lives and pay the man a visit. We can't make snap judgments based on Colin's shenanigans."

"Very mature, Errol. I'm shocked you're not suggesting castration."

"That's always an option if I find out de Gris is a pedophile."

"At least you have a backup plan," Bash said ruefully.

I snorted.

"We should consider paying him off."

"Now who's being ridiculous? The man is accomplished in his own right. I doubt there's enough money in the world to keep him away if he's after an innocent like Colin."

"Right," Bash said succinctly. "There's got to be something he wants. Once we find out, we can make him an offer he can't refuse."

"A bit premature, considering we have no idea what's going on between the two of them."

"Which brings us back to square one. We need to question Colin," Bash insisted.

Out of habit, I reached into my pocket, fishing around for the cigars I no longer carried. "God, I need a smoke so bad. You wouldn't happen to have an emergency stash, would you?"

Bash sighed. "No, but I know some people in high places. I'll be right back."

"Thank you, love."

After Bash departed on his mission of mercy, I tried to analyze my feelings again. What if I was wrong and this person wasn't a predator? Colin had as much right to find a love match as we did, and if that was with another man, then so be it. Except his current choice was in the wrong age bracket. This was a rebound affair, and Colin was asking for trouble. He'd sink into a deeper depression if Alain broke it off. Because it was a given. A successful guy his age didn't need the long list of rules and obligations associated with a royal marriage.

I sank into my recliner and shut my eyes. Our summer vacation had barely started, and we were already facing a crisis. Unfortunately, even a good cigar wouldn't work to calm my nerves or lessen the sting. We'd made a mistake in assuming Colin's personal life was resolved when, in fact, it was falling apart. Bash and I were to blame for this turn of events.

COLIN NEVER SHOWED up for dinner, and as the clock struck ten, we realized he wasn't coming home. Once again, he'd given his security the slip, and they couldn't account for his whereabouts. Bash had been apoplectic, ranting for the last hour, and threatening to personally yank Colin out of de Gris's bed, diplomacy be damned. It was time to do something constructive before he alienated our son or had a heart attack.

I suggested a walk on the beach with Snow. Our bodyguards gave us a wide berth, affording us the privacy we badly needed. The moon was full, and the rhythmic sound of waves rushing to shore and then pulling away had a soothing effect on both of us. By mutual agreement, we decided not to pursue Colin right then. Whatever was going on with our son would still be there in the morning. The scientist might not be our first choice, but Colin had to have feelings for the man if he'd gone back for seconds. We had to shrug it off, lower the blood pressure, and enjoy our peaceful surroundings.

Back in our room, Bash and I reached for each other. Going at it like randy teenagers had always been our default, a convenient and enjoyable form of pain management, but we were in our late forties and mentally exhausted. After lazily sucking each other off, we fell asleep.

When I woke up, the sun was out and our butler had just wheeled in the breakfast trolley. The smell of newly baked bread and strong coffee was powerful enough to pull Bash into a sitting position.

He accepted his first cup gratefully. "Please ask His Royal Highness to join us for coffee."

The butler paled. "I'm afraid Prince Colin hasn't come home."

Bash carefully put his cup down and ordered me to get dressed.

"Why?"

"We're going to get some answers."

"Aye."

We were in our car in less than twenty minutes followed by two SUVs, filled to capacity with heavily armed and well-trained security.

"Does anyone know where de Gris lives?" I asked.

"According to the information we plugged into the GPS, he's not too far from us," Bash replied.

"That's convenient."

Bash's mouth flattened into a severe line. "We'll see about that." He was angry again, but it was on simmer rather than full boil.

"Try to contain your temper," I suggested. "Until we're better informed."

"You mean I can't decapitate the man and ask questions later?"

"Bash."

Glaring at me, he ordered, "Don't try to dilute this, Errol. We have a right to be upset."

"Yer aff yer heid," I murmured, reverting to my Scottish roots. "Colin will never forgive us if we unman him in front of de Gris. Stay calm and I'll watch your back."

"Fair enough," he replied.

It only took twenty minutes to reach our destination. The man's home was as impressive as his credentials. Even Bash looked mollified after setting eyes on the Italian-style villa.

"Can't fault the boy for his taste," Bash murmured.

Bash was out of the car before it came to a complete stop. In an instant, he was banging on the front door with the lion head knocker. Patience was in short supply at the moment, and I sincerely hoped de Gris would open the door before Bash had security break it down with their handy battering ram.

My nerves were strained to the limit by the time the door opened, and an arresting man with tousled black hair and striking catlike eyes appraised us coolly.

"May I help you?"

"I'm looking for my son," Bash blurted. "Get Colin now."

"Sorry?"

Inserting myself between Bash and the man I assumed was de Gris, I inquired, "Is Colin available?"

"Are you talking about Colin Maitland?" de Gris asked with infuriating calmness.

"Don't you mean His Royal Highness, Prince Colin of Sendorra?" Bash retorted angrily.

"Do I?" de Gris asked, a smile tugging at his lip.

Now I was getting upset. He was far too smug and our fatherly hysteria was amusing him. "Aye, ye ken well who we're talking about."

"I'm afraid you're too late. Colin left at midnight."

"I don't believe you," Bash said.

"You're more than welcome to search my home," de Gris said, stepping aside and motioning us inside.

Bash gave his security the order to find Colin while we stood our ground.

"Would you like a cup of coffee while they check my property?" de Gris asked.

"Not now," I replied. "But we're going to sit down with you some time in the future. After we find Colin."

"Feel free to call my office and make an appointment."

My hands curled into fists. I was tempted to wipe the icy disdain off his face, but I couldn't expect Bash to remain in control if I lost my mind. "Aye, we'll do that."

The security team informed us that Colin was nowhere in sight.

"I told you," de Gris said. "Are you sure I can't offer you any refreshments?"

Bash stepped forward and got right in the insufferable man's face. "I don't know where you're hiding Colin, but I'll find him, and when he's back where he belongs, we'll deal with you."

De Gris's mask slipped slightly. "Is that a threat?"

"Nay, it's a promise." Clutching Bash by the hand, I pulled him toward the car. Glancing back, I noticed de Gris had already disappeared behind the massive carved door.

"I'll strangle Colin the next time I see him," Bash grumbled.

We meshed fingers and said nothing more on our way home.

Chapter Eight

COLIN

Loud voices came from downstairs, and my pulse sped up dangerously. What on earth was happening? One minute, I was fast asleep, and then Alain was shaking my shoulder and telling me to be as quiet as possible while he dealt with the intrusion. The urge to follow him was abruptly curtailed after I recognized Da's rough Scottish burr accompanied by Papa's demanding voice inquiring about my whereabouts.

Panic set in, and while I struggled to remain calm, anger and embarrassment quickly replaced the fear. That my family would dare to barge into Alain's home without advance notice was outrageous. Granted, I should have left word that I'd be gone for the night, but the real question was, how did they know to look here? Had my fathers' surveillance team had eyes on me all this time?

I never questioned Alain's instructions and listened to him murmuring some incantation in a language I didn't understand before throwing the duvet over my naked form. Expecting an ordinary blanket to conceal me felt unrealistic, but for reasons I couldn't explain, I trusted him. Angry voices preceded the heavy tread of boot-clad security invading Alain's private sanctuary. I didn't have to see them to know these were the specialists entrusted with my safety. I held my breath, waiting to be discovered, but it didn't happen. By some miracle, they couldn't see me, and the sound of waning footsteps signaled their departure. How was that possible? I threw back the covers and padded over to the large window overlooking the driveway. I was barely in time to see the last SUV in the three-man convoy speeding down the driveway. What in the hell?

A familiar purring caught my attention, and I spun around in time to see Alain stroll in with Merlin padding lightly behind him.

"You're up," he noted unnecessarily.

I must have looked a right mess as I gaped at him. Running my fingers through my bedhead, I reached for the coverlet and wrapped it around me like a sarong.

"Do you want to explain how you managed to keep me hidden in plain sight?"

Alain's self-satisfied smile was contagious.

Grinning, I prompted, "How'd you do it?"

"Let's talk over breakfast."

"Give me a minute to throw on some clothes."

"I rather like naked you."

"What about your staff?"

"There's no one around except me."

"You cook too?"

"I'm a man of many talents," Alain teased.

"Way to make me feel like a slacker."

"Come on, gorgeous. I'm dying for a cup of coffee."

I trailed behind him, still wrapped in my makeshift gown. In the kitchen, coffee was ready to pour, and the rectangular oak table was set for two. A platter of scrambled eggs—steam still rising—accompanied by a mound of bacon made my mouth water. Several slices of buttered toast were snug on a silver bread rack with crystal containers of apricot and strawberry jam at the ready.

"Are you some kind of magician?" I asked wonderingly as I took in the feast.

"Eat first, talk later."

There was something about his tone and demeanor that brooked no argument. Even in a dressing gown, with unruly curls tumbling around his face instead of his normally sleek style, Alain de Gris had a commanding presence. I nodded and picked up a fork.

We ate in silence, which gave me time to go over the events of the last twelve hours.

After yesterday's tennis game and subsequent session at the sauna, Alain had asked me to dinner. We'd driven to the restaurant in his Porsche, where he ordered a bottle of wine—2004 Sierra Cantabria Amancio Rioja— and convinced me to join him. I ended up having two glasses with my flame-broiled steak. After dessert, Alain asked me to spend the night. I accepted eagerly but insisted he drive us back to the club so I could retrieve my car. Alain only shook his head and gave me an enigmatic grin.

"What?" I asked, confused by his behavior.

"Are you still afraid of me?"

I flushed, ashamed to be so transparent. "It's not that—"

"I know who you are," he clipped.

Terror shot through my veins. Had I misplaced my trust and fallen into the wrong hands? "Sorry?"

"You're the heir apparent to the throne of Sendorra," Alain recited in a bored voice. "If I had any intention of hurting you, I would have done it straight away, instead of spending a small fortune on our dinner."

Fear quickly evolved into anger. "When did you find out?"

"The morning after you snuck out like a jewel thief."

"I told you I had issues," I blustered.

"You did, but I hoped your fears might be dispelled after our memorable encounter." Alain quickly added, "Unless you weren't feeling it the way I was. You didn't even stick around for a conversation, Colin. You're lucky I bothered to call you back for seconds."

I stared at my lap.

"Look at me," Alain said softly.

Raising my eyes, I blinked rapidly. "I ran because I was in over my head."

Alain cocked his head. "How so?"

"I've never been in a relationship with a guy before."

"You told me you've been with other men."

"Schoolmates. None of them made any kind of impression. You're in another league altogether. I was afraid I'd disappoint you if I stuck around."

"Yet here we are."

I looked him full in the face. "Do you want me to disappear?"

"No," Alain said, "But I would like you to try to relax."

"The wine helped," I admitted.

"Good. Your car will be safe at the club, Colin. Come home with me."

"Okay."

And despite my initial misgivings, Alain had set me at ease by being the perfect host. We'd shared another bottle of wine in his great room, and I asked him questions about his research, which was the right move. As a member of the royal family, proper etiquette had been instilled at a young age. People enjoyed talking about themselves, I was informed, and inquiring after one's career was always a good ice breaker. It seemed to be working like a charm with Alain. Most of the information he shared on pharmacology and genetics was far above my pay grade, but his enthusiasm and pride was unmistakable. Alain clearly loved his profession, and I resolved to learn more so I wouldn't appear so uneducated the next time.

After my second glass of wine, I was ready for some action. Alain didn't initiate sex so I clambered on his lap like a kitten and plied him with kisses. I'm not sure how we ended up naked in his bed, but we did. After that, it was all an erotic dream I planned on revisiting.

Finished with breakfast, I crossed my utensils on the plate and looked at him expectantly.

"I suppose you want some answers," he guessed.

"Let's start with this wonderful meal. Who cooks around here?"

Alain smirked. "Do you believe in magic?"

That was unexpected, but I wasn't going to lie. Not when I had supernatural abilities of my own.

"As a matter of fact, I do."

"I'm not talking about extravagant Las Vegas showmanship," Alain clarified.

"Do you mean witchcraft?"

He paused, looking surprised by my nonchalant query. After a minute, he replied, "Yes, that's exactly what I mean."

Undeterred, I asked, "Are you a witch?"

His eyes bored into mine, and I didn't flinch under his gaze. My nonresponse appeared to be acceptable, and Alain let down his guard. "My mother, Isabelle, is the high priestess of the Simon Coven. I inherited all her powers and acquired some of my own. Some people call me a warlock, but that has a bad connotation. I'm actually a lone or gray witch, depending on who you ask, and I promise you I don't dabble in black magic. I'm much happier using my skills for the common good."

"I see."

Eyebrows raised in surprise. "Any other man would be running out the door by now."

"You should stop underestimating me, Alain. Tell me about your father. Was he also a witch?"

He shook his head. "He had no magic."

"How did he die?"

"I'd rather not discuss him at this time."

"Fair enough."

Despite my outward calm, I was worried. His gender and our age gap would pose a challenge in terms of my future reign, but this new information might tip the scales in the wrong direction. How would Granny take the news? Did she know Alain's mother? What would these two covens make of our relationship if it ever progressed?

Granny will explode!

"Get out of my head!"

"Colin?"

I started. "Sorry, I zoned out. This is a lot to take at face value."

"Do you need proof?"

"Sure. Can you offer something at a moment's notice?"

Still looking amused, Alain flicked his wrist and murmured an incantation under his breath, again in an ancient language I couldn't discern. Water flowed from the spigot and soapy bubbles rose up in the atmosphere, hovering over the room in an incandescent kaleidoscope of colors. It was magical, and a childhood memory rose unbidden—Granny and me in her flower garden, chasing butterflies and bubbles on a warm summer afternoon. She'd used magic to entertain me, and being exposed at such an early age wiped away any fear I might harbor in the presence of this talented witch.

His smile grew wider after seeing the unadulterated pleasure. "You like what you see?"

I leaned forward on the table and nodded. "Would you like to see one of my own magic tricks?"

Alain's expression grew quizzical. "Are you going to pull a rabbit from underneath the table?"

I took a deep breath and called upon psychokinetic skills I hardly ever used. Hopefully, I'd pull it off without embarrassing myself. One by one, our breakfast dishes floated toward the sink and landed in the water. I focused all my attention on the next task, and clean dishes slipped out and onto the drying rack, sparkling in the morning light.

"Impressive," Alain remarked. "I thought I caught a whiff of magic the other morning. At first, I assumed you were adept at picking locks, but then I realized that no ordinary human could break any of my spells. Tell me about your lineage."

"My granny comes from a powerful coven, and apparently, the witchy gene skipped my father and landed in me."

"Are your fathers aware of your power?"

"Hell no. Magic is a bad word where I come from. My grandda, Emile, made Granny give it up as soon as they married. She taught me as much as possible on the sly, but I know there's a lot more we haven't covered."

"What's your personal opinion on witchcraft?" Alain asked curiously.

"I don't know enough about it to have one."

"Would you like to learn more?"

"I'd have to think about it, Alain. There's a chance I'll alienate my fathers if I delve deeper. What's the point in gaining knowledge if I can't use it openly?" I asked. "At least your magic helped you win a Nobel Prize."

Alain's expression darkened. "My magic has nothing to do with my accomplishments. Years of hard work and research are the only reason for my success."

I was taken aback by his indignation. "I'm sorry. I just assumed you had the upper hand over your fellow researchers."

"Let's resume this discussion another time," Alain said dismissively. "You're going to have to return to the palace and explain your whereabouts."

Sighing, I nodded. "Don't remind me."

"I'll drive you to the club to get your car."

"Why not drop me off at home, which is closer. I'll have someone fetch my car later."

"As you wish," Alain said formally.

"You sound angry."

"No, Colin. I'm being thoughtful. We have a lot in common, and yet we're nothing alike. It's going to take more than good sex to unravel this mysterious connection that seems to be binding us together."

"Did we fuck last night?"

His eyes glimmered. "No. We'd had too much to drink."

"But I'm sure I was more than willing."

"That was never in question," Alain said softly.

"Thank you for being such a gentleman."

"You're welcome."

"Do you think I'm worth the wait?"

"I don't know," Alain replied. "Time will tell."

"That's not reassuring."

"I'm sorry," he replied. "It's best to leave the sugarcoating to greeting cards. I'm a man of science, and making assumptions without a fair amount of research can only lead to failure."

"Aaand there goes the last of my confidence," I said dejectedly.

"Buck up, sweet boy. I'm definitely interested, but we have a lot to think about before our next meeting."

"How soon?" I asked eagerly.

"I'll text you."

I pushed away from the table and stood. "I'm not good at waiting."

Alain's upper lip curled, renewing my determination to have this man despite my misgivings about the future.

"Your impatience is no secret," he teased. "I'm more interested in uncovering your other layers."

"Text me," I echoed.

Chapter Nine

DOWAGER PRINCESS ALEXANDRA

My Parisian shopping expedition had been abruptly ruined by Sebastian. After his frantic phone call the previous night, I ordered my ladies-in-waiting to pack my things, and we took the train back to Biarritz. All for naught because my darling Colin walked into the palace over an hour earlier—giving no explanation as to his whereabouts—and locked himself in his room.

Although he was unscathed and the immediate crisis averted, I was determined to get more information. If he was in trouble, I wanted to know all the details. Not to relay my findings back to his fathers, but Colin and I had a special connection that started the day the doctor placed him in my arms. Due to the unusual circumstances surrounding his conception and birth, I was much more than a grandmother, and I swore to guard him with my life.

This vow was solidified as soon as I felt the unnatural tingling between kindred spirits. I didn't share the news with the men in my life for many reasons. Emile's bitter disappointment at the death of Andrew, the firstborn twin, would only be magnified if I announced that Colin had inherited my supernatural genes. Errol, already suspicious of magic after the way he'd been selected as consort, would be horrified, and Bash would side with his husband and father because he always did.

Fear was a powerful emotion, and my sister's ability to foresee the future and alter present events with ancient spells had spun a growing web of suspicion around our coven that transferred to my husband. Some of the stories were greatly exaggerated, but a few were true, and that was all it took to turn Emile against the Bradfords and all they stood for.

Hazarding a falling-out with my husband, a certainty if I was discovered, Colin was surreptitiously introduced to his complicated genealogy. I didn't want him to grow up in the dark in case his supernatural powers manifested unexpectedly. Since his tutorial had begun at such a young age, it was hardly surprising that he took most of his abilities in stride. His sixth sense and otherworldly impulses weren't frightening evidence of the occult but a special skill set he barely acknowledged and only used in my presence.

While most boys veered away from their female relatives the minute hormones kicked in, Colin continued to confide in me throughout puberty. He considered me the voice of reason whenever he felt bogged down by tradition. Understanding his need to see life without protective filters, I became his willing accomplice and enabled him to slip away from a thousand watchful eyes at least once a year. To my mind, it was an essential part of his education that would make him a better ruler. Sebastian had grown up in a privileged bubble, and it had taken time and the love of a good man to erase most of his bad habits. I didn't want Colin to suffer the same fate. What if he didn't meet someone as patient and loving as Errol? He needed to grow into his own without relying on a future partner who might or might not bring out the best in him.

Blending into crowds without being spotted wasn't easy. Colin had been in the spotlight since birth, and his features were easily recognizable in our principality. Rather than resorting to theatrical makeup and hair dye, I chose magic to cloak my grandson in anonymity. The spell never lasted longer than a few hours, but it was enough to give him a taste of life as a commoner.

After Bash and Errol recounted Colin's most recent hijinks, I had to wonder if he'd slipped on a new identity to go trolling. He'd never done it without my help before, but the boy did like his secrets. Had he stored the proper spell in his memory bank and used it for his night out on the town?

Colin had revealed his bisexual orientation to me a while back and asked me to keep it to myself until he was ready to share the news with his fathers. I told him there was no need to be uneasy as his homosexual fathers would certainly understand, but he insisted his reasons were more out of respect for Charlotte than anything else. Their breakup had been disappointing, and gossips were already speculating on the reasons. He didn't want to compound the rumors by announcing he was bisexual.

Glancing at my wristwatch, I realized that two hours had slipped away since Colin's return. By now, he should have settled down and prepared for the inevitable inquisition.

"Please let me in," I asked after knocking on his bedroom door and getting no reply.

Colin unlocked the door and gaped at me. "I thought you were in Paris."

"I came home as soon as your fathers called."

"Fuck."

"Colin…"

"Sorry, Granny. I didn't want to ruin your holiday."

"My sweet boy. You're far more important than the Boulevard Saint Germaine. What's been going on?"

He threw himself on the bed and made a nest with his pillows while I perched near his feet.

"I think I'm in love with a gray witch."

Of all the scenarios I'd been anticipating, this wasn't even close. Masking my concern, I prompted, "Tell me more."

"Have you ever heard of Alain de Gris?"

"Not until your fathers mentioned him."

"How about the Simon Coven?"

Terror lanced through me like shards of glass. The Bradfords hatred for the Simons was well known throughout the Wiccan world, but Colin didn't have to hear the horrific details of my family's ancient feud. This was not his fight, and he shouldn't be caught in the middle.

Instead of lying to him, something I'd never done in the past, I asked, "Is Alain related to the Simons?"

"His mother is Isabelle."

Fumbling with the pearls around my neck, I did my best to guard my features, but Colin saw right through me and demanded an answer.

"Is she that bad?" He reached for my hand. "You look like you've seen a ghost."

"In a way, I have," I said haltingly. "Her name has always given rise to fear. Before I go into details about the Simon family, can you tell me how far this relationship with Alain has progressed?"

"It's early days, Granny. We just met, but there's a powerful connection I don't understand."

"Were you in disguise?"

"No."

"Does he know who you are?"

"Now he does, but not the night we met. It wouldn't have mattered anyway, because David and Sam dragged me back to their apartment before anything happened. They were pretty shocked to see me at a gay bar."

I made a mental note to cross-examine David at my earliest opportunity. How dare he keep this information from me? "I'll bet they were. What happened next?"

Colin recounted the sequence of events. I grew more agitated after hearing he'd spent the night with de Gris. This relationship was moving too fast for my liking, and it was confirmed by his next question.

"I can't get him out of my mind, Granny. Is it love at first sight, or has he cast a magic spell I can't seem to break?"

"Perhaps a little of each."

"You know how I feel about male pregnancy."

"You're getting ahead of yourself, Colin."

He looked sheepish. "It's what I do best."

"You always were a worrywart. Tell me more about Alain, sweetheart."

"You still haven't answered my earlier question, Granny. Why did you react so badly after I mentioned Isabelle?"

I took a deep breath and blurted out the truth. "My grandfather killed Isabelle's husband."

Colin sat forward. "Alain's father?"

"To be honest, I'm not sure. I'd heard that Isabelle had a son, but I never cared enough to learn anything about him. It was her first husband, Randall, who died by my grandfather's hand."

"Why?"

"It was a hunting accident," I explained, "but it had devastating results."

"If it wasn't intentional, they should have been able to get past it, right?"

"You would think so, but there were some who believed it was premeditated."

"Because?"

"Randall was a womanizer and had been making overtures to my sister, Laura."

"But he was married."

"That never stopped him. Isabelle didn't believe the rumors at first, but after the accident, she was convinced her husband was murdered. Things just escalated after that."

"How?"

"It's ancient history, Colin, and shouldn't be relevant to you."

"The hell it isn't!" Colin exploded. "Once Alain tells his mother we're dating, it'll all come out. I want to be prepared so I can defend myself and your family's reputation."

"Do you honestly think Alain will pursue this relationship? You're thirteen years his junior, and if that isn't bad enough, your status comes with a long list of obligations. This isn't just a question of chemistry, Colin. He would have to make huge compromises, and I can't imagine he'd be remotely interested, unless this is part of Isabelle's plan to get revenge."

"Even more reason to be coached on this bullshit vendetta. Why am I just learning about this now?"

"There was no reason to bring it up before. Besides," I reminded him, "you know how your grandda felt about my family. Witches were a dirty secret and a blight on your genealogy."

Colin frowned. "That is wrong on so many levels. If it weren't for you, I wouldn't be here."

"Your parents will argue that magic had nothing to do with their romance."

"But weren't you enlisted to cast some spell?"

"Yes, but Colin, they don't know I've shared this with you. You can't use the magic pebbles to defend your current choices."

"Why don't we table this for now, Granny?"

"Promise me you won't see him again."

Colin shook his head. "I can't do that."

"You've already made your decision, haven't you?"

"No, but I won't be handled like a brainless child. This is my life, and no one gets to decide my future except me."

"And if I'm right, and you're wrong, how will you protect yourself?"

"You forget I have considerable powers of my own."

"Colin, I'm ashamed to admit this, but I'm the least savvy witch in my family. There's a good reason Emile made me put away the grimoire. If you're going to rely on your powers, you need a much better teacher."

"Do you still have the book?"

"Of course. It's under lock and key."

"I'll study it front to back and top to bottom. Make sure you bring it to me as soon as possible."

"Absolutely not."

"Why?"

"It's dangerous to hone your skills without proper guidance."

"Then find me a good tutor," he insisted.

"If this goes awry, your fathers will never forgive me. And I'll never recover if anything happens to you."

"Get real, Granny. Learning my craft isn't an extreme sport. Nothing bad will happen."

"Maybe not, but don't expect to get caught up in days. It takes time and patience to perfect your skills. I'm in my late sixties and still have much to learn."

"That's because you put your magic on hold."

"You're letting your hormones get in the way of common sense."

Colin gave me an indulgent look that was eerily reminiscent of Errol. "I love you, Granny, but I'm old enough to know my own mind. Please help me, or I'll figure this out on my own."

DAVID LOOKED UP from a stack of papers on his desk, and his eyes widened in alarm after he realized I was in a rage.

"Why didn't you inform me that you and Sam rescued Colin at a gay club?"

"I'm sorry, ma'am. He asked me to respect his privacy."

"You have been my event planner for years. Do I have to remind you who pays your salary? I don't need an excuse to fire you, David. Don't give me another reason to show you and your husband the door."

David looked devastated. "Has anything happened since that night?"

"You tell me," I snapped. "Apparently, you and Sam know more than anyone else around here."

"Sam and I were just as surprised to see Colin at the club. We had no idea he was gay."

"Bisexual," I interrupted. "It was no one's business but his."

"Right," David agreed. "Nonetheless, he appeared intoxicated, and we were concerned he was doing something against his will. The next morning, he assured us that it was a random incident and we had nothing to worry about."

"Didn't it occur to you to mention it to me or His Royal Highness?"

"He asked me to respect—"

"You already said that!"

David appeared crestfallen but resolutely stuck to his original excuse. "I thought it best to keep the line of communication open in case Prince Colin decided to explore gay life in the city."

"What can you tell me about this Alain person?"

"We know he isn't a serial killer or some club boy stalking Colin. After getting his name from the manager, we discovered the man is an accomplished Nobel Prize winner, someone with an impeccable reputation in the scientific community, and on a personal level, no evidence of addictions anywhere."

"That's a lot of information from one source."

"Actually," David said, removing his glasses and polishing them until they gleamed, "Sam has a buddy who is a private investigator. We asked for a basic profile so we knew what we were dealing with."

"What else did you learn?"

"Alain is a private person who leaves the club as soon as he's pulled someone of interest."

"How often does this happen?"

"I can't say."

"Where does he live?"

"In a villa not too far from here."

"Does he have an office in town?"

"I believe so."

"Find out," I ordered. "You need to get as much information as possible, starting with his family. Is that clear?"

"Yes, ma'am."

"I'll leave you to it then."

"Ma'am?" David called as I got ready to walk out.

"Yes?"

"Alain de Gris has a stellar reputation. If I had to pick anyone for Colin, this man would rank high on the list."

"Except for the huge age difference and the ever-present issue of procreation."

"His father found a way around it. Why should it pose a problem now?"

"Colin isn't in favor of male pregnancy."

David looked surprised.

"It's a conundrum," I remarked, acknowledging his confusion, "But one we'll have to deal with if this relationship progresses into something serious. Meanwhile, you and Sam should get as much information as possible. I'll pay for any additional expenses if you have to hire the PI to keep an eye on de Gris."

"Yes, ma'am."

"For my eyes and ears only," I ordered.

"Understood."

Chapter Ten

ALAIN

Colin's supernatural demonstration at breakfast had me wondering what other powers the boy might have. By his own admission, he was unschooled in witchcraft, and yet he was able to move objects with hardly any effort. There was no telling what he'd be able to accomplish with proper training— or me by his side.

That he'd managed to get me thinking in such terms was astonishing, but magic had tipped the scales in Colin's favor. Suddenly, he was far more interesting. Physical attraction, however powerful, was short-lived, but a meeting of the minds was a rare thing and couldn't be dismissed so easily. I wasn't in the market for romantic entanglements, and even if I were, Colin was far too young. But...I wouldn't object to playing Higgins to Colin's Doolittle. We could part ways at the end of summer with a deeper, more meaningful friendship, and perhaps Colin would have learned something about himself that had remained buried due to his grandfather's prejudice.

Throughout history, witches had been persecuted because humans feared what they couldn't comprehend. It was much easier to attribute otherworldly impulses to demonic intervention than acknowledge there were people who were born with the ability to manipulate metaphysical energy. I knew next to nothing about Colin's family, and his granny in particular, but if they'd forbidden the use of her "special" skills, it was obvious they shared the mindset that witchcraft was wrong, and it bothered me to no end. Call it pride or my natural distaste for idiocy, but it wasn't fair to let Colin continue in a state of oblivion. His late grandfather's notion that magic, in general, was inherently bad was preposterous. Like any other preternatural gift, it could be used for good or evil, and I'd be doing Colin a disservice if I allowed the myths to obscure the truth.

Fortunately, Colin was more substance than fluff. He'd already proven that several times by doing the unexpected, and now I wanted to know everything about him. My online search had only revealed the basics. Seeing his royal parents in full protective mode had only reiterated the sad truth of his tightly structured life. He was on vacation, for pity's sake, and should have the opportunity to enjoy himself before the heavy mantle of responsibility was laid on his broad shoulders.

And thinking of his shoulders—and other parts of his delicious body—brought to mind my unexpected reluctance to carry our physical relationship to its natural conclusion. Using alcohol as a convenient excuse had spared Colin's feelings, but my reasons were far from altruistic. Penetration might be meaningless to other men, but not to me. Holding off had been my own defensive mechanism. I knew I'd be in serious trouble if I took that step, and I had no intention of falling in love, no matter how much I craved the intimacy. Colin's unguarded reaction to the new experience might be worth the risk, but I'd learned to ignore my needs. Listening to my inner voice had been the key to my success, and right now, it was telling me to hold off on that final step.

On my way into town, I called my mother to get a weekly update. Although I'd purposely chosen to keep the Simon Coven at a distance, I was my mother's only child, and I tended to be protective. She'd had me in her thirties, a product of her second marriage, and even if she appeared healthy, sixty-nine was nothing to sneeze at. The climbing numbers meant she was slowly approaching the twilight of her life. The thought of anyone shoving her aside, before she was ready to relinquish the chain of command, was disturbing. I didn't want to step into her shoes, but on the other hand, losing the power and prestige associated with my coven didn't sit well either. By all rights, it was mine for the taking, but the other twelve members wouldn't agree since I'd been an absentee witch for too long. All hell would break loose if I waltzed into a meeting and announced my candidacy. Not that I had any intention of throwing my name in the hat, but what if there was a crisis and she flat out asked me to intervene?

"You're troubled," Isabelle said the moment our connection was established.

"I don't even know why I bother to call," I murmured scornfully. "We could just communicate via mental telepathy."

Her peal of laughter reassured me. She still sounded youthful and in good spirits right then. "You know it's so much easier via Bluetooth."

"What did we do before technology?" I teased.

"Double, double toil and trouble," she whispered in a reedy voice.

"Oh, stop. You're only scaring the mice in your hovel."

"A forty-five-hundred square-meter chateau on five acres is no hovel. What's the problem, Alain?"

"You'll choke on your tongue if I tell you."

"I'll do my best to keep that from happening."

"I've met someone."

"Does this person have a name?"

"Colin."

She sighed in disappointment. Homophobia wasn't in play here but a burning desire to have a grandchild. If I kept hooking up with men, she wouldn't live long enough to see the next generation.

"Hear me out, Maman."

"All right."

"It started out in the usual fashion..."

By the time I got to the end of my story, I could tell she'd lost interest.

Until I mentioned the magic.

And Colin's last name.

"He's unsuitable in every way," she said flatly. "Set your sights on someone else."

"I don't need you to tell me all the reasons he's wrong for me. I've already figured that out for myself."

"Then why on earth are we even discussing the boy?"

"He needs a friend and a mentor. I think I can provide that."

"For heaven's sake, Alain. Get a puppy if you have this burning desire to care for a helpless creature. Better yet, find yourself a nice girl, get married, and give me a grandchild. I'm running out of time, and your reluctance to do the right thing has been a thorn in my side for years."

"Are you ill?"

"No," she snapped. "But I'm not getting any younger."

"About that," I said reluctantly. "Have you given any thought to your replacement once you step down?"

"I'm old," she snarled, "not dead! The subject of my succession hasn't come up."

"That you know of," I corrected. "Is the coven going to wait until you pass before they start jockeying for power? Won't they shove you aside the minute they see any sign of weakness?"

"There's no imminent danger. I'm healthier than most of the old biddies in my inner circle."

"Okay, let's drop this topic. Tell me about the feud between the Simons and Bradfords."

"I thought you weren't interested in that brat!"

"I'm curious about his relatives."

"I'll put a spell on him if you don't stay away."

"Maman, you know better. I stopped following your orders a decade ago, and furthermore, you'll never see me again if you do anything to hurt the boy. Instead of issuing empty threats, why not tell me what's behind the bad blood between our families?"

She sighed. "What motivates people, Alain?"

"Is this a trick question?"

"Yes and no. After parsing out the psychobabble, it all boils down to lust and greed. Most human beings are driven by an unquenchable need for money and power, and let's not forget lust. We're all looking to get laid."

"That's rather simplistic, and horribly jaded, I might add. I can mention six other reasons that motivate us."

"Glam it up all you want, but most people don't give a shit about their fellow man."

"I do."

"You're an anomaly."

"Perhaps, but what's this got to do with the Bradfords? Did some ancient crone seduce someone's husband or run off with a prized bull?"

"Colin's great-grandfather murdered my first husband, Rand, and called it an accident."

"How long ago?"

"I was in my late twenties. We'd only been married a few years, and it tore me apart."

"What happened next?"

"I did a little investigating and found out Rand was having an affair with Laura Bradford and that's why he was killed."

"What did you do?"

"I needed proof so I cast a wasting spell. She would survive if the rumors were false."

"And?"

"She died within the month."

"Shit..."

I don't know why I was so surprised. My mother was a vindictive woman who preferred to mete out her own justice. Whenever she nonchalantly mentioned a revenge spell, I knew she was deadly serious. Her motto had always been an eye for an eye, and killing off the woman who'd caused her grief wasn't unexpected.

"Who was Laura?"

"Princess Alexandra's sister."

"Now we're getting to the central plot. Alexandra is Colin's grandmother?"

"Exactly."

"I don't agree with your methods, Maman, but you got your revenge. Why didn't it end there?"

"The Bradfords put a curse on me."

"What kind?"

"They made sure I never found happiness in my next marriage."

"Are you accusing them of murder as well?"

"Let's just say they accelerated your father's death."

"Didn't he have a heart attack?"

"That was the official diagnosis, but I know they had something to do with it. Why would a man in perfectly good health drop dead so unexpectedly?"

"Did you ask for an autopsy to determine the cause of death?"

"No."

"So you're just assuming the Bradfords were behind his sudden demise."

"It's what I would do if I wanted to get back at someone who hurt me."

"Not everyone is a killing machine."

"Don't call me that! I do what I must to protect my own."

"Your methods are Draconian."

"But effective," she snapped.

"Perhaps it's time to move on," I suggested. "It's been decades and most of the key players are dead."

"Only if you promise you won't see him anymore."

"I already told you this isn't a romance, and I insist you stay out of it."

Her silence was telling. Our conversation had taken a turn for the worse, and the high priestess was not going to be strong-armed into backing off. No one told my mother what she could or couldn't do, and I nearly apologized for overstepping, but then I thought of Colin. There was no predicting her next move if she determined he'd become a problem. Instead of backing down, I waited her out.

"I'll keep my distance unless you do something incredibly stupid," she pronounced.

"I don't do stupid."

"Except when you're thinking with your cock."

"I've had enough of this conversation, Maman. I'll catch up with you later in the week."

"Have dinner with me."

"Let me check my work calendar."

"Don't put me off, Alain."

"I won't," I promised before disconnecting the call.

Chapter Eleven

SEBASTIAN

After we'd been informed that Colin was back in the palace, Errol persuaded me to unwind before confronting our son. A few laps in the pool helped, as did the full-body massage at the gifted hands of Patrick, our in-house masseuse.

We were having a light meal on the balcony outside our bedroom when Colin finally sauntered in, looking remarkably innocent. If I'd ditched my bodyguards at his age and remained incommunicado for hours, I would have had the good sense to look guilty, but Colin seemed more self-assured than ever. His confidence was a quality I secretly admired, but not if Errol and I were on the receiving end. Nonetheless, I resolved to keep my temper in check, no matter how this conversation played out. Good advice would fall on deaf ears if it was accompanied by hateful accusations.

"Can we talk?" Colin asked.

"Pull up a chair," Errol said. "Do you want something to eat?"

"I'm not hungry."

"A drink?"

Colin shook his head and sat down. Turning his attention on me, he said, "I think I may be having second thoughts."

"About what?"

"My future."

"Care to elaborate?"

"I've met a guy," Colin stated.

"We heard," Errol remarked.

"From who?"

"Does it fucking matter?" I snapped. "Did you really think your inappropriate behavior would go unnoticed?"

Colin frowned. "Have you been having me followed?"

"Of course we have," I admitted without reservation. "It's our prerogative to make sure you're safe. Anything could happen, and from what I understand, *it did*!"

"That's fucked up."

"Deal with it!" My anger spiked, good intentions notwithstanding.

"It's an invasion of my privacy," Colin fumed. "Stop treating me like a child."

"You're not just anyone," I reminded him. "Put yourself in our shoes for a second. As the heir apparent and our only child, you have no business hooking up with strangers. Anyone you date must be thoroughly vetted. And don't get me started on the PDA. "

"Is that the problem, or were you blindsided by my choice?"

"A little of both," Errol interjected. "We didn't know you were bisexual until yesterday. It would have been nice to hear it from you rather than others. And if you want to explore a same-sex relationship, someone closer to your age would be more appropriate, ye ken? De Gris is too old for you."

"You don't get a say!"

"I'm afraid we do, and I would tone down the attitude if you want to get your point across," Errol scolded.

"There's no winning with you and Papa."

"Colin, listen to reason, lad. We're open-minded about many things, especially your sexual orientation, but safety is another matter entirely."

"Alain would never hurt me," Colin said stubbornly. "Don't make assumptions about him because he's older."

"How long have you known him?" I asked.

Colin flushed. "Only a few days."

"Which isn't enough time to get the true measure of someone's character."

"And I'll never get a chance if you forbid me from seeing him."

Colin's debating skills were on point today, and I was running out of patience. "Why waste your time on someone unsuitable?"

"I'll admit my attraction to him is unexpected, but I'd like the opportunity to date him without constant interference."

"What do you propose?" Errol asked warily.

I glared at my husband. "You can't be serious?"

"Let the lad have his say, Bash."

"Thank you, Da," Colin said. "Alain told me you guys showed up at his place uninvited, so you've already seen how he lives. The guy isn't a scrub;

in fact, he has way more accomplishments under his belt than anyone I know. And for the record, he's been a perfect gentleman so far."

"How can you say that after your performance at the tennis club?" Errol asked. "A true gentleman would have stopped you."

"We were horny!"

"I ken that, but you're a public figure. And there's the health issue." Errol added. "Are you being safe?"

"We've had numerous lectures on this subject, Da."

"You have to use a condom at all times. Do you understand?"

Colin rolled his eyes. "Not that it's anybody's business, but we haven't had that kind of sex yet."

"Why not?" I asked. "I thought you were attracted to him?"

"This is what I'm trying to tell you," Colin replied, turning in my direction. "Alain has treated me with respect from the beginning. We've messed around some, and although I've pushed for more, he's resisted. The guy isn't a predator, and I know I'm safe in his company. You have to trust me on this."

Errol and I exchanged glances. Perhaps I was wrong to jump to conclusions about de Gris, but it didn't change the numbers. A thirteen-year age gap was noteworthy.

"Maybe now that this is out in the open, you'll have a change of heart," Colin pleaded. "Let us date like ordinary guys and see how it pans out."

"There's nothing ordinary about either of you," Errol groused. "What if you fall in love with him? Have you thought about the repercussions?"

"Of course I have, but there's no love involved. I just want to have fun."

"Papa and I fell in love within a matter of days."

"It's true," I voiced. "It'll be much harder to give him up if that happens."

"I'll have to risk it," Colin said stubbornly.

"And here's where I must object," Errol said. "You've never wavered in your belief that male pregnancies are unnatural and endanger both father and child. I'm only throwing this out to keep this conversation real, but if you fall in love with Alain and he reciprocates, where do you go from there?"

"I don't know." Colin's shoulders slumped and he picked up a croissant and began shredding it. He looked confused and miserable. "I shouldn't have to be facing these decisions," he muttered.

"You're the heir," I reminded him.

"Actually I'm the spare."

"Don't prevaricate, Colin. Andrew's death pushed you to the head of the line, and there's no getting around it."

Colin stood abruptly, knocking his chair down in the process. "I'm so fucking tired of being levelheaded and responsible. Give me three months of happiness, and I promise I'll go back to Sendorra at the end of the summer and resume my predictable life."

"Don't rush off yet," Errol begged. "This conversation isn't over."

"It is for me," Colin uttered with complete finality. "You can give me some leeway or continue to be meddling jerks, but in either case, I'll find a way to get around the tight security. I always do."

"Sit your ass back down and look your sovereign in the eye while you're making threats."

"That wasn't a threat," Colin said, picking up the fallen chair and perching on the edge. His eyes, so similar to mine in color, were bright with anger. The confused kid who'd shown up briefly was replaced by a determined young man.

"I will not be ignored or placated, Papa. It's my right to explore my future on my terms. You, of all people, know what it's like to live with such high expectations. Don't you dare lie to me and pretend you marched to Grandda's tune like a good little soldier. I've heard about your wilder days, and I demand equal rights. For once in my life, I'd like to be afforded the same privileges you enjoyed."

"We've given you everything your heart desired from the day you were born," I said. "You've never wanted for anything."

"Except my freedom," Colin blurted. "I'm tired of being the heir apparent, Papa. Let me be the spare for three months. Please."

I turned to Errol for help. There was no way I could cut Colin some slack without having a nervous breakdown. What if something irreversible happened? He wasn't the goddamn spare and never would be, no matter how much he wished it.

Errol leaned back in his chair and shook his head. "We had no idea you felt so strongly about your position."

"Was there even a point in bringing it up?" Colin asked desperately. "We can't change the past, and I realize my future was preordained from the moment I took my first breath. Knowing our principality depends on my ability to produce an heir has weighed on me for years, but voicing my concerns would have been futile. I've already checked; the law is immutable. All I'm asking is that you give me the opportunity to explore my options in any way I choose."

"That's a big ask," Errol said.

"I disagree," Colin replied.

"Despite all his accomplishments, de Gris is a stranger. We can't allow you to see him without your security detail. They can be discreet, but they have to be close."

"And if I refuse? Are you going to bury a tracking device under my skin like you did to Snow?"

"Colin, please be realistic," Errol said.

"You've obviously forgotten what it's like to be young," Colin accused. "Knowing I'm under constant surveillance is the worse buzzkill in the world. Anyone remotely interested in dating me will turn around and walk away."

"Let's compromise," I suggested. "Ask Alain to have dinner with us tonight, so we can feel him out on our own. If things go well, you might get some concessions."

Colin looked hopeful for the first time since he walked in our room. "For real?"

"Yes."

"Okay," Colin said. "May I call him in private?"

I waved him away. "Go ahead."

He walked out of the room, and I muttered, "That didn't go the way I expected."

"Aye."

"Who knew he had such a stubborn streak?"

Errol guffawed.

"I know what you're thinking. The apple doesn't fall far from the tree, and I shouldn't be the least bit surprised."

"Your words not mine," Errol said indulgently.

"Except I never dated an older man. My father would have had a stroke if I'd even mentioned it. And I sure as hell didn't get on my knees in public."

"We have to accept that Colin is mature beyond his years. He seems to have a clear picture of his role as heir apparent, and after his passionate plea, I don't have it in my heart to refuse. Let him have his fling, Bash. De Gris will certainly tire of him in three months, and this will be a nonissue."

I shook my head. "Don't be so sure. What if this escalates into something serious?"

"Let's cross that bridge if and when it happens."

"But we can prevent this from developing by withholding consent," I stressed.

"We can also alienate our son forever by taking a hard line."

"Fuck me."

"As soon as Colin returns with Alain's RSVP."

"It was a figure of speech, Errol, but now that you've offered, I expect to be rendered boneless."

"Have I ever disappointed you?"

I reached across the table, and he met me halfway. Squeezing his hand, I assured him. "You've always surpassed my expectations."

"Aye, and I'll keep doing that until you ask me to stop or the good lord calls me home."

"I'll never stop wanting you, and I command you to live longer than me. You're not allowed to die before I do."

Colin was back with a smile on his face. "Alain will be here at seven."

"Good. Now go away and let me and your da have some privacy."

"Code for fucking."

"Be gone before I bend you across my knee and give you the thrashing you deserve."

Colin gave me a kiss on the cheek instead. "Thank you," he said softly.

I looked up at him and couldn't prevent the swell of pride filling my chest. Despite my misgivings, I had to admire the boy. "I love you, son."

"I know, Papa. Just...for a few months, love me a little less."

Chapter Twelve

ALAIN

I'd been summoned to the summer palace for dinner so the royals could interrogate me in their own environment. All understandable, given this new development with their son, but unnecessary in my opinion. Anything they wanted to learn about me could be found online, and we'd already met, in a manner of speaking.

The whole "meeting the parents" business was incongruous given our non-status, but I found it impossible to refuse Colin's request. If our friendship had any hope of surviving without constant interference, getting to know the royal family under better circumstances was a good idea. The researcher in me was curious about the man who'd risked his own life to create Colin. The big Scot had been dangerously intimidating when he'd shown up at the villa, and I had to wonder what lay beneath the gruff exterior.

And what of the dowager princess? Would she be around to voice her objections given my family history? Colin had mentioned her magic was a bone of contention, and even if she was aware of my relationship to Isabelle, would she dare to bring it up? If the reigning prince shared his father's disdain for the supernatural, he would automatically dismiss Alexandra's fears about my lineage as irrelevant. The prospect of being mentally poked and prodded as a potential suitor was distasteful; nonetheless, it would be the perfect opportunity to figure out if this member of the Bradford Coven was friend or foe.

My research firm had just wrapped up an enormous study involving botanicals and their effectiveness in combating symptoms associated with aging. Most of the major work—lining up volunteers, interviewing, testing, checking, indexing, and collating laboratory results—had already been completed. It was my job to make sure the paperwork was in order. The minutiae required for government funding was a critical part of the process, and it was usually at this point that mistakes were made, jeopardizing months of hard work. It was incumbent on me to make sure nothing had slipped through the cracks. So I stayed in town, instead of jetting off to exotic locales, while the majority of my staff left on a well-deserved six-week break.

To take my mind off my disappointment, I changed the music, selecting a particular set from my varied playlist that was teeming with classical guitars, rhythmic foot stomping, clapping, and the unmistakable sound of castanets. It stirred my senses, invoking flamenco dancers, Rioja wine, paella, and a cozy table for two in a candlelit club I frequented in Ibiza. The Spanish resort town was a favored retreat for many reasons. Aside from the weather, food, and outstanding eye candy, Ibiza offered anonymity. Biarritz was wonderful in the summer, but it was my home, and I couldn't take a piss without being recognized. Not that I had anything to hide, but living under the watchful eyes of my mother's spies, and, worst yet, paparazzi, a by-product of my newfound celebrity, was uncomfortable. Knowing that Colin was in the same situation, on a much grander scale, planted a tiny seed that took root with surprising clarity. Vacationing with him in a remote location sounded immensely appealing at the moment.

In my fantasy, we were lying side by side on colorful beach towels, soaking up the rays. Colin's well-developed chest and finely shaped arms and legs were slick with suntan oil. His lush blond hair, a shade lighter than the soft pelt covering his chest and groin, tumbled around his face.

I rolled over to my side and thumbed Colin's pouty lower lip. He gave me an enigmatic smile that was equal parts come-on and fuck off. He was a haughty shit, but the unspoken challenge cranked my chain like nothing in recent memory. Hearing him beg for release was a huge part of my attraction to this sensuous boy.

In my vision, I sucked on his lower lip and freely explored the enticing landscape until my fingers curled around his engorged cock. Lingering over his face, I delighted in watching my well-bred captive turn slutty before my eyes. The coconut-scented oil and tangy sea air were astonishingly real as I continued to enjoy my reverie. Colin reciprocated, engulfing my cock in one slick move, and the illusion was so realistic I was on the verge of spilling. *Merde.* I had to do something quick or go home and change my pants.

I pulled into a gas station and killed the engine. The facilities were reserved for customers, so I had high hopes they were relatively clean. I swiped my credit card and set the hose to fill my tank while I went to get the restroom key. On my way back, I completed the gas purchase and removed the hose before entering the tiny restroom and locking the door. I jerked off in record time. It was embarrassing in the extreme, but the alternative was worse. Colin would die laughing if I confessed I'd reverted to a horny teenager who couldn't control his impulses.

The rest of the day was uneventful, and I took one last look at my office to make sure I'd addressed all the particulars before confidently dispatching the reams of paperwork that would eventually bring the study to a triumphant conclusion. I had no intention of stepping foot in there until September, three months away. I paused for a second, racking my brain to determine if I'd covered all my bases. Satisfied, I powered off the computers, set the alarm, and walked out the door.

Surprisingly, or not so much after factoring in my juvenile slip at the gas station, I was behaving like a guy on a first date while I scanned my wardrobe. Did I want to appear younger to avoid the criticism regarding our age gap or dress the part of a Nobel Prize winner? I opted for a comfortable middle ground instead—stylish brown pants and a pale gold button-down to complement my dark hair and eye color. At the last minute, I shrugged on a toasted-brown linen blazer. I could always remove it if the royals were in casual attire, but it offered a certain amount of respectability if they dressed for dinner.

I knew I was being foolish. There was no reason to be intimidated by the royal family, but I did want to make a good impression and pave the way to better relations. It would make Colin's life a hell of a lot easier if I could prove that I was an honorable man.

Colin was waiting at the porte-cochere. I'd texted before leaving home, and the sight of him in a casual summer suit made me glad I'd worn the blazer. He shook my hand by way of greeting, acting like the royal he was, instead of a love-struck boy. That role had been mine all day, and I resolved to do better going forward.

"I'm sorry about this command performance," he apologized, "but it's unavoidable if we want any semblance of privacy."

I handed over my car key to the valet and followed him into the palace. "Your parents have a right to be concerned."

Once we were inside, Colin took my hand, and ducking into a private alcove, he pressed his body against mine and gave me a resounding kiss. "Thank you for being so understanding."

I cupped his face in my hands and spent another few minutes enjoying the feel of his mouth on mine. "If this meeting will make your life easier, then I'm doing us both a favor. And thank you for the kiss. You have no idea how much I needed it."

"For real?"

I chuckled. "More than you know."

"Tell me later."

"Definitely. Let's get this over with."

I slid on a protective shield to guard my inner thoughts in case the dowager was present. Even if she was capable of mind reading, I doubted she'd break through my barriers. To date, the only person who had succeeded was my mother, but that had been years ago. As I aged and perfected my craft, she'd stopped being invasive.

Colin led me to the drawing room, and I froze in the presence of the enormous white dog that looked more like a small bear. He growled and bared his teeth until a firm hand landed on his head.

"Don't worry," Colin assured me from the rear. "Snow is harmless."

"Snow?" What a gentle name for such a ferocious creature.

The consort snapped his fingers, and the brute sank down and watched me warily.

Tearing my eyes away from the dog, I asked, "Will it rip my throat out if I make a sudden move?"

"Aye, she will. If I give the command," the consort added in his distinct Scottish burr.

The implication was clear. Do right by my son, or this fluffy bitch will take you down in an instant.

I nodded and turned my attention to the other father. The Prince came forward and extended his hand. "Nice to see you again. Welcome to our home away from home."

"Thank you, Your Highness. I appreciate the invitation."

"Colin insisted we meet under better circumstances."

"Our first meeting wasn't exactly ideal."

"True," the Prince replied. "May I introduce you to my mother, the Dowager Princess Alexandra."

I hadn't noticed the other person in the room until she stepped out of the shadows. She was an older version of the Prince, who Colin also resembled. Her hair was silver, though, and pulled back in a low knot at the base of her head. Fine wrinkles around her mouth and eyes were to be expected, given her age, but they hadn't diminished her classic beauty. She was dressed in a long gown of blue silk, and strands of creamy pearls intertwined with gold chains circled her neck, strategically camouflaging the inevitable loose skin.

Alexandra regarded me with such loathing, I recoiled. She obviously knew I was Isabelle's son. I tried to reassure her by casting a silent peace offering, but she was either too frightened by my presence or unreceptive to magic. Colin had mentioned she wasn't a practicing witch, and I supposed her elemental skills were rusty from disuse. Still, there was no reason for her to be afraid. I tried lowering my shield somewhat, so she could glean my good intentions, but she continued to view me with suspicion.

Finally, she reverted to diplomacy and offered her hand and a stilted greeting. "Thank you for coming."

I was shocked to feel her icy fingers. Fear was leaching out of her and slithering up my arm like a poisonous snake.

Frustrated by her unwarranted reaction, I forced a smile. "I hope we can be friends."

Blinking rapidly, she murmured, "I doubt it."

"Granny?" Colin asked in alarm, having observed our exchange.

Snatching back her hand, the Dowager remarked, "I'm fine, sweetheart."

"Are you sure?" he asked.

Before she could reply, the consort intervened. "Shall we have a drink before dinner?"

"That sounds wonderful," the dowager replied. "Make mine a double."

Gripping her by the elbow, Colin helped her to her seat before sitting down beside me on one sofa. His fathers viewed us from the three-seater across the square cocktail table, which was covered with a large tray of finger food. The dowager's high-back chair in-between the sofas allowed her to follow our conversation like an observer at a tennis match. I could feel her fixed gaze on me the entire time, and she only looked away when I returned the favor.

Instead of ignoring her, I tried engaging in a neutral conversation.

"Did you enjoy your shopping spree in Paris?"

"Until it was cut short," she replied stiffly.

Without hesitating, Colin threw out the first bomb of the night. "Now that you've met Alain, I'm sure you'll agree there's nothing to fear."

She fidgeted with the pearls at her neck and worried her lower lip.

"Colin," Prince Sebastian warned. "There's no need to bring that up now."

Stubbornly, he forged ahead. "Isn't the purpose of this meeting to determine if Alain and I can date without the usual security?"

I put my hand on Colin's thigh and gave a light squeeze. "The evening has barely started, Colin. Why don't we wait until after dinner to continue this discussion?"

"An excellent suggestion," the Prince replied. "Shall we?"

We stood and followed him out the door and into the dining room. The table was beautifully set, and our meal commenced with a garden salad, followed by a bowl of cool gazpacho.

Colin pushed his food around, and it was obvious he was only going through the motions. I ignored him and tried to engage the rest of the family in a conversation about their principality, always a safe topic. They, in turn, asked about my job and research in general. The long meal passed without incident until the crème brûlée was presented in individual ramekins.

"Why are you interested in dating our son?" the consort asked bluntly.

"Da!" Colin protested.

"I'd like an answer as well," Prince Sebastian seconded. "He's far too young for you."

"Do share your thoughts," the dowager chimed in frigidly. "Surely you can find someone who's more your age."

I cleared my throat and viewed my rapt audience. "Excuse me for being frank, but I find your questions insulting. Not to me especially, but to Colin. You're suggesting he's not my equal, which isn't true, but your assumption that he's incapable of handling himself without constant supervision is unfounded."

"He's inexperienced with people like you," the dowager remarked.

"Granny!"

I gave Colin a reassuring smile. Returning my gaze to the royals, I asked, "Do you consider me some kind of monster?"

"Of course not," the consort interjected. "Our primary concern is that Colin has never been in a same-sex relationship. In fact, we weren't even aware that he was bisexual. I think this is what the dowager meant to say."

"Colin's reluctance to confide his orientation with you is disturbing on many levels," I opined. "Perhaps you should be asking yourself why he's kept his feelings to himself, rather than trying to find fault with me."

"How dare you," the Prince lashed out. "We have an honest and loving relationship with our son."

"Do you? Then why are you so blindsided by his interest in the same sex?"

"It's you we find objectionable," the dowager hissed. "Not his orientation."

Colin jumped up and focused all his anger on his grandmother. "Stand down, or I'll say something we'll both regret."

Tears flooded her blue eyes, and she bit down on her quivering lower lip. "Forgive me."

"If it makes you feel any better," I said, trying to bank my anger, which had flared at her unexpected attack. "I have the utmost regard for your grandson, but marriage isn't in play here. At the moment, we're friends. If that changes, you'll be the first to know."

"That's good because it'll take more than one dinner to convince us you're the right choice," the Prince interjected.

Colin flushed, and I was sure he was about to lose it and storm off before anything was resolved.

"Colin," I said softly. "It's all right."

"No, it's not," he snapped.

"We want Alain to understand the implications of dating you," the duke reasoned.

"Do you have any idea how much you're embarrassing me?" Colin raged. "I agreed to this interrogation to get you people off my back for three months. Subjecting Alain to this level of scrutiny is inappropriate on every level. We're friends. That's all."

"A part of me understands your concerns," I addressed the group evenly, "but I can assure you that Colin is safe with me."

"I hope so," Prince Sebastian replied. "You won't live long enough to talk about it if you do anything to hurt him."

"I give you my word."

"Are you opposed to the idea of marriage?" Colin asked me. "Not that I'm in the market either, but I'm curious now that this ridiculous topic has been introduced."

"Not in principle," I replied.

"But?"

"We can talk about this in private, Colin."

"Of course," he said, nodding. "I'm sorry. This whole evening is a disaster."

"No, it's not," I assured him. "Meeting your parents was necessary."

"Thank you," the Prince agreed. "You seem to have more sense than my son."

"I'm afraid I have to disagree," I argued. "Colin is as level-headed as possible, given his circumstance, but you coddle him like a child. Why not allow him the freedom to prove his mettle, rather than swaddling him until he chokes on your good intentions?"

The silence was deafening, but in the end, the royals relented. I might have given them a little push with my powers of suggestion, but I wanted to back Colin. They needed to cut the ties before he went off the deep end. As for the dowager, she wasn't convinced. She continued to glare at me like I was an incubus instead of a fellow witch. I'd have to figure out a way to reach her, or she might cause more trouble. Perhaps a private meeting would be a good idea. I sent her another silent nudge, but she looked the other way.

"Very well," the Prince pronounced. "Leave all your contact information so we can reach you at a moment's notice."

"Fair enough," I agreed.

"And Colin?"

He shifted in his seat but answered the question. "Yes, Papa?"

"Don't make me regret this."

Part II

The Novice

Chapter Thirteen

DOWAGER PRINCESS ALEXANDRA

With a heavy heart and impending sense of doom, I was back on the train with Fiona, my lady-in-waiting and loyal companion of thirty years. Colin's so-called friendship with de Gris went beyond my worst nightmare. My grandson appeared bewitched, and I had to call in reinforcements if there was any hope of averting a crisis. My two remaining sisters, Maura and Brigid, agreed to meet in a neutral location, and the City of Lights was far enough from prying eyes and ears to satisfy their request.

Most people who lived past their sixties had a few regrets, and I was no different. Despite my long and happy marriage to Emile, I'd given up a part of myself to make it work. My family felt betrayed after I turned my back on witchcraft, and, by extension, the entire coven. I'd been a newlywed then, and working to fulfill my duties as wife and mother had influenced my decision. Ours was a good marriage, and I would have done anything to make Emile happy, but his prejudice against magic had created an insurmountable rift between me and the coven that I'd never tried to repair.

Having lived under different circumstances, my sisters, only a few years older than me, looked their age. I felt a pang of guilt at seeing their unfashionable clothes, gnarled hands, and wrinkled faces. Fiona was shocked to learn that Maura and I were only eleven months apart, and Brigid, who was seventy-two, looked like a woman in her eighties. We studied each other warily, and I tried not to judge, but I was clearly unable to keep the surprise off my face. My shallow reaction to their appearance must have been obvious because Brigid lashed out.

"We can't all be Coco Chanel, sister."

"I wasn't expecting that," I said lamely.

"Then stop gawking."

I averted my eyes and nodded.

"What can we do for you that money can't buy?" Maura coldly inquired.

Rattled by the hostility, I reverted to good manners instead of engaging in a sisterly battle, inappropriate given our age and the long list of transgressions I'd accumulated through years of neglect. Unable to participate in family functions, I'd become one of those people who sent monetary gifts during the holidays but rarely asked about their daily hardships. I knew next to nothing about the family dynamics and swore to do better going forward.

Ignoring Maura's question, I suggested, "Why don't we have some refreshments first?"

I signaled for Fiona, and she rang room service, asking them to deliver the high tea I'd preordered. The mood improved exponentially as we enjoyed the lavish array of French pastries and delicate cucumber-and-cream-cheese sandwiches. I ordered a pot of coffee for myself, and one of black tea in case my sisters preferred the latter. After the food was consumed and the tray wheeled away, I dove into the heart of the matter.

"My grandson, the heir apparent, is in trouble."

Brigid's expression softened after she realized this meeting was about Colin and not me. As far as I knew, she had no children, but I could have been wrong. Nonetheless, I was encouraged by her body language.

"Go on," she prompted.

"I should have said something the minute I realized Colin had magic in his blood, but I was too intimidated by Emile and his irrational distrust of witchcraft."

Maura grimaced. "I never liked that man."

"I'm sorry I let things get so out of hand," I said softly. "Can we try to move on?"

"Does the current prince share his late father's views?"

"The last time Sebastian was subjected to magic of any kind, and it was two decades ago, things worked out rather well."

"How so?" Maura asked curiously.

I reminded them of the time Sebastian was in need of a consort and my sisters had given me pointers on using magic to guarantee the right choice. Errol's reaction after it was revealed he'd been selected through witchcraft elicited genuine laughter for the first time since we'd sat down to converse.

"After their marriage, I was ordered to put away the grimoire."

Brigid scoffed. "You were a fool to listen to your idiotic husband."

I shrugged. A spinster would never understand the concessions one made to sustain a good marriage.

"Continue your story," Brigid said.

"I tried to school Colin in a craft I'd never perfected, but it was a mistake. A little bit of knowledge is worse than none at all."

"You're finally starting to talk sense," Maura said tersely. "Go on."

"Colin has started dating Alain de Gris, Isabelle Simon's son."

The collective gasp was reassuring. "He's no match for Alain, but telling Bash and Errol that we're dealing with a powerful witch will only result in a battle of epic proportions. Colin has threatened to reveal my secret if I tell his fathers about Alain's connection to Isabelle Simon."

"What secret?"

"That I've been instructing him in the rudiments of magic."

"Let's back up a minute, sister. Your grandson shares his fathers' orientation?"

"Didn't I mention that?"

"No," Brigid replied.

"Do you have a problem with it?" I had a natural aversion to conflict, but if my sisters made the slightest homophobic remark, I would surely lose my mind.

"Not anymore," Maura said. "When we heard about Sebastian years ago, we were surprised, but now it's old hat. There are gays everywhere."

"Colin is bisexual."

"Same difference," she said disparagingly.

I leaned forward. "It's not the same, but that's beside the point."

"We're not here to debate human sexuality," Brigid argued. "But don't leave out the facts if you want our help."

Resentment flooded my veins as I listened to my older sister scolding me. Had she forgotten who she was dealing with? As a member of the royal family, I commanded respect, yet Brigid and Maura were treating me like a hapless younger sibling. I bit my tongue to hold back a vicious reprimand and concentrated on the task at hand.

"I'm not sure if you know the details surrounding Colin's birth, but I feel the backstory is relevant to our current dilemma."

"Whatever we know is secondhand."

Another reminder that I'd kept them and the entire Bradford family out of the royal loop. Humble pie tasted horrible, especially if it was my own creation.

Searching out the last vestige of my patience, I continued. "Colin's birth was a joyous occasion, but it was overshadowed by the death of his twin, Andrew."

"I assume it was the consort who was artificially inseminated?"

"Yes. Errol was marvelous throughout the ordeal, but there were complications in the end. Colin swore he would never put himself or a loved one in the same position. After he announced his engagement to Princess Charlotte, a childhood friend, we logically concluded that he was heterosexual."

"A mistaken assumption but quite understandable given his actions," Brigid remarked primly.

"Correct. They broke off the engagement recently, and now he's dating Alain."

"It has to be a rebound romance," Maura determined. "It'll fizzle out before it becomes a problem."

"Perhaps, but I'd like to nip it in the bud. Colin appears besotted, and if he stays the course, there's a question of future progeny. Colin will be confronted with the same dilemma Sebastian faced two decades ago. Knowing the extent of Colin's phobia of male pregnancies, there's a possibility he'll insist on carrying the child himself. An unthinkable option for a royal."

"Why?"

"He can't put his life at risk. The onus of responsibility has to lie with his consort, and de Gris would never put himself in that position. Even if he's fool enough to fall in love and take on the challenge, we don't believe Colin will give him the option."

"How refreshingly unselfish," Maura said.

The jab did not go unnoticed, but I refused to engage. Colin's future was more important than asserting myself.

I continued in an even tone. "We—his fathers and I—want Colin to find a love match, but not at such a high price. Maybe we'd have been better prepared if he'd shown the slightest interest in the same sex, but the fact was he'd been fully invested in Charlotte. This new development has changed everything."

"What are you hoping we can do?" Maura asked. "Change his mind through witchcraft?"

"I don't know," I said truthfully.

"Finding someone in our coven who's willing to get Colin's otherworldly impulses up to speed sounds like a good beginning," Maura concluded. "At least he'd be a better match for de Gris if he's as gifted as you say."

"His blood sings with magic," I said proudly.

"That's all well and good, sister, but it's useless if he can't control it," Maura stressed.

"I agree."

"And learning his craft might protect him if Isabelle decides to wreak her usual havoc."

Incredulous, I leaned forward and asked, "Why would she attack an innocent?"

"Because she can, and Colin would be the perfect target," Brigid chimed in.

Her words were spoken with such conviction I knew they weren't exaggerating. The magnitude of this situation was making me light-headed. Bash and Errol would never forgive me for hiding the truth about Alain's connection to a rival coven, but I would lose Colin if I broke his trust.

"Who are you proposing to act as Colin's tutor?"

"My grandson, Drake," Maura revealed.

Surprised, I blurted, "I didn't know you'd married."

"I didn't." She waited to see my reaction, and I didn't even blink. "My daughter Sarah was born out of wedlock, and she, too, had a son without the benefit of marriage."

"I see."

Maura glared. "Don't judge."

"Stop being paranoid. I couldn't care less about marriage—yours or Sarah's. I do want to make sure your grandson is a gifted witch and cognizant of Colin's royal status. Being well-mannered and appropriately dressed will also be helpful."

"You're unbelievable," Maura said with a ferocious scowl on her lined face. "Would I mention him if he wasn't perfect for the job?"

I took a deep breath. "I'm sorry. That came out wrong. I know what you must think of me, and most of it is probably true, but if we can put aside old grievances and stick to the present, things will go more smoothly. I mentioned Drake's wardrobe because I'm more than happy to pay for anything he needs to pass himself off as Colin's equal."

"He's not Colin's equal," Maura said disdainfully. "Drake is superior in every way."

Oh dear. I was a tactless, insensitive old lady, so out of touch I'd forgotten how to communicate without trampling on feelings. Her opinion of Drake might be questionable, but he was her grandson, and I had no right to judge.

"Once again, I must apologize. You know best and I have to trust that you'll have Colin's best interest at heart."

"Damn right I do, but if you belittle Drake in any way, shape, or form, you'll never see us again."

"I promise to do better. May I meet him?"

Maura pulled her phone out of an ugly black purse and dexterously sent off a text. I'd never mastered the art of finger typing and was impressed. After a few minutes, there was a knock on the door.

Surprised, I asked, "He's here?"

"He drove us and has been waiting in the lobby this whole time." She hurried to the door.

To my surprise and utter confusion, Drake Bradford could have been Colin's twin. The genetic stamp of our clan was unmistakable. Also over six feet tall and blond, there was much about him that was familiar, until our eyes met and held. Dark brown instead of Colin's startling blue, and most importantly, coldly calculating. If his eyes mirrored his soul, then Drake Bradford was a force to be reckoned with.

He kissed Maura on the cheek and murmured, "Granny."

"Come and meet my sister, Alexandra," Maura urged, taking Drake by the hand.

He bowed and extended his hand deferentially. "I'm pleased to meet you at last, Dowager."

"Likewise," I responded, reaching for his outstretched hand. He kissed it in an old-fashioned gesture that elevated him in my eyes. "My, you're charming. How old are you, Drake?"

"Twenty-six, ma'am."

"You're a little older than Colin."

"Colin?"

"My grandson is only twenty."

"Our age gap might be advantageous if you want me to teach him."

"How do you know the plan?"

He smirked. "Magic."

I appraised Drake once again. His powerful aura swirled around him in a tantalizing mix of red and orange. Strong colors that suggested infinite possibilities. Was I doing the right thing by introducing this obviously gifted relative into Colin's life? Would he be of help or make things worse? Then again, what choice did I have? I couldn't, in good conscience, stand by and let things between Colin and de Gris unfold naturally. The momentum had to be stopped as soon as possible, and maybe Drake was the right person to do it. He certainly appeared capable, and his charming manner might make all the difference in gaining Colin's trust. With that in mind, we moved back toward the sofas and formulated a plan.

Chapter Fourteen

COLIN

The large tub in the corner of Alain's bathroom was flanked by uncovered windows that allowed an unfettered view of the city and the harbor beyond. I voiced my concern about the lack of privacy, and Alain pointed out that his hilltop villa was guarded by an electrical fence and a powerful protection spell. The exclusive area was off the beaten path, too remote for hikers, and even if anyone managed to break through his first and second line of defense, they'd have to fly or scale the rough granite wall to peer through the windows, only to find they'd been specially treated to reflect the sun and block the inside view from prying eyes.

Tonight, we'd opted for candles instead of electricity, and there were dozens scattered on ledges and counters. The subtle aroma of honeysuckle—one of Alain's favorite scents as it turned out, and the chief ingredient in catnip he informed with a naughty grin—added to the alluring atmosphere. Outside, stars glinted in the cloudless sky, and a full moon illuminated the tub's ornate gilt fixtures. This secluded sanctuary was conducive to romance and magic, two items high on my wish list. I concentrated on the dolphin-shaped spigot and directed the water to flow.

Nothing happened.

Alain stepped closer, encircling my naked chest from behind, and whispered in my ear. "Envision a waterfall."

"I'm trying," I muttered, "but I can only move solid objects. I've never been able to conjure up something inanimate like air or water."

"Close your eyes and block out all distractions. Focus on your desire."

I snorted and whirled around. "It would help if you stopped touching me. At the moment, the idea of blowing you is far more appealing than a warm bath."

"Slutty boy," Alain teased in a husky voice. His arresting tiger eyes flared with hunger as he surveyed me possessively. "Under normal circumstances, I would yield to your irresistible pull, but I don't want to get derailed."

"Can't this wait?" I purred, wrapping my fingers around his impressive erection. "Who's grading me?"

"I am."

Disappointed, I released him. "Tell me why this is so important to you?"

"I'm determining if your skills are learned or hereditary."

"Why?"

"You've had the worst teacher on the planet, and I would like to wipe out whatever your grandmother taught you. Most anyone can cast a spell with a proper grimoire and a modicum of interest, but someone who comes from a long line of witches, like you, has magic in their genes. With proper guidance on my part, your natural abilities should flourish and increase on their own."

"My father, Sebastian, has no magic."

"So you've said," Alain said dismissively.

"I'm not so sure I'm one of the gifted ones," I said. "Wouldn't it have manifested at a younger age?"

"Maybe it did, but your grandmother blocked it in case the other royals got wind of your skills. I don't know what she did or didn't do, but I can feel your power, so I know it's somewhere inside you."

"Leave poor Granny out of this," I warned. "She's trying to make amends."

Alain frowned. "How?"

"By looking for someone who can teach me."

"She need look no further; I volunteer."

"Unfortunately, she doesn't trust you."

"I've given her no reason to doubt me," Alain protested. "If it's my mother she's worried about, tell her to rest assured. Isabelle has been warned to stay out of my affairs. Her ancient feud with your granny's coven has no relevance to our generation."

"That might be true, but there's also the question of our age gap. Granny doesn't approve of our relationship. Period."

"Our *friendship* shouldn't be a cause for alarm. Being young and unattached entitles you to fuck around. It's all part of growing up."

My heart sank upon hearing that remark. I wasn't sure what I was expecting, but his casual dismissal of a pivotal moment in my life was disheartening. I retaliated angrily. "We're not exactly fucking, are we?"

"I already told you there's time for that in the future. Right now, I'm enjoying the foreplay."

"What if I want more?"

"You can always go back to that club on the strip if you're interested in getting laid," he lashed out. "I'm sure you'll find lots of guys who are willing. Despite your granny's low opinion of me, I don't do casual, Colin. Blowjobs are one thing, but penetration would take this to another level. We barely know each other, and I won't be pushed into anything because you're feeling deprived for some reason. Which is crap. I bet you've had more orgasms in the last week than you've had your entire life."

"You don't know shit about me," I said furiously.

Alain's eyes narrowed. "Have you ever been fucked by something other than a dildo?"

The disrespect was humiliating, and I closed my eyes, wanting to banish the sneer from his otherwise attractive face. I wished I could sweep the candles off their ledges and walk out of the room. No one talked to me like that. I opened my eyes to the sound of splintering glass and was shocked to see candleholders tipping over and landing on the marble floor. Flames sputtered and died, leaving trails of hot wax in their wake. I stared in horror after seeing the disastrous consequences of my actions.

"Oh my god."

Alain's smile was rueful. "I apologize for my crude remarks, but I'm enjoying your royal tantrum."

"Asshole," I muttered. "Say another word and I'll flood your bathroom."

And just like that, water began to flow out of the stubborn spigot that had given me so much grief earlier. Was it anger that brought out my powers or being around Alain?

"Come here," Alain said softly, drawing me into an embrace. "I've been treating you like a child when you're far more mature than a lot of my contemporaries."

"Don't ever talk to me like that again."

He kissed me on the forehead. "I promise."

The sound of splashing made me turn in alarm. The tub had overflowed and the resulting deluge was alarming.

"Do something," I cried.

"Why don't you?" he dared.

I waved my hands around, hoping that would put an end to it, but water kept flowing. Alain laughed in the background, enjoying my confusion.

Desperately, I asked, "What shall I do?"

He held me by the shoulders and stared into my eyes, his own amber and green orbs crinkling in amusement. "Think of the Sahara or any other arid landscape. There's nothing but sand as far as the eye can see. Hundreds of feet below, tiny creatures are crying out for nourishment. Allow your water to do some good."

I closed my eyes and concentrated on his words. Little by little, the sound of running water subsided. In my mind's eyes, I could see the lifesaving liquid soaking into the dunes and disappearing from view. I opened my eyes and Alain was smiling widely.

"Did it work?"

"See for yourself," he said.

The tub had stopped overflowing, and the gurgling indicated the water was slowly draining away. With a flick of his wrist, Alain whisked away the shattered candleholders and somehow managed to restore order to the chaos. After he was done, we held hands and padded out of the bathroom.

Standing by the bed, Alain looked at me questioningly. "Did I ruin the mood with my boorish behavior, or do you think some makeup sex is in order? Since you're the injured party, I'll let you decide the form of repayment."

I smiled, relishing my tiny victory. Fucking was off the table. He'd made that abundantly clear, and I wasn't going to beg. However, his insult had inadvertently planted a seed.

At the risk of embarrassing myself, I murmured, "I've never used a dildo."

Alain lifted my chin and peered at me. "Seriously?"

"We couldn't keep that sort of stuff hidden in school, and that's the only place I've had sex with guys."

"This is the second time you've alluded to encounters with your schoolmates, but it seems you didn't do much of anything."

"I might have lied a little bit."

Alain stiffened. "Are you telling me you're a virgin?"

"Only with men."

"That explains it."

"What?"

"Your hesitation when I first tried to kiss you."

"Busted." I chuckled, trying to laugh it off. "Circle jerks and expeditious blowjobs were the sum total of my vast experience before I met you. Kissing was usually reserved for girls."

Alain's features softened and he cupped my cheek. "You've rallied quite remarkably."

"I'm going on pure instinct."

"You're a natural," he praised. "But now that I know what we're dealing with, I'll be less demanding."

I fumed with impatience. "There's no need to handle me with kid gloves. Treat me like any other hookup."

"Don't put yourself in that category," Alain scolded gently. "What I meant to say was that my tutoring will now extend beyond magic. I want all your firsts, in and out of my bed, to be memorable."

Backing down, I released a pent-up breath and unclenched my fists. "That sounds much better."

"Where's this combative side coming from?" Alain asked. "Did you learn how to fight in school?"

"Pretty much. I attended an all-male academy in the Scottish Highlands with rules up the wazoo. Our curriculum included survival skills."

"That's surprising," Alain remarked. "Shouldn't you have been homeschooled?"

"My other dad, Errol, wanted me to experience as normal a life as possible. Granted, my mates were all privileged, so normal was just a word in the dictionary." I stopped and grinned. "I did learn how to play with others."

"Were you a spoiled brat before they sent you away?"

"I suppose I was. Things would have been different if my twin hadn't died. For one thing, I would have been the spare, and my life would be far less demanding."

"You want to talk about it?"

Tell him about our connection!

I shook my head. "Nope, I'd rather have sex."

"Of course you would. Cheeky boy," Alain added indulgently. "Would you like to try a little anal play?"

My breath faltered. "I thought you wanted to wait?"

"More than ever," he replied. "But a dildo will give you a taste of what's to come, plus it's something you can enjoy when I'm not around. Let me show you."

Before I could formulate an intelligent reply, Alain kissed me, teasing my mouth open with his tongue. My pulse quickened while he gently guided me onto the bed.

"On your stomach," he ordered.

I rolled over without resisting, my heart thudding loudly in my chest. Belatedly, I thought about personal hygiene and what I should have done to prepare for this, but all thoughts escaped when Alain dribbled a generous amount of oil on my back and laid his hands on me. Using long and firm massaging strokes, he glided up and down the length of my back, shoulders, neck, and scalp. Warmth spread throughout my body as little by little I began to relax underneath his touch. His hands moved lower to my thighs, legs, and feet, and my breath quickened in anticipation of the next step. His thumbs slid down my crack and pressed against my hole. I shuddered as newly awakened nerve endings tingled. He parted my ass cheeks, and without warning, buried his face against my warm skin and pierced my hole with his tongue. I whimpered and he paused.

"You like that?" he asked in a muffled voice.

"Yes," I responded shyly, and he resumed the intoxicating, rapturous torture. I lifted my hips, silently begging for more. My leaking cock pressed against the mattress, and I knew I would come if he kept this up, but then a drawer scraped open. I peered over my shoulder and watched Alain pull a rectangular box out of the drawer on the nightstand.

"What are you doing?"

"Wait and see."

I buried my face in the pillow. The suspense was killing me, and I wondered what would happen if he inserted a finger or an actual dildo. Would it be better than his tongue? It was hard to concentrate when he was playing my body like a virtuoso. I knew he was being extra cautious after my stupid confession, but this glacial pace was driving me nuts. He responded to my silent complaints as if he could read my mind.

"A good lover will take his time to prepare you," Alain said clinically. "And I'm determined to make this experience as enjoyable as possible."

The next thing I felt was a lubed finger making its way inside me. I clenched automatically, and Alain's soft laugh was reassuring. "Relax, Colin. You'll cut off my circulation at this rate."

"Sorry," I mumbled. I blew out a breath, and my muscles loosened their death grip.

"That's better," Alain said soothingly. After a few seconds, he inserted another finger, and then a third. My body was slowly adjusting to the unfamiliar invasion, and soon I was rocking and clutching the bedsheets.

He inserted the dildo just before I started to beg. It felt weird at first, and I couldn't decide if I liked it or not until the blunt tip grazed something inside of me that sent shock waves throughout my system. I'd never felt anything like it and bit my lower lip to keep from crying out.

"Don't hold back on my account," Alain urged.

His go-ahead was all I needed to let out a stream of porn-worthy filth as I begged and whined for more. I spooged all over his sheets in a shuddering gasp and tiny squeaks of contentment escaped from my throat as wave after wave of pleasure swamped me.

Chapter Fifteen

ALAIN

Colin was beautiful in the throes of passion—sleek muscles distended, tousled strands of gold swaying while he rocked back and forth, seeking more and more friction. The cries of pleasure were enough to make me wish it was my cock grazing his prostate instead of the hard silicone. Knowing I could bring him to such heights made it difficult to follow my own rules, but in the end, I resisted temptation and humped his leg like an oversexed teen as soon as he released.

Thankfully, he was too sated to realize I'd lost control, and he fell asleep shortly after I wiped us down with a warm washcloth. I gathered him in my arms and sighed in a satisfied stupor. What on earth was I going to do with this man-child? I didn't need his granny to tell me he was too young for me—I could do the fucking math. After years of evading a committed relationship, I never thought I'd find myself in such an unlikely scenario. Was it the forbidden aspect of our pairing or plain old lust?

I tried pushing the conflicting thoughts out of my head, but I was too wound up to sleep. A drink might help, or I could cave and resort to magic to find the answers I was seeking. The power of precognition was one of many tools in my supernatural arsenal, but one I rarely employed. As a man of science, I knew that delving into the future and rerouting the present to realize a better outcome could only lead to disaster. But the temptation to sneak a peek into Colin's destiny was irresistible.

Extricating myself from our tangle of limbs, I took the stairs down to the library. Merlin sensed my presence and exited one of his hidey-holes to keep me company. The fire I'd lit earlier in the evening had long gone out, and even if temps were mild this time of year, I was uncomfortable, having left my robe at the foot of the bed. Living alone gave me the freedom to walk around naked, and I often did, but gooseflesh was a distraction, and I needed to concentrate. With the flick of my wrist, the ever-present logs stacked on the grate burst into flames. Problem solved, I poured myself two fingers of whiskey and sank down on the sofa, covering my groin with a throw pillow, and just in the nick of time. Merlin's claws were already extended and he claimed his favorite spot on my lap within seconds.

I scratched behind his ears, and the contented purrs combined with good whiskey and leaping flames were hypnotic. I closed my eyes and brought Colin to the forefront of my mind. The man who materialized was nothing like the sleepy boy I'd left in my bed. Astride a white horse and draped in a blue-and-gold tartan, Colin looked older and far more regal, a character straight out of a romance novel. Flanked by Errol, also in full Scottish regalia, and Sebastian, the reigning monarch, resplendent in black and silver, the party of eight included strangers I hadn't met. In the distance, a large castle materialized, complete with turrets and flying banners. I'd never been to Sendorra so I wasn't sure, but it seemed like a fitting residence for the royal family.

The setting shifted, and now we were inside a church, festooned with pine and holly wreaths, red velvet ribbons, and lit candles. The pews were filled to capacity with elegantly dressed men and women while organ music played Handel in the background. Colin's family was seated in front, but the dowager was missing. At the altar, Colin fidgeted, pulling at his collar and glancing nervously at the procession slowly making its way up the aisle. I tried to see the image of the bride—or groom—but the scene evaporated in a luminous shower of red just as I caught a glimpse of scattering rose petals.

My heart began racing as darkness blanketed the wedding scene, and I was catapulted into a frigid hospital corridor. Men and women in white scurried around while sirens blared in the distance. Behind curtained cubicles, lifesaving machines hissed and bleeped in regular intervals. Sounds of distress were coming from one such space, and I moved closer to get a better look, but an invisible barrier impeded my progress. No matter how hard I tried to break through, I was from another place in time and bogged down by laws of physics. Frustrated, I glanced around, hoping to spot a familiar face. The royal couple were huddled near an elevator, consulting with several doctors. Errol's face was a rigid mask while Sebastian was weeping openly.

My uneasiness grew, and fear changed the natural rhythm of my breathing. Ice water rushed through my veins and I began to shiver. I pushed Merlin aside, ignoring his indignant yelp, and I rose from my present spot on the sofa to get closer to the fire. The heat was restorative, blanketing my frozen limbs as I peered into the flames; however, the familiar scent of burning wood was replaced by the metallic tang of blood. It was so strong I gagged and retreated a few steps. The pungent fumes enveloped me like a noxious cloud, settling in my nostrils. Within moments, I was choking, desperate for clean air. Anxious to end the nightmare, I muttered an incantation, but a wave of brackish liquid seeped into my open mouth. The taste was as foul as the smell, and I flailed against an invisible enemy. My body rejected the viscous fluid, and it rose unbidden, pouring out of my throat and onto the floor in weighty splats. The gray linoleum in my dream was covered in a thick layer of crimson, more in keeping with a slaughterhouse than a hospital.

Errol rushed forward and grabbed me by the arm, pulling me along with such force I practically flew down the corridor. This time, we swept past the troublesome barrier with no problem, and I stopped dead. Tangled up in white sheets streaked with blood and other life sustaining fluids, lay the fragile body of an infant still attached to the umbilical cord. A bloody hand was wrapped around the babe's leg, and a disembodied voice begged the doctor to save the child no matter what. I couldn't see the mother, but I sensed her desperation, and when the same bloody hand shot out and grabbed me by the wrist, I screamed.

"Alain, wake up!" Colin ordered, shaking me roughly. Worry had transformed his beautiful face, and I felt sick for having been discovered in what was obviously a bad place.

"I'm okay," I lied. "Stop fussing over me."

"Bullshit! You're covered in sweat and look like you've seen a ghost. What on earth happened?"

Desperate to purge the horror from my mind without revealing the details of my unfortunate sojourn into the future, I struggled to my feet and hurried over to the sideboard. It was lined with cut-glass decanters, and I poured myself another stiff drink. It went down smoothly but landed in my roiling gut like a ball of fire. I retched and the amber liquid shot back up my throat with a force that left me winded. Grimacing at my mess, I swirled my hands around, conjuring a mop and disinfectant to clear the stench.

Colin was by my side in a few seconds and wrapped me in his arms. "You'll feel better once we get you back in bed. I think you might have been sleepwalking or something."

"Or something," I said vaguely, too shaken to reveal the truth. There would be no more poking around in places I didn't belong and, as such, didn't understand. I had to live in the moment or go mad trying to ascertain the future.

After brushing my teeth, I climbed into bed, pulled Colin close, and wrapped us both in a protective shield. Sleep came with surprising ease, and when I woke the next morning, the sun was already high in the sky. My lover was nowhere in sight.

Puzzled, I made my way to the bathroom for the usual ministrations, and this time, I threw on a robe before heading down the stairs. Colin was seated at the kitchen table, in boxers and a T-shirt, sipping coffee while scrolling through his phone. He looked up and gave me a level gaze.

"Good morning," he said, continuing to examine me from head to toe. "How do you feel?"

I pulled a mug off the rack beside the coffeemaker, filled it, and moved to join him at the table. Before sitting, I ruffled his hair and kissed him on the forehead.

"I'm fine," I assured him. "Sorry about last night."

He put his phone aside and continued to stare as I sat across from him. "Do you sleepwalk a lot?"

"I wasn't sleepwalking," I corrected.

"Then what happened?"

"Give it a rest, Colin."

"You scared me, Alain. I thought you were having a seizure or something."

I sipped my coffee, trying to come up with a reasonable explanation. In the end, I went with a partial truth. "I was bored and thought I'd play around with a few spells. For practice, you know? Magic is like any other skill. You lose it if you don't use it."

"Did you short out a magical fuse?"

"Sorry?"

"Does this happen whenever you dabble in sorcery?"

"What makes you think it was black magic?"

"Finding you in the throes of a panic attack might be a good indication."

"I don't have anxiety issues, and there was nothing sinister about the spell I was invoking."

"Then what in the hell happened?"

I shrugged, going with a nonanswer.

Colin's phone buzzed, and he picked it up with an irritated frown, but not before he issued a warning. "Don't think this conversation is over."

Refilling my now empty mug, I listened to Colin telling his granny he was too busy to go back to the palace to meet some long-lost cousin. Her shrieks of anger came through the tiny speaker, and Colin slammed his fist on the table.

"Enough!"

My eyes widened at the unexpected outburst. I watched with interest as Colin struggled for control. Within minutes, the respectful grandson was back in place, and he apologized, albeit reluctantly.

"I'm sorry, Granny, but you need to keep your voice down."

There was much eye rolling as Colin listened to her rebuttal, and he made a few more attempts to refuse the dowager's command, but he gave in with a caveat I hadn't expected.

"I'll meet this relative on one condition," he said. "Alain's coming along for the ride."

She said something, but Colin persisted. "If he's as gifted as you say, Alain will confirm your recommendation. I'm not going to put myself in the hands of an amateur again."

That statement made me pay closer attention. What was the dowager up to now?

"Don't negotiate with me, Granny. Those are my terms," Colin said firmly. "We'll be there in a few hours."

The buzzing from the other line resumed.

Colin sighed. "We're still at breakfast, and I will not be rushed."

"That was unexpected," I remarked after he put his phone aside. "Who are we meeting?"

"Some Bradford cousin she convinced to hone my magical skills."

"I thought I was going to be your teacher?"

"It's what I'd prefer, but you know how she feels about you. Let's go and meet the guy to make Granny happy. I can always send him packing if you think he's a fraud."

"What if he won't go?"

"He'll do as I say," Colin said, reverting back to his royal persona.

There was something about this side of him I found immensely attractive, and I could feel a stirring in my groin. "You're all kinds of hot in princely mode."

He smirked. "Is that right?"

I stood abruptly and was by Colin's side before he could blink. I lifted him by the armpits and propelled him toward the wall. We were evenly matched at the moment, the clumsy pupil replaced by a man imbuing a sense of confidence that had previously been dormant. After yanking the flimsy belt keeping my dressing gown in place, Colin had me naked and exposed with little effort. He grabbed me by the ass cheeks and rubbed against me with unbridled passion. Last night's tenderness had been replaced by wanton need, and I tore off his T-shirt and nearly shredded his boxers, craving bare skin against my heated flesh. Our tongues tangled for supremacy while I joined our distended cocks with both hands. Finesse was ignored in favor of friction, and I squeezed and stroked while Colin's harsh breathing and demands for more sent sparks of energy flying around the room like fireworks on Bastille Day. There was no longer any doubt in my mind that we were evenly matched—age difference and experience notwithstanding. Colin would be formidable if someone unleashed his power.

We slumped against each other after we released and sank to the floor in a satisfied heap. Reluctant to let him go, I held him close and whispered the sweet words that had been missing during our rush to get off.

"That was pretty amazing."

"You mean it?"

"Why would I lie about something so indisputable?"

"I'm surrounded by sycophants, Alain. Sometimes, it's hard to separate the truth. I don't mean to lump you in that category, but I've come to view most compliments with suspicion."

"There's a lot we don't know about each other, Colin, but I promise you I will never lie."

"You're not telling me the truth about last night," he persisted. "It doesn't take a genius to figure out you've been spinning the facts to protect me."

Whatever doubts I had about Colin's insight were quickly dispelled by this observation. "I may keep certain truths to myself for reasons I can't get into right now, but I swear on all I hold dear that I will never disrespect you with a brazen lie."

"Are you ever planning on telling me about these so-called truths?"

"In due time," I said.

"You do realize I'm falling for you," Colin said softly.

"You've hooked me as well," I admitted. "Against my better judgment."

"Don't start with the age gap again," Colin scolded. "It's no reason to deprive yourself if I'm the one you want."

"We should table this discussion for later. Let's not keep your granny waiting too long."

"Crap. I forgot about that."

"What are you going to do if you can't persuade your relative to disappear?"

"He can't teach me if I'm not around."

"You can't stay away forever," I reminded him. "As much as I enjoy your company, we do have separate lives and obligations."

"Didn't you say you were free until September?"

"Yes."

"Then I can hang out with you until then."

"Let's not get ahead of ourselves," I said cautiously. "We can discuss future plans after we meet your cousin."

Colin's face soured, and I knew he wasn't happy with my answer. Nonetheless, I wasn't prepared to make any kind of commitment.

Chapter Sixteen

COLIN

I chattered inanely on our way to the palace, mindful of Alain's mood. He was distant and answered in monosyllables, clearly annoyed at Granny for dragging in a third party since he was more than capable of instructing me.

Frustrated by this turn of events, I blurted, "This could have been avoided if I'd taken my father's hard stance against witchcraft."

"That's absurd," Alain remarked, taking his eyes off the road for a second. "Would you stifle a natural ability for art or music to avoid conflict?"

"You can't lump witchcraft and artistry in the same category."

"Why not?" Alain asked, gripping the steering wheel like it was someone's neck. "You're either born with talent or you aren't. No amount of money in the world will turn one into a Rembrandt without an artistic gene. And by the same token, you can chant spells until you're hoarse and come up short if it's not in your blood."

"What good can possibly come of having a witch as a ruler?"

"You'd make better decisions for your people if you're in tune with your sixth sense."

"Please, Alain. Are you saying I can prevent a drought or keep a pandemic away because of my uncanny foresight? I'm not god."

"No, you're an inexperienced prince who's been indulged at every turn. Imagine a scenario where one of your leading engineers proposes a new bridge or tunnel to improve your infrastructure. Rather than signing off on the project without a second thought, you can harness your precognitive skills and look deeper. What if there's a geological fault where they lay the pilings and this weak spot causes the bridge to collapse? You could steer him in another direction and prevent a disaster."

"Is that how you won the Nobel?"

"I already told you my magic had nothing to do with it," Alain snapped.

"You use magic all the time," I reminded him. "I find it hard to believe you weren't guided by instinct rather than research."

Alain shifted in his seat, unconsciously bristling at my observation. I could enumerate several instances where he'd resorted to magic for convenience. Why would he suspend his natural talent if it helped with his work? Instead of clarifying, he defended his earlier statement in a combative tone that was off-putting and did nothing to reassure me.

"I've spent thousands of hours hunched over a microscope, and even longer entering data from clinical trials. My otherworldly impulses can't conjure up a cure for cancer or diabetes—"

"Maybe not consciously..."

"Perhaps my instinct led me in a different direction, one I wouldn't have chosen if I were born without the ability to see beneath the surface," Alain admitted, picking up the thread. "But that's neither here nor there. We're talking about you, not me."

"Can I change the future?"

"That's debatable."

What about the past?"

"No."

"If you're making a case for witchcraft, you're failing," I said irritably. "There's no point in mastering my craft if I can't alter anything."

Alain glanced at me with a raised eyebrow. "What would you change if you could?"

"My life."

Alain activated the hazards and pulled over at the first opportunity. We were alone in a designated turnaround and free to have a conversation without endangering anyone.

After unhooking his seat belt, he faced me and reached for my hand. "That's a broad statement, Colin, and quite disturbing. What's so terrible about your current existence? From where I sit, you have everything money can buy, parents who love you, and a brilliant future. Is the thought of ruling your country so abhorrent?"

"I wasn't meant to rule," I said bitterly. "If I could go back in time, I would make sure my twin didn't die."

"Even if you could time walk, and I doubt you can, tampering with the past is forbidden."

"Is there such a thing?"

"What?"

"Time walking."

Alain sighed. "There are some witches who have the ability, but they're the exception, not the rule."

"Can you?"

"No," Alain replied.

"I thought you were a powerful witch."

"It takes more than spells to be able to go back in time and return safely. Time walkers are born with a special gene that enables them to cross through different dimensions. These witches are uncommon, and many of them dabble in the darker arts. Even if I could go back in time, I wouldn't. Trying to change the course of history, or alter someone's fate, is a disaster in the making. It shouldn't be attempted."

"If there was a way for me to go back to the day I was born, I'd make sure the doctors who attended my father knew my twin was in distress. They might be able to save him."

"You mean your mother," Alain clarified.

I blinked a few times and shook my head. "There was no female involved, Alain. I thought you knew I was created in a Petri dish and implanted in Errol's uterus."

"Right," Alain replied, shaking his head. "I forgot your father was intersex."

"And here I thought you were a genius."

"Put a lid on the sarcasm and clear up my misconceptions."

"Sebastian insisted on a love match, and after tests confirmed that Errol was capable of carrying children, they agreed to produce an heir through in vitro rather than involve a surrogate. My twin should have been the heir, but he was stillborn."

"These things happen, Colin. What on earth do you think you can accomplish by going back in time? There's no way to change the outcome of that tragedy."

"You can't know for sure. If the doctors are forewarned and on the lookout for signs of distress, Andrew would become the heir and I'd have the freedom to love whomever I choose."

"Don't you have that right now?" Alain asked, looking confused. "Your parents wouldn't force you into a loveless marriage, or would they?"

"I won't subject the man I love to a male pregnancy, and even though I'm intersex like my father and more than capable of carrying a child, the constitution won't allow it. Apparently, I'm not expendable."

Alain frowned, and I ducked my head, embarrassed that I'd dropped the L word so casually. I assumed he cared, but I could be totally wrong. What if I was just a summer fling? I was the one tripping over my feet to get his attention, not the other way around. My line of succession and the future of Sendorra was the least of his problems. Backpedaling, I tried to downplay the conversation with laughter that sounded false to my ears. Alain withdrew his hand and started the engine.

"We'll talk about this again," he said smoothly. "Your logic is flawed for one thing, and you have people waiting. We've already wasted enough time."

"What's wrong with my assumption?"

"It doesn't hold water," Alain said succinctly. "You wouldn't be you if your twin didn't die."

If I wasn't already regretting my weak moment, his casual dismissal only reinforced my doubts. There would be no more discussions about my future until Alain made his feelings clear.

We were quiet the rest of the way home, and my peace of mind, unsettled by our conversation, received another blow when I set eyes on Drake for the first time. He was sitting with Granny on a sofa and stood the minute Alain and I walked in. We looked alike, but his thinly disguised arrogance rubbed me the wrong way. If Drake expected me to grovel in gratitude because he agreed to become my tutor, he had to work on his body language. I was getting the wrong impression and so was Alain.

It didn't take a clairvoyant to see they hated each other at first sight. Dominant personalities locked eyes and silently challenged like territorial beasts. The atmosphere was thick with tension, and currents of magnetic power, ever-present in Alain, crackled and swirled around Drake in equal measure. I had to wonder if Granny might be right for once. My cousin appeared to be a powerful and competent witch. He'd have no qualms teaching me what I needed to know, providing we could get past this meeting.

Putting on my most diplomatic face, I greeted him warmly. "Welcome, Drake."

"Thank you. I hear you're in need of a teacher."

"Yes he is," Granny agreed, taking me by the hand and leading me to the sofa. She and Drake sat on either side of me while Alain had no choice but to take the opposite seat.

Remembering my manners, I introduced the two men who were still glaring at each other. "Drake, this is my friend, Alain de Gris."

He nodded but didn't rise or extend a hand.

Alain stood and offered a hand in greeting. "My pleasure."

"Is it?" Drake asked with a cock to his head.

Alain scowled and withdrew. He motioned for the door. "May I talk to you in private?"

"Now?" Granny asked. "You men just arrived. Surely it can wait."

"No," Alain said decisively. "It can't."

I followed him, and he whirled on me the minute we were out of earshot.

"Get rid of him."

"I don't think I can," I said, taken aback by his vehemence. "What's the problem?"

"He has some twisted agenda, and I won't rest easy until I figure out what he's about."

"Maybe you're just jealous."

"Don't insult me, Colin. I'm only trying to protect you."

"I have to go through the motions for Granny's sake. She would raise holy hell if I did otherwise."

"You know where to find me."

"Don't go, Alain."

"I'm not sticking around to watch this train wreck. Call or text if you come to your senses."

I didn't try to stop him since I knew it would be futile. Once Alain made up his mind, he wasn't going to budge unless it was life-threatening, and I couldn't lump instant dislike into that category. Shrugging, I returned to the great room, hoping to learn more about my cousin.

He seemed a lot more amiable now that Alain was no longer present, and we spent a few hours finding some middle ground that didn't involve jealous boyfriends or magic. It was presumptuous on my part to call Alain my boyfriend, but we were seeing each other exclusively, and that qualified as a relationship of sorts. It might be more wishful thinking than fact, but boyfriend sounded way better than friend or lover. It carried more weight, to my way of thinking, and might keep Drake from badmouthing him. Not that he'd tried, but I knew Granny wasn't a fan of Alain's, and there was no telling what had transpired between her and my cousin while she was in Paris. My thoughts were all over the place, and Drake broke into my internal monologue.

"I'm straight," he announced, a useless piece of information, since I had no intention of cheating with him. Maybe he hoped I'd pass it along so Alain's hostility would ebb. Not a chance.

Aside from our physical similarities, I learned that Drake and I had little in common. Raised by a single mother who worked as a chocolatier in Bruges, Belgium, he was fluent in four languages—Flemish, Dutch, French, and English—and used to fending for himself. His primary and secondary education were unremarkable, but living on a tight budget had fueled his need for a better life. Street smarts accounted for much of his resilience, and the magic in his blood added the extra element he needed to pursue higher education in Antwerp. After getting his bachelor's in Applied Economics, Drake had been working as assistant manager in a five-star hotel in Brussels. It would explain why he was so comfortable with strangers and new situations.

"Are you hoping to become general manager one day?" I asked after he finished briefing me on his background.

"Unless something better comes along."

"Such as?"

"I don't know," he said, shrugging his shoulders. "Who doesn't dream of winning the lottery or marrying an heiress to have a better life?"

"Is money that important to you?"

"Having an endless flow of cash would allow me to make choices based on desire rather than need."

"You've had to work hard to get this far," I deduced.

"Unlike you," Drake pointed out. "What's it like to grow up in the lap of luxury?"

"I don't know any other way," I admitted. "Working in a hotel sounds much more exciting than training to rule a principality."

"I guess it depends which side of the fence you're looking over."

"How were you able to get away from work?"

"I had vacation days."

"Enough time to get me up to speed?"

"Our grandmothers were vague regarding your needs. What exactly do you want to learn, and why have you waited so long? I could cast spells before I got my first two-wheeler."

"It's a long story," I said. "Why don't we continue this by the pool? Are you up for a swim?"

"Sounds wonderful."

"I'll meet you poolside in about thirty minutes. Ask one of the servants to show you the way."

"Don't worry," Drake said. "I'm sure I can find it on my own."

Chapter Seventeen

ALAIN

All my instincts were urging me to turn back and hang around Drake to get a better read on the guy, but I would appear weak if I showed up at the palace after issuing an ultimatum. I had to let this first meeting between the cousins run its course. Even though I felt the dark magic swirling around Drake like an electrical storm, I had no proof he was there to wreak havoc.

Perhaps Isabelle would be a good resource. She kept tabs on all the covens in Europe through an intricate network of informants. If anyone could shed some light on Drake Bradford, it would be my mother.

Bracing for the inevitable third degree, I pulled up her number and hit connect.

"Alain," she purred. "How nice to hear from you."

"Good morning, Maman."

"What can I do for you this fine day?"

"Do you know anything about Drake Bradford?"

"Apart from his relationship to Maura?"

"Yes."

"May I ask why the sudden interest?"

"I've just met him at Colin's, and my first reaction is pretty negative. Am I being overly sensitive?"

"So you're still involved with the brat?"

"Yes, but I didn't call to get a lecture. Give me the hard facts on Bradford."

"He's an opportunist as well as a womanizer."

"What about his craft?"

"Maura has been grooming him for years, so you can assume he knows what he's doing. Rumor has it that he's more interested in acquiring wealth and power than heading his coven."

"He could do both."

"Not if he's too busy climbing the social ladder. One of the words commonly associated with Drake is pretentious. Apparently, he and his mother went through hard times, and Drake is dedicated to overcoming his past. He's been known to juggle multiple relationships while always on the lookout for the next best opportunity."

"He sounds like a bona fide asshole."

"Sociopath is a more apt description."

"Why would the dowager bring this sort of person into Colin's life?"

"Perhaps she doesn't know what she's dealing with?"

"The more I learn about Colin's grandmother, the less I like her. She's utterly self-absorbed."

"Her sisters don't have much regard for her either."

"Is this another rumor or fact?"

"All true. She cut them out of her life after she married royalty, and they never forgave her."

"And yet Maura has graciously lent her beloved grandson to teach Colin how to be a proper witch." I was beyond furious, and Isabelle had to notice my change in temperament.

"The boy has magic?"

"Yes, but he's unschooled. Now he's determined to learn it all at once. The fool has even asked about time walkers."

"You know as well as I that they are as rare as unicorns."

"Except unicorns are mythical creatures while time walkers actually exist."

"That's true, but it takes more than desire to make it happen. He has to have the gene, for one thing, and learn basic magic if he hopes to ever attempt time walking—"

Irritated, I cut her off, "Tell me something I don't know."

A string of French expletives was unleashed by my rudeness.

"Sorry," I said automatically. "I'm in a foul mood."

"Obviously." Sounding placated, Isabelle asked, "Why use Drake when he has you at his fingertips?"

"The dowager doesn't trust me. Now Colin is stuck with Drake, and I have to suck it up or break off our...whatever this is."

"What is it between you two, Alain? Are you actually in love with the boy?"

"I've got to go, Maman. Nice talk."

I disconnected while she was still spluttering and didn't bother picking up the next call. There was no way I could deflect because I had no answers. Instead of going home and brooding, I drove down to La Marine on the Rue de Mazagran, where I could grab a light lunch and people watch. As I was perusing the menu, I spotted an old acquaintance and raised my hand in greeting. Jack Parsons was my age, a charming Brit I'd met at a conference a few years back. We'd ended up shagging after a particularly boring lecture and parted on good terms. He was quietly attractive, in a rumpled academic sort of way, and I would have welcomed any overtures if I didn't have Colin on my mind. Nonetheless, I didn't push him away.

"Fancy meeting you here," he joked after sauntering over to my table.

"How are you?" I replied, standing to give him the requisite bro hug. "Are you in town for the summer?"

"I wish," he said. "Why aren't you off to some exotic locale as usual?"

"I'm biding my time," I hedged.

"If you're in the mood for something different, try the Seychelles. Breathtaking landscape and the eye candy isn't half bad."

"I'll keep that in mind," I said, grinning at his enthusiasm. "Would you care to join me for lunch?"

"If I'm not intruding."

"I wouldn't ask if you weren't welcome."

Over lunch, Jack gave me more information on his recent diving trip to the Seychelles, and he pulled up several videos on his phone to entice me. Although I'd never tried scuba diving, I wasn't opposed to the idea, and a largely French-speaking populace was a huge plus. The remoteness of the islands guaranteed anonymity, and if I rented a private bungalow, Colin and I could enjoy our vacation without worrying about intrusive paparazzi.

By the time I crossed my utensils over my plate, I was convinced it might be the perfect place to get away with Colin, providing he could convince the royals to let him go. I had no doubt he'd be on board with my plan, but his fathers' paranoia over his safety and Drake's sudden appearance posed an obstacle. If I gave them a detailed itinerary and we promised to check in daily, perhaps they might relent. It was worth a try. I wanted time away with Colin to figure out where I intended to go with this acute obsession. There was no other word to describe my irrational interest in the boy, but I was tired of lying to myself. If my need for Colin survived and continued after two weeks of intimacy, there would be some intense reckoning on life choices for both of us.

Jack shared his resort contacts, and I promised to keep in touch. We were both slaves to our schedules, and the odds of bumping into each other again were slim, but not impossible. He asked who I was planning on taking on the trip, and I gave him some vague answer rather than explain the inexplicable.

It was four in the afternoon by the time I pulled into my driveway. Colin was sitting on the doorstep, looking irritated.

"How long have you been here?" I asked after I removed the security spell that allowed entry into my home.

"Where in heck have you been?"

I was surprised but secretly flattered by his possessive tone. "Out."

"Alone?" he asked.

"How was your tête-à-tête with Drake?"

"Fine, I guess."

"You're not sure?"

"Answer my question, Alain. Were you with someone else?"

"If you must know, I had lunch with an old friend."

"What kind of friend?"

I gave him a pointed look, and he had the good sense to drop the subject. We were in the great room at this point, and we sank down on the sofa to continue our conversation.

"Tell me about your dear cousin," I said, dripping sarcasm. "Is he as gifted as the dowager believes?"

"I suppose, but I don't feel any sort of familial connection. I doubt I'll learn anything from a total stranger. It's more an intrusion than anything."

"Let your grandmother know how you feel."

"We've already had a few words."

"I gather they fell on deaf ears?"

"This is bullshit," he said, frowning.

"Come here," I said, pulling him close. He came to me with the eagerness of a puppy, and I couldn't help throwing out the much-needed bone. "I missed you too."

We made out like teenagers, but I put the brakes on before we ended up in bed. "How would you like to go away for a couple of weeks?"

His eyes widened in surprise. "For real?"

I nodded and gave him an idea of my plans. By the time I was done, he looked upset rather than pleased.

"What is it, Colin?"

"They'll never let me go," he surmised. "Not even if I brought security, which I won't do."

"Why don't we go and talk to them together?"

"What about Drake?" he asked. "Granny will have a fit if I abandon him so soon."

"Maybe a monetary contribution might entice him to back you on this escapade," I suggested, remembering Isabelle's earlier assessment of Drake's avarice. A few bills might go a long way to easing his pride.

"You think?"

"We won't know unless we ask him."

"Let's go," Colin urged.

"Now?"

"The sooner, the better."

Back at the palace, we found Drake in the customized movie theater, enjoying the latest Oscar contender with a bucket of buttered popcorn at his side. He was alone, which was perfect.

"Drake," Colin whispered. "Can we interrupt you?"

He hit pause on the gizmo, and the room brightened as the pin lights automatically engaged.

"What's up?"

Colin started babbling, and I could tell Drake wasn't buying into the plan to send him back to Brussels so soon.

"I'll be more than happy to compensate you for this favor," I interjected. "It'll only be a two-week delay."

"I'm already enjoying my stay," Drake said, looking around the plush surroundings. "I'd rather not leave if that's okay with you."

"They'll never let me go," Colin murmured. "Not if you stay."

Drake looked me in the eye, and I knew what he was going to suggest before the words even left his mouth.

"No," I said adamantly. "Don't bother suggesting it."

"It would solve the problem," Drake pointed out. His eyes sparkled with malice. "Don't you think I'm up to the task?"

"What's he talking about?" Colin looked mystified.

"If I'm not mistaken, Drake is planning to switch places with you."

Colin's face lit up, and he excitedly asked Drake, "You can do that?"

"It's a simple disguising spell," he said nonchalantly. "I did it all the time in school to cut class—left my doppelganger in place while I went off and had fun. Since you and I look so much alike, it'll be a walk in the park."

"But Granny has to see both of us, or she'll wonder what happened to you."

"Please," Drake said with an eye roll. "I'm more than capable of pulling the wool over the dowager's eyes, considering how clueless she is."

"My fathers aren't quite as dim," Colin said defensively. "They'll catch on in a minute."

"Let's put it to a test," Drake challenged. "If I pass muster, you can start packing your bags. Oh, and while you're there, Alain, please teach this boy some magic so he can perform some respectable tricks. I don't want his granny to think I'm a slacker."

All my instincts were telling me this was a terrible idea, but my hormones were leading me astray. The thought of having Colin to myself for two whole weeks without worrying about constant interference from the royals tipped the scale in Drake's favor. Colin's next plea was impossible to ignore.

"Alain?" Colin pressed. "Please let Drake show us what he can do."

I nodded, and we followed Drake out the door.

Part III

Utopia

Chapter Eighteen

DRAKE

After Colin's departure, I moved into his room, bringing essentials like toiletries and underwear, leaving the rest of "Drake's" belonging in the guest room. As assistant manager in a five-star hotel, I was no stranger to excess, but the opulence of Colin's suite, tailor-made for royalty, triggered hidden emotions. I admired his sound system and gaming paraphernalia, checked out his vast collection of shoes, fondled pricy *objets d'art*—a jewel-encrusted letter opener and a creamy marble replica of that monstrous dog they called Snow. The bed linens alone made our hotel's highest thread count look and feel like the cheapest poly blend.

Jerking off and defiling such splendor had to be the ultimate rush. I tested my theory the moment I opened my eyes that morning. It was better than good. I wondered what level of luxury awaited in Sendorra—if I got that far. My life to date had been an interesting mix of magic, luck, and hard work, but this new adventure, which had fallen into my lap through no effort on my part, might result in the biggest payout of all.

There was a knock on the door, and thoughts of my endgame were cut off as I contemplated my next move. "Who is it?"

"It's Granny, Colin. Let me in."

"Give me a second."

Putain. What could she possibly want so early? I sat up, trying to gather my wits. I'd neglected to ask Colin if he was a pajama user or not, and this minor detail might be my undoing. Throwing the duvet over the obvious wet spot, I went in search of clothes. There was a silk robe hanging on a hook behind the bathroom door, and I wrapped it around my naked body while murmuring the disguising spell. Despite my bedhead and the two-minute warning, I must have passed inspection, because the dowager only gave me a cursory glance.

"What's so urgent?"

"Drake is missing," she said, pushing past me. "Where could he be?"

"He's probably out running."

"Really?"

"Yeah, it's his thing," I explained. "You can't control him, Granny. Drake isn't our prisoner. We should be grateful he's taking time off to help us."

Color rose to her cheeks, and I wondered if perhaps I'd overstepped. Before I could figure out how to correct my mistake, she muttered, "I suppose you're right."

"I am right," I said, glad I'd established some boundaries. "Drake and I have worked out a schedule to meet for a few hours each day. Other than that, I plan on enjoying my vacation and so will he."

"But he's only here for one reason," she spluttered. "I'm not paying him to have a good time."

Anger pulsed through my veins upon hearing her words. She was treating Drake like a servant, not family. I had to tamp down my need to lash out; Colin would never reprimand his granny for being a haughty bitch. Instead, I attempted a few ground rules to keep her temper in check.

"You're being unreasonable, Granny. I can only assimilate so much knowledge at a time. Drake and I plan to make the most of our two weeks, but don't expect us to stay locked up in the palace all day."

"Fine." She pursed her lips, but I could tell I'd won this round. "Does Drake have everything he needs?"

"I thought I'd take him shopping later. He didn't bring a lot of clothes."

"Excellent idea. Put all his expenses on your credit card, and make sure you stop by David's office before you leave."

"What for?" *Who in hell was David? Colin didn't say shit about this person.*

"Drake should have some cash in case he wants to go out in the evening. We settled on an amount in Paris, and I'd like him to have half. He'll get the balance at the end of his stay."

"Okay." *David must be her accountant. Easier to deal with a minion than another relative.*

"Will you join your fathers and me for breakfast?" she asked, breaking through my train of thought.

"I'll be down in a few minutes."

She offered her cheek, and I bent to kiss her. It would have been odd if I refused. She and Colin were uncommonly close, and I had to keep up pretenses. I locked the door behind her and stepped out on the private balcony to soak up the view. The dowager was going to be a problem if this was a preview of her level of interest. I'd done what I could to keep her from micromanaging my—Drake's—life, but she was accustomed to blind obedience.

There was a time my mother and I were just as tight. She'd done her best to raise me properly while trying to earn a living, but there were days she'd come home exhausted, too tired to make dinner or ask how I was faring in school. As my magical powers increased, I became more independent and took matters into my own hands. She had never asked where I got the money to buy our daily staples. Hunger always trumped curiosity.

The first time I'd heard about our connection to the royal family of Sendorra, I was confused. Over the years, it had morphed into anger. How could we be related to such a distinguished line and still lack for basic necessities? Other than Granny Maura, no one else in our family had extended a helping hand. I suppose my being born out of wedlock had something to do with it, but my mother wasn't the first woman in history to pay the price for a moment's indiscretion. Why punish us for the sins of a man I didn't even know?

This lack of support had made me more determined to succeed. Decency and fair play no longer factored into my decisions, only the end result. After countless attempts at turning fantasy to reality, namely straw to gold or the more impressive water to wine, I honed my craft until I became an expert illusionist. Even as a young boy, I had realized that magic was my salvation. People didn't bother to investigate an anomaly unless their lives were disrupted in some form. Learning how to replace a stolen loaf of bread or a wheel of cheese with a shadowy image of the real thing had changed the course of my life.

When I'd accepted this job, I wasn't sure what to expect. I'd disliked the dowager from the first, but Colin was another story. I might actually feel sorry for the guy if I didn't resent him so much. Sure, he had it all, but was he better off? The only time Colin seemed genuinely happy was in the company of the witch.

Which brought me to the crux of the matter. Alain de Gris was the only reason the dowager had sought my help. Her desire to get Colin up to speed with his craft had nothing to do with good intentions. Her inherent distrust of Isabelle Simon had transferred to Alain. Refusing to accept the genuine attraction, the dowager believed that Colin was bewitched. The idea that de

Gris would resort to magic to lure Colin into his bed was as improbable as my spinning gold out of straw. Isabelle's presumptive heir had all the qualities necessary to forge his own love connection. From what I'd learned before leaving Brussels, de Gris wanted nothing to do with his mother's legacy. Good-looking and accomplished in his own right, Alain had purposefully distanced himself from the machinations that swirled around any clan. That didn't mean he wouldn't pose a problem. I'd have to deal with him eventually, once I figured out what I wanted out of this charade. At the moment, I'd given Colin what he wanted—two weeks alone with his lover.

Board shorts, a David Bowie memorial T-shirt, and comfortable boat shoes were more to Colin's taste than mine, but I put aside my feelings and donned his clothes like I would any costume. He'd agreed to leave his mobile so the royals could stay in touch, so I slipped the latest iPhone into my back pocket and grabbed his wallet as well. There was no way Colin would leave the palace without these items in hand.

Facing Prince Sebastian and his consort at breakfast would be interesting. I'd breezed through the experiment when Colin and Alain had watched on the security camera the previous night, but in my experience, disguising spells were harder to pull off when the audience was sober. People were naturally inquisitive in the morning, and an alert mind was more challenging. If asked about Drake, I'd tell the royals the same thing I told the dowager. He was a health nut and jogging was a daily occurrence. It would eliminate future subterfuge if Drake never showed up for breakfast. I'd arrange a chance meeting between "Drake" and the royals some time during the day. Having us both present at the same time was manageable, but it was powerful magic and sapped my energy. Keeping us separate was a better plan.

"How's your cousin settling in?" Errol asked in between mouthfuls of his porridge. I'd seen it often enough at the hotel to know it on sight. The consistency and flavor made me gag, but our Scottish guests insisted it be included in the breakfast menu.

"Great so far," I replied noncommittally. "I plan on showing him the sights later today."

"Why is he here again?" Sebastian asked his mother.

"I bumped into my sister Maura in Paris, and Drake escorted us around town. He's her only grandson and she dotes on him. I thought it would be nice if he and Colin finally met."

"Why have you waited so long?" Errol asked. "How many other mysterious cousins are out there?"

"None that Colin would be interested in," the dowager replied stiffly.

"How do you know I won't like them?" I asked, daring to contradict her. She'd be forced to answer a difficult question in front of the royals, and I had no qualms asking it. If Granny Maura was right, Prince Sebastian and Errol had no idea I was there to teach Colin the family trade.

"I don't see how any of this is relevant," the dowager replied dismissively. "Most of your cousins are women anyway and they're married with children."

"That doesn't make them bad people, Granny. I like girls, and I'd like them even more if I was related to them."

"It would be nice if you would make up your mind, Colin."

"What on earth is going on, Mama?" Sebastian interrupted. "Are we talking about female relatives, or are you still upset about his breakup with Charlie?"

"We're going to miss Charlie, but that's neither here nor there," Errol interjected. "Colin has made his decision, and we'll respect it."

Charlie? What was I missing? Colin never mentioned that name.

"Thank you," I remarked. "Drake seems like a great guy. Maybe he can help me arrange a reunion. What do you think, Father?"

Errol raised an eyebrow. "Father?"

Oops! I used the wrong honorific. Colin had left me a list of names and I'd picked the wrong one. I laughed, trying to pass off the slip as a joke. "Come on, Da. You know my brain is mush at this hour."

"Are you hungover?"

"We did have a few glasses of wine before bed last night."

"And yet your cousin is out there pounding the pavement?"

"He's a gym rat."

"Maybe he'll teach you a thing or two," Errol said. "You spend too much time on video games instead of sports. At your age—"

"Enough, Da. I'll make sure to ask Drake about exercise. Now, can we get back to the reunion? What do you think?"

"Bash?" Errol asked the Prince. "Wouldn't it be great to meet the rest of the family?"

"Not now," the dowager interrupted. "Perhaps we can arrange something at a later date."

"Why not?" I persisted, just to see her squirm. There was no way the dowager could subject herself to the Bradford clan after ignoring them for so long. They would come, but friendship would be the last thing on anyone's mind. Verbal evisceration or worse was a more likely scenario.

"Let's revisit this conversation another time," Sebastian said diplomatically. "We've waited all these years. There's no sense in making a quick decision now."

"Why did you keep them away in the first place?" I asked the dowager. "Didn't it occur to you that I was lonely and a cousin or two would have been welcome?"

"That's enough, Colin," Errol said. "I'm sure there's a good reason we aren't close to your granny's side of the family."

"I'd like to hear it."

"Another time," the dowager replied. She stared at me, trying to figure out why I was badgering her. I could feel her probing, sneaking into my brain to get more info, and that wouldn't do. I counterattacked with my own weapon and relished her grimace of pain as the debilitating migraine struck.

"Will you...excuse me?" she said haltingly. "I need to lie down."

"Are you okay, Granny?"

"I have a terrible headache all of a sudden."

"Let me walk you to your room."

"Thank you, Colin. That would be helpful."

The concerned royals were both standing at this point.

"Shall I call a doctor, Mama?" Sebastian asked.

"No need," she said, waving him off. "An ice pack will do the trick."

"Colin, see Granny to her room," Errol ordered.

"Don't worry, Da. I've got this."

Chapter Nineteen

DRAKE

I used the dowager to fill in the blanks. Charlie, David, and a broken engagement were details Colin had left out of his narrative before leaving town, and I needed to know it all to avoid another situation. In her befuddled state, "Granny" answered all my questions without hesitation, and after she swallowed the migraine medicine, I wiped out the memories of our little chat. She'd wake up with no recollection of anything but the food she'd had for breakfast.

David, the person I was supposed to see before leaving the palace, was queerer than a three-legged dog. Not that I was a homophobe or anything, but the men in this place were predominantly gay, and I found it interesting that the dowager objected to Colin's liaison with another man. Or was it only Alain who posed a problem? Would she have reacted similarly if Colin had shown up with some random dude he'd met on the beach? I tucked the thought away for future use. There was no telling if it might come in handy or not, and I never discarded useful bits of information.

In the meantime, I planned to extract as much information from David as possible. He certainly had no qualms asking me what was going on in my life.

"How are things going with Alain?" he asked while he counted out the cash for Drake.

"Fine."

"I understand you've been seeing a lot of each other."

"Don't start with me, David. I've already had enough lectures from Granny."

"She's only concerned for your future."

"And I'll tell you the same thing I told her—butt out!"

"It's hard to let go of a dream."

"Which dream are you referring to?"

"The one where you and Princess Charlotte get married and fill the nursery with great-grandchildren."

"The stuff of fairy tales," I said with an edge to my voice.

"You don't have to convince me, Your Royal Highness. I'm married to a man; however, I was around at the time of your birth. The dowager doesn't want a repeat."

What was he talking about? "My fathers are happily married."

"I meant the medical issues," David said. "It's my duty to warn you that your grandmother wishes to prevent anything permanent with Monsieur de Gris."

"Thank you for telling me, David."

This guy was playing two sides of the coin, and although I was the last person in the world to judge, I found his obsequiousness irritating. On the other hand, the dowager wasn't going to be around much longer, and Colin would be ruler someday. So David deserved points for hedging his bets.

"I feel responsible in a way," David blundered on. "After all, Sam and I were there the night you met Alain, and I did advise you to explore your orientation if you felt the need."

"Right."

So David was feeling guilty. More to the point, Alain was Colin's first homosexual experience? If this was true, it didn't bode well for dear old cuz. The witch couldn't be strong-armed into anything against his will. I hadn't even tried to read his thoughts the last time he was around. The protective shield around him radiated like moonbeams, and I knew I was no match. Poor Colin was wasting his time if he was hoping to tie Alain down. And why did the dowager feel that magic would tip the scales? None of it made any sense.

"Now I'm wondering if I should have dissuaded you somehow," David said apologetically.

"Don't be absurd," I snapped. "You know that's impossible."

"Are you certain you can't find a compromise with Princess Charlotte?"

"I'm not a fucking charity case, David. My life isn't up for negotiation."

"Charlie would never think of you that way, Your Highness. She's loved you for years."

Charlie was Charlotte. One less thing to figure out.

Before I could venture a reply, David added, "I heard she's having second thoughts over the breakup."

"Where'd you hear that bit of slander?"

"On Twitter."

"Oh, please."

"Rumors are usually based on fact," he defended. "She may have mentioned it to a friend."

"I don't have time for this crap. Is the money all there?"

He handed me the envelope meant for Drake. "I hope you're not upset with me."

"Not at all," I assured him. There was no sense getting on his bad side. "Let me know if you hear anything more about Charlie."

"Will do."

I left the palace in Colin's BMW convertible. The tantalizing smell of leather upholstery and a top-of-the-line navigation and sound system, coupled with the reliable purr of a powerful engine, were a tangible reminder that I inhabited another man's space. To own a car of this caliber had been an elusive dream, one I chased whenever a highborn guest pulled into the hotel and tossed the keys at our valet with entitled ease. It was impractical to own a vehicle if you lived in a bustling city, where public transportation was dependable and parking fees were astronomical. Nonetheless, my physical and financial constraints had never stopped me from taking lessons and applying for a driver's license. Preparing for any eventuality was a credo that governed my life. As I guided my dream car around the hairpin curves leading to the center of town, I wondered what it would be like to switch places with Colin permanently. He was clearly miserable in his role as heir apparent while I was soaking up the whole experience.

Granny Maura hadn't had to twist my arm to take this job. Knowing I'd be living like a prince for two weeks was inducement enough. The dowager wanted Colin schooled in witchcraft while the coven was more interested in payback. Years of indifference deserved some retribution, and Granny had no qualms dishing out revenge in the form of a grandson who was prone to mischief on a grand scale.

"Spend as much of their money as you can," she'd advised before we parted. Bitter much?

Now that I'd met the players, I realized I'd be doing Colin a favor by taking his place—if I convinced him it was the perfect solution. He'd continue being Alain's lover and I would pick a bride—maybe change Charlotte's mind for real, if I could get her between the sheets—and knock her up before anyone was the wiser. Presenting the royals with a pregnant fiancée was a fait accompli, and there would be more rejoicing than hand-wringing. Why not shoot for the stars if they were aligning in my favor?

The sheer novelty of buying anything my heart desired, on top of being treated like a prince, was a heady experience, and I expanded on my idea as the day flew by. Any doubts I had were wiped out after Colin's phone chimed and Charlie's name showed up on caller ID. It was an omen, a virtual go-ahead from the goddess, and I wasn't about to turn it down.

Me: hey you!

Her: wassup?

Me: same ol shit. kind of miss you ;)

Her: o_o

Me: for reelz come visit

Her: when?

Me: tomorrow

Her: are u sure?

Me: yeah

Her: \o/

Me: ☺

Disconnecting, I ordered another glass of wine and worked out a plan. It would have to be a done deal before Colin got back, but it depended on the chemistry between Charlie and me. I brought up Colin's photos to see what she looked like. Not that it mattered, but it would be an additional perk if she was attractive. As luck would have it—and mine continued to be stellar—there were many shots of Colin with a gorgeous brunette who could only be Charlie. They made a cute couple and appeared to be genuinely happy. I was more interested in her solo shots, and as Colin had been foolish enough to give me full access to his phone, I had no qualms swiping through the wide selection, even the ones meant for his eyes only. She had a killer body and wasn't ashamed to show it off. Her tits were on the small side, but I was more interested in her ass and legs, and hers were first class. Luscious lips pouted or smiled in alternating poses, sending my thoughts straight to the gutter. She was sexy as fuck, and I wondered how on earth Colin couldn't make this happen. Then I remembered he was into cock and I answered my own question. Definitely, his loss was my gain.

Upon my return to the palace, I checked on the dowager for a couple of reasons—to make sure she hadn't suffered any residual damage from my subliminal attack and to prep her for Charlie's visit. She might be a senior, but she wasn't stupid. For Colin to abruptly shift his interests from Alain back to Charlotte would be entirely unrealistic. But I was no stranger to unusual situations, and handling women, regardless of their age, had never been one of my problems. They loved me as much as I enjoyed them.

I knocked on her door and entered after getting clearance. She was reclining on a chaise lounge and smiled at me.

"How are you feeling?"

"Much better, sweetheart. How was your day in town?"

"It was great. Drake went a little crazy shopping, but I knew you wouldn't object. He seems like a good guy and outfitting him is the least I can do."

"By all means," she agreed. "Where is the dear boy?"

"He's taking a shower. We're going out tonight, but I wanted to check on you first. You scared me this morning."

"That's so sweet."

"Can't have anything happening to my favorite lady."

"Don't worry. I'm as strong as a horse. Is Alain joining you for dinner?"

"We're meeting downtown."

"Won't Drake feel like a third wheel?"

"He'll hook up soon enough. The guy's got moves."

"I suppose he does. Working in the hotel industry tends to add a bit of panache to anyone."

"Guess who called?"

"Who?"

"Charlie. She's coming to visit tomorrow."

"That's a surprise," the dowager voiced, sitting up straighter. "Did she say why she's coming?"

"I guess she's bored. Drake and I can entertain her."

"That sounds like a good idea. Make sure you bring her by for a visit. Is she staying here?"

"I'm not sure."

"Tell her she's welcome. You know how much I enjoy her company."

"Don't get your hopes up, Granny. She's just visiting as a friend."

"Maybe you'll have an epiphany," she teased. "You never know."

I rolled my eyes in a perfect imitation of exasperated Colin. "I doubt it." This irritating mannerism was going to give me migraines if I didn't find an alternative. Maybe shrugging would work next time.

"Go on and get dressed. Mustn't be late for your date."

I stood and kissed her one more time. She was an easy mark, and I had no doubt things would go my way if I pursued my plan. A lot would depend on Charlie, but I'd never met a female I couldn't seduce. It was another form of illusion, and I was a master at my craft. Tomorrow would be another interesting day.

Chapter Twenty

COLIN

The plane banked left as we began our final approach to the international airport in Mahé, the largest island in the Republic of the Seychelles. My nose was pressed to the window like a child as I viewed our destination from my cushy seat on the jet Alain had chartered for our trip. The reason for his extravagant gesture was twofold, he'd explained after I asked why we weren't flying commercial. It was easier to stay under the radar by avoiding traditional methods of transportation, and he could afford it. If anyone spotted me in a security line at an international airport, it would end up on social media with the usual who, what, and where attached to my name. Although Drake provided the perfect cover, it was incumbent on us to do our part to assure that our getaway was a success.

Thoughts of my witchy cousin came to mind as I recalled the events leading up to this unexpected vacation. Alain had been reluctant to put our fate in the hands of a stranger, but I was wildly enthusiastic with Drake's plan to assume my identity. The first and most important step was wardrobe. Like any good actor, he required a change of clothes. He was into suits and the latest in fashionable, but casually chic, attire while I favored skinny jeans, T-shirts, and boat shoes. Drake tried on several of my shirts, all the while muttering on the poor selection and settled for a blue linen button-down Granny had purchased for me on her last shopping spree. It still had the store tag hanging from one sleeve. Next came the jeans. Mine were too tight, but he managed to squeeze into a pair of old chinos. Finally, he shampooed the stiff product out of his hair and let it air dry, the finishing touch necessary to turn him into my clone.

Drake instructed us to observe him by accessing the security feed on my phone. The public rooms in the palace had cameras in place, and it was simply a matter of logging in. Alain peered over my shoulder, and we watched Drake's performance at dinner. In the short time Drake had been around me, he'd managed to pick up a few of my mannerisms, and he played his new role with surprising aplomb. Granny and my fathers were completely unaware they were dining with an imposter. They asked after Drake, and my clever cousin informed the family he was resting after his journey. They accepted the explanation and moved on to another topic of conversation. It was hard to tell if magic was creating the illusion or Drake's superb acting, but it was working.

Seeing him in action convinced me to ignore my misgivings after he suggested a communication blackout. There was less chance of discovery if we eliminated random texts or calls, and the less I knew about palace activity, the easier it would be to have a good time. I left my mobile with him. It was an extension of my brain, and I was reluctant to give it up, but Drake pointed out my fathers or Granny wouldn't be able to communicate with the persona staying behind, so I gave in. All my life, I'd missed my twin, someone who could share the burden of our royal lineage, and right then, Drake was offering to watch my back.

As expected, Alain wasn't keen on the idea. He was a control freak, and Drake was basically a wild card, someone we hardly knew. How could we put out any fires if we were kept in the dark? His inherent distrust was about to ruin a perfectly good plan. Drake was doing us a huge favor, I argued, and begged Alain to give Drake the benefit of the doubt.

After much cajoling on my part, Alain finally relented, and we left Biarritz with no fail-safe in place. A couple of hours into our trip, the trench between Alain's eyebrows disappeared, and he reluctantly admitted that relinquishing control for two weeks might not be such a bad thing. I might have sealed the deal with a leisurely hand job while we huddled underneath a blanket in the secluded bedroom.

Now, in the dawning light of day, with an island paradise sprawled ahead, I was euphoric. Even if Alain and I ended up parting ways at the end of the summer—a thought too horrible to contemplate but rooted in reality—I would always have the memories of this special time to comfort me.

"It looks just like Jack described," Alain's quiet voice sounded in my ear. "He said it was heavenly."

"I'm dying to explore. Can we leave the unpacking until much later?"

"Anything you want," he said warmly. "This is as much your vacation as it is mine."

The arrival area for private jets was tiny but efficient. There was one official who gave our passports a cursory glance, and no one bothered to inspect our luggage. We were done in record time, and after thanking our pilot and arranging for the return trip in two weeks, we walked into the sunlight and boarded the waiting Jeep, which would take us to our accommodations at the Hillcrest Villas located on the northwest side of the island. Although it was a bit of a hike, privacy was paramount, and we'd been assured the area was exclusive and only occupied by a few other guests. In addition, the higher elevation would mean a drop in temperature thanks to seasonal trade winds.

As we drove through the capital city of Victoria, the driver dutifully pointed out architectural landmarks and other points of interest. After hours in a climate-controlled plane, my body was reacting to the sweltering heat. I could feel moisture pooling in my pits and groin, and drops of sweat dotted my nose and forehead. We'd been warned that summer wasn't an ideal time to visit as temps were high with humidity factors in the eighty percentiles, but weather hadn't been our priority. The air conditioner in the car wasn't doing much to cool me off, so I rolled down the window, hoping to catch a breeze. Instead, a waft of cooked food redolent with unfamiliar spices seeped through, reminding me that our last meal had been hours ago. Alain sniffed the air like a curious cat and turned to me with wide eyes.

"What is it?"

"There's magic in the air," he pronounced.

"You can tell by inhaling?"

Alain nodded. "It's unfamiliar but ancient and powerful. I can actually picture a few people gathered around a fire pit."

"Sheesh, all I'm picking up is the delicious smell of food."

Alain laughed. "I'm hungry too."

"Let's hope we'll find a well-stocked larder at our rental."

"They promised we'd have everything we need and then some."

"I wonder if I can learn anything from these local witches."

"Patience, *mon chaton*. We need to work on the basics before we delve any deeper."

Chaton? Calling me his kitten wasn't much by way of endearments, but I treasured the implication. Alain's reluctance to embrace his feelings for me had been falling away in tiny increments, and although I was less experienced in matters of the heart, I knew we were moving in the right direction.

At our destination, I was glad we'd opted for a villa rather than the duplex the rental agent had first suggested. Yes, it was too much space for a couple, but Alain and I were used to palatial accommodations and would have been uncomfortable in anything smaller. We'd filled out a questionnaire online to help them determine our needs, and the section pertaining to food was surprisingly detailed. Taking the time to reply had paid off now that I was confronted with a variety of our favorites lining the cupboards and refrigerator shelves.

Someone had kindly left a bowl of seafood salad with a note stuck to the plastic wrap mentioning it had been made only a few hours before. This same person recommended we throw away any leftovers as daily specials were part of our package. A short menu had been supplied so we could tick off our preferences. There were baskets of fruit and freshly baked bread, along with the usual staples such as milk, cheese, yogurt, and butter. Several varieties of tea and coffee were within arm's reach of the machine, and beverages ranged from high-end booze to bottled water and juices. The kitchen appeared well-stocked and highly functional. Anything we lacked could easily be ordered.

After our light lunch, we hit the shower, and then crashed in the comfortable king-size bed. The sheets were silky smooth, the air conditioner cooled us off admirably, and sleep came within minutes.

I reached for Alain upon waking and came up empty. After twisting and stretching tight muscles that had been dormant for hours, I made it to the bathroom without bumping into walls. Afterward, I followed the light seeping in through the open bedroom door and found Alain sitting on the sofa going through a stack of brochures. He had a pen in hand and was scribbling notes on a small pad as he scanned the information.

"Hey," I greeted as I padded barefoot across the room toward the kitchen, separated by a wraparound counter. After pulling a bottle of water from the fridge, I took several deep gulps and went to sit by Alain. "What are you doing?"

"Planning our itinerary," he said. "There's a lot to see, and I'm trying to map out a daily schedule so we don't miss anything."

"Can't you put that analytical brain of yours on hold while we're here? The best part of being on vacation is having no schedule."

"We won't keep a rigid timetable," Alain explained sheepishly, "but it's always good to have a general idea or we'll waste precious time dithering."

"And we mustn't have that," I agreed. "What's caught your interest so far?"

We put our heads together and came up with a rough plan for our stay. As we got more familiar with our surroundings, we'd add or subtract items. One thing we both agreed on was learning how to snorkel. The photos of white sand beaches and crystalline water were too tempting to ignore.

"Are we going island-hopping?" I asked.

"There's a three-island snorkeling tour we could try if you're interested."

"That sounds good," I said, folding my legs underneath me and snuggling closer. "Don't forget to pencil in some time for lovemaking, or we'll be too tired to get it up."

Alain smiled indulgently. "I'm trying to remember if I was this horny at your age."

"What were you like growing up?" I asked. "We never talk about your childhood."

"It seems so long ago."

"You're not that old," I pointed out. "Some would say you're in the prime of life."

"It's all relative. You weren't even born the first time I jerked off."

"Maybe not, but I bet I was younger than you when I first discovered my dick."

"Why would you think that?"

"I was a precocious child," I admitted.

"How old were you?"

"Eight or nine."

"Hah! I was only six."

"You can't jerk off at that age," I argued.

"Why the hell not?"

"Can you?"

Alain laughed and pushed me onto my back. I spread my legs, and he slid over me to fall into the perfectly constructed slot.

"You are definitely good for my ego," he remarked.

"How's that?"

"You're ready to rock and roll in no time flat. Makes me feel irresistible."

My gaze settled on his smiling face to see if he was serious. "Was there ever a doubt?"

I wanted to say much more—that he was beautiful inside and out, and I couldn't look at him without wanting to touch, and being treated like an equal instead of a child was more than I'd ever hoped for, and saying *I love you* was always on the tip of my tongue—but it was way too soon, and so I poured my feelings into the kiss instead . He responded with equal fervor and I had to believe he gleaned the truth. We pulled down our boxers, and the feel of skin against skin was heavenly. Soon we were arching and squirming for release. I wrapped Alain in a cocoon of arms and legs and keened with pleasure as we shuddered to completion.

Later, after we cleaned up and were back in bed, I brought up the subject of his childhood again. "Tell me about your magic. When did your mother first start teaching you?"

"As a toddler."

"Isn't that kind of young? You could have set your house on fire or changed the cat into a dog?"

"First of all, the things you mentioned aren't accomplished by waving a wand and chanting *presto chango*. If it were that simple, the world would be full of magicians. Isabelle's teaching techniques were fundamental. She'd demonstrate and I would imitate her. We started out with the easy stuff: moving my bottle of milk from dresser to bed or setting my stuffed animals in motion to dry my tears. I remember watching a toy elephant flying around the room like Dumbo and wishing I could join him. I may have hovered a few inches off my mattress before crashing back down again. When I was old enough to read, she cracked open the Simon grimoire."

"Is it a thick book?"

"Over a thousand pages."

"How long did it take to master?"

"Years. I'd study a spell, and she'd test me before we moved on to the next page."

"Did you memorize the spells?"

"The ones that pertain to this century. Witches add spells as they're created and pass them down to their offspring. Some of them are hundreds of years old. There's no point in learning how to prevent conception with herbal teas if one can buy a packet of birth control pills."

"Why not toss the dated stuff?"

"A grimoire is more than a book of spells. It's a historical document, a tangible record of a family that's irreplaceable."

"Can you have yours scanned and copied?"

"I've done that, but copies aren't the same."

"How can ordinary paper have any kind of power?"

"It's not the paper as much as the magical threads within."

"So all I'd have to do is steal your grimoire to learn the family secrets."

"Not necessarily," Alain replied. "If it fell into the hands of an amateur, someone with little or no magical power, it would be interesting reading and nothing else."

"But if I were to read it?"

"You'd learn a thing or two after studying it for years."

"Years?"

"It takes the right teacher and a lot of patience to perfect our craft."

"Weren't you destined to head the Simon Coven?"

"I chose a different path."

"You're lucky Isabelle gave you that option."

"She's not happy about it, believe me. Now she's set her sights on a mythical grandchild to step into her shoes."

"You're under pressure to get married and reproduce?"

"In a manner of speaking."

"I guess we're in the same leaky boat."

"Except my failure to comply won't generate a constitutional crisis."

"My biggest fear is putting someone else's life in danger."

"I don't follow."

"If I were to marry a woman, the point is moot, but if I follow my heart and marry a man, history will repeat itself, and I can't risk it."

As I expected, Alain didn't reply. There wasn't much he could say without revealing his hand. I'd often heard that one should never ask for anything unless you were willing to accept a negative response. At the moment, I didn't have the internal fortitude to press for answers. It was too soon to end our relationship, and there was no doubt in my mind that Alain would walk away if I boxed him into a corner.

"You have years to make a decision," he murmured into my ear. "Let's enjoy the moment."

"I'll be twenty-one soon, and the pressure will mount."

"When's your birthday?"

"Sixth of July."

"That's right around the corner."

"I know."

"Isn't there some sort of protocol associated with it?"

"A party has been mentioned."

"You're not going to be around for the planning," Alain pointed out.

"I'm sure Drake can improvise; he's in the hotel industry."

"What if they ask him questions he can't answer?"

"Like what?"

"Oh, I don't know," Alain mused. "Something mundane like your favorite cake."

"You worry too much."

"And you act like you don't have a care in the world."

"You're wrong. I worry, too, but I'm trying to concentrate on the here and now. God knows I'll never be able to do this again. We'll be back in plenty of time to stave off disaster."

"I hope you're right," Alain replied.

Chapter Twenty-One

ALAIN

I waited until sleep overcame Colin and quietly left the bedroom. Once my internal alarms were triggered, I couldn't put aside my questions for another minute. I'd agreed to keep my nose out of Drake's business, but no one said anything about avoiding the internet. That would have been like asking me to have a lobotomy. I pulled my laptop out of my carryall and booted up.

History will repeat itself was going around like a loop in my jet-lagged brain. What was up with the historical reference? How was I supposed to circumnavigate a problem if I had no idea who or what I was dealing with?

A little over an hour later, I had most of the gruesome details of the Duke of Maitland's near fatal pregnancy and the death of Colin's twin. My brief glimpse into the future had no meaning at the time, but now I was sure it had been a premonitory symptom of another male pregnancy. Who was the poor creature bleeding out on the bed? It couldn't possibly be me— I would never subject myself to such horror, and even if I could be persuaded, I wasn't intersex and therefore not a viable candidate. Colin had made it clear that he would not be allowed to carry a child, so that left a gaping hole in my need-to-know brain. Who would the royals enlist to carry on their line?

And if that wasn't enough to give me insomnia, the idea of Drake running wild in Biarritz planning a celebration that was much more important than Colin let on was pushing all the wrong buttons. My protective instincts, already on simmer since the beginning of this trip, climbed to dangerous levels.

I sent Isabelle an email to let her know I was out of town. Regardless of her feelings for Colin, Isabelle would never betray me, and she could be counted on to ferret out the truth. I needed eyes and ears on the ground in Biarritz to make sure Drake was behaving. My mother was suspicious of everyone, and this disturbing attribute had been instilled in me from an early age. As much as I wanted to trust, accepting anything at face value went against my nature.

As I was getting ready to shut down the computer and return to the bedroom, Isabelle's reply landed in my inbox.

Her: Why didn't you tell me you were going on vacation?

Me: It was a spur of the moment thing.

Her: Do the royals know?

Me: They have no idea. Colin asked Drake to front for him and this is what's keeping me up.

Her: DRAKE BRADFORD!

Me: Yup.

Her: Stupid move.

Me: Possibly.

Her: What are you worrying about?

Me: Anything and everything.

Her: Typical.

Me: Shitcan the lecture. Maybe I'm misjudging him.

Her: I doubt it.

Me: Let me know if you hear anything.

Her: Like what?

Me: No idea.

Her: You're being impulsive.

Me: I'm not.

Her: That boy is melting your brain.

Me: Without a doubt.

I disconnected before reading her reply. Humiliation sent blood rushing to my cheeks. No amount of denying would convince Isabelle that I wasn't acting like a fool. Her snide comment about my liquefying brain was particularly insulting. I was acting like a starstruck fanboy lusting after an untenable movie star. There were many adjectives I could attach to my feelings for Colin—irrational and impulsive came to mind in an instant.

Instead of embracing the truth, I was convinced it was a mistake to fall in love with someone so young. People would accuse Colin of having daddy issues, and I'd be the pervert reaping the benefits. It was a lie, but my success had been hard won, and I couldn't subject either of us to ridicule. Would any other Nobel Prize winner put themselves in such a delicate position? Or was I overthinking as usual because my mother was a witch and our coven attributed my accomplishments to magic rather than hard work?

On display from a young age, I was used to being scrutinized by members of our coven. They were jealous of anything Simon-related and waited in malicious anticipation for me to fail. I'd proved them wrong, but that didn't mean they'd stopped hoping I'd crash and burn. Falling in love with Colin might destroy whatever credulity I'd accumulated so far.

Even worse than hiding from my truth was the yearning in Colin's eyes. The boy was in love and searching for a commitment I was unwilling to give. He probably put whatever qualms he'd had about Drake aside in the hope that this trip would force me to confront my relationship demons once and for all. Whatever Colin might have lacked in experience was overlooked by his pugnacious determination to have me at any cost. He was relentless, and I had to give him the highest marks for trying.

Back in our room, I found Colin spread out on the mattress, bedsheet thrown off to the side. He was naked, and I devoured him hungrily while I stepped out of my boxers to join him. Perching on the edge of the bed, I paused for a few minutes. He was stunning, an enticing combination of his fathers' genealogy that set my pulse racing whenever he was close. I toyed with his hair, carding the golden strands, and imagined a not-too-distant future where I would yank on said locks and listen to his cries of pleasure as I breached him for the first time. Goose bumps rippled across my flesh, my body reacting predictably. I caressed the curves of his perfect ass and dipped a finger into his crack, teasing the tight furl that clenched automatically.

He raised his hips in silent invitation. I slid into bed, my cock throbbing with need, and reached for the lube I'd placed under the pillow. Spooning against him, I pumped him a few times, relishing the instant response as he thickened in my hand. I pushed between his legs, dragging my cock against his taint and balls.

"Do it," he whispered urgently. "Fuck me."

I would have given my left nut to comply, but I'd sworn to hold off until I was convinced this was right. Stifling a frustrated groan, I stroked him in tandem with my jerky movements, a parody of the act we were both craving, but which I was stubbornly avoiding. I sped up at his urging, and the heat from multiple pressure points pushed me over the edge. He spurted hotly into my hand while I covered his legs with my seed.

On cue, he rolled over and looked me in the eyes.

"You're going to fuck me before we leave these islands."

Unable to hold back a comment at his cheeky assumption, I said, "We'll see."

"Prevaricate all you want, but I will have you in the end."

I fell silent. This wasn't the first time Colin had read my mind. Was it magic giving him this power over me or plain old lust? Whatever trick he employed was working. My resolve was crumbling around my feet, falling away in tiny increments like an eroding landscape. Emotions were betraying me, completely out of sync with my logical brain. I had to find a happy medium if I didn't want to end up hurtling over a cliff. I knew Colin was more than a fling, but I'd given myself a timetable and wouldn't be rushed. This was one study that deserved all the attention and experience in my learned arsenal, because there was no going back once I made up my mind.

But.

There was always a "but" whenever it came to Colin. He'd snuck through my defenses and laid waste to my original plan to keep him at arm's length. Loving him was so much easier than pushing him away. I kissed him softly.

"Go to sleep, *chaton*. We can argue tomorrow."

Colin put a hand on my cheek. "Have you always been this stubborn?"

"All my life."

"No wonder you're so good at what you do."

"Sorry?"

"You're probably the kind of researcher who would rather go hungry and be sleep deprived than throw your hands up in the air in resignation."

"I don't stop until I'm out of options."

"Don't quit on me, Alain. Despite your misgivings, and I know you have several, we were meant for each other."

"How can you be so sure?"

"Fate would have never put you in my path."

"That's it?"

"It's enough for me."

Merde. How could I argue with that kind of logic?

I didn't reply, and he rolled over, and we were back in our favorite position, with me taking the spot of the big spoon. He never let go of my hand, clutching it to his chest possessively. The innocence of youth was on his side, and I found there was no defense in the face of his certainty. I would have to stop fighting every step of the way. It would make for a more enjoyable vacation, and maybe for the first time in my life, I would allow logic to take second place to the life-giving muscle that sped up whenever Colin was around.

THE NEXT FEW days were straight out of the tourist guidebook. We tackled the big island first, exploring Victoria's quaint shops, fish and fruit markets, the colorful Hindu temple, museums, and botanical garden. We hiked, zip-lined, snorkeled, sailed, sunbathed, and ate a wide variety of foods in the tiny cafés that lined the cobblestone streets.

I insisted on visiting the Bel Air Cemetery, one of the Seychelles national monuments, built around the time the city was first established. Colin's surprising reaction when we approached the area gave me pause. He clutched my hand and refused to step foot onto the hallowed ground, swearing he felt bad juju. I explained that it was the living we had to fear, not the dead, but Colin wasn't convinced. Something or someone had provoked this inexplicable dread. I gave the area a careful sweep to see if I caught a whiff of the preternatural and came up empty.

"You know what?" I said, disappointed, "I'll come back another day."

"Hell no," he argued. "I'm not going to let you do this on your own."

"Why not wait for me outside the gates?"

He chewed on his lower lip, looking undecided for a few moments. I waited patiently while he made up his mind, noting the tightness of his shoulders and visible pulse in his neck. He was staring at a crumbling tombstone in the distance, fixating on the innocuous jumble of rocks as if anticipating some ghoulish apparition. He moved closer and, with a brisk nod, took my hand and pulled me into the cemetery.

Shady trees blocked the sun in many places, lowering the temperature considerably. The smell of newly turned earth and lush vegetation was overpowering, and I mentioned as much as we strolled on the verdant grass that carpeted the area.

"It's creepy as fuck," he remarked, oblivious to the beauty.

We wandered around, and I paused occasionally to study the names and dates etched on the ancient stones. I'd hoped Colin would relax once he realized there was nothing here except history, but he seemed more agitated than ever. His focus darted around like a trapped animal, and my soothing tone did nothing to assuage his fear. Finally, after thirty minutes, I decided he'd had enough. I would have liked to stay longer, but his face was twisted in terror.

On our way home, Colin confessed he had the ability to see spirits, and the cemetery was overcrowded with uneasy souls looking for closure.

Shocked, I scolded him for keeping this to himself. "Why didn't you tell me?"

"I don't want you to think I'm nuts."

"For heaven's sake, Colin. I'm a witch."

"But you're so normal."

"I may look conventional, but I'm genetically linked to a powerful coven that's centuries old. I'm not sure what you imagine a witch should look like, but most of us are quite ordinary. We learned long ago that drawing attention to ourselves can only lead to death. Plus, I'm not just anyone, Colin. I'm supposed to be your mentor, and it would have been nice if you'd shared this important piece of information. How long have you been able to see the dead?"

Colin avoided my eyes and picked at a loose thread on his shorts.

"Answer my question."

He lifted his chin and stared, eyes bright with excitement. "Since I was a kid. Andrew visits all the time."

"Andrew?"

"My twin."

I tried to mask my surprise, but something in my expression must have put him on the defensive.

"Don't you believe me?"

"Why wouldn't I?"

"You're looking at me like I'm crazy."

I shook my head. "Does your grandmother know?"

"I've never told anyone but you."

"Thank you for trusting me," I said, hoping to ease his discomfort. "What do you guys talk about?"

"It's more a stream-of-consciousness thing than an actual conversation. Lately, I've been mentioning you."

"Does he approve of our friendship?"

"I think Andrew is straight. He makes a face whenever I tell him what we do in bed."

"What we do is private," I snapped. "You don't need to give your brother a running commentary."

Colin burst out laughing.

"What's so funny?" I snarled.

After he calmed down, he gleefully admitted, "The two of us talking about my conversation with a dead person. Who knew it would be so easy?"

"Are there others in your circle of spiritual friends?"

"Not really. Andrew has buddies that tag along once in a while, but I wouldn't necessarily call them friends. I only communicate with my twin."

I shook my head in wonderment. "You've got layers I haven't even begun to explore."

"Now that it's out in the open, I'll be glad to share anything you want."

"What other secrets have you been guarding?"

Chapter Twenty-Two

COLIN

My other worldly connection to Andrew might have been unnerving to some, but I was counting on Alain's familiarity with the preternatural to pave the way for this discussion. As expected, Alain treated my revelation like a failure on his part to have recognized this important aspect of my personality. Which was just as well. I was acutely aware that my relationship with my dead brother was unusual, and I'd never shared this aspect of my life. All the same, I now sympathized with Alain's need-to-know attitude and decided to be as truthful as possible, even if I was slightly uncomfortable under his intense gaze. There was no room for mystery in a relationship that had more hurdles than an Olympic event. If I wanted Alain beyond sex and magic, I had to let him pick at my brain like a vulture.

"Go ahead and ask me whatever you want," I prompted.

"Why not start from the beginning," he countered.

"It was long ago," I began. "I must have been two or three years old. I didn't know he was my twin, and I sure as shit didn't know he was dead. I was just excited to see another kid. My nanny reported that I was conversing and playing with an invisible friend, and my parents assumed he was imaginary, a supposition confirmed by the pediatrician on retainer. He assured them it was entirely normal for an only child."

"Your grandmother never suspected?"

"She was too busy being my grandfather's right hand to notice."

"Were you isolated as a young boy?"

"Yes and no. My fathers spent most of their free time with me, but there were some weeks I'd be all alone. It took a lot of persuasion on Errol's part to convince my other father to send me off to boarding school. Even then, I had a bodyguard. They wanted to shield me from the harsher realities of life, so having Andrew in my limited arsenal of friends was a gift, and one I wasn't about to share."

"Everything I've learned about your father's pregnancy, and your subsequent birth, explains why they're overprotective."

"You've been researching me?"

"How could I resist? Dropping ambiguous statements about birthrights and history repeating itself lends itself to further investigation. The laws of succession in your principality are clear-cut, but what I don't understand is why your parents didn't opt for surrogacy."

"You'll have to ask them."

"Maybe someday I will," he stated. "Did Andrew die in utero or shortly after he was born?"

"Does that make a difference?"

"I'm detail oriented."

"No shit."

"It's not a bad trait," Alain defended.

"Except, I'm on the receiving end of your inquiring mind."

"Didn't you give me carte blanche to dig into your interesting past?"

"Am I that interesting?"

"Stop fishing."

"Sorry, not sorry," I joked. "Andrew was stillborn. I don't have the exact medical details other than we were born premature. My father, Errol, has a scar from sternum to groin. He considers it a battle wound and never did anything to repair the unsightly reminder. I find it disturbing as fuck."

"What bothers you the most?" Alain asked gently. "The physical deformity or the wisdom behind his decision to carry a child?"

That was a good question. Alain was gifted at so many things, and getting to the heart of the matter was one of his many talents.

"I honestly believe it was wrong for Papa to ask Da to risk his life in such a manner. I'd never force someone I love to gamble on a long shot."

"Errol doesn't appear to lack a backbone. I can't imagine anyone twisting his arm."

"You're right," I agreed. "But he was mad for Papa—still is actually—and would have grown feathers and learned how to fly if it was required to become his consort."

"Love and common sense don't always go hand in hand," Alain said with deprecating honesty.

"Is that a quote or a confession?"

"Let's get back to your spiritual connection with Andrew," Alain prompted, ignoring my question. "Countless studies have proven there's a bond between twins that goes beyond the logical. Even those separated at birth exhibit the same characteristics or preferences no matter how or where they were raised. The ability to silently communicate or to use a different language altogether isn't uncommon. I assume you were identical?"

"Yes."

"That makes it more compelling. Sharing the same space for nine months, and then having it brutally wrenched away can leave a soul in limbo. Now that I know the facts, I'm not at all surprised that he continues to be a part of your life. How often does he visit?"

"Whenever I'm upset."

"He must be a huge comfort."

I nodded, eyes brimming. "I'd give anything to bring him back. This is why I have to learn how to time walk."

"You can't change the past without affecting the future," Alain explained. "I know it sounds like a great idea, but even if you could go back—a rare ability in the world of witchcraft—you shouldn't. Use reason to work through your questions instead of your emotions."

"I could at least warn the doctors to keep a closer eye on Da."

"And in doing so, you might save your twin but cause your own death or Errol's. Have you thought about that?"

"That's not possible," I said. "How can I be dead if I'm back in time advocating for Andrew?"

"The tiniest change can have severe repercussions. Let's say, for the sake of argument, the doctors resort to drastic measures to save both babies."

"Like what?"

"Allowing Errol to die."

"Papa wouldn't let that happen. He'd rather slit his own wrist than lose Da."

"And maybe that's what happened, Colin. Before you run off half-cocked and try to change the past, why not ask important questions that pertain to the present? What was the actual cause of Andrew's death? Was Errol's life in jeopardy at any time? Did the Prince make the hardest decision of his life and choose his beloved husband over an unborn child?"

"I don't think they'd answer that last question."

"And they have every right to refuse. Why would you think to challenge a decision that was made two decades ago? Because that's exactly what you're doing by forcing their hand. What does Andrew think of your cockamamie plan?"

"He's skeptical."

"Huzzah! What you're trying to achieve is impossible. It would only create chaos and might possibly end your life or that of others in your inner circle. Promise me you'll put this idea to rest."

"It's a moot point since I haven't the first clue how to time walk."

"And you can rest assured I'm not teaching you."

"Do you know how?"

"I refuse to answer on the grounds that it will incriminate me."

"Come on, Alain. Stop being so damned responsible."

"Someone has to be," he bellowed, fresh out of patience. "You are clearly incapable of making the right decision."

"How about if we go back in time and be a fly on the wall?"

"To what end?"

"I'm not sure. Maybe there's something we're missing."

"That still doesn't change the fact that you can't tamper with the past."

"Will you consider it?"

"No."

"Okay," I said, dragging out the word. "Let's find a reasonable alternative. A powerful seer might be able to give me answers. If I'm satisfied nothing could have been done to change the outcome, I'll stop bugging you about time walking."

He took a few deep breaths, and I feared he was about to unleash the anger he'd been bottling since I first mentioned Andrew. To my surprise, he sank down on the sofa, leaned against the throw pillows, and closed his eyes. What the hell?

I waited several minutes and eventually grew impatient and shook his arm. "Alain?"

"Yes."

"Are you napping or what?"

His eyelids fluttered open, and I felt the intensity of his gaze before he replied. "You are getting on my last nerve."

"Why?"

"Because you never take no for an answer. There's always an argument before you give in. I don't know if this has to do with the blue blood running through your veins or a generational lack of respect for authority. I'm thirteen years older than you, with two degrees, and a Nobel Prize to back up my opinion. Most people hang on to my word like it's the gospel, while you question the slightest thing. What do I have to do to earn your trust and respect?"

His observations felt like a blow to my solar plexus. I sank to my knees in between his splayed legs and buried my face in my hands. He didn't move, but his harsh breathing made me lift my head, and I was caught in the glare of his arresting eyes.

"I'm sorry, Alain. There's no one I respect more than you."

"Then what is your fucking problem?"

I bit down on my lower lip to keep from blurting the wrong words. I'd never heard this harsh tone focused on me, even during the early days of our friendship. Back then, he was more amused than anything, but a lot had changed since our first kiss. I wanted much more and could only hope he felt the same. Somehow, I had to convince him that my dogged pursuit for answers had nothing to do with a lack of trust and everything to do with my future monarchy.

"A good ruler has to be a combination of many traits," I replied evenly, hoping to bring his anger down a notch. "One of them is to be steadfast in my beliefs. Exploring all my options before making a final decision is embedded in my DNA. I've often been told there's no such thing as impossible—it's simply a question of finding another means to the desired end. Obviously, I've taken it a step too far."

Scowling, Alain lobbed his reply. "Any world leader worth their salt will surround themselves with experts to advise them when answers aren't forthcoming. You don't have enough life experiences to be so unyielding. It would be in your best interest to keep an open mind, especially with anything magic related. Enlisting the help of a necromancer to find your answers goes against everything I believe. We are not dabbling in the occult to solve your problem."

"Who said anything about black magic?"

"People who have the ability to communicate with the dead are called necromancers, and we've just discovered you're in this special category. Now, you can choose to go either way. Ignore your ties with the afterworld or hone it until you become a master. I want nothing to do with it!"

"Hold the fuck on! I have no desire to chat with random dead people. Didn't you see how creeped out I was at the cemetery?"

"Be that as it may," Alain replied tersely. "You have the gift, if you can call it that, and now is the time to decide how you plan to deal with it."

"I choose to ignore it, except with regards to Andrew. He'll always be a part of me, and I'll remain open to him until he ends our connection."

"Fair enough," Alain said, visibly relieved. "Since we're being so damned honest, I have my own confession to make."

My eyes widened in surprise. "Oh?"

"Remember the day you found me on the floor in my library?"

"What about it?"

"I'd been poking into your life to try to find out more about you."

"That's an invasion of privacy," I accused.

"Yes, it is, and I'm sorry. You were a mystery back then, and I'm inherently cautious. A person with hardly any social media presence in this century is an anomaly. I couldn't find anything useful on the internet so I resorted to magic."

"Not a good reason to pry; you could have come right out and asked me."

"I got my just deserts."

"Is that why you were on the floor? Did an electrical volt zap you for being Curious George?"

He looked grim. "The truth is I saw something so disturbing my brain couldn't handle it. I fainted."

Terror shot through my veins. My worst nightmare was coming to life through Alain's memory. I should have ended the conversation then and there, but I was searching for answers, and he might have them. "What did you see?"

"A bloody hospital scene with a dead baby still attached by the umbilical cord."

I gasped. "Who was the mother?"

"I don't know."

"Was there a man in the bed?"

"I don't know."

Shaking him, I demanded, "What in the hell do you know?"

He reached for my hands and held them tightly. "I'm not sure if I was looking into the past or the future. Either way, it was none of my business. Something was telling me in no uncertain terms to leave it alone. I shouldn't have attempted it, and the only conclusion that makes sense is that tampering with fate in any shape or form is wrong."

"Easy for you to say," I muttered. "It's not your life on the line."

"Isn't it?" he asked.

Chapter Twenty-Three

DRAKE

There was a knock on my bedroom door, and without waiting for permission, the dowager pushed through with David at her heels. For the umpteenth time since I'd swapped places with Colin, I wondered why he tolerated such disrespect. Granted, she was his grandmother and a monarch to boot, but Alexandra was the most vexing woman I'd ever met, and her lackey was no better. I rewarded her rudeness with a chilly smile while throwing some mental shade to put her in her place. She faltered for a second, grimacing at the sudden onslaught of pain.

Rushing to her side, I asked, "Granny, are you all right?"

"I...think so."

"Why don't you sit for a minute?" I suggested, taking her by the elbow and leading her to the chaise lounge. "Your blood pressure must be off again."

"All right," she agreed weakly. "I've been having a lot of headaches lately."

If you would stay out of my affairs, then perhaps your health might improve.

"Is Drake jogging again?"

"He runs every morning, Granny. Nothing has changed in eight days."

"More's the pity. I wanted to talk to both of you about this sudden urge of yours to have a party."

"It's not unexpected, is it? Turning twenty-one is a milestone."

"When your fathers and I broached the subject months ago, you considered it another duty, rather than a cause for celebration. What's different?"

"Charlie's back in the picture," I admitted. "A public gathering will be a good time to announce our reunion without the usual fanfare."

The dowager's eyebrows rose, and she fixed a dubious look in my direction. It wasn't the first time she had questioned Colin's sudden reversal, and each time it happened, I sent a tiny zap to her brain. The dizziness and momentary confusion were a good diversion. These spells, as she called them, were happening more and more as I accelerated my program. I was running out of time, and I wanted it all in place before Colin and Alain showed up.

"What about de Gris?"

I shrugged. "He's not interested in a future with me. Drake taught me how to break through Alain's defenses and reveal his true intentions. Why should I waste my time on a losing proposition?"

"Why indeed," she said primly. "I'm so glad your cousin is useful after all. He's been quite free with my credit card, and I was starting to doubt his sincerity. It seems I've misjudged him. Now, let's put your unfortunate relationship with the witch behind us and get down to business. David, take notes."

"Yes, ma'am."

Turning to me, the dowager asked, "How many people were you thinking of inviting?"

"You're much better at this than I could ever be. I do have one request, though."

"Anything, dear boy."

"Invite as many of my relatives on the Bradford side as possible. It's time we mended some fences."

"I'm not sure that's such a good idea, Colin. Those people have no idea how to mingle in high society."

This insult—the second one in less than a minute—demanded immediate retaliation. Her bowels could use a good dose of my medicine, and I twisted the imaginary knife until she hunched over in discomfort.

"Granny?"

Her face was ashen as she raised her eyes to meet mine. "I think I'm coming down with something."

She looked miserable, and satisfaction oozed through me like a thirty-year-old single malt. I gave the knife one final shove before I eased up. I didn't want to do irrevocable damage—there would be plenty of time to deal with her in the future. At the moment, she was a useful ally to Colin.

A few minutes passed before she recovered from the severe cramps, but her attitude toward my family remained unfazed. "I don't think it's a good idea to invite strangers to such an important occasion. They don't know any of our friends and won't know how to mingle."

I dug my fingernails into my palm to keep from slapping her. "I'm afraid I have to insist. They might surprise you by actually using a napkin and lifting a pinkie at the appropriate moment."

"Hold your tongue," she scolded.

"You should hear yourself sometimes, Granny."

"I'm too old to change," she said irritably. "And I don't need any lectures from you. Getting back to the guest list. Who should we ask?"

"I'll send David my contacts. He can text or email instead of wasting time on a written invite."

David actually gasped at my suggestion. "Your Highness, I beg to disagree. Celebrating your birthday is a grand occasion and should be treated as such. How will guests RSVP?"

I rolled my eyes. "You need to get with this century, dude."

"Will they actually text a reply?"

"They will if you tell them you need a head count."

"Then that's what I'll do for your friends. The rest will get a standard paper invitation."

"Knock yourself out. And one more thing," I said, certain his head would explode. "Let's make it a masquerade ball."

"It's a lot to put together on short notice," David protested weakly.

I wasn't interested in hearing his nonsensical reasons why this couldn't be done. What else did he have to do? It would be far easier to do a bait-and-switch while in costume. I'd still have to orchestrate my moves, but it would be less taxing than messing with apparitions. They tended to get wonky in a crowd.

In a tone that brooked no argument, I said, "This isn't a request, David. See that it gets done, and do it right."

"Yes, Your Highness. Should I arrange a fitting for a proper costume?"

I blinked at him. I hadn't thought that far, but he did have a point. "That would be great. Thank you."

He gave me a hopeful smile. All was restored in his world now that he was back in my good graces.

The dowager looked amused. "You remind me of your papa, Colin. He also had a masquerade ball for his twenty-fifth birthday. That's when he met your da."

"Then I'm following a time-honored tradition," I pointed out. "Let's party!"

"As you wish," she agreed. "David and I will compile the guest list as well as other essentials for your approval."

"That sounds great, Granny. Are you feeling any better?"

"Yes," she nodded. "David can escort me to my room."

"No need," I said. "I'll tuck you into bed myself."

"Thank you, sweetheart."

After she was settled, I took off in *my* convertible. I'd fallen into the role of prince with remarkable ease and the trappings of royalty continued to bring a smile to my face in spite of the daily interference by the dowager. Colin's fathers were remarkably chill, and I'd grown fond of them despite my initial misgivings. The damn dog, though, wasn't fooled by my disguise and sniffed around me suspiciously, raising a few eyebrows. Fortunately, she couldn't talk, and I'd taken to carrying treats in my pocket to solve the immediate problem.

I'd agreed to meet Charlie and her friends at the tennis club. She had refused to stay at the palace, claiming our network of spies would track her moves and report back to the dowager. As Colin's childhood friend and ex-fiancée, she was privy to the inner workings of the royal machine, whereas I wasn't.

It didn't take a genius—or a witch—to figure out why the engagement had been called off. The physical attraction between her and Colin had to have been lukewarm at best. This was confirmed after I kissed her the first time we went dancing. She looked at me in stunned confusion.

"Wow," she remarked. "What in heck have you been smoking?"

I held her gaze for a long time and broke it with a throaty laugh. Instead of answering the question, I drew her closer, grinding my hips against hers so she could feel the undeniable level of interest.

Against the soft skin behind her ear, I whispered, "Let's just say I've come to my senses."

After that, it didn't take long to persuade her to let me into her bed. Our genuine attraction was the best and worst part of this game. After spending eight days with Charlie, I was unequivocally invested in her. Knowing she'd be caught in the crossfire if this game blew up in my face was my biggest fear. She was everything I could have asked for in a partner, but I knew I was playing with fire.

Charlie was of royal decent, and even if she could persuade her parents to let her marry a commoner, she would surely hate me for taking her under false pretenses. Nonetheless, I couldn't stay away. I was falling for her as quickly as Colin had fallen for Alain. How ironic. I'd been hired to teach him the necessary skills to break away from Alain's spell, and I'd fallen into a honey trap of my own making.

Granny Maura would tell me to get my head out of the clouds and focus on the endgame—bringing down this royal family regardless of the consequences. Easy for her to say. She wasn't the one whose heart melted when Charlie called out Colin's name at the height of passion.

I pushed all thoughts of consequences aside and did my best to live for the moment. That skill set had been my salvation for years, and it was in my best interest to revert to form. Growing a conscience this late in the game was counterproductive. Best case scenario, this would work, Colin would agree to relinquish his position, and Charlie and I would live happily ever after. If that didn't pan out, I'd figure out something else. I always did.

Chapter Twenty-Four

COLIN

Alain's disturbing revelation brought forth the feeling of unease I've lived with since I was old enough to grasp the implications of a same-sex relationship. The murky future had never felt so immediate. My twenty-first birthday was rapidly approaching, and I was in love with the slumbering man to my right. There would be no sidestepping the consequences of my choice once I made a public announcement. Would I have answers when my fathers and the ministry posed the hard questions?

Even without any declarations on his part, I knew it was only a matter of time before Alain voiced his true feelings. I could see it in his eyes and feel it in his touch. Moreover, our daily lessons in witchcraft and spell-casting had strengthened our bond and shown me another side of his character I found irresistible. Far superior in book learning and experience, Alain was a kind and caring instructor, a true mentor in every sense of the word. There were no flashes of temper or grumbling impatience if I fumbled a step or questioned the need for certain spells. His answers were measured and left me more certain that knowledge of any kind, whether it was useful or not, wasn't a waste of time.

Although he still hadn't given in to my repeated requests to experience what I considered to be the ultimate act of joining, I instinctively knew it was the life-altering step he had to cope with, rather than a lack of desire. He'd said as much one night after I'd nearly broken his resolve.

"To love you the way you're asking is to embrace every aspect of your life. I'm not sure I can make that kind of commitment, Colin."

"Aren't you getting ahead of yourself? We're not talking marriage, Alain."

"I will not give in to you until I'm prepared to take that step."

The snarky rejoinder was on the tip of my tongue—no one made as big a deal about fucking as he did—but putting our lovemaking in that tawdry category was doing us both a disservice. If he respected me enough to hold off until he could commit, then I damned well better learn how to wait.

I rolled over to see if Alain was asleep, and his even breaths proved he was out for the count. I slipped out of bed. It was time for some brotherly advice. There was no guarantee Andrew would find me in this location, but I hoped his ghostly GPS would track me down.

Sitting on the sofa with nothing but a bottle of cool water, I called his name, the way I'd always done in the past.

"Andrew? Can you hear me?"

Nothing happened for several minutes. Discouraged, I leaned against the cushions and closed my eyes. I don't know how long I was asleep before I heard his voice.

Colin...wake up.

He might as well have used a Taser. I jumped out of my skin as the air crackled around me. On the opposite sofa, Andrew glowed, sparks of blue, yellow, and green circling around him like fireflies. He was in beach attire, complete with flip-flops and a straw hat.

"I see you're dressed for the occasion as usual."

You could have told me you were in the bloody Seychelles.

"Sorry, it was a last minute thing. Shall we take a stroll along the beach?"

In a minute. First, tell me who's the imposter in your rooms back in Biarritz?

"That's our cousin, Drake. He's covering for me."

And doing a bang-up job from what I could glean. Drake practically fainted when I materialized.

"He saw you?"

No, but he felt me.

"Wow. I guess he is as powerful as he claims. What's he been up to?"

We'll talk about Drake in a minute. Do you want to tell me why you've called me up like a pizza?

I chuckled, amused as ever by his wit. "Alain had a disturbing vision."

The witch.

"My boyfriend."

Do tell.

After I finished recounting what little I knew, I waited for Andrew's reaction. "Well?" I pushed. "Was he seeing the past or the future?"

I'm not sure.

"Not helping, brother. You're supposed to be omniscient."

You must be thinking of god.

"Why can't you see my future?"

I'm not part of His privy council.

"So there is a god?"

In a manner of speaking.

"Must you be so vague?"

Yes.

"What about your friends? Are they better informed?"

No.

"Don't dead people always see the big picture?"

There is nothing beneficial to being dead.

"It would have been so much easier if you'd lived."

You are repetitive and boring, Colin. Tell me something I don't know.

"I told Alain I was interested in time walking."

I hope he shot you down.

"Forcefully."

Good man. You should marry the guy.

"He hasn't asked, and even if he did, I won't subject him to the procreation nightmare."

Shouldn't it be his choice?

"It's too much to expect."

Advocate for change. The laws of succession in Sendorra are outdated.

"Can I do that?"

You can do whatever you want. I hope your boyfriend is smarter than you.

"He is."

Then he'll come up with a solution. You need to stop pestering me about this crap—I was never meant to exist. Wishing and hoping won't change anything. Live your life and have fun.

"It's so unfair."

What else is new?

"I'm in love."

More than you were with Charlie?

"I don't believe I was ever in love with her. She's a dear friend and I care for her immensely, but what I feel for Alain is completely different."

That's a relief.

"Why? What's happening back home?"

Do you really want to know?

I leaned forward in concern. "Shouldn't I?"

When does your vacation end?

"Not for another week."

This can wait.

"Are you positive?"

I'll be back if anything changes.

"Colin?" Alain called out. "Who are you talking to?"

Turning toward the bedroom, I yelled, "I'll be right there."

Andrew vaporized into the mist before I drained the bottle of water and went to bed.

"Were you talking to someone?" Alain asked sleepily.

"Andrew."

"That's nice," Alain muttered, falling back into sleep.

He probably wouldn't remember anything in the morning, which was just as well. Andrew's words of advice seemed more in line with Alain than me. I was still conflicted on how this was going to be resolved.

AFTER EXPLORING MAHÉ for six days, we made the short trip to the island of Praslin in an island-jumper prop plane. Born and raised in a landlocked region of the world, I'd always been fascinated by the sea. It was one reason I loved our residence in Biarritz. The hydrangea-covered hillsides, meandering walkways, and close proximity to the ocean were a huge draw. But nothing had prepared me for the paradise known as the Seychelles. As much as I loved to people watch from my cozy seat on the sidewalk bistros back in France, I'd never realized a vacation could be so much better with hardly any people around. Nothing but miles of pristine white sand and an ocean so clear one could see the colorful variations of fish and coral hundreds of feet below our glass-bottom boat.

Vacationing with a man of science had proven to be more than mindless sunbathing and snorkeling. Alain was constantly in search of new information, and since he'd spent the better part of three years immersed in botanicals, we had to see anything plant related that was out of the norm. One of the main attractions on Praslin, a palm tree called coco de mer, was the first item on his agenda.

"What's so different about this tree?" I asked as we made our way to a thick grouping of palms.

"See for yourself," Alain replied, mouth curving into a smile.

I burst out laughing after I saw the phallic-shaped flower protrusions and the extra-large fruit resembling another distinct female body part.

"Told you it was worth the trip," Alain quipped. "These palms are dioecious, which means they come in two genders. You can easily distinguish the male from the female by the—"

"Humongous dick and noteworthy approximation to the female genitalia."

Alain grinned. "Exactly."

I returned his smile. "Are all scientists weirdos like you?"

"Only the good ones."

"Sheesh. Can we eat one of those amazing fruits?"

"I doubt it," he said. "They're an endangered species, and the fruits take six to seven years to mature. There's not enough to go around."

"Do they taste like a regular coconut?"

"Let's go find out."

Alain was correct to assume they weren't readily available. According to our tour guide, if we were lucky enough to get our hands on a ripe fruit, we were told not to pass on the experience. Supposedly, they were "refreshing and sweet with an earthy, spunky aftertaste."

"Not your ordinary coconut," Alain mused.

"Maybe a little sexier," our guide joked.

That only made us more determined to seek out the elusive fruit. The next few days found us wandering all over the island, enjoying everything from coral reefs to rushing waterfalls and even a pearl oyster farm. Alain never detoured from his original list, painstakingly planned the night we'd first arrived. He was meticulous and organized, and yet there was something about him that was also spontaneous and fun loving. He didn't pass on a chance to try something new, even if it was out of his comfort zone, like zip-lining or dancing around a fire pit in nothing but a native thong. I certainly experienced more on this trip than I ever had in my short life.

The best part of each day was watching the sunset from our terrace. After a refreshing shower and light dinner, Alain and I would expound on every topic imaginable. That night, we talked about Andrew. I should have known he wouldn't forget about the nocturnal visit. Alain's mind was like an ever-expanding sponge, soaking up information and storing it for future use.

"Was Andrew's visit a random event, or did you call for him?"

I sighed.

"Answer the question."

"I told him about your vision and wondered if he could explain it."

"Did he have any insights?"

"None."

"Then I'd stop trying to figure it out. It will all be revealed in the end."

"He intimated that something was going on back in Biarritz."

"What?" Alain pounced.

"I don't know. He disappeared when he heard you call my name."

"Drake is probably up to no good."

"And you're letting an ancient feud color your opinion of someone who, by all appearances, is doing us a favor."

"We'll find out soon enough."

"I can't believe we've only got a few days left. Can't we stay here forever?"

Alain chuckled. "Even paradise gets old after a length of time."

"Everything will change after we leave."

"Don't be so pessimistic."

"I can't help it. My own brother thinks I'm a brooder."

"We'll have to change that."

"How?"

"By working on it...."

"As a couple?"

"Two minds are better than one."

Part IV

Reckoning

Chapter Twenty-Five

ALAIN

We left Praslin with a heavy heart, determined to revisit the tiny island at our earliest opportunity. Aside from the natural beauty of the landscape, the atmosphere was teeming with magic. Without doing a thorough investigation, I could only guess the source, but I was certain that Voodoo played a huge role. I'd studied the origins at my mother's side, and the proximity of the Seychelles to Africa, where Voodoo originated, led me to surmise the religion had accompanied the early settlers.

Reinforcing my assumption was an artifact we stumbled across during one of our hiking expeditions. Thanks to my eidetic memory, I recognized the wooden post—integral to most of their temples—carved with the serpent gods Damballa and Ayida-Weddo. I explained the word origin for Voodoo—vo (introspection) and du (into the unknown)—but stopped short after Colin rolled his eyes and called me a nerd. Abashed, I admitted to being a bookworm and couldn't help myself. My embarrassment was quickly erased after Colin threw his arms around my neck and kissed me, swearing he was my love slave, no matter how pedantic I might be at times.

The sheer volume of information I had to impart was mind-boggling and would take a lifetime to absorb if one wanted to be a practicing witch. The dowager's hope that Drake would get Colin up to snuff in two weeks was utter rubbish. It had taken me years, and there was still much to learn. If the old bat hadn't been so determined to keep our relationship from progressing, she would have realized the futility of her plan.

During our time in the Seychelles, Colin displayed a strong affinity for fire. Not surprising, considering he was born at the height of summer. This particular element—one of four utilized in spell casting—was associated with the sun, the giver of life, and it governed passion, intuition, a strong will, and power. Fire was also related to motivation and creativity. The basic energy could be positive and uplifting, promoting courage and strength, but also frightening if uncontrolled.

I'd already witnessed Colin display several of the characteristics associated with a fire personality. Charming and passionate, Colin relied heavily on his instincts and intuition, enjoying stimulation and challenge in equal measure. However, if left unchecked, too much fire could lead to selfishness, egocentricity, and unrealistic expectations of others.

It was my goal to guide my fledgling magician by showing him how to control himself and channel his resources evenly and productively. Going by our past experience, Colin's powers were heightened as his temper flared. We'd already had a couple of minor accidents during practice sessions—a charred hibiscus trellis and a blackened fruit tray—and I couldn't, in good conscience, teach him more without some proper guidelines.

Colin needed to find inner balance. He was conflicted about many things, but mainly his ponderous role as future monarch and any relationships he might establish leading up to the day he was crowned. His sexual orientation, previously on the back burner, had been shoved to the forefront, now that he and I were firmly entrenched in a satisfying physical relationship. He continued to struggle with thoughts of what might happen if he asked for my hand in marriage. I had given him no verbal indication that I would consider a proposal, but I'd witnessed his relentless nature and known from the early days of our friendship that he was dogged in his pursuits. He would stop at nothing if he wanted me as his consort.

Perhaps Andrew could talk some sense into his brother. After rehashing past conversations between the two, I'd come to the conclusion that Colin's twin was his soulmate in the truest sense of the word. Andrew appeared to be less serious, but he was also able to see the big picture, whereas Colin tended to have tunnel vision. Interestingly enough, Andrew's advice was sacrosanct, and Colin accepted his suggestions without a heated debate. It was a sore point I didn't hesitate to mention, but in Colin's defense, I couldn't compete with a brotherly bond that went beyond the grave. Andrew was a loving, benign spirit who appeared in and out of Colin's life whenever he teetered over an abyss, and I was willing to swallow my pride and defer to the "older" brother if it kept Colin safe.

Our current situation—jetting home in the private plane I'd recalled a day early—started that afternoon, shortly after we'd arrived back in Mahé. While Colin was in the shower, I had made the stupid mistake of checking my emails. Isabelle's caught my attention immediately. Her subject line was in block letters, and I would have been an irresponsible fool to ignore anything labeled IMPORTANT.

Her spies had informed her of the recent flurry of activity regarding Colin's upcoming birthday party, one he was supposedly planning with the approval of his parents. He'd intimated on Twitter that an announcement of importance would be forthcoming at the end of the evening's celebration. Since the birthday boy had been by my side for the last twelve days and he never used Twitter, I could only conclude that Drake was behind these machinations. At the risk of incurring Colin's wrath, I told him we had to cut our trip short by a day.

Thankfully, Andrew agreed with my decision after Colin sought him out. That didn't make our sudden departure any easier, and he was still seething an hour into our flight. I took my attention off my laptop for a minute, hyperaware of Colin's unrelenting gaze. The temperature in the Lear's cabin was rising uncomfortably.

"You promised a communication blackout," Colin snarled.

He sat across the narrow table I was working on, arms crossed over his chest. Defiantly, he stood and pointed in my direction. "You lying sack of shit."

I'd never seen him this angry, and his fingertips glowed like dying embers.

"Lower your hands," I warned him. There was no way I was going to risk first-degree burns from an out-of-control witch. I'd douse him with gallons of water first, property damage notwithstanding.

He looked at his offending digits, and his eyes widened in surprise. "What the fuck?" he mused, distracted for a split second.

"Please calm down, or you'll set something on fire."

He frowned, curled his fingers into fists, and continued to rant. "I told you to stay out of Drake's affairs."

"I was uncomfortable leaving the area without informing Isabelle of my whereabouts. I'm all she has, as you know, and we're always tethered electronically. In the process, I asked her to keep an eye out for unusual activity coming from the palace. This would have been a nonissue if Drake had kept his side of the bargain."

"She spied for you?"

"Aren't you glad? Drake is neck deep in something nefarious, and we need to stop him before it's too late."

"You're exaggerating."

"That's not my style."

"No, you're the methodical airhead who always does the right thing."

Colin's reference to air, the element that was most prevalent in my particular DNA, was galling because it was true. I *was* rational and analytical, a clear thinker who didn't rush into things. I enjoyed mental stimulation, a good debate, and an exchange of ideas. But Isabelle had warned me that too much of a good thing could make me critical, with a bookish attitude bordering on tiresome. So sue me. I'd rather err on the side of caution than dive into a void and hope for the best.

I didn't refute Colin's statement, so he grew bolder and explained how he was going to resolve our current situation.

"All I have to do is get down on my knees in front of Papa and Da and confess. They've always forgiven me in the past. Why should this be any different?"

"Your past transgressions will pale in comparison to a calculated deception in order to run off with your lover."

"I suppose you're right," Colin agreed despondently. "They'll blame you, and Granny won't hesitate to call you out."

"Of course, they will."

"But once I explain that I was behind this crazy plan, they might relent. Hopefully, they'll throw Drake's ass out of the palace, and life will go back to normal."

"I doubt they'll listen to reason. Your parents warned me that I was on shaky ground, and I won't be surprised if they press charges for kidnapping, adding rape in the bargain. You are the heir apparent, Colin. Letting this go unpunished would be setting an example, and you would be put in a vulnerable position for future extortion schemes."

"What a load of crap. Our relationship has always been consensual, and they know it. The only thing I've lost in this adventure is my heart."

I swallowed my angry rebuttal. He'd basically declared his love and deserved some kind of reassurance.

"*Chaton*," I called out softly. "Come here."

He stepped into my circle eagerly and wrapped his arms around my waist. His generous heart thundered in his chest, and for a split second, I imagined a life without him by my side. It was inconceivable. Lifting his chin, I kissed him softly. His familiar taste propelled me back to our romantic villa on the hilltop, evoking a combination of love, hope, and endless possibilities. Images of days and nights spent in complete harmony flashed across my mind's eye like a movie trailer. Our vacation had surpassed my expectations, and it was time to loosen the inflexible cords of reason that dictated my life.

I wasn't surprised to hear myself whisper, "I love you too."

Tears flooded his eyes, turning the blue into an azure so pure it reminded me of the waters we'd played in for the last two weeks, minus a day.

"No matter what I have to endure at the palace, hearing those words made this trip worthwhile," Colin said solemnly. "I love you, Alain. I think I have from the beginning."

I kissed him again, and this time it lingered. The popping in my ears, as well as the distinct sound of wheels engaging for a landing, signaled our plane's descent. We broke the kiss and held hands while the plane made its approach toward Biarritz airport.

"What's your plan?" Colin asked just before we touched down.

"Your parents might not see things our way for a while. Before we barge into the palace with guns blazing, it would be in our best interest to get all the details so we can assess the damage."

"I'm listening."

"Let's sit down with Isabelle first. See if the damage is irreversible or if it can be contained."

"Your mother?"

"Yes, all three of us."

"What a terrible way to meet a potential in-law."

"Let's not get ahead of ourselves, Colin. We'll have no future if we can't fix our present."

Colin bit down on his lower lip and nodded. It was obvious he was struggling to hand over control, but after my lecture on trust the other night and what just happened between us, he knew better than to insist on having his way.

After they checked our passports, we picked up our luggage, and stepped out of the building. Isabelle's favorite limo driver was waiting for us.

"Hello, Guy. I wasn't expecting you."

"Madame is in the car."

"Alain?" Colin held back, sounding panicked.

I gave his arm a reassuring squeeze. "Relax."

"I'm not ready for her yet."

"Don't go royal on her and it'll be fine."

"I'll try," he said, sounding decidedly unprincely. I didn't blame him. The dowager had already poisoned Colin's mind in regard to my mother, who was, in truth, a formidable enemy. Isabelle, in turn, had made it clear that she disapproved of our relationship. Hoping to get her support to clean up our mess would be a stretch. Still, I was her only child, and I counted on her love and loyalty to see beyond her irrational hatred for the Bradford Coven.

She gave us both an icy smile when we slid into the limousine. I sat by her side, and Colin took the seat directly opposite her.

"Isabelle, I'd like to present His Royal Highness, Prince Colin of Sendorra."

She studied him for a few moments and then commented, "You're but a child."

Anger flashed across Colin's features, but he swallowed what might have been a vicious retort and replied in a quietly controlled voice. "Appearances are deceiving, Madam. Alain is quite happy with my level of maturity."

In fact, I was damned proud of my prince. He hadn't succumbed to name-calling or tried to set Isabelle on fire, not that he would have succeeded. She would have turned him into a statue before he threw the first spark. Instead, Colin respectfully challenged her to prove she wasn't dealing with a child. An ambitious move I never thought I'd witness and one my mother definitely appreciated.

A bemused smile creased Isabelle's cheeks and disappeared just as quickly. Turning to me, she muttered in a barely audible voice, "I'm inclined to give him the benefit of the doubt."

"Thank you," I said sincerely. "We can use your help."

Chapter Twenty-Six

COLIN

Isabelle never took her eyes off me as the limo weaved through traffic. Instead of avoiding her gaze, I studied her with equal fascination. She was stunningly beautiful, hardly what I expected. I assumed she and Granny were contemporaries, but Isabelle appeared at least a decade younger. Maybe she *was* in her sixties—it was hard to tell in this age of Botox and fillers—but the woman sitting across from me didn't strike me as the type who wasted time and money on plastic surgeons. She exuded the kind of confidence one only found in people who'd been beautiful their entire lives. No lowering of the eyes or nervous gestures to mask her insecurities. This was a woman who'd been blessed by the goddess Aphrodite and was at ease with her effect on the opposite sex.

Her jet-black hair was woven with gray, and her upturned eyes, as catlike and alluring as her son's, had deep-purple irises. The effect, so close to her black pupils, was a little unnerving. I forced myself to hold her invasive stare so she wouldn't think I was a poor match for her son, but it was a questionable victory as her lips curved in a knowing smile. Isabelle was trespassing and I didn't like it one bit.

Stay out of my head, witch.

She crossed her legs and grinned. *Neophyte.*

Alain caught the tail end of our mental tussle and shot her a poisonous look. "Cease your games, Maman. Now is not the time."

"Colin and I were just playing," she said sweetly. "Don't be such a bore."

"Save it for another day."

Her eyes continued to sparkle with mirth, but she held her tongue, and the mind games were put on hold. Even Isabelle knew Alain wasn't in the mood to be pushed.

The car sped along the AutoRoute toward the Spanish border. I had no idea where we were heading, but I memorized a few landmarks in case I had to return one day. The driver veered off the main road before we got to the border checkpoint and began the switchback route up the mountain. After ten minutes, we arrived at a granite structure that looked like an old French chateau. I wondered if this was the ancestral home or a new acquisition. I couldn't remember if Alain had ever shared his ethnicity. Was he French or English? Didn't he attend university in Edinburgh? Some boyfriend I was if I couldn't answer the most basic questions about the man I loved.

The moment we stepped into the cavernous foyer, a white owl with black-tipped wings flapped down from one of the exposed wooden rafters and gently perched on Isabelle's shoulder. I stood, amazed, as she crooned a greeting while the bird responded by nuzzling Isabelle's neck and emitting soft mewling sounds. We followed her into the living room with the owl firmly seated on her shoulder.

"What's that all about?" I asked Alain curiously.

"Bibi is her familiar."

"Her what?"

"I don't have time to explain," Alain muttered under his breath. "For the moment, consider Bibi a pet, and for heaven's sake, don't touch. Let her make the first move."

"She looks harmless."

Alain's raised eyebrows made me rethink my hasty assumption.

"Not true?"

"She's fiercely protective of her mistress and a carnivore. If you want to save your fingers, I suggest you keep your hands to yourself."

"Do you have a familiar?"

Alain looked at me with disdain. "Merlin."

"Right," I replied, drawing out the word. "You'll have to expound on this topic someday."

"I'll be glad to, Colin. Right now, we have a mess to untangle."

A fire was blazing in the stone hearth, and an assortment of refreshments were laid out on the sideboard. I wasn't hungry, but I poured myself a cup of coffee to jump-start my brain, which was getting sluggish from the journey. Apparently, Alain had the same idea. I settled on the sofa, facing Isabelle across a coffee table that might have been a barn door in an earlier incarnation. The redwood was polished to a high gloss, but there were plugged holes on one end where the iron door hangers must have been removed. It was an interesting conversation piece, and I would have commented, except Alain joined us with a cup of coffee in one hand and a brioche in the other. After parking his loot on the table, he urged his mother to proceed with her report.

"Where should I start?"

"Since we already know how this began, I'm interested in hearing how our simple plan went sideways," Alain replied. "Do you know any of the details?"

"Of course," she said emphatically. "Bibi has been keeping a close eye on Drake since I received your first email."

"Sorry?" I was completely thrown by that response.

"You heard right," Alain said. "She and Maman make an excellent team."

"The bird is her spy?"

Isabelle visibly bristled. "Don't insult Bibi. She is not some lowly *bird*. My snowy owl is an excellent astral traveler that has been my familiar for years. I utilize her skills all the time. The how is not important, Your Highness. It's the results that matter."

"Please dispense with the honorific."

"As you wish. May I continue, Colin?"

"Yes, please."

"Drake, in his guise as the heir, has been seen in multiple locations around town with Princess Charlotte on his arm. They have been freely demonstrative, quite obscene if you believe the gossips."

"Wait—what? He's tapping Charlie?"

"If tapping means being intimate, then the answer is yes."

I stood so abruptly my knees knocked the low table, and the bone china wobbled precariously. "I've got to put a stop to this."

"You are not going anywhere," Alain thundered. He clamped his fingers around my wrist and pulled me back down on the sofa. "We will rescue Charlie in due time. Let Maman finish her report."

"This is a disaster," I exclaimed. "Could she possibly be in love with him? Do you think he wore a condom? And if he didn't, what if she's pregnant? Does this mean I'll be obligated to marry her? What in the fuck was Drake thinking?" I rose again, desperate to get away, and once more, Alain drew me back down. This time, he put his arm around my shoulder to keep me in place.

"Take a deep breath," he said, trying to reassure me. "All your questions will be answered eventually. It might take time, but we'll fix this."

"How can we possibly?"

"There's more," Isabelle stated coldly. "Drake has been using black magic to harm your grandmother. The foolish woman has been walking around all these years without a protection spell. Drake has taken advantage of her innocence and rendered her incapable of coherent thought."

"Oh my god. Can he kill her?"

"Dying would be a blessing."

"What can be worse than death?"

"He's destroying her brain in tiny increments. She'll end up a vegetable at this rate."

"What about my fathers?" I asked shakily. "Are they okay?"

"As far as I can tell."

"You don't know for sure?"

Terror was gradually being replaced by impotent anger. Thinking of my family and Charlie in harm's way because of my selfishness was making me nauseous. My hands tingled, a recently discovered prelude to a fiery meltdown, and heat shot through my veins like an accelerant. I had to get out of there and warn my family. There would be hell to pay, and god only knew how Alain would react after he realized I'd gone, but I couldn't let Drake get away with this.

Isabelle observed me silently. She would be digging into my private thoughts any second now, and I conjured up a protective shield, hoping this would be enough to keep her away. Alain's theory that my magic was fueled by need or anger never felt truer than it did right then. I was not about to be tag teamed by this powerful duo. They had no right to keep me from protecting the people I loved.

Curbing my hysteria, I cleared my throat and asked, "Why don't we call the police so they can check on Granny? Better yet, give me a phone, and I'll call one of my fathers. Once they know what's going on, they'll take care of the problem."

"You don't want to tip off Drake," Isabelle advised. "A trapped animal will chew off its own leg to escape or kill anyone who tries to stop him. Your fathers may end up as collateral damage."

"He wouldn't dare commit regicide," I argued. Turning to Alain, I asked, "Is she serious?"

"I'm afraid so," Alain said. "At the moment, there's nothing preventing Drake from incapacitating your fathers or anyone else in the villa. If he's got Charlie under his spell, she'll go willingly, and then he can use her as a bargaining tool. No one will touch him once that happens. And if you think he'll hesitate to hurt a royal, think again."

"But he's family," I protested weakly. "Why would he do such a horrible thing?"

Isabelle snorted. "The bad blood must run deeper than I thought."

"What are you talking about? Isn't the stupid feud between your family and ours? Drake is my first cousin, Madame. This makes no sense."

"You can drop the honorific as well," Isabelle said before proceeding. "How much do you know about your sweet granny?"

"Don't," Alain snapped. "He's upset enough."

I glared at him. "I swear I'll torch this house if you people don't fess up."

"Tell him, Maman."

"It seems the dowager let her royal status go to her head, and she neglected her own family. The resentment has been building for decades. Drake is Maura's only means of getting back at her sister."

"That's fucked up!"

"Revenge usually is."

"Why can't we sit down like civilized people and work something out? If it's money they want, I'm sure my fathers would pay it."

"I don't think that'll appease the bloodlust."

"They want to see us dead?"

"Or ruined…" Her words trailed off, and I didn't ask for clarification.

I had to get away from there as quickly as possible before I became a walking flamethrower. Fire dancing under my skin should have weirded me out, but the sense of power trumped the fear. I couldn't wait to give Drake the worst sunburn of his miserable life.

"I need to lie down," I muttered. "Maybe things will look better after I've had a chance to rest. The combination of jet lag and shellshock has wiped me out."

"Of course," Isabelle said. "Alain, show him to your room upstairs."

I started to follow Alain but stopped before my foot hit the first rise. Glancing over my shoulder, I asked Isabelle, "Is there any kind of spell you can cast to protect my family?"

"We're a little too late."

"Please? Anything is better than nothing."

"Follow me," she said, heading down the hall.

Midway out of the room, I tugged on her arm. "Wait a minute."

She gave me an appraising look. "Having second thoughts?"

"It's just, well, you know...I'm thinking..."

"Spit it out," she dared.

"What about this feud between you and Granny's family. Isn't this situation playing right into your hands? You must be happy we're going down."

"I'm going to give you a pass because you've had several shocks in the last few hours. However, I must tell you that you insult me by assuming I'll be dancing on your family grave with the cretins who've perpetuated this sordid affair. Don't ever put me into that category."

"I had to ask."

"Yes, I'm certain you are confused right now. You've heard alarming things about me, and although most of the accusations are true, there were always extenuating circumstances that led to my actions. I'm not an evil witch, Colin, but I've been in charge of my coven for years. People in power have to make decisions that aren't always palatable, but they're necessary to protect the group. You'll realize this after you ascend the throne. Just so we're clear, I don't practice black magic. Nothing good ever comes out of wishing ill on others. It'll come back threefold and you're worse off.

"I looked in the mirror the other day, and I saw several new wrinkles. I'm getting old, Colin, and holding on to my anger is bad for my general health. I don't want to be that person anymore. For whatever reason, and I still have a difficult time admitting this, you make Alain happy. I can finally envision a future where he's surrounded by love, so why on earth would I do anything to jeopardize you or your family?"

"Do you swear on whatever you hold sacred that you're telling the truth?"

"On Bibi's life," she said. Her familiar had been hovering around like a helicopter. Hearing her name, the big bird landed on Isabelle's shoulder gracefully and clapped her beak repeatedly. She was looking at me with those creepy yellow eyes, daring me to hurt her mistress.

"Stand down," I warned. "I'm one of the good guys."

Isabelle stroked the ruffled feathers, murmuring soothing words in their shared language.

"So?" she asked, after the owl settled. "Shall we try to cast a protection spell after the fact?"

I nodded. "Can you show me how to do it?"

"Do you want this to work or not?" she asked, amused.

"I meant can I watch? I'm not risking my family on my mediocre skills."

"Follow me."

Chapter Twenty-Seven

COLIN CONTINUED...

As we moved farther into the chateau, Isabelle answered some of my questions regarding her home. The edifice was built in the late eighteenth century and remodeled several times before it fell into her hands. The thick stone walls were made to withstand a siege, comforting in years past, but impossible to insulate in the present. As such, fires blazed in main rooms, and thick woolen carpets from all over the world were strewn over the stone pavers to soften the impact on her aging musculature. There were antique tapestries and paintings hanging on the walls while the furniture was eclectic, combining exquisite pieces crafted by master carpenters of a bygone era and newer chairs and sofas that were much more comfortable. The kitchen was modern and there were flat-screen TVs in all the central rooms. I assumed there was Wi-Fi as well.

Isabelle's workshop was in a turret only accessible through her boudoir, an old-fashioned term she used to describe her bedroom. It was fitting in this case and mirrored her alluring personality. There was the requisite fireplace warming the large room and throw rugs scattered on the hardwood planks. The window hangings, bed coverings, and multiple throw pillows were an amalgam of textures in different shades of amethyst, gray, and white. The wide four-poster was calling to me, and I would have given anything to dive under the fluffy duvet, but we had a disaster to avert.

Alain and I had been holding hands the entire time and only separated as we stepped through an ornate carved door to climb up steeply winding stairs. The stone treads were worn and narrow, the rise uncommonly high, and the missing balustrade made the grueling assent that much harder. If I had any doubt about Isabelle's general level of fitness, it was dispelled as soon as I reached the top landing. I was winded and she wasn't. Alain managed to keep up without breaking a sweat, and I had to wonder what super gene kept mother and son in such good shape.

It's a question of healthy living and exercise, Isabelle answered in my head.

"Will you quit it?" I complained. "It blows my mind whenever you intrude unexpectedly."

"Pardon me," she said out loud. "Alain and I communicate silently all the time."

"Let's stick to verbal until I get used to you."

"As you wish."

Bibi was flying overhead, making loud clapping noises with her beak, and she circled the area a few times before landing on a window ledge above what appeared to be an altar. From a distance, she looked no different from hundreds of other owl statuary crowding the small room.

"You must have a thing for owls," I said lamely.

Isabelle looked scornful.

"Sorry, I didn't mean any disrespect."

She hissed and put her finger over my mouth. *Be quiet!*

"Right."

Alain reached for my hand to give it an encouraging squeeze. I didn't know much about spell casting. We hadn't covered this topic during our lessons in the Seychelles, because I was still working on the first step in the witches' pyramid—to know. Understanding and learning my craft on all levels—rituals, herbs, candle magic, astral travel, spell work, psychic awareness, and divination—would take more than two weeks. To will, to dare, and to keep silent were the other steps in the pyramid we'd barely explored. On the surface, I felt I already had the desire to learn and the courage to step out of my comfort zone. Silence meant more than keeping my trap shut. It included mastering the art of self-awareness and introspection, attributes I sorely lacked. To be worthy of calling myself a witch, I had to watch and learn, and who could be a better role model than the woman in front of the altar. She'd certainly proven her mettle by raising the exceptional man I could finally call my boyfriend.

And yet, despite Isabelle's goodwill and seemingly benign personality, I knew she was keeping a watchful eye on me. Mistrust for anything Bradford-related couldn't be swept away that easily. Even I knew that a grudge this old had to have taken root. Just because Alain and I were in love didn't mean all was forgiven, conciliatory speech notwithstanding. It would be a long time before the animosity subsided, and she would consider me worthy to join her family.

I looked around the small room adorned with nothing but the accoutrements of witchcraft. Candles were the main source of illumination, and there were hundreds already burning when we'd walked in. Dried herbs in marked canisters lined one wooden shelf. Desiccated plants and flowers were hanging upside down from racks within easy reach. Isabelle prepared to cast the protection spell by lighting aromatic incense and dipping her fingers into a small pot of essential oils. She touched her forehead, eyelids, mouth, and ears as she whispered words only she could hear. Bibi cawed and flew down from her perch, landing gracefully on Isabelle's shoulder. The bird swayed in time with the rhythmic incantation.

I was about to ask Alain if it was old French, but he said Basque before I could form my sentence. My eyes widened. They were French Basque?

"Sort of," he replied out loud.

"We need to talk," I whispered in his ear. This ability to read my thoughts was pissing me off. There had to be some sort of blocking spell to keep them out of my head.

"There is," Alain said, trying to hide his smile. "But you have to improve your skills before it'll work on people like us."

"I hate you."

He chuckled and squeezed my hand.

"What's she saying?"

"As night becomes day, keep Drake Bradford away. Move on from our lives for now and evermore. As I say, so let it be."

"She didn't mention Granny or my fathers."

"Don't worry. This is just the first spell. There will be more."

Alain wasn't wrong. Isabelle repeated the moves, and this time, I heard the names Alexandra, Sebastian, and Errol mixed in with the strange words. I had no idea if this would work, but it gave me a small measure of comfort that wasn't there earlier.

With the spell casting completed, Isabelle snapped her fingers and snuffed out most of the candles. We left the room with Bibi leading the way.

At dinner, we weighed the benefits of "bumping into" Drake in town or confronting him in the palace. I was all for the latter, but Isabelle and Alain remained firm in their belief that we take a wait-and-see attitude. I made a concerted effort to clear my mind, so they had no inkling I disagreed. With escape in mind, I insisted on another tour of the chateau before retiring. Isabelle refused to accompany us, claiming exhaustion.

"I'll show Colin around," Alain offered.

"By all means," she replied. "I'll see you men at breakfast. And I would appreciate it if you kept the sex sounds to a minimum."

"Put your earplugs in," Alain rebuked.

"I'll take a sleeping potion instead."

"Even better."

The three-car garage was attached to the main house, an anomaly for this type of structure, but I was relieved. This meant easy access after Alain fell asleep. There was a Range Rover and a Mercedes sedan. Two cars I could easily drive, and the keys were conveniently hanging on wooden pegs beside the burglar alarm.

"Do you have a problem with theft this far out of the way?" I asked, pointing at the electronic box.

"You can never be too safe. Maman lives alone and she's getting old. I had the entire chateau wired for her protection."

"Doesn't she have any sort of staff?"

"They're day servants. She's alone at night."

"Isn't she a powerful witch, though? Won't a protection spell ward off trespassers?"

"Having one more line of defense is a precaution."

"What's the code?"

Alain raised an eyebrow. "Why do you need to know?"

"What if she sends me to town on an errand?"

"That'll never happen." Alain yawned, and I knew he'd fall asleep as soon as his head hit the pillow.

"Let's go to bed," I suggested. "We can both use a good night's sleep."

"I thought you'd never ask."

Alain couldn't even muster the energy for a blowjob. I waited until his breathing evened out completely, and I stole out of the room. If Isabelle took the sleeping potion, I was safe. Although her familiar was an owl with supersonic hearing, I hoped she was off somewhere hunting field mice for dinner. The thought of her sharp beak crunching down on a fresh kill was hair-raising, but it was nature's way, and I needed to stop being so squeamish.

I felt a little guilty inside the garage, imagining Alain's anger and justifiable fear once he realized I was gone, but this situation was largely my fault. I had put Charlie in Drake's path, an unforeseen complication I never dreamed possible. There was nothing ambivalent about our breakup. How had Drake lured her into his bed? What had he promised her?

Charlie's trusting nature was about to be destroyed due to my impulsive decision. It was time to right the wrongs I'd committed in the name of love.

My heart thudded loudly as I approached the alarm box. Breaking and entering was such a foreign concept, I had no idea where to even begin. I punched in some random numbers to see what would happen. The light flashed a few times and Access Denied stared me in the face. I tried keying in Alain's birthday and the same thing happened. Frustration was making me angry, and I could feel the fire beginning to dance under my skin. Maybe magic was the answer.

My conscious mind had to will this to happen, so the subconscious could tap into the stream of energy. All I needed was a little spark to short out the entire alarm system, but I was so inept, I might end up razing the chateau to the ground with Alain and Isabelle inside.

"Andrew, can you hear me?"

If he was able to zone into me in the fucking Seychelles, then locating me in the southwest of France wasn't that improbable.

I tried again, sounding more desperate. "Andrew!"

For god's sake, brother. I'm not a microwave. It takes a few minutes to cross over the divide.

"Help me."

Where the hell are we, and what's so damn urgent?

"I'll explain while we're in the car. Right now, my problem is getting out of this place without raising the alarm."

What's the code?

"Da fuck? If I knew the answer, your services wouldn't be required."

You put a lot of faith in me.

"If you can't help me, then nobody can."

Why not use magic?

"You know about that?"

I didn't initially, but hanging around you and Alain has been eye-opening.

"Tell me you haven't been watching us have sex."

Gross. I'm not interested in seeing you two bump uglies. It's the magic that's intriguing me.

"So? Any suggestions?"

You need a familiar to empower you.

"I can't find one on short notice."

I'm right here.

"Aren't familiars supposed to be animals?"

Ghosts are preternatural. I'm probably a better conduit than Bibi.

"You might be right. Alain says a familiar, whether astral or physical, can help to enhance a witch's power. They're also supposed to defend us against harm. A personal guardian who brings strength, love, and above all, unflinching loyalty."

Blah, blah, blah. Don't I do that already?

"Damn straight."

Set your mind to the task, brother. Visualize the wires that make this thing work. I'm going inside the machine to see what's what. After I find a vulnerable spot, you'll zap it with your fiery fingertip.

"Andrew, I'm scared this will blow up in my face."

Listen to me, Colin. If this is a life or death situation, there's no time to hesitate.

"I know."

Go ahead then. I'm right here.

Having Andrew by my side and hearing his words of confidence set me at ease. Clearing my mind, I imagined the inner workings of the alarm. It had to be a simple network of wires, nothing as complicated as my laptop. I had no fancy rhyming words or candles to help in this project, only a strong desire to succeed. In my mind's eye, I could see red and blue wires intertwined like a puzzle piece. There was a place where they met up, and I knew this was the weak link, the spot I had to zap.

"Andrew, I think I found it."

I think so too. Right there at the crossroads.

"Shall I try it?"

Hell yeah!

I pointed my finger and heard a soft sizzle as the wires melted, emitting a soft puff of smoke and a faint odor. The breath I'd been holding escaped my lungs in a relieved gush. "Holy shit."

Good job, brother. Let's take the Range Rover. It'll probably get better traction.

"You're coming?"

You promised to catch me up on the drama, and to be honest, this is the most excitement I've had in years. I wouldn't miss it for the world.

"Let's go."

Chapter Twenty-Eight

COLIN CONTINUED...

Getting out of the garage was easy enough, but I kept looking in the rearview mirror, certain that Isabelle or Alain would chase us down. The section of my brain that was still under construction—the one advocating caution and forethought—was telling my foolish and impulsive side to slow down and rethink my decision. It would have been so much easier with Alain by my side, but since he'd made his feelings clear, I was left with no choice. Having never dealt with black magic in any form, I wasn't sure what to expect. On the plus side, Andrew was watching my back. The power of two had to be more potent than one, especially with right on our side.

Can you get into the palace without being spotted?

"Why should I hide?"

Because this is a stealthy commando operation.

"You've been watching too many movies."

Maybe, but as your familiar, I'm in charge of your safety, and I'm telling you to sneak into the palace and take Drake by surprise.

"Can't you do a fly-by and tell me what's happening right now?"

I can try.

"Do it. It's going to take thirty minutes to reach the outskirts of town. That should give you enough time."

He was gone before I finished my sentence. Sheesh. Must be nice to have that kind of power. Someday, I wanted to learn how to astral project the way Isabelle did with Bibi. It couldn't be any more difficult than zip-lining or parasailing, two sports I enjoyed on our vacation. The avenues available to a good witch, one who excelled at their craft, were infinite. I planned to spend the rest of my life delving into Alain's vast stockpile of knowledge.

Resentment toward Granny and Grandda for keeping witchcraft out of my reach—as much my birthright as the royal line of succession—would have derailed my good intentions if I wasn't feeling so guilty about Charlie. This current mess was as much Granny's fault as mine. She should have jobbed out my magical education if she was incapable of teaching me. Moreover, introducing evil into my life, albeit unknowingly, for no other reason than to break up my relationship with Alain was inexcusable. My love for her could and would override the anger, but there would be much groveling on her part going forward. Part of her penance would be pushing for my union with Alain. I still had no answers regarding the succession, but there was time to figure it out if Drake didn't destroy us first.

The atmosphere in the heated car grew frigid, a prelude to Andrew's return. He was like a moveable glacier most of the time, but he also had the power to startle me with a blast of heat when I least expected it. The duality of his nature would come in handy as my familiar.

"Learn anything useful?"

It's as bad as I expected.

"I already know he's sleeping with Charlie."

Are you sure that's not all he's doing?

"What could be worse than that?"

There's a velvet box on his dresser with a diamond ring inside.

"That blowhard! We have to stop him before he gets a chance to propose." I clenched the steering wheel in a death grip while fire danced under my skin. Envisioning Charlie's humiliation was wreaking havoc on my composure. "It'll be a bitch trying to justify my actions."

She may never forgive you.

"I know. What else is going on?"

The palace is a hive of activity. Did you know he's planning a masquerade ball for your birthday?

"How could I possibly know what he's planning next?"

You do remember that tomorrow is our birthday.

"I haven't given it much thought."

You have to attend.

"Seriously?"

There's no getting around it. Our twenty-first birthday is a milestone, and I plan to celebrate in whatever form I can.

"If I throw a sheet over your ghostly form, some hapless fool might actually see you."

Ooh, I never thought of that. Shall we give it a shot?

"Don't lose your focus, Andrew. We have a job to do first."

Nervous much?

"Aren't you worried?"

I'm untouchable.

"But I'm not! I don't want him to turn me into a zombie."

I'll kill him if he tries.

"Can you do that?"

I've never done it before, but it shouldn't be that hard to snuff out a life.

"According to Isabelle, a good witch should walk an ethical path. Whatever energy I send out will return threefold."

Even if the end justifies the means? We're dealing with a madman who's intent on stealing your life.

"We'll have to find some other way to stop him."

Let me know if you come up with a solution.

I huffed out a frustrated laugh. "The blind leading the blind."

Don't go Gandhi on me, and it'll all work out.

"How's Granny?"

A wilted shell of her old self.

"Jesus. Do you think there's permanent damage?"

I'm not a doctor.

"But—"

You need to stop giving me so much credit! I'm the dead guy, remember?

"Sorry."

Let's get serious, brother. Is there a way to your room that won't involve multiple checkpoints?

"Alain taught me a disguising spell that'll allow me to walk right past the palace guards without being spotted."

Fantastic. It'll be fun having a witch for a brother-in-law.

"Do you think we're a good match?"

He's attractive and super smart but a bit too controlling. Can you live with that?

"Apparently I can't get enough."

Then you'd better snag him before he changes his mind.

"He says he loves me."

Let's see how he feels after tonight.

"I'm hoping he'll forgive me."

Only if you succeed.

"Not helping, brother."

A little reality check is part of my job as your familiar.

"Don't take this the wrong way, but this is your first day on the job. Try not to fuck things up too badly."

Moi?

"You've been a know-it-all since I was peeing in my diapers. Follow my lead instead of assuming command. *That's* part of your job."

And you should park the damn car and stop lecturing me. I know what I'm supposed to do. Being a familiar is intuitive, and I've had your back since forever.

I let that register for a while. Andrew had never let me down, and there was no need for me to give him pointers. My job was to stay out of Drake's magical crosshairs and keep my composure until we could figure out how far the asshole intended to go with this charade.

There was a turnaround leading to the palace, and I decided to park the Range Rover and close the short distance on foot. Before approaching the checkpoint, I murmured the disguising spell and was relieved the sentries didn't even look up as I walked past. Andrew gave me a silent high five and cackled gleefully. I grinned back. My life had taken such an unexpected turn. I was surrounded by witches, a balls-to-the-wall familiar, and a new resolve. The fear I'd been carrying since I melted the burglar alarm in Alain's garage evaporated with each step. My entire body was tingling in anticipation, but I reined in the anger, knowing I needed a sound mind and cool head if I was going to survive this challenge.

Sounds of snoring seeped through the door as we got closer to Papa and Da's room. I hissed at Andrew and pointed at our feet to warn him to tread lightly, a needless precaution since he was floating several inches above the pavers.

My bedroom was on the opposite end of the palace, closer to Granny's room but far enough from my fathers to allow maximum privacy.

"Should I check on Granny?"

Why not pull the alarm while you're at it?

"Sorry. Nerves are messing with my functioning brain cells. I'll try to keep it together, or we'll both go down."

We approached the door to my room, and I froze for a second.

What's the matter?

"I'm gathering my energy."

Remember what we did back at the chateau. Visualize the end result, and I'll do the rest.

"Are you sure he can't hurt you?"

Positive.

Drake was slouched on the bed, scrolling through messages on *my* phone. He snarled at the intrusion and was about to unleash a blistering tirade, but the words died in his mouth when he saw me instead of a servant. It took barely a minute for him to adjust to my unexpected appearance. He got to his feet in one fluid motion.

"I wasn't expecting you for a few more days."

"I had to cut my vacation short because of your shenanigans."

"My what?"

"Don't play the fool, Drake. I'm on to you."

"You asked me to stand in for you, and I have. Quite well, I might add. Nobody missed you."

"You had no right to involve Charlie in your plot. What's your endgame?"

"I'm taking her off your hands. You didn't want her and I do."

"You bastard. What have you promised her in my name?"

"Don't call me that."

He dropped all pretenses and stepped into his role as heir apparent with frightening ease. There wasn't a flicker of remorse in his cool gaze.

"Charlie has agreed to marry me, and there's nothing you can do to stop this. We've been sleeping together since you left, and I'm certain she's already pregnant. That'll cement our union."

"How could you?"

"I'm doing you a favor, Colin. You never wanted to be the heir. You've said it often enough, so it has to be true. I'm going to unburden you by stepping into your shoes. This way, you and Alain can take off to parts unknown and live happily ever after. It's a win-win for all of us."

"You're insane."

"Am I? You're the confused kid, not me. I know what I want."

"My life?"

"In a nutshell."

"I can't let you get away with this." Invisible flames swirled around me like a funnel. All I had to do was raise my hand in his direction and he'd be toast. But I had to try diplomacy first. "I'll pay you whatever you want to make up for your loss."

Drake's eyes widened as he felt the power of my magic. "Your skills have improved."

"Damn right. I'll turn you into a pile of ash if you don't pack up your stuff and go."

"You wouldn't want your loved ones to suffer because you're too cowardly to be the ruler you were meant to be. The title was wasted on you, Colin. Why not let a real man take over?"

Zap him!

"Not yet."

My evolution from clueless human to apprentice witch didn't include wiping out my conscience. I couldn't bring myself to commit murder regardless of the provocation.

"Who are you talking to?" Drake demanded.

"My familiar."

"Why can't I see him?"

"He's a ghost."

Drake looked at the empty space to my right, and Andrew stuck out his tongue and blew a raspberry. A gust of frigid air hit Drake squarely in the face and he stepped back.

"Tell him to back off, or I'll destroy the dowager with the flick of my wrist. She's already on the brink of death, and a little push will end her misery."

"Leave her out of this."

"She started it all."

"Aren't you too old to be blaming others for your decisions? Whatever Granny did or didn't do is history. Why don't we start fresh, and I promise to treat you and your family with the respect you deserve."

"Too late," he said bitterly. "I've already had a taste of your life, and I don't intend to give it back."

I zapped the smoke alarm on the ceiling and the deafening screech reverberated throughout the palace. Security guards were tumbling into the room within seconds, fire extinguishers in hand.

"Arrest him," I said, pointing at Drake. "He's an imposter."

Drake let out a mocking laugh and leaned against the wall, one hand on his hip. In his fashionable attire, he looked like a prince, whereas I was still in the rumpled outfit I'd worn on our flight home. If anyone looked like a fake, it was me.

"Open your eyes," Drake reprimanded as the head of security appeared conflicted. "My cousin has ingested too many pills and is quite delusional. He needs to sleep this off in another location. Take him away."

"Where should we take him?"

"Put him on a train back to Brussels."

"Like hell you will," I said loudly. "I'm Prince Colin. Touch me and you'll live to regret it."

A show of force would be a good idea right now.

"Ya think?"

Torch the curtains or something to show Drake you mean business.

I raised my hand in Drake's direction and stopped dead when I heard Papa's voice.

"Where's the bloody fire?"

Chapter Twenty-Nine

COLIN CONTINUED...

Da, wearing nothing but his white linen nightshirt, slipped in behind Papa with Snow bringing up the rear.

Arms akimbo and legs planted a foot apart, he surveyed the scene and asked, "What's going on?"

"Drake has accused me of impersonating him," I replied.

Unperturbed, Drake remarked, "As you can see for yourselves, my cousin is out of his mind."

"Yer both aff your heid," Da accused.

Papa looked Drake in the eye. "Explain yourself, Colin."

"I'm Colin," I said, touching Papa's arm. "You're talking to Drake."

"He's the imposter," Drake stated. "Look at us. Which one doesn't belong here?"

"One of you is lying." Papa's gaze darted between us. "I demand to know which one of you is the culprit."

"Aye," Da seconded, scratching his head and looking at the two of us. "Ah dinna ken who's telling the truth."

I was equally frustrated by the standoff. There was one thing that might work, and I whispered in Da's ear. "I'll gie ye a skelpit lug."

I'll give you a slap on the ear was one of his favorite threats whenever I misbehaved. He never followed through, of course, but it didn't stop him from using the old Scottish saying.

He started upon hearing the familiar refrain and pulled me closer as awareness dawned. Snow rubbed against my legs, and her feathery tail wagged in recognition. I patted her on the head, grateful for her loyalty. With his arm over my shoulders, Da proclaimed, "This is our lad, Bash. Arrest that imposter."

Papa motioned to the guards. "I'm not sure what's happened here, but security will escort Drake off the premises and straight to the police station."

"Not a chance," Drake said, shedding his Colin persona. Without magic to enhance our similarities, it was easier to spot the differences in our appearance. His hair was more stylish, as were his clothes, but the most notable difference was the malice glinting out of world-weary eyes. "I was hired by the dowager, and then Colin modified the deal. You can't arrest me for that."

"Part of that is true," I admitted, "but Drake failed to mention he's a witch. I think he's been hurting Granny."

Both fathers looked at Drake in horrified fascination.

"Yes, I'm a witch, but so is your son and the man he's dating. The dowager asked me to improve Colin's magic, but he decided to go on a vacation instead. He practically begged me to cover his tracks. Did you know he and Alain were in the Seychelles for the last two weeks? Having a grand old time while I had to put up with the dowager and her infernal meddling."

Da frowned at me. "Is that true?"

"I can explain."

"This better be good," Papa jeered. "You're in so much trouble—"

"Both of you have to listen," I cut him off. "Granny is dying and Charlie is pregnant. All because of Drake. You need to stop worrying about my sins and concentrate on punishing this guy."

"He's talking nonsense," Drake said. "The dowager is fine, and Charlie's pregnancy hasn't been confirmed yet."

Da turned several shades of purple. "Have you lain with Princess Charlotte?"

"On every flat surface, and what of it? We're both adults."

"If you didn't tell her the truth, then you took her under false pretenses," Papa countered.

"Perhaps, but I can assure you it was a two-way thing. She loved each minute. Colin never satisfied her the way I did."

"I've heard enough," Papa said tersely. "Impersonating Colin is one thing, but luring an innocent girl into your bed is unforgivable. We can't let this go unpunished."

"I hate to remind you, but I'm not under your jurisdiction. Furthermore, consensual sex is not against the law. Charlie will stick by me no matter what you say."

I scoffed. "You tricked her into sex, so you can forget the consensual defense. Do you think she'll stay with you after she learns the truth?"

"Why wouldn't she?"

"You're not her equal," I said bluntly.

Drake's instant response didn't give Andrew or me time to prepare. The water sprinklers were activated with a snap of his fingers, showering cold liquid onto my body, effectively dousing the fire underneath my skin. Since we hadn't worked out a plan B, I wasn't sure what to do next. Andrew tried to help by circling around Drake like a whirling dervish, but the damn witch didn't even flinch. I could try kickboxing, something I'd learned as an adolescent, but I found myself rooted to the floor. I struggled to free my legs from the imaginary rope to no avail. All of us were under the same spell, endeavoring to escape the invisible bonds but getting nowhere.

"Do something!" Papa bellowed at his security.

"We can't move, Your Highness."

Snow howled in frustration, tugging on her non-existent leash while Da threatened to pickle Drake's balls if he ever got free. My failure to stop Drake was a bitter pill to swallow. I should have listened to Alain and Isabelle instead of trying to save the world on my own. It was stupid and irresponsible, and the anger built again. Deep down in my core a spark was lit and caught. Like an engine that had stalled and restarted, my magic thrummed to life.

"You'll pay for this," I swore. "We'll find you eventually."

Drake snatched the blue velvet ring box from atop the bureau and stuffed it into his pocket. Then he dragged a suitcase out of the closet. Calmly, as if he had all the time in the world, he started emptying out his drawers and pulling shirts and suits off hangers. Most of the clothes still had tags on them, expensive souvenirs of his days as Prince Colin.

After he was done, Drake took one last look around the room and dropped his next bombshell.

"Try to stop me and the dowager dies. Your paltry magic is no match against my skills."

"Leave her alone," I begged.

"Her good health depends on you, Colin. Wouldn't you prefer to leave her death off your growing list of failures?"

"How dare you."

"I've lived your life for the last thirteen days," Drake contented. "Those who've crossed my path have remarked on my newly found confidence. The truth is you're a whiny loser and have no business hanging on to your title. Pass it on to someone worthier."

"Like you?" I scoffed. "Your smarmy moves don't qualify you to shine my shoes."

Now you've gone and done it. The asshole will turn you into a toad.

Andrew's warning didn't go unnoticed. I pulled up my imaginary shield and waited for Drake's next move while the heat inside my body continued to rise. There must have been a glow around my persona only a witch could see, because Drake appeared to be considering his options. Well-honed survival skills came into play, and rather than engage in anything physical, Drake hit below the belt.

"That insult cost the dowager her life. There's a blood vessel in her puny brain that just burst. Even if the paramedics manage to get here in time, she'll never survive."

"Bastard!" Papa screamed. "You'll pay for this."

Drake threw him a disdainful look and began to walk out of the room.

Colin, don't let him go. Zap the motherfucker.

"Help me."

Let's melt his fancy shoes first.

I focused on the tasseled loafers, and they started to smoke.

Drake stopped and wriggled out of his shoes in the nick of time. The fine leather curled in on itself as a shower of angry red flames incinerated the Gucci's. My pulse sped up as something dark and knotted exploded inside me. I glared at Drake, silently daring him to take another step.

"Your juvenile magic can't touch me," Drake said.

His mocking tone acted like an accelerant and fire swept through my veins like smoldering lava. I turned my attention on the suitcase, filled to bursting with Drake's ill-gotten possessions and watched with deep satisfaction as it went up in smoke.

The familiar face twisted into an unrecognizable mask, and he lifted both arms in my direction. Something deadly entered through the base of my skull and spread. I covered my ears in a futile attempt to keep Drake out, but his evil was unstoppable, creeping though my brain like a malevolent vine. I cried out and dropped to my knees, effectively felled by powerful black magic I couldn't ward off. As the toxic plant grew thorns, drawing blood from tender gray matter, the metallic taste seeped into my mouth, and I coughed, choking on life-sustaining fluid. My fathers were hollering for help while Andrew's otherworldly friends—ghosts, vamps, and demons—gathered around my failing body to offer their support.

Limbs no longer responded to my commands, and I crumpled to the floor in a heap. I was dying, and there wasn't much I could do about it. My only consolation was knowing I'd be with Andrew shortly.

Don't give up, he urged in my ear. *Help is on the way.*

"Alain will be too late."

We can't let Drake get away with this.

Excruciating pain forestalled my reply. I had to escape this torture, and if dying was the only cure, then so be it. The last thing I remembered was someone shouting orders and then the horrific pounding on my chest.

I was on my four-poster the next time I opened my eyes. A cool cloth was pressed to my forehead, and the debilitating ache in my head had subsided. My fathers were anxiously pacing at the foot of the bed while Alain perched on the edge of the mattress and held my hand. Andrew snuggled up on the other side, whispering words of encouragement.

"Am I dead?"

Not quite. Remind me to perfect my skills before we engage the enemy again.

Alain raised my hand to his lips and kissed me tenderly. "I thought you were a goner."

"About that..."

"We can talk later, *chaton*. Right now, you need to regain your strength."

"Where's Drake?"

"He's disappeared."

Panic stricken, I tried to rise, but Alain pressed me down gently.

"We have to stop him," I argued.

"Let me take care of Drake."

"I failed."

"You were extremely brave."

"No, I wasn't," I said bitterly. "This entire mess is my fault. Go ahead and admit it."

"I wish you had listened to me."

"You were right all along. Did Granny survive?"

"Isabelle is attending to her."

"Your mother's here?"

"Yes. She's doing what she can to help the dowager, but the damage was extensive. We're not sure of the outcome."

I bit down hard on my lip.

"Stop blaming yourself," Alain sympathized. "She's the one who brought Drake into your life."

"May we speak to him?" Da asked, approaching the bed with Papa in tow.

"Of course," Alain said, leaving my side. "I'll be waiting outside."

"Don't go far," I begged.

"I won't."

As soon as the door closed, Da said gruffly, "He saved your life. I dinna ken what he is, so long as he protects you."

"I love him, Da. And he loves me."

"It's pretty obvious," Papa remarked. "We'll have to think of a way to repay him and his mother properly."

"I'm sorry for the deception."

"Now's not the time for recrimination."

"I feel so guilty."

"You're alive," Papa said. "That's the only thing that matters."

My throat clogged, and I quickly closed my eyes to keep the tears at bay, but it was useless. They overflowed and ran down my cheeks. My fathers left the room, and the moment I felt Alain by my side, I clambered onto his lap and quietly fell apart.

Chapter Thirty

ALAIN

Colin's gut-wrenching sobs filled me with sadness, but the alternative was unthinkable. Drake had managed to kill him by the time I arrived, and if Colin hadn't been in the peak of health, and I wasn't qualified to administer CPR—while Isabelle shocked his stalled heart with her magical version of a defibrillator—we would be dealing with a corpse and a monastic crisis instead of a guilt-ridden prince.

His genuine grief over his recklessness was reassuring. Life lessons were especially harder on people who were used to giving orders and being instantly obeyed. Despite his bellyaching about his role as heir apparent, Colin was a natural-born leader, and relinquishing control, however sensible, went against his nature. I hoped this incident would remain forever etched in his memory bank, a permanent reminder that bravado wasn't always the answer.

It had been eight hours since the showdown. Four hundred and eighty minutes since Drake vanished in a spectacular display of lights. He could be anywhere in the world by now, or holed up in a local establishment to keep an eye on the royal family he'd been determined to penetrate and destroy. While Colin was recuperating from his brush with death, the royals had caught me up on the situation with Princess Charlotte. Colin's childhood friend would suffer the most if Drake wasn't stopped. Even if she was in lust with Drake's version of Colin, she would be repelled by him once she learned the truth. The police had checked on her whereabouts, and the apartment she'd been renting was empty.

My nerves were frayed, and I would have given anything for a rejuvenating nap, but knowing that monster was somewhere in the world made it impossible to relax. Colin slumped against my chest, wiped out from his catharsis.

In a barely audible croak, Colin said, "He said I wasn't worthy of the crown."

"Why do you care what that asshole thinks?"

"Maybe he's right," Colin replied. "How can you be so sure I'm not a fuckup?"

"I couldn't possibly love a loser."

He snorted, then laughed against my chest, a wonderful sound I never thought I'd hear again. "I would give anything to have a tenth of your confidence."

"It didn't happen overnight, Colin. You forget I've got a thirteen-year head start. I told you I was an idiot at your age."

"It's hard to imagine."

"Isabelle can tell you all about my wayward youth. My acts of rebellion were a sore point and the main reason I stayed away from the coven. I wanted to prove I could succeed on my own merits, whereas she was more interested in shaping a subservient clone who would step into her shoes one day."

"Was she pissed?"

"For a long time, but she never cut me off financially. I don't think we'd have as good a relationship if I hadn't made a clean break first."

"The feud between the Simons and Bradfords will probably escalate now that we've stopped Auntie Maura's golden boy."

"Anyone who relies on a sociopath for revenge has got to be missing a few screws herself."

"I dunno. Drake is a charmer who probably had his best foot forward in his grandmother's presence. She'll never believe he's capable of murder."

"Sociopaths *are* charming, but they're also manipulative, narcissistic, and prone to lawlessness and sexual deviance. Furthermore, they lack empathy, and the result is a cold and calculating personality with delusions of grandeur, which can't tolerate any form of criticism."

"No wonder he lost his mind after I told him Charlie would dump him if she finds out he's nothing special."

"You kicked him where it most hurt without realizing it."

"I guess I'm lucky to be alive."

"You have no idea."

"Was I clinically dead?"

"Your heart had stopped."

"I could sense the separation from my body as soon as it was happening."

"Were you frightened?"

"No, on the contrary. It was peaceful and I was looking forward to being with Andrew."

"I was scared out of my wits," I admitted. "Promise me you'll wait until you're ninety before you die."

"What I can promise is a change in attitude. No more complaining about being the heir apparent. Drake's takeover made me appreciate my birthright for the first time in my life."

"Then you're better for the experience, although I wish you'd had your epiphany in some other way."

"This doesn't mean I've forgotten the succession issue."

"You have years to resolve that problem."

"Will you help me?"

"I'll put all my resources into finding a solution."

"I want you to marry me, Alain. Would you ever consider it?"

"Falling in love with you wasn't in the plan, yet here we are. Marriage is a daunting prospect, but I'm more open to the idea than I've ever been. How's that for an answer?"

"I'll take it as a yes."

"No, don't do that. Consider it a new level of commitment."

"What's the next step?"

"We'll get engaged a year before our marriage."

Colin pushed away from me and stared. "Do you have a timetable?"

"I'd like to wait until you're mentally prepared."

His eyes widened. "What the hell, Alain? Who's going to judge my personal growth?"

"Who do you think? I'll be by your side through most of it."

"This arrangement has too many loopholes. I need a date."

"Today is your twenty-first birthday," I pointed out.

"I'm aware."

"If it goes according to plan, we can make the announcement on your twenty-fourth birthday and get married after you turn twenty-five."

"You're asking me to wait four years?"

"That's not unrealistic, is it? We've just started dating and we need to spend more time together. After seeing what Drake did to you, I'm more determined than ever to help you improve your craft. You never know when it might prove useful. And although it goes without saying, I'm reminding you that governing isn't easy. I want to make sure you can handle the responsibility of being a ruler, as well as a husband and father."

Colin rolled his eyes. "Why do you have to be so methodical?"

"Because I love you and we can't afford to be hasty. I'll be going through a learning curve as well. A reliable and loving consort is crucial to your success as a monarch."

"And I suppose you plan on being the valedictorian of husbands?"

"You deserve nothing less."

"I'm going to agree to this ridiculous plan with one important caveat."

"Penetration."

"How'd you know?"

"You've been thinking about it for weeks."

Colin shrugged. "If you quit withholding, then perhaps I'll stop obsessing. For all I know, I'll hate taking it up the ass."

"Oh, you'll love it."

"Awfully sure of yourself, aren't you?"

"Isn't it part of my appeal?"

Colin knew how much I enjoyed our verbal tussles, and egging me on was one of his guilty pleasures. I wasn't surprised by his querulous reply.

"Yeah, but this time you'll have to back up your words with some action. I'm not taking your word for it."

"You've got a deal."

"When?"

"After you're fully recovered."

"I'm fine," Colin insisted.

"We'll see."

"Alain-speak for no way, no how."

"This is the sort of childish behavior I can't tolerate."

Colin ducked his head and murmured, "Sorry."

"You died, *chaton*. Anyone else would be in the hospital for observation. Instead you're whining about lovemaking. Let's see how you feel after the party tonight."

"Is that still happening?"

"Too late to cancel according to David."

There was a knock on the door and Isabelle appeared, looking grim and disheveled. There were bags under her eyes, and right then, she looked every one of her sixty-nine years.

"What is it?" I asked, bracing for the bad news.

"The dowager has passed away."

Colin gasped and shook his head in denial.

"I'm so sorry," Isabelle said gently.

Still holding on to Colin, we shuffled out of his room and down the short walk to his grandmother's suite. It had been set up as an intensive-care unit after the specialists determined her condition was terminal. Rather than have her die among strangers at the local hospital, Bash made the decision to bring the necessary equipment to the palace, so she could remain in familiar surroundings. A combination of drugs and Isabelle's healing potions had kept the dowager comfortable. Her death, officially ruled as a massive stroke, had been expected. Although we'd all been praying for a miracle, and Isabelle did everything in her power to repair the damage created by Drake's parting attack, it had proven fruitless in the end.

The room was crowded with medical personnel gathering up equipment. Errol and Bash knelt beside the bed, heads bent in grief, while Fiona, Alexandra's lady-in-waiting, and David, her faithful assistant and event planner, stood weeping in the background. Colin joined his fathers and clutched his granny's hand while tears rolled down his cheeks.

I was gutted by the fact that we couldn't save her.

"We have to find Drake," I whispered angrily in Isabelle's ear. "Are you up for a witch-hunt?"

"I need a gallon of coffee and a shower first. Then I have to send out a group email to inform the covens of this turn of events. I'm not chasing down a rogue witch without their blessing."

"It's none of their business," I hissed.

"Nonetheless," Isabelle maintained, "the Bradford Coven will retaliate if we mete out punishment without giving them the facts. They can officially deny their involvement or stand behind Maura and her grandson. In either case, we have to observe protocol."

"We're not in the bloody United Nations, Maman."

"You might not think so, but witches don't go around randomly killing each other. It would be akin to a foreign nation dropping an unexpected bomb. You're too young to remember the last war between our kind. Innocent people were hurt, and I refuse to make that my legacy. We do it my way or not at all."

I fumed in frustration, but logic won out. She was right, and I was too involved to put this in perspective.

"How long is it going to take to get the go-ahead?"

"I would give them twenty-four hours."

"The trail will be colder than ice by then."

"I'm sorry, Alain. I know how much Colin and his family mean to you. It would be satisfying, and well within your rights, to exact revenge, but let's do this right or you'll only make things worse."

Admitting defeat was a foreign concept and one that chafed like ill-fitting shoes. However, Colin's safety, and the royals' by extension, had to be my top priority.

"You know where to find me when you're ready."

"Are you going to tell Colin?"

"No."

"He has a right to know."

"The bastard almost killed him! I won't risk his life again."

She snorted. "Men..."

Chapter Thirty-One

ALAIN

Prince Sebastian issued an official statement to the press announcing the untimely passing of his mother and the cancellation of the masquerade ball. The dowager's funeral, to be held in a few days, would take center stage for the time being.

Before departing for Sendorra, the royals insisted on answers. They were in turmoil over the dowager's death, and the events leading up to the disastrous altercation with Drake deserved some explanation. Maman had already left for home and promised to check in with me later in the day.

The peaceful atmosphere in the library was a welcome relief after our stressful morning. Food and beverages were laid out on a sideboard, but I was too wound up to eat. Colin and I held hands on the sofa while his fathers faced us across the coffee table in individual club chairs.

The Duke of Maitland was the first to speak.

"Before anything else, I'd like to thank you and your mother for saving Colin's life," he said. "Losing our lad alongside the dowager would have been unbearable."

"I agree," Prince Sebastian said. "We're in your debt."

"There's no need to thank me. I would have gladly faced Drake myself, but things got out of hand. Colin's safety has always been my first priority."

"That's why I'm willing to hear you out," the Prince replied. "What in the hell were you thinking, man?"

"I take full responsibility, sir. Leaving town was a bad decision."

"Alain," Colin protested. "You know that's not true. I'm the one who insisted on getting away."

"It doesn't matter, Colin. I knew better."

"Will you let me explain?"

"I'm capable of speaking for myself."

He squeezed my hand in supplication. "Please? There's a lot of backstory on Granny that needs to be addressed first."

"All right."

"If you'll bear with me," Colin began. "I need to start from the beginning."

"Go ahead." The duke gave him an encouraging nod.

"You were aware that Granny was a witch, right?"

"Yes," the Prince replied. "But your grandda put a lid on her witchcraft."

"What you might not know is that I inherited the gene."

They both leaned forward. "So that bastard wasn't lying?"

"Not about this—I am a witch. Granny was aware of my abilities from the beginning, but she was too afraid to say anything."

"Perhaps it would have been better if she'd informed us," the Prince remarked.

"Your father would have lost his mind," the duke pronounced.

Prince Sebastian shrugged. "Better the devil you know—"

"Granny had her reasons," Colin clipped. "We'll never know if they were right or wrong, but it was Grandda's fault that she began teaching me in secret. It was also the main reason she cut ties with her family, which led to a lot of anger and resentment. Drake is the weapon they used to get back at us."

"That's preposterous," Prince Sebastian blustered. "We never hurt them."

"She ignored the entire clan, which was even worse."

"Keep going," the duke urged, warning the Prince with a sidelong scowl so he wouldn't interrupt.

"Through the years, I learned a few tricks, amateur stuff that barely scraped my true potential. And then I met Alain."

"Who is also a witch?"

"Yes, but he's not a practicing one. Alain is a scientist first and foremost. Granny disapproved of our union because Alain is a Simon, and there's some ancient feud between the two covens."

"Isn't your last name de Gris?" the duke asked me directly.

"I changed it to distance myself from the Simon Coven."

"Why? You seem to be on good terms with your mother," Prince Sebastian asked.

"It's a long story."

"You'll have to enlighten me another time," the Prince said dismissively. "Let us deal with Colin first."

I didn't argue. It was more important they see the big picture through their son's eyes. I listened with half an ear as Colin methodically explained our relationship from its inception to the present. His honest description—starting with our meaningless hookup and his dogged pursuit for something more meaningful by suggesting Drake impersonate him—elevated him in my eyes. It would have been so much easier to point the finger at me. I was the more experienced partner and should have known better. But Colin didn't do that, and I wasn't going to let him bear the brunt of his fathers' anger.

"May I interrupt?"

Colin appeared hesitant but gave in nonetheless.

Having never proposed marriage before—to a royal no less—I wasn't sure how this would play out. Even though it would be years in the making, my love and commitment were front and center, and I wanted them to hear it from my lips.

I took a deep breath and began. "You've been given all the facts, but there's one thing you should know. I've fallen in love with Colin and hope to marry him sometime in the future, if you give us a nod of approval. The start of our relationship was a little rocky, but I can assure you it was consensual. I made some poor decisions by going along with Colin's madcap plan, but as Maman has mentioned several times in the last few weeks, love and smarts don't always go together."

The duke cracked a smile, but the Prince went for the jugular. "Are you even intersex?"

"No, sir."

"Then your proposal is denied unless witchcraft can overcome the problem."

"I'm not sure I understand."

"Our principality would become a protectorate of Spain should Colin die without fathering an heir. Although he is intersex and could carry a child, our constitution forbids the reigning monarch to be put at risk."

"I see."

"We're not getting married tomorrow," Colin clarified. "It'll be five years down the road, which will give us time to explore alternatives."

"For sure, but wishing and hoping won't change the facts," the duke commiserated.

"We don't need to dwell on this for now," Colin snapped.

His demeanor switched from apologetic son to the inflexible heir apparent I'd come to know and love. I knew we'd have years to figure this out, but it wasn't the right time to start a debate on the future of Sendorra.

The Prince must have realized that arguing over a nebulous future was less important than our current problem. "What I want to know is how we're going to bring Drake to justice?" he asked. "Do you have any ideas, Alain?"

"Maman feels it's necessary to inform the coven, given how Drake is a witch, and there's protocol that needs to be observed before we can hunt him down."

"Were you planning on telling me?" Colin interjected.

"Eventually."

"If you think I'm going to let you go off on your own, then think again."

"Let's talk about this in private," I insisted.

"You're not going anywhere except home," Prince Sebastian announced. "Granny deserves a royal send off, and I expect you to walk behind her casket with your da and me. Playing the avenger is not your job. I can provide Alain with all the security and resources he needs, but you, dear boy, are staying put."

They rose in unison and left the room.

Colin didn't attempt to follow. Instead, he sat and stewed. My witch's eye could see colorful flames racing up and down his arms and fingers, and his ragged breaths were always a prelude to disaster.

"Calm down before you do any permanent damage."

"They continue to treat me like a child!"

"Since you were left for dead, I get where they're coming from. Humor us by staying out of harm's way."

"On one condition."

"What's that?"

"You fly back to Sendorra with us."

"I have to attend to some other matters first. I'll catch a commercial flight in a couple of days and be there in time for the funeral."

"Unacceptable," Colin said. "Today is still my birthday and you made me a promise earlier. I might be able to live with Papa's decision if you keep your word."

Squeezing my eyes shut, I tried to come to terms with his obsession. "How can you think of sex at a time like this?"

"You just reminded me, I was clinically dead. Granny is in a coffin. You're planning to go on a witch hunt without me. Do you think I'm letting you go anywhere while I'm still a virgin?"

"Colin, please. This isn't the time or the place."

"I agree. We're going back to my ginormous palace where you can pop my cherry in style."

"Your stubbornness is only matched by your bravery. I'm sure I can live without both."

"You're a terrible liar, Alain. You'd be bored if I didn't challenge you."

"It seems I've fallen in love with the whole package."

"Speaking of package..."

I swallowed his words with a kiss.

A few hours later, we were on a private plane to Sendorra. With a glass of whiskey in hand, Prince Sebastian grew maudlin and began reminiscing about his mother.

"Has anyone told you about my own masquerade ball?" he asked Colin. Colin perked up. "Not all of it."

"Bash," the duke remonstrated. "They don't want to hear our story."

The Prince ignored him and recounted the many steps it had taken to find his love match. The magic pebble and all it entailed made me crack up.

In between wheezes, I asked, "Are you telling me the dowager used witchcraft and got away with it?"

"She sure did," he replied. "My father was repulsed by the idea but desperate enough to allow her one chance to get it right." He reached for the duke's hand and smiled. "As you can see, it worked out just fine."

Encouraged, I brought forth another question. "So, witchcraft doesn't frighten you?"

"Not as much as it did my father. I realize there's more to magic than love potions, and it can be used for evil as well as good."

"Aye," the duke concurred. "Recent events have made me a believer, but I'm not sure how comfortable I would be with a practicing witch in residence."

"You will keep an open mind, though?"

"I'll do my best," the duke said. "My primary concern is Colin's safety."

"One I share with all my heart," I agreed. "Colin's brush with death has put everything into perspective."

The duke gave me a measured look. "That's all well and good, but don't get too complacent. I'll sink a dagger in your chest if you disappoint our lad."

"Da! Don't threaten my boyfriend."

"Just so we're clear, ye ken?"

"Crystal," I confirmed. "Are you willing to give me time to find a solution to our biggest hurdle?"

"Can you?" Prince Sebastian asked dubiously.

"Alain can do anything once he sets his mind to the task," Colin noted enthusiastically.

Prince Sebastian looked skeptical, as did the duke, but gratitude tipped the scales in my favor. Colin was alive thanks to my efforts, and time seemed like a small price to pay for a miracle. From where I sat, the opportunity to come up with a viable alternative to a seemingly insurmountable problem was a gift in and of itself. At the moment, I had no solution, but I would do everything within my power—human and preternatural—to find the answer.

A stretch limousine was waiting at the airport, along with the hearse to transport the dowager's coffin to the mortuary, where they would prepare her body for the public viewing. Once that was accomplished, she would lie in state in the palace chapel until it was time for the funeral.

Despite its proximity to Biarritz, I'd never had the opportunity to visit Sendorra. It was popular among skiing and hiking enthusiasts, and for those who preferred indoor sports, there was the casino, a chief source of revenue. From the clear air to the towering mountains and lush green pine forests, it was picture-perfect. We drove through the charming town center and continued on until the Imperial Palace was seen in the distance. I was struck by a powerful sense of déjà vu after seeing the guards patrolling the area astride horses. Even the palace, rising majestically out of the mist, felt familiar. Perhaps it was the men's attire that stirred my memory. The uniforms were typically Scottish, in deference to the duke's heritage, but these men weren't in place for a photo op. Their straight-backed posture and ferocious scowls lent gravitas to their surroundings, and I knew they were present to defend the royal family. Certain disaster would befall anyone who attempted to break through this daunting human barrier.

David was at the head of the long line of staff waiting to welcome the royal family home on this solemn occasion. They were standing at attention in two rows. The men wore black armbands, and the female staff members had small black ribbons pinned to their left breast. It was a moving tribute to the dowager but depressing as hell. Colin's eyes glittered as he shook hands and accepted condolences. This was the first time I'd observed him in an official capacity, and I couldn't help the swell of pride as I watched him master his emotions.

The royals didn't ask about our accommodations, and their uncharacteristic lack of interest led me to believe they didn't care if I slept in Colin's bed or the stables. They had more important things on their mind and making small talk at this juncture would have been awkward.

Before dinner, Colin gave me a brief tour of the palace. It was far too large to take in all at once, so we stuck to the ground floor. I viewed the throne room, the impressive library, the official dining room, which could easily accommodate twenty-four guests in one sitting, the ballroom, and finally the quaint chapel. Once again, I felt I'd seen the wooden pews and ornately carved altar before. It was such a strong feeling I had to pause at the entrance.

"What's the matter?" Colin asked. "Are you going to burst into flames if you enter a non-Wiccan chapel?"

"Don't be ridiculous," I countered. "I'm an agnostic not a Wiccan."

"But you're a witch."

"Not all of us are Wiccans."

"Okay," he said, looking at me curiously. "You can clarify another time. Right now, I want to know why you're acting all squirrely."

"Am I?"

"Yeah."

How could I tell him I'd been here before?

"Perhaps I'm feeling the effects of our long day and need some rest."

"You have to do better than that, Alain. I can tell when you're leaving out something important."

I sighed and drew Colin closer. "There's something very familiar about this chapel."

"You must have seen it in a picture somewhere."

"That's always a possibility, but my sixth sense is telling me there's more to it. I'm not overly fond of mysteries," I admitted. "It'll nag at me until I come up with an answer."

"A glass of wine and a comfortable mattress might clear the cobwebs."

I snorted. "It'll put me to sleep."

"Don't even think about it," Colin warned. "You're making good on your promise before you pass out."

This time, I was the one who did the exasperated eye roll.

Colin's crestfallen look upon seeing my reaction filled me with remorse. The dowager's death had overshadowed the significance of two milestones—his twenty-first birthday and our future engagement—and it fell on me to put a smile back on his face even if the timing wasn't ideal.

I reached for him and felt marginally better when he melted into my embrace.

"Go ahead and start our bath," I whispered close to his ear. "I'll be up in a minute."

Colin drew back and looked me in the eyes. His lips parted, and I expected the usual inquiry, but his expression shifted and renewed hope brightened his features, erasing the melancholy. I was never more cognizant of my role in his life and silently vowed to measure up to his every expectation. Without saying a word, he gave a brisk nod and headed upstairs.

I enlisted the help of a cooperative chef and his eager kitchen staff to come up with a fantastic three-course dinner, which included an impromptu birthday cake. The finished product would be delivered to our suite by the time we were done with our leisurely soak.

Hundreds of lit candles greeted me when I pushed through the door of the royal accommodations. Colin had been busy with his own surprise, and my excitement picked up as I passed through the large sitting room and into the bedroom. In the en suite bathroom, I found him immersed in a large sunken tub, covered in aromatic soap bubbles, with a flute of champagne in one hand.

"There you are," he exclaimed happily. "I was worried you might be having second thoughts."

I studied him while I undressed, trying to determine if he was joking or not. Was there ever a moment when he expected me to cut and run? The last forty-eight hours had been a horrific reminder that the only certainty in life was death. Embracing happiness while it was within our grasp superseded everything, and it was crucial to profess my love in the clearest of terms to assure Colin I was in this relationship for the long haul. I lifted the bottle of champagne out of the ice-filled container, filled my own flute, and joined him in the tub.

Smiling, I raised my glass in a toast. "Happy birthday, my love. Let's drink to your continued health and our new understanding. Long may we reign."

"Hear hear," he responded, beaming with happiness. He drained his flute and scooted over to my side.

After that, there was no need to fill the silence with small talk. We'd considered our options, examined our motives, and come up with the same conclusion. Love would prevail, no matter what obstacles we'd have to endure. When the champagne was consumed and the last of the suds disappeared down the drain, we dressed in matching blue silk robes and moved on to the next phase of our celebration.

The cook had outdone himself, producing a gastronomical feast fit for my prince. Colin's birthday cake, a chocolate concoction complete with twenty-one candles, melted in our mouths. We exchanged sugary kisses and consumed another bottle of champagne. By the time the footmen wheeled away the food trolley, we were ready for the main event.

We stood at the foot of the bed, and I pulled on Colin's sash. The robe parted, and I skimmed over his chest and shoulders as the rich fabric fell to the carpet. Following my lead, Colin undressed me. He was surprisingly gentle, considering I'd put him off for so long, but his ability to see beneath the surface was on point tonight. Colin knew how much this meant to me, and instead of hurrying me along as I'd expected, he was treating me with the sensitivity of a mature lover. Suddenly, it felt like our roles were reversed; I was the virgin instead of the teacher, and I fell in love with him a second time.

With thoughts of love and commitment running through my mind, I savored the body that was as familiar to me as my own. Colin's quiet exhale and nod of encouragement was all I needed to proceed with this monumental first. He gripped my arms, wrapped his legs around my torso, and whispered words of love whenever I hesitated. Thanks to many practice sessions with our trusty dildo, I sank into him with hardly any resistance. The affirmation in his sparkling blue eyes was everything I'd hoped for, and we moved together easily, as if we'd been doing this for years.

We crested as one, and the atmosphere crackled with our combined energy. The fire within Colin simmered dangerously, and I was reminded that his powers increased with strong emotion. I released him, giving him room to breathe. After our hearts slowed to a normal rhythm, Colin asked if it would be this good each time we had penetrative sex.

"I don't see why not."

"Can I top the next time?"

I huffed out an exasperated laugh. "Way to ruin the moment."

"Aw, that wasn't my intention at all. You were right all along. I loved everything about it and hope to return the favor someday."

"We'll see."

"I'm beginning to detest those words."

"I have no doubt you'll wear me down like you've done so often in the past."

"You bet I will."

"I love you, Colin."

"It took you long enough," he complained.

"Wasn't I worth the wait?"

"More than worth it, but we'll have to work on your spontaneity."

I smacked him playfully on his spectacular ass. "You've already upended my meticulous life. Don't push your luck."

Before I could protest, Colin managed to roll me over. With a soft sigh, he lay on my back, nose buried in the crook of my neck. I could hear the thundering of his heart and feel his cock stirring against my thigh.

"What are you doing, *chaton*?"

"Biding my time..."

Once Upon a Mattress

Chapter One

SEBASTIAN

"Find a husband, or we'll do it for you," my father said, giving me the stink eye.

I knew I was in trouble whenever he used the royal "we" instead of the less formal "I." Granted, His Royal Highness, Prince Emile of Sendorra, had every right to call himself whatever he wanted, but I bristled on the rare occasions Papa treated me like a subject instead of Heir Apparent to our small principality tucked away in the mountains between Spain and France.

"You've been given enough time to play the field," my mother, Princess Alexandra, seconded in a prissy voice that set my teeth on edge. "Every gay man of child-bearing age within our borders has seen fit to grace your bed, and yet you remain single. It's high time you get serious, Sebastian. You'll be twenty-five in a month, and our patience has run out. The stakes are too high."

"I'm aware of my duty, Mama. You don't have to remind me that Sendorra reverts to Spain if I don't crank out a kid before Papa dies."

"Must you be so crass?" she shrilled.

"The subject at hand lends itself to prurient remarks," I argued. "Stop treating me like a prized bull."

"Bash," Papa said, using my nickname in a conciliatory tone. "You know that's not the case. We've respected your wishes, allowing you to find a love match, the perfect partner who would provide the requisite child but also one who'd bring joy into your life. Ruling is hard enough without the right person by your side, but it's been three years since this quest started."

"Tell me about it," I grumbled. "If I were to judge someone on physical attributes alone, the nursery would be full by now. But you're asking for the impossible, Papa. Making me swoon in bed is only part of this mythical person's job. Granted, it's a necessary component, but I'm not marrying a booty call. My special man needs to be princely, and someone with an engaging mind, as well as a body that'll make me stand up and take notice."

Mama gasped and covered her mouth with a shaky hand.

My eyebrows shot up when I realized what I'd said. I'd forgotten my mother was a bit of a prude. Poor father.... It wasn't surprising I had no siblings.

Clearing my throat, I tried another approach. "I apologize if I've made you uncomfortable, Mama, but it usually boils down to one thing. The lookers are almost always vapid and the brainiacs leave me cold. I've exhausted the available gene pool."

"Nonsense," she argued. "There has to be someone out there who will meet your specific criteria. We should have a ball to celebrate your birthday. Send invitations to royal families all over the world. Surely someone suitable will turn up."

"Why limit our selection to royals?" I asked. "No disrespect to either of you, but I think I've already checked out the small group of blue bloods, and none of them have passed muster."

"You'd consider a commoner?" she asked, looking horrified.

"Get real, Mama. There's too much inbreeding as it is. What I need is someone intelligent and healthy—regardless of his pedigree—who is willing to be my consort with all the bullshit it entails. Put your scruples aside and think of the possibilities."

I could practically see the gears in her brain whirring with images of wedding invitations, flower arrangements, and ultimately, the cooing fat-cheeked grandson she could dote on.

"If we agree to your terms," Papa said evenly, "I expect a viable candidate by the end of your birthday festivities, or the decision is out of your hands. Do we have a deal?"

"Absolutely," I lied. Anything to get them off my back.

In truth, there was every possibility this would be more of the same—failure but on a grander scale. What if I changed things up? Do some prep work before the actual event. It would give me the opportunity to study each candidate, go beyond the physical, and put the contenders at the front of the line. There was no harm in wanting to learn more about someone who'd be sharing my life. After all, this was a forever match, not a one-night stand. Most dating sites demanded full disclosure; why shouldn't I?

Choosing my Prince Consort wasn't just a question of chemistry. He could be the best fuck in the universe, but what if he hated kids? More importantly, how would he feel about getting pregnant? Breeding between two men was generally a complicated business and required medical intervention. Not everyone was willing to be benched for months. Mr. Right had to be smart enough to know the end game would be worth the aggravation, but some guys were squeamish and unwilling to take the risk regardless of the payout. Granted, male pregnancy *was* dangerous, but fortunately, they'd made great strides in the last few years. There were far more successes than failures, thank Christ, which made my situation less of a problem. If not for the remarkable changes that had taken place in the last decade, I'd be married to a woman for the sake of our small country. Not that I had anything against females in general. I enjoyed their company, but never in my bed.

Resolved to make this work, I posed the question. "Would you consider it a breach in etiquette if we have our guests fill out a short form prior to receiving invitations to the ball?"

My mother's blank look was frustrating. "Whatever do you mean, Bash?"

"I'd like to hear more before I decide," Papa interjected.

"Gladly," I said. "I'm as tired of these never-ending first dates as you are. Meeting someone for the first time—with hardly any pertinent information—and expecting me to propose marriage within a few days is unrealistic. A questionnaire will help me weed out the losers before we issue invitations to the party. Plus, it'll cut down on costs. Why spend money on a lavish event when we're only seeking a handful of potential candidates?"

"People will think we're destitute if we don't have a large ball," Mama whined.

"Your mother's right, Bash. We mustn't put ourselves in that position. You're the Crown Prince and deserve the best celebration money can buy. This selection process needs to be discreet, and it can't happen with a bloody questionnaire."

"Could you possibly put your scruples aside for one time and consider my request?" I begged. "Let's make it a masquerade ball, and then we can disguise the questionnaire. Make it more about their needs than ours."

Puzzled, Papa asked, "How on earth will you be able to vet contenders with a one-size-fits-all form?"

"I'll throw in a few key questions only gay men will understand."

My mother grimaced.

"Don't worry, Mama. I won't ask for dick pics."

"Bash!" she squealed indignantly.

"Sorry," I said, stifling a grin. My poor parents were trying their best, and I was being a total shit. "I promise to keep the questions as polite and impersonal as possible."

"I insist on seeing them first," Papa said. "Have them on my desk by tomorrow."

"Your wish is my command."

This time he growled at me. "You're an insufferable boy. I don't know why I put up with you."

"Because you love me," I sang. "You really, really love me."

"Oh, Bash," my mother chimed. "You know we do."

Ashamed, I stepped forward and hugged her. "I know, Mama. I'm sorry for giving you such a hard time. Isn't there some magical way to figure this out?"

Pushing me back, Mama huffed indignantly. "Weren't you the one who forbade the use of magic in selecting your consort?"

"Yes," I conceded. "But my methods are failing on all fronts. Perhaps one of your magic potions might do the trick. Nothing drastic, mind you, but a little nudge in the right direction?"

Mama's stiff composure broke, and the regal features so similar to mine changed dramatically. Sapphire eyes twinkled with excitement and her mouth curved into a smile, causing the dimples in her cheeks to make a rare appearance. Even her normally drab blonde curls took on an effervescent quality.

My mother was one of five sisters born into a powerful family of witches; however, she'd shelved her talents in favor of marriage and motherhood. Papa had insisted she curb her natural inclination to "fix" problems with a flick of her wrist after a disastrous event at court. She'd turned several villagers into braying donkeys when they'd demanded he lower their taxes. Mama had panicked when she heard the raised voices and inadvertently caused quite a scandal. On another occasion, she'd refurbished the décor from stodgy to ultramodern giving Papa hives. He'd walked into his library in search of a good book and his favorite armchair but ended up having to make do with a giant flat-screen TV and console filled with gaming paraphernalia. His favorite recliner had been replaced with a squishy bean bag that was as uncomfortable as it was ugly. His indignant roar was heard through the thick walls, and after Mama set everything back to normal, he insisted she never use her magic again.

It had been a bone of contention for a long time, but eventually the urge went away, and Mama had learned how to live as a mere mortal. Which is why she was delighted when I asked her to crack open her book of spells for the greater good.

"Remember what I said, Mama. A subtle sign is all I want. Don't go overboard."

"Very well," she said, bobbing her head in agreement. "I'll be a model of discretion."

Papa gave me a look that spoke volumes.

"I know what I'm doing, Papa. You'll have to trust me on this."

"I only hope she doesn't turn my future son-in-law into a prancing unicorn."

"Emile, really," Mama fumed. "Have a little faith. I'm as invested in this project as the two of you."

"Can you think of anything off the top of your head, Mama?"

"It'll involve bedroom antics."

I waggled my eyebrows. "I'm always up for that."

"Not in *that* way," Mama scolded.

"What then?"

"Something to do with your bedding," Mama said thoughtfully. "I'll have to do some research before I can give you an answer. Maybe I should call one of my sisters."

"God, no! They'll turn this into a monumental project, and I can't deal with the hovering. I just want a little sign that I'm picking the right guy."

"I understand," Mama said. "No bells or whistles when he walks through the door, but something profoundly meaningful you'll be able to glean on the spot."

"Now you're getting it," I encouraged. "Remember, Mama. Less is more."

"Get cracking on those questions, Bash," my father commanded. "I have more faith in that than your mother's magic. God only knows what'll happen now that I'm letting her off the leash."

"One more word and I'm turning you into a toad."

"I would challenge you to give it your best shot, my dear, but I'm afraid it'll actually work this time. I have no desire to spend the rest of my life croaking on a lily pad."

Mama's laughter filled the throne room. The noticeable change in her demeanor was astonishing, and I had to wonder if the person I'd been living with my entire life was a fraud, and this animated version was the real Alexandra. Like a prisoner who'd finally been set free, my mother was blooming in front of my eyes. I had no idea that stifling her magical powers could be such a downer. Maybe she wasn't actually a prude but wound so tightly by my father's iron rule she'd been withering on the vine. Note to self. Don't be that kind of husband.

And with that in mind, I made my way out the door and through the labyrinth of corridors leading to my bedroom. At my desk, I opened up my laptop and typed in a query. How to find the perfect match.

A million answers popped up, and I squinted at the screen filled with good advice. Most of them catered toward heteronormative relationships, but there were a few that might pertain to me. Gritting my teeth, I began the tedious process of formatting the infamous questionnaire.

Chapter Two

ERROL

The invitation to the masquerade ball in honor of Crown Prince Sebastian's twenty-fifth birthday lay among a pile of papers scattered haphazardly on the step near my front door. I'd never gotten around to repairing my mailbox someone had knocked over the month before, but since most of my bills were delivered online, the need to find suitable housing for junk mail seemed superfluous. However, the unsightly mess bothered me more than I cared to admit, and I vowed to set matters straight over the weekend.

Living alone made it a lot easier to ignore certain things that could potentially start an argument. I wasn't a slob by any means; in fact, the complete opposite was true. My ex had often accused me of having OCD tendencies—when I gave him shit for his own messiness—and this uncharacteristic disinterest in a simple home repair was my lame attempt at proving him wrong. Not that it mattered anymore. We'd broken up six months ago, and I'd stopped missing him about an hour after he left.

I tossed most of the sale flyers in the trash bin beside my garage door, but I clung to the large navy blue envelope with the Crown's signet embossed on the red wax seal. After hanging up my jacket, I grabbed a beer out of the fridge and gravitated toward the recliner in front of the TV. I turned it on for background noise, more interested in the invite than the news. Toeing off my chucks, I sank down on the well-worn leather chair and ripped open the envelope.

My legal name—Errol Leith Maitland—was penned in fancy calligraphy at the top of a questionnaire tucked inside the formal invitation. Whoever had thought to include me was making this as personal as possible, a nice touch, even if the entire event was a thinly disguised attempt by the royals to find a bridegroom for their finicky son.

The quest had gone viral among gay men after the royal family had announced they were including commoners to the pool of contenders. It was unprecedented, a once in a lifetime opportunity, and eligible bachelors from every corner of the globe had been issued invitations. I couldn't figure out how I got on the list since I'd never posted a profile on dating sites and had yet to meet Prince Sebastian or any of his cronies. My temperament was more suited to candlelit dinners than clubbing—apparently one of his favorite things—which led me to believe we'd be a terrible match. Granted, he was easy on the eyes, more than passable, truth be told. I'd always been attracted to blonds, perhaps because they were my exact opposite, but there was something about this particular royal that went beyond good looks.

Photos of him ladling soup at homeless shelters or handing out winter gear at the same location struck a chord when I'd come across the news on the internet. It wasn't the first time he'd spearheaded charitable events and appeared to be genuinely engaged. Aside from his kindness, Sebastian had a beautiful smile with deep dimples in both cheeks that made me want to reach out and touch the guy. He was charming, in a playful sort of way, and the public and paparazzi loved him. I had to admit I found him quite intriguing. Enough to glance at the questionnaire and start filling it out.

What's your occupation?

Didn't these people already know? To be fair, I wasn't much of a partygoer and didn't socialize with the prince's crowd, but my sculptures graced buildings and museums all over the world. Maybe this form wasn't tailor-made for me after all. I frowned, wrote down sculptor, and moved on to the next question.

What is your genetic background?

I'm a transplanted Shetlander whose veins bleed red whenever I injure myself on the job. As unroyal as you can get but hardworking and healthy in every way.

I underlined healthy twice. Put that in your data bank, sweet prince. If this was his subtle way of asking if I had any mutated genes that might produce a hemophiliac or worse, this would clear up the issue.

Do you like children?

Who doesn't?

Who's your favorite historical person?

William Wallace.

Will you portray this figure at the ball?

I hadn't really thought about my costume, but I could play Sir William in a flash. I already had the kilt and could find war paint anywhere. Do the whole *Braveheart* thing and look fiercely sexy. Maybe the thought of what was underneath my plaid might inspire the prince. I wrote down yes.

Are you willing to relocate?

I already have!

Pet peeves.

People who ask dumb questions.

Guilty pleasure.

Hearing someone beg…

Breakfast or dinner?

Depends on the company.

Can you climb stairs; i.e. are your knees healthy?

Oh, that's a good one. I thought about my answer for a second, then wrote my knees work just fine, thank you very much. Never had any complaints. I drew a big heart instead of a period. Hopefully he'd get a woody reading between the lines. Serves him right, tricky wee bastard.

Do you like games?

Can't you tell by my answers? My favorite is hide the pickle. LOL.

I snorted out a laugh when I realized I was getting hard thinking about the possible scenario. Hopefully, he'd get the same reaction instead of shredding the paper.

Are you willing to submit to any and all medical procedures necessary to produce my heir if and when the time is right?

I wasn't sure what all was involved, but I realized this was the deal breaker. A negative reply would take me out of the running. Gnawing on the end of my pen, I tried to formulate an intelligent reply. Finally, I scribbled that I would only agree after a thorough briefing by the physicians in charge. *I won't go into anything blind.* That would be irresponsible on my part. *If all my questions are answered to my satisfaction, and I'm confident the docs know what the hell they're doing, then I don't see a problem.*

Do you believe in love at first sight?

Yes.

Describe your ideal partner?

Impossible to do in one sentence. Sometimes a song can evoke the right feelings, and these are a few of my favorites. They're an eclectic mash-up of old and new but reflect my needs. "The One" by Elton John; "Sometimes When We Touch" by Dan Hill; "Queen of My Heart" by Westlife; "Who I Am With You" by Chris Young; "Truly Madly Deeply" and "I Knew I Loved You" by Savage Garden; "Another Lonely Night" by Adam Lambert; "Somebody to Love" by Queen.

Shit. The last two selections were kind of pathetic. I didn't want the prince to think I was a needy fuck, then again, I had a reputation to maintain, and inserting these two songs might give a clearer picture. I stuck the questionnaire in the self-enclosed envelope and put it on the table beside my car keys. It could have gone in my own mailbox if the damned thing wasn't out of commission.

With thoughts of weekend chores on my mind, I made myself breakfast for dinner—buttered toast and a mushroom, sausage, and cheese omelet with a pile of hash browns on the side. My pooch, Snow, was by my legs within seconds, waiting for a chance to lick the plate when I was done. I didn't usually feed her people food—I'd go broke if I did—but she had a nose for eggs, and I indulged her shamelessly.

Weighing in at a hundred and ten pounds, my Pyrenean had almost met her death under the wheels of my truck the winter before, around the same time my relationship fell apart. Some heartless bastard had dumped the wee puppy—she was a tiny ball of white fluff back then—and she'd wandered out to the highway in search of food and water. It had snowed the night before, and white on white was a disaster in the making. It was a miracle she wasn't crushed, but I managed to stop in time. I wrapped her in a woolen blanket I kept in the boot for emergencies and brought her home. We bonded over the next few months, and my little "Snowflake" was renamed "Snow" as she expanded in height and girth. I wasn't familiar with the Great Pyrenees breed and was astonished when my little darling turned into a woolly mammoth. Talk about a good appetite! I was constantly refilling the storage bin and eventually started buying her food in bulk. Even though she was huge and could probably rip out a predator's throat in one bite, my girl loved a good cuddle. Her favorite thing was draping herself across my lap when I sat on the sofa in front of the fireplace. Her fur was so thick she kept me warmer than the flames.

With Snow on my mind, I pulled the questionnaire out of the unsealed envelope and wrote a follow-up question of my own on the bottom.

P.S. DO YOU LIKE DOGS? TEAR UP THIS SHEET IF YOU DON'T. I COME WITH HEFTY BAGGAGE.

Folding up the paper, I slid it back into the envelope and sealed it this time. Snow padded softly behind me as I closed up for the night—locking the front and back doors, turning off the lights, and setting the alarm. Most of the people in my neighborhood were aware I had a living, breathing bodyguard, but it never hurt to be careful.

I put my foot down when it came to our sleeping arrangements. There was no way in hell Snow was allowed on the bed. Aside from ruining my sex life—can you imagine anyone interested in sharing space with her furry arse—I had no desire to get crushed in my sleep or end up on the floor, which was the more likely scenario because Snow would rather bite off her foot than hurt me.

She turned around a couple of times in her plush-lined bed in the corner, sank down, and laid her big head on her front paws.

"Sweet dreams, baby," I muttered softly.

My life would be so much better if I could whisper those same words into a human's ear, but I'd given up trying to fill the void with losers. My new motto was quality versus quantity, and if a blue blood could provide the physical and mental stimulation I needed to stay interested, then so be it. There was no reason to turn my nose up at a high-ranking member of society because of my own self-imposed rules. I'd made it a point to date men who were my peers, guys who shared the same humble beginnings but weren't afraid of hard work to improve their plight. Unfortunately, these same men weren't interested in broadening their horizons. Content in their ordinary jobs, with money to blow on the weekends, they didn't need more. Unlike me. There were so many places I wanted to see, so much to learn, so little time, and never enough money. My bucket list was a mile long.

Being an artist meant learning how to budget. Commissions were generous and sales were good, but the money didn't show up every two weeks like a regular paycheck. It came in fits and starts and planning was critical to my piece of mind. It would be counterproductive to blow my profits on a trip to Ibiza if I wasn't sure what was around the next bend. This tendency to scrimp had been one of the factors that broke up my last union.

You have to be more spontaneous I was told on more than one occasion.

Bullocks. If I didn't have to pay for everything, then maybe I would entertain a trip out of town, but for whatever reason, these guys thought I should pick up the tab. Yeah, I made good money, but I wasn't a chump either. Bunch of losers. It would be nice to date someone who might actually put himself on the line for more than sex.

I closed my eyes and tried to imagine what it would be like dating a royal. Would he be different—generous in and out of bed—or was I delusional? He was probably a lazy fuck and would expect me to do all the work. Not happening. I liked control in the bedroom, or at the very least, I enjoyed men who were open to a power exchange. It didn't matter if the guy was a prince or a pauper, but while he was in my bed, he'd have to learn how to bend, even temporarily, or it wouldn't work.

Chapter Three

SEBASTIAN

In my eagerness to prescreen my future consort, I'd forgotten that someone had to read and sort through hundreds of questionnaires arriving daily. Unfortunately, I couldn't delegate the job if I wanted this done right, but I did enlist Mama to help sort the trolls from the lookers. Every contender had been instructed to enclose a photo or a link to a dating site, where I could check out his appearance. I could be diplomatic and say that physical beauty didn't factor into my decision, but it would be a lie. There seemed no point in considering a man I found unattractive, regardless of his inner beauty or worldly accomplishments. Mother knew the type of men I'd dated, and she was pretty good in separating the keepers from the rejects, but the pile of eligible men was growing.

"I'm counting on your magic to keep me from making the wrong choice," I said, glancing up at Mama. "How can I possibly do that when I have a smorgasbord of men at my fingertips?"

"You'll have to prioritize your needs," she said wisely. "I know you're hoping to fall in love at first sight, but that's the stuff of fairy tales. Set your sights on someone who intrigues you, a man who engages your mind as well as your body. He needs to be the sort of person who will challenge you and make you want more, or you'll be bored to tears after the passion fades."

"I don't want a loveless marriage," I stated emphatically. "The whole point to this stupid masquerade is to find the perfect match."

"There's a spell I found that might whittle down the selection process," she said uncertainly.

I put down the questionnaire and gave her my full attention. "I'm listening."

Glancing around to make sure we were alone, she leaned toward me and whispered, "It's simple enough, Bash. All you have to do is get him in your bed."

My eyebrows shot up. "You're not seriously about to give me sexual pointers, are you?"

"Heavens no," she said, breaking into nervous laughter.

"What then?"

"I'm going to put something magical underneath your mattress."

"Sorry?"

She gave a quick smile and continued, "The object in question is a tiny pebble. Ordinary men won't even know it's there, but your Mr. Right will insist something is poking him, making it impossible to sleep comfortably."

Grimacing, I implored, "Please don't use the word poke in my presence."

She wrinkled her nose. "Get your mind out of the gutter, Bash."

"It's difficult when we're talking about luring someone into my bed."

"To verify your choice...."

"God, Mama. It sounds positively medieval."

She looked uncomfortable but resolute. "It's an old spell, to be sure, but very effective. My sisters swear by it."

Knowing she'd consulted with her witchy brood about my sex life creeped me out. "It's been tried and tested on family members?"

"Absolutely," she said.

"All right," I agreed. "Don't tell me anything else. I intend to forget this discussion as soon as you walk out the door."

"We're spending an inordinate amount of time and money to get this right," she huffed indignantly. "I don't understand why you're being so squeamish. You were the one who suggested magic in the first place."

"It was in the abstract, Mama. Having you mess around in my bedroom before I lure someone into my bed is a bit...weird. Don't you find it uncomfortable imagining a naked man in my arms?"

"I try not to think about it," she said.

"Do you and Papa still have an active sex life?"

She stood immediately. "You're being inappropriate, Sebastian."

"Sorry." I felt like a jerk. What did it matter if they did or didn't burn up the sheets? It was none of my business. I tugged on her wrist. "Please, sit down. I promise to behave."

"I doubt it," she bemoaned, "but there's too much to do, and we can't waste time bickering. Let's get back to the task at hand."

I nodded and picked up the next sheet of paper on the pile. *Errol Maitland*. As I started to read, I became more and more interested. There was something about this guy's answers that caught my interest. He'd neglected to send a photo or a link, but when I put his name into my search engine, a photo popped up that literally took my breath away.

Holy. Fucking. Shit.

Where in heck had he been hiding all this time? He lived in our principality for the love of God. And he was quite famous. How come we'd never met? There was this monstrous white creature by his side, and I assumed this is why he'd added the postscript. Was that thing really a dog? I zoomed in so I could get a closer look at the guy. He was wearing a loose white shirt tucked into a green and black kilt that sent my mind racing back to the gutter. My mother wasn't far off the mark in that regard. Was he naked underneath the folds?

I might have whimpered out loud because Mama snapped, "Are you all right?"

I nodded, unable to come up with a coherent answer. Errol's broody gaze had sucked the words right out of my mouth. His black hair fell in messy waves to his shoulders, and the dark scruff on his cheeks went far beyond the five o'clock shadow, but it wasn't an actual beard. The top of his shirt was open, and I caught a glimpse of chest hair. It led me to believe his entire body was covered in soft fur.

Trying to determine his eye color through a computer screen was difficult. They could be brown or possibly hazel—it was hard to tell—but there was no mistaking his thick eyebrows or his curly lashes. They were as dark as his hair and definitely striking. If his guilty pleasure was hearing someone beg, then he need look no further. Despite my royal status, I loved being subdued behind closed doors and had yet to find a man with the guts to take me on. Most guys assumed I would be outraged if they suggested such a thing. The few that had made the attempt were clearly uncomfortable in that role.

I shut my eyes and imagined a scene where my hands were bound in leather and Errol stood over me, knowing instinctively that I would bow to his commanding presence.

Shoving the paper over to my mother, I prompted, "Take a look at this one. He's supposedly a resident, but I've never seen him around town. Have you heard of him?"

She picked up the questionnaire and began to read. Impatiently, I fidgeted, hoping to speed her up with my body language. Finally, she put down the paper. "Why are you so interested?"

I spun my laptop around so she could see his photo. "Look at him, Mama. He's imposing as hell and I love his answers."

She leaned in and peered at the screen. "He looks rough around the edges."

"I know," I said with an exaggerated moan. "Scorching hot."

Straightening up, Mama gave me the once-over. "You're thinking with the wrong body parts, Bash. There's more to being your consort than servicing you in the bedroom."

"I'm aware."

"Then perhaps we can agree Maitland is a poor choice. Artists are quite temperamental and I've heard this one is demanding and intractable."

"So you do know him," I accused. "Why don't I?"

"Dear boy, I stopped monitoring your friendships years ago. As for me, the museum committee contacted him at one point, but his schedule wouldn't allow him to accept the commission. He refused to give us alternative dates so we chose another artist."

"For what?"

"Busts of your Papa and me."

"So you never actually met the guy."

"No," she conceded. "We dealt with his agent."

"Then you can't judge him fairly."

Pink lacquered fingernails tapped the shiny tabletop. "I don't think he'll have time to perform all his duties if he's got such a thriving career."

"Why would he bother to fill out the questionnaire if he didn't think he was up to the task?"

She crossed her arms over her chest and pouted.

"Mama?"

"I'm not a mind reader, only a concerned parent. Maybe it's the thrill of the chase that's motivating him," she said tersely.

"There's no need to get defensive," I pointed out. "I realize you want my marriage to succeed as much, if not more, than I do, but your choices won't necessarily be mine."

"True," she replied. "This is why magic is so important. Your father and I have agreed to abide by the results of my spell regardless."

"Fair enough," I said. "In the meantime, I'd like to gather as much info on this man as possible. Do you think you can arrange that without invading his privacy or getting caught?"

"I'm sure it won't be a problem," she said. "Is there anything specific you'd like to know?"

"It would help if I learned more about his background. He says he's a Shetlander. I know it's somewhere in Scotland so why not call himself a Scot? Did he leave home on his own volition? Does he still have family back there? Where was he educated? Maybe your guy can find out something about his love life. He's not on any dating sites so I'm curious. Has he ever had a serious relationship? Details like that."

"All right."

"Thank you."

"Isn't there anyone else in that stack of forms who has piqued your interest?" she asked curiously. "Surely there's more than one eligible bachelor."

"This is the first one to merit a second look."

Her eyebrows knit in confusion. "Your interest in him is astonishing. I thought someone more refined would be better suited to your lifestyle."

"In theory, you're right, but guys who say and do the right thing aren't necessarily the ones who get under my skin."

"I'd rather not have a barbarian for a son-in-law," she said testily.

"Stop stereotyping, Mama."

"Look at him, Bash. He exudes testosterone."

I licked my lower lip, imagining the taste of his—

"Sebastian!"

I started, blinking rapidly. "What?"

"It's obvious you're besotted with a man you've never even met."

"Right?"

"Get your head out of the clouds and be serious. This is not a game."

No, it wasn't a fucking game. This was my future, and if Errol Maitland could hold my attention from a distance, I seriously doubted I'd be able to resist him when I saw him up close. I stared down at the piles and piles of questionnaires and was tempted to dump them into the fireplace and set a match to the entire lot. As far as I was concerned, the hunt was over, but my parents would have coronaries if I didn't go through the motions.

Chapter Four

ERROL

On the day of the masquerade ball, I decided to go into town for a haircut. More often than not, I trimmed my own hair, but for this special occasion, I thought it more prudent to put myself in the hands of a professional. I still intended to show up as Sir William Wallace but changed my mind on the war paint. If I was going to woo the prince, it would be in my best interest to dress like a nobleman rather than a bedraggled freedom fighter.

There was something about a properly kitted Scot that turned men and women into compliant piles of mush. One could have the craggiest features and the mental acumen of a pumpkin, but once the shirt, tie, jacket, kilt, sporran, and footwear were in place, we were hard to resist. Unless the person you were trying to sway had preconceived notions about men in skirts or an ice cube for a heart.

There had been many conquests in the past whenever I put my best foot forward. I had no qualms using every trick in the book to get Sebastian's attention, even if it meant parlaying my heritage to my advantage. It was imperative I stand out at first glance—among hundreds of eligible bachelors—and there was only one night to leave a lasting impression.

I don't know when this contest had become so important. Perhaps the hype surrounding the event was a contributing factor, but I suspected it was loneliness propelling me out of my comfort zone. All the hours I spent holed up in my studio with no one to talk to, except Snow, had begun to take their toll. The danger signs of depression were starting to manifest: lack of appetite, sleepless nights, and talking out loud. If that wasn't bad enough, my artistic endeavors were uninspired, a calamity far worse than all the other symptoms rolled into one.

Bed-hopping was no more satisfying than jerking off. Trying to explain my needs to a one-night stand without sounding like a controlling asshole was tiresome. BDSM clubs were always an option, but I didn't want anyone who officially participated in the lifestyle. Meting out pain wasn't my thing, and most of the guys who were available on short notice craved the sting of a flogger or wanted to be tied up and humiliated. None of it was appealing, but neither was dating someone as bland as bread pudding. There was no evidence to suggest the prince understood the subtle power exchange I was craving, but my intuition told me Sebastian was the one. A day of primping seemed like a small price to pay for a slice of happiness.

Snow was strapped into the passenger seat of the SUV as we careened down the mountain road into town. She appeared serious as if she understood the importance of our expedition. Normally, her head would be out the window, tongue lolling in the wind, scattering drool over the side of the vehicle, but not today. She was sitting straight up like a tour guide at the head of the bus.

Amused, I tugged on her ear. "Don't worry, baby. I know what I'm doing."

She glanced my way but didn't look convinced. Did she have some sort of sixth sense that I was about to do something completely irrational? I had no idea what was involved once you'd been chosen by the heir to the throne. Would the prince expect me to pack up and move my shit to the palace without some sort of trial period? How would we know if our union was the forever kind after only one night? It was absurd, and yet here I was joining ranks with hundreds of other hopefuls.

It seemed like everyone in town had the same idea, judging by the line outside the hair salon. I managed to squeeze through the crowd and wave at Barb, my sometimes stylist.

She looked shell-shocked, mouthing "I'm sorry" when I pointed at my hair. My frown must have been daunting because she yelled, "Come back in a couple of hours."

"Okay," I said, gladly leaving the mob behind.

Because of her size, I didn't always bring Snow into business establishments, unless I had prior permission. Barb loved her, and on a normal day, I wouldn't have thought twice, but today was anything but. Streets were crowded with strangers—gay men had arrived in droves—gearing up for tonight's celebration. The party atmosphere was already in full swing even though the actual festivities weren't until nightfall. I stopped for a minute to check out the competition. Same old stuff, from what I could see so far. If none of them caught my eye, then it was safe to assume the prince would turn them down as well. Then again, I didn't know what set his pulse racing. He might be into men who were my complete opposite. It would be foolish to assume I knew his tastes.

Snow barked enthusiastically as I approached. Before exiting the car earlier, I'd rolled down the window partway, and her big head stuck through the opening, sticky drool hanging in strings. Pedestrians swerved when they walked by, daunted by her ferocious appearance. Anyone fool enough to get too close would regret it the instant she bared her canines, and although she had yet to bite someone, it was good to keep them guessing. I unlocked the door and she hopped out gracefully.

We headed over to La Brasserie, a favorite café, and somehow managed to be seated at my usual spot within five minutes. It was a table for two in a corner, where no one would be bothered by the presence of my furry companion. I ordered a full English for myself with a side order of scrambled eggs for Snow. The waitress always plated her portion in a throwaway container, so no one would give us grief if they happened to catch me laying her dish on the floor. Not everyone was an animal lover—I knew that much—but Snow was the only family I had and fuck anyone who said otherwise.

I broke off a piece of sausage and handed it down to my wee darling. It was impossible to resist when she turned goo-goo eyes on me. The whole begging thing was my Achilles' heel, and she'd learned it when she was no bigger than a hamster. I wasn't sure how or when this need of mine developed, but I attributed the broken parts of me to my past. My story wasn't that uncommon, though; in fact, it was a goddamn cliché. Mum and Dad had asked me to rethink my orientation or get the fuck off the island. It was as simple as that. No son of theirs was going to embarrass them, and if I stayed in the area, they would be subjected to all kinds of slights, real and imagined. It broke my heart to leave, but I wasn't switching to the other side to make them happy. I swore I'd never be that kind of father if I was ever lucky enough to have a child. Which brought my thoughts back to the present.

Whenever I dreamed of my future family, I never considered being the one who'd go through nine months of discomfort, ten if you counted the preparation. Now that science had made it a possibility, I knew I'd do an outstanding job. Because that was the way I rolled. Snow had been my litmus test, and she'd turned out great. Granted, I didn't pop her out of my body, and she wasn't human, but I sure as shit spent sleepless nights worrying about her survival.

I came across a motivational poster once that said relationships didn't die from natural causes. It was selfishness, neglect, unwillingness to compromise, and lies that were the culprit. True enough, but wasn't love the glue? Perhaps I was being naïve, but loving someone unconditionally—for better or worse as the vows suggest—was the only way to see it through to the end. The timing was right for me, but I had to make sure Sebastian was in step. It all hinged on him.

After our meal, we walked around until it was time to head back to the salon. The damn place was still crowded, but Barb's seat was empty, and as she flapped her big white cloth and draped it over my shoulders, she apologized for the delay.

"I promise to make you gorgeous."

"You don't need to go overboard," I responded. "Just enough to catch the prince's eye."

"I'm surprised you're even considering this," she remarked.

"Why do you say that?"

"I'm a great resource," Barb confessed. "As soon as I bring out the scissors, people can't help barfing out their truth."

I snorted. "What nasty stories have you heard about me?"

"Hmm," she pondered, looking up at the ceiling then back down at me with a naughty smirk. "You're arrogant, opinionated, a control freak, and deliciously sexy. A guy like you could have anyone in the world. Why throw yourself at the mercy of the royal family? You'll just be another flunky."

"That's where you're wrong, lassie. I don't take orders from anyone."

"You'll do as you're told or be out of the running."

"I'm not a citizen of Sendorra."

"So what?" she challenged. "You've been passing through for the last ten years?"

"I'm still a Scot but with a permanent resident's visa."

"Which they can revoke if you insult them."

"I wasn't raised in a barn, lassie. Only a desolate island in the middle of the North Sea. I can mind my Ps and Qs and lift my pinkie with the best of them."

"The prince can be rather churlish when he doesn't get his way."

"And I can be an ornery bastard when I'm crossed."

"Wow, we'll have fireworks tonight," she crowed, "and not the kind you buy at the store."

"I'm certain this event has been planned and double-planned, so the chances of things going wrong are slim to none. His Royal Highness and I will size each other up and part ways amicably if the sparks don't fly."

"If he doesn't pan out, I have lots of customers who are interested in dating you."

"And why haven't you mentioned them before?"

"My bad," Barb apologized. "You don't strike me as the type of guy who enjoys hooking up."

"I don't advertise."

"Apparently not," she replied, thumping me on the head gently. "How short do you want to go?"

"Half an inch."

"You may as well have stayed home."

"Come on, Barb. Nothing drastic, just a little clean up."

"Are you going to let it hang loose or tie it back?"

"What do you think?"

"Tie it," she suggested. "Let him undo the ribbon himself. Then he can run his fingers through these gorgeous thick locks and—"

"Let's not be getting ahead of ourselves," I interrupted. "Keep your wild imagination under control for the moment."

"You're no fun at all," she said.

"I'm a bag full of laughs in the right situation."

"Want me to do your eyebrows?"

"Do what?"

"Trim, pluck, or wax maybe?"

"None of the above."

"They make you look fierce."

"Good."

"Are you planning to court him or scare him into submission?"

I leered at her through the mirror we were both staring at and waggled the culprits. "Wouldn't you like to be a wee bug on that wall?"

"I'd pay to watch."

"You're a depraved woman."

"Said the man who's putting himself on the auction block."

"No one is paying for my services."

"Don't kid yourself, Errol. Once you step foot in the palace, you're basically selling yourself to that family."

"I'm going of my own volition and can walk out just as easily."

"God, I hope you know what you're doing."

"Let's hope they do."

Chapter Five

SEBASTIAN

I studied my reflection in the full-length mirror and was pleased. I'd gone full retro, choosing the *Phantom of the Opera* as my theme. The black suit and cape highlighted my blond hair to perfection, and the half mask accentuated my full lips. At my request, the tailor had paid special attention to my pants, which were tight enough to show off the goods, but not to the point where they'd rip if I bent over. He must have used spandex or some other stretchy fabric because they were extremely comfortable. Mama would probably have a fit, calling it unseemly, but I had no more fucks left to give. This extravaganza had been her idea, and if I wanted to dress like a rent boy, albeit operatic, then she'd have to bite her tongue.

My friends were aware of my outfit, but the contenders had no idea. It would give me an opportunity to mingle and check out the guys I'd put on my favorite pile. So far there were two. The Scot, and an American banker, Carl Perkins, whose answers had intrigued me. He was nothing like the stodgy financiers I dealt with here at home. The guy had answered most of my questions with witty double entendres. He might be nothing but a poser, but there was only one way to know for sure.

I still hadn't made up my mind on how this would play out. If I was going to use the mattress test as final validation, I'd have to coax the chosen ones into my bedroom. Not exactly princely to fuck on a first date, but how else would I know if we were a match? Mama hadn't thought this through. There must be a way we could hold off on sex until we were both comfortable, although...I'd never been a big proponent of waiting.

This unwarranted bout of scruples was the product of my environment. Lessons in nobility had been drummed into my lizard brain since I was a toddler, and while it was fine to give in to my baser instincts at a club or hotel, it seemed utterly wrong to go flat-out slutty here at the palace. My ancestors would be rolling in their graves watching me bump uglies with two gentlemen in one night. But wait. Was I really going to do them both on separate beds, or would I pick one and hope he was the right choice? That made no sense. How on earth would I find out if there was good chemistry if I didn't take a test drive?

With new resolve, and a final glance in the mirror, I headed to Mama's suite. She was already dressed when I barged in.

"We need to make some adjustments," I said without preamble. "Pour some of your witchy brew on another pebble."

She looked at me in astonishment. "How dare you barge in here and start issuing orders."

Abashed, I apologized sincerely, "Sorry, Mama. I'm in a bit of a rush."

"At this rate, you'll be worn out before your guests arrive."

"It occurred to me that our plan is flawed," I explained. "This is why I'm a bit anxious."

"In what way?"

"I have two contenders, Mama. You can't expect me to pick one over the other without your magical seal of approval."

Examining my costume, her gaze faltered when it arrived at my crotch. "You make a fetching phantom except your pants are obscene," she pronounced royally.

I grinned. "But it'll get the job done."

"Dear God," she exclaimed, putting her hands over her ears. "I don't want to hear another word out of your mouth."

"I'll be as silent as a monk if you'd get to work on your magic."

She huffed and turned in a swirl of purple satin and lace. There was a wooden reading stand close to a window with a ponderous leather-bound book on display. It had a red ribbon marker sticking out from the middle, and she opened it up to the selected page.

Curious, I stepped closer. "What is that, and why haven't I seen it before?"

She looked up, lips pursed in annoyance. "If you must know, this is my grimoire, and it's been in the vault for safekeeping until now."

"Your personal guide to casting spells and wreaking havoc on the unsuspecting," I observed dryly. "Papa probably had it under lock and key."

"He took it away from me a while back."

"Can't you remember how to cast this particular spell? You just did it a few days ago."

"Bash, you're irritating me to no end," Mama said testily. "I'm not a practicing witch, and I don't remember a thing I did the other day. And furthermore, I'm fresh out of pebbles. I don't suppose you brought one along?"

"Fuck, no."

"Language!"

"Sorry, Mama. Use something else."

"Such as?"

"I don't know," I whined. Scanning the room, I pointed at her sewing box. "Don't you have anything useful in there?"

"Buttons?"

"There you go," I said excitedly. "Pick the smallest one, and after you're done doing whatever you need to do, place it underneath the mattress in the guest room adjoining mine."

Her eyebrows rose so high they almost hit her hairline. "Tell me you're not going from one bed to the next in the same evening."

"Don't ask for details if you're afraid of the answers," I warned.

"Quite so," she said. "Please go before you say anything more."

"You'll take care of the button?"

"I'll handle it," she promised. "Go out there and start mingling."

I kissed her on the cheek and headed toward the gardens. The weather gods were on our side, it seemed, with a starlit sky and warm summer breezes wafting through the branches of the surrounding trees. The live band was already in motion, and liveried waiters were walking through the crowd with silver trays filled with champagne flutes. My gaze flicked from man to man, looking for my Scot, but I wasn't seeing him. Maybe he hadn't arrived yet, I thought, trying to curtail my disappointment. The evening had just started, and perhaps he chose to be fashionably late.

Papa hailed me from afar, and I weaved my way through a sea of men until I arrived at his side.

"How's it going, my boy?"

"It's just started."

"See anything you like?"

I snorted in amusement. "A veritable bounty of manhood."

He observed me with a gimlet eye. "I'm expecting some progress by the end of the evening. We've tarried enough on this quest of yours."

"Don't worry," I assured him. "You'll have a future son-in-law by sundown tomorrow."

He gave me the once-over and, like Mama, didn't much approve of my attire. "I would hope so seeing as how you're practically naked."

"There's no harm in advertising, Papa."

"Except the ones who should be on display are your guests, not you."

"I want to make sure they like what they see. How can they make informed decisions if I'm covered up in a shroud?"

"Isn't there a happy medium between ballet dancer briefs and a robe?"

"Certainly, but I choose to put it out there in case there's any doubt I'm up to my marital duties."

"There's no room for error in that getup," he grumbled. "See that you don't get too excited, or you'll embarrass us."

"Enough," I said dismissively. "I think I just spotted my American."

I couldn't see the look on Papa's face as I walked away, but I'm sure he was none too pleased. Accustomed to being in charge, he had become increasingly frustrated as I grew more and more independent. This business of choosing a consort should have been wrapped up years ago.

Too bad, I thought ruefully. It was my life, and I wasn't going to be led around like a lamb to slaughter. If I made the wrong decision, it wouldn't be for lack of trying. Luck, and a little help from Mama, should help me circumnavigate this challenge.

There was a group of men hanging around the bar in a variety of outfits that belonged in a PRIDE parade. I could spot pirates, gangsters, Doms, ingénues, Chers, Madonnas, Dolly Partons, beauty queens, slaves, jockeys, cops, firemen, but only one cowboy. I assumed this was Carl.

"I don't see your horse anywhere," I teased as I sauntered up to him.

He gave me a classic aw-shucks look that suited him perfectly. His cheeks pinked up with pleasure, and I could tell he was flattered by my attention. The photo he'd submitted had obviously not been recent, or he'd photoshopped the heck out of it, because this cowboy had less hair and a few more wrinkles. Not that I minded an older gent on occasion, but truth in advertising was crucial to the success of this mission, and I already felt duped.

He stretched out his hand for a shake. "Howdy, partner. Carl Perkins here."

"Pleased to meet you," I said, reaching for his hand. "Are you enjoying yourself?"

"So far so good," he said, taking a sip of his drink. "I can't wait to meet the prince."

"I've heard he's a real handful."

"Is he?" Carl replied, showing more teeth. "I'm not worried about it."

"You seem pretty confident, considering you've never met the man."

He waggled his eyebrows, a stupid move that got under my skin. "Once I get that boy between the sheets, he'll know who's in charge."

My blood rushed to my head. How fucking dare he? I took a huge calming breath and remarked, "Is that right?"

"Never met a pony I couldn't tame."

"Good luck, Carl."

"Hey, buddy. You didn't give me your name. Maybe we can get together if this thing with the prince doesn't pan out."

"The name is Sebastian and your window of opportunity has just closed."

I spun around before he could bluster out a useless apology. No longer interested in that group, I made my way to the other side of the garden, stopping several times to greet friends and acquaintances. There was a buzz of anticipation every time I got close to a bunch of guys, and I could almost see them mentally raising a hand and screaming pick me! Why anyone would be so eager to step forward was a mystery. I supposed the honor and prestige were enough of a draw, not to mention the cushy life of a royal, but it was disappointing to think love didn't factor into their plans.

Leaving yet another group, I headed toward the palace. My head was lowered, and therefore I didn't see the body until it was too late. I ran into an impressive chest covered in creamy ivory with a dark jacket over a green and black kilt. When I lifted my head, a set of hazel brown eyes looked down at me in amusement.

"Going somewhere?"

My mouth dropped open. It was him, my Scot, and holy mother of God. He was magnificent, every bit as gorgeous as his picture. "Um, no. I've been waiting for you."

He grinned. "I have a date with a prince, not a phantom."

Slowly, I removed my mask, never dropping my gaze. "You're looking at Prince Sebastian of Sendorra."

The grin broadened into a full smile. "Is that right?"

I was tongue-tied and my heart fluttered dangerously. Always adept at flirting, Errol's physicality threw me off my game. He was everything I imagined times ten. I couldn't catch my breath and was getting light-headed as a result. My face must have shown my distress because I felt strong hands guiding me toward the inside of the palace.

"I think you need a glass of cold water," he said solicitously.

"More like a shot of whiskey."

"Aye, there's nothing a wee dram can't cure," he said, smiling. "Why don't you lead the way?"

Chapter Six

ERROL

Sebastian whipped off his cape as we walked toward the palace, and I soaked up the vision of his enticing backside. Cinched in some kind of fabric that hugged him like a second skin, each purposeful step down the long corridor caused his glutes to shift and my mouth to water. I envisioned dragging those skintight britches down his long, long legs and burying my tongue in his cleft. My outfit was much more forgiving, thank Christ, as my host had given me a raging cock stand. Nothing a strategically placed sporran couldn't hide, but if he didn't plant himself in a chair soon, I wouldn't be able to concentrate on anything else.

We ended up in a book-lined room, a surprising choice, but one that afforded maximum privacy. None of the partygoers would wander in here, unless they were drunk or lost, but we were alone for now. He tugged on a cloth pull before sinking down on the leather sofa facing a massive stone fireplace. A butler appeared in under five minutes.

"Fetch me a cool cloth," Sebastian ordered. "But before you go, pour us two whiskeys, please."

With a bob of his head, the butler walked over to a mirror-backed cabinet lined with cut-glass decanters and glasses in every shape imaginable.

Turning toward me, Sebastian gestured to the empty space by his side. "Please, have a seat."

"Thank you," I responded, perching a few feet away. "Are you feeling better?"

"I'll be fine," he said, trying to laugh it off. "You seem to have a devastating effect on my composure."

Flattered, I teased, "I'm sure it's only temporary."

The butler returned with our drinks and left the room silently.

Sebastian held out his glass, and I met him halfway, clinking the fine crystal together.

"Thank you for accepting my invitation," he said in a low voice, studying my features. "A man who looks like you shouldn't have any trouble finding a date."

"Correct me if I'm wrong, but I thought this meeting was far more than a date."

"Indeed it is," he admitted. "I'm pleasantly surprised that someone of your caliber is even considering my proposition."

"Don't sell yourself short, Your Highness."

"Please, call me Sebastian or Bash. Leave the title out of this."

"Fair enough. Is today really your birthday?"

He nodded.

"Am I supposed to be one of your presents?"

A rosy tinge crept across his cheeks before he lowered his head. It was incongruous, given his position, but I was elated. The rumors regarding Sebastian's arrogance were turning out to be pure slander, or was this behavior reserved for me? If so, we were a match made in heaven.

I lifted his chin with my forefinger. "Look at me."

Striking blue orbs bored into mine with intent. His face was still flushed and his mouth parted, but he didn't veer when I slanted my mouth over his and took possession. His soft moan set fire to my neglected libido, and I had to contain the urge to press him down on the sofa and ravage him then and there. Gathering the last of my reserves, I broke the kiss.

"Why did you stop?" Sebastian asked, looking disappointed.

I thumbed his lower lip, now slick with our combined saliva. "I'm not sure if there's some sort of protocol I need to follow when it comes to my next move."

"Sorry?"

He looked dazed and incredibly sexy, but I forced myself to answer the question. "If you were anyone but a prince, there would be nothing in the world that could stop me."

I reached for his hand and pressed it against my cock, so he could feel how desperately I wanted him. "See what you're doing to me? I'd like nothing more than to carry on, but we're in your bloody palace, and the royal guards are one scream away."

Instead of nodding in agreement, Sebastian licked his lips and began to explore the folds of my plaid. "Is it true what they say about Scots and underwear?"

"Aye."

"There's nothing under here except you?"

I shifted when I felt his hand creeping up my naked thigh. "Don't go any further, or you'll pay the price."

"And what might that be?" he flirted.

My hand moved of its own volition, collaring his neck. His breath caught, and the rapid pulsing of his heartbeat against my thumb did all kinds of strange and wonderful things to my psyche. I wanted this man.

In the worst way.

Right now.

Not tomorrow, or the day after, but this very minute. "I'm going to carry you off like a sack of spuds and spend the rest of the evening showing you what's in your future—if I agree to your terms. I'd like to take you home, so we can explore to our hearts' content without worrying about interruptions."

He didn't say another word but continued his slow journey toward my cock, which was on the brink of erupting. A brush of his hand and I'd be a goner. I stopped his progress by clamping down on his wrist with an iron grip. His whimper almost made me reconsider, but when I noticed the bulge in his crotch, I realized he was just frustrated, not scared.

"Will you come with me?" I asked.

"To the ends of the earth," he replied in a husky voice. He stood in one fluid motion, and I followed him out the door. We retraced our steps back to the garden, where the party was in full swing. There were several food tents to accommodate the crowd and a raised dance floor packed with revelers.

Sebastian stopped abruptly and spun around. "Where are we going?"

I grabbed his hand and walked down the patio steps. We were swallowed up by a surge of hopefuls who pestered Sebastian for a dance or a word in private. He demurred as diplomatically as possible, and most of them backed off, but there was one guy who set my teeth on edge. He was dressed like a cowboy, and when he opened his mouth and hailed Sebastian with a familiarity completely unsuited to his rank, it grated on my last nerve.

"There you are," the cowboy twanged. "Why'd you run off before we could get better acquainted?"

"I told you I wasn't interested," Sebastian replied stiffly.

"Now, that just ain't nice. I've come too far to be brushed off. You have any idea who you're dealing with?"

"I'm sorry," Sebastian said, "but there were no guarantees when you accepted my invitation. I think that was pretty clear on the questionnaire."

"You implied we'd have a one-on-one conversation."

"I'm sorry, but you misunderstood," Sebastian said. He was backing away and the asshat stepped forward instead of retreating. My patience ran out the minute he reached for Sebastian to try to hold him in place.

"Take your hands off him," I growled.

His jaw jutted in a bulldog-like stance. I could smell the booze on his breath and I realized he was bladdered.

"Who in fuck are you?" the cowboy asked churlishly.

"Bugger off, mate."

"Fuck you," he said, lunging toward us.

"Guards!" Sebastian hollered.

A clutch of uniformed men were on the bastard like flies on shit.

"See that Mr. Perkins is escorted back to his hotel. He shouldn't drive in his condition," Sebastian ordered.

"Yes, Your Royal Highness."

Sebastian turned to me. "Shall we?"

I grinned and reached for his hand, folding his fingers with mine. We headed out toward the parking lot and were stopped once more. This time, it was the Prince and Princess who asked where we were going.

"I'll be back," Sebastian assured them.

"Bash, you know this isn't part of the plan," Princess Alexandra said, looking worried. "You have to sleep here tonight."

"Don't worry, Mama. I know what I'm doing."

"Who is this man?" she asked, examining me like I was a pheasant under glass.

"Errol Maitland at your service," I said, bowing with flourish. "I promise you that Prince Sebastian is in safe hands."

"You're the sculptor, correct?"

"I am."

"Where are you taking him?"

"To meet my dog, Your Royal Highness."

"Your dog?" she asked in horror. "Now? Surely that can wait."

"I'm afraid not," I said apologetically. "It's imperative that Snow weighs in on this proposal."

"I beg your pardon?" Prince Emile asked, looking confused.

"Papa, give it a rest," Sebastian said impatiently. "I'll be back later."

Sebastian grabbed my hand and tugged. "Let's go while we can."

We raced across the lawn and out to the lot. Fortunately, I remembered the general direction in which I'd parked, because most of the vehicles were black like mine. I hit my remote to get a clearer idea and heard a horn honk.

"There it is," I said, dragging Sebastian at a fast clip.

"Are we really going to meet your dog?" he asked when we strapped in.

I gave him a side look. "I told you it was a deal-breaker."

"And if we hate each other on sight...."

"I'll bring you back untouched."

His mouth gaped. "You're not going to have your way with me after all this?"

"Not if Snow doesn't like you."

"Then I guess I'll have to turn up the charm," he said, winking at me.

I leaned forward and kissed him. "She'll fall hard and fast like her daddy."

"Is that right?" he teased, slipping his hand under my kilt again.

"Behave yourself," I said sternly.

"I would except you've made this too easy by wearing that getup. I can get you off before we leave the parking lot."

"I'm sure you can, but that's not what this is about," I said, softening my stance.

Sebastian retrieved his hand and gave me a half smile. "What's this about then?"

"Becoming a family."

He smirked. "Just like that?"

I nodded.

We didn't speak after that. It was a twenty-five minute drive through winding roads with only the moon to guide our way. I turned right when I saw my exit, and the wheels of the SUV gripped the unpaved dirt road that led to my house and attached studio. I expected Sebastian to say something as we drove through the unlit pine forest—a daunting experience in and of itself—but the sense of alarm wasn't forthcoming. He was relaxed in my company, and that made me care for him even more.

Snow must have heard the car, because she began barking the minute we unbuckled our seat restraints and I turned off the engine.

For the first time since we got into the SUV, Sebastian looked worried. "Will she bite me if she doesn't care for my company?"

"Of course not," I assured him. "She might look like a polar bear, but she's got the manners of a lady."

"Some of my best friends are women, but I would hardly call them ladies. They're rather vicious when crossed."

I laughed, imagining the catfights. "Don't worry about a thing."

"Easy for you to say," he murmured. "My future is in the hands of a bloody dog."

Chapter Seven

SEBASTIAN

As soon as we stepped through the front door—with me bringing up the rear—a mass of white fur sprang forward. Rising on her hind legs, Snow placed her front paws on Errol's chest and licked his face enthusiastically.

"That's enough," he laughingly scolded as he scratched behind her ears and cavorted with Snow for a few minutes. "I want you meet a friend."

Terrified to make the wrong move, I stepped back, pressing against the door. I'd never had a dog growing up. Papa had his bloodhounds, and Mama's yappy lapdogs were always underfoot, but I was more a polo pony kind of guy. I wasn't sure how to ingratiate myself with this enormous creature. I'd have offered her cut up carrots or an apple if she were a horse, and little by little, we'd become friends, but I had nothing in my pants except a flagging cock. This wouldn't do at all. As ludicrous as it sounded, my future depended on Snow's good opinion, and I was going to win her over, ignorance notwithstanding.

"Come here, Bash," Errol coaxed, sliding an arm around my waist. "She won't bite."

And just as suddenly, I was no longer afraid. I'd known Errol for less than two hours, and I already felt certain he'd never put me in harm's way. His earlier reaction to Carl was all I needed to convince me I was safe.

"Tell her to stand down."

"Sit!" Errol commanded, and Snow plopped down, looking up at her master adoringly. Her long tail waved back and forth on the floor like a feather duster.

Errol held my hand and slowly brought me to my knees so I was more at eye level with the dog.

"Hi there," I greeted softly.

She sniffed my outstretched hand and lapped my fingers with her warm tongue. It tickled and I wanted to pull back, but then she might pounce, so I didn't budge. After a few minutes, I turned my attention to Errol. He was beaming at my interaction with Snow, and I imagined a similar reaction if and when we had a child. How that vision bloomed so clearly was a mystery, but everything about this matchmaking venture had been surprising. I'd expected the worst and assumed it would be a waste of time, but Errol had surpassed my expectations and was living proof that good things actually happened if you held out long enough.

"She likes me," I pointed out.

"Aye," Errol nodded. "I reckon she does."

Emboldened, I reached out to scratch behind her ears and laughed when she rolled over to bare her stomach.

Joining in the fun, Errol scrubbed her belly and mentioned, "She's an absolute slut for tummy rubs."

I blurted, "So am I."

Suddenly the air around us sizzled with anticipation. The attraction that had been propelling us forward—and contained pending Snow's approval—was back in full force. Once again, my heart was racing, and the blood pooled in my groin.

The desire to jump Errol's bones was so intense my voice cracked when I spoke. "Do you think—?"

"Aye," he said, cutting me off unequivocally.

He pulled me up, motioning Snow to stay put. As we walked out the front door, I asked, "Where are you taking me?"

"To my studio next door," he said.

"Don't you have a bedroom in your house?"

"I don't want Snow pawing at the door while we're busy."

I stopped and grinned at him. "Are you serious?"

"Of course. She might get the wrong impression," Errol confided. "She's a virgin, ye ken? There's no telling how she'll react."

My smile grew wider. "You're assuming I'm a screamer?"

"Aye, and if not, I'll turn you into one," he growled, reaching for me.

Our mouths crashed together in a desperate need to taste and explore. He cupped my ass and lifted me up, knowing instinctively I was ready to get on with business. With my legs wrapped around his waist, and our tongues still entwined, we inched our way across the yard to his studio. Wood splintered, but we didn't break the connection. I was too far gone to care that Errol had kicked his door open, and even if the entire structure fell into pieces around us, I would be oblivious so long as we both got off before we died.

He laid me on a wide featherbed, a luxurious touch, although weirdly out of place. Later Errol would explain he'd often nap in his studio after immersing himself in a project. Right then, I was grateful for the comfort but much more interested in ripping off his clothes than trying to figure out the whys and wherefores of his furniture.

My fingers ached to delve underneath the folds of his kilt, but he'd moved away to pull off my boots. Tossing them over his shoulder, he was back within seconds, unbuttoning my britches and rolling them down my thighs. Eyes shining, he exclaimed with pleasure when my cock sprang up, unimpeded by underwear.

"I knew you were naked underneath these ridiculous pants."

"A time-saver to be sure," I said, shrugging out of my shirt.

His tongue darted out to lick his lips. "You're beautiful," he said reverently.

Subconsciously, I lifted my chin to expose my neck. He cursed under his breath, and I almost cried out with relief when I felt his large hand clamp around my throat. "Will you lie still while I taste you?"

I nodded.

He grabbed my cock with his free hand and held it steady while he wrapped his lips around the engorged head and slowly slid it into his mouth.

I must have made a noise because he paused and looked up. "Are you okay?"

"Don't stop."

He pressed his thumb gently against the quickening pulse in my throat and smiled with satisfaction. His unspoken mastery was greatly appreciated. I'd endured fawning sycophants who were simply going through the motions as well as clumsy lovers eager to take their pleasure without giving much thought to mine. It was a welcome change to put myself in the hands of a man who was obviously in control of both his mind and body. Errol resumed his efforts and swallowed my shaft until my balls rested against his chin. No one had ever sucked me in so deeply, and I bit my lower lip to hold back my scream. When he increased the suction, I couldn't stifle the sound effects any longer. I could tell he was enjoying my reaction, because he renewed his efforts, sliding his lips up and down my length while sucking greedily. As much as I was enjoying this, the need to reciprocate became too powerful.

I sat up, and when he let go of my shaft with a look of surprise on his face, I tugged him onto the bed, plucking at his waistband to get him naked.

"Help me out here," I demanded urgently.

"Why not wait until I've pleasured you?"

"Because I want us to come together."

He looked gobsmacked by my refusal but acquiesced, making short order of the sporran and kilt. By then I was on my side, watching his every move. He was a vision come to life, lightly furred with dark whorls covering his chest and leading down to the tantalizing prize jutting from his groin. He scooted next to me, kissed my lips, then dragged a wet trail to my ears and down my neck. In one slick move, he pinned my arms to the mattress on either side of my head and continued downward to feast on my nipples. I moaned loudly and tried to squirm away, but he was much stronger and kept me in place.

"Don't you like this?" he asked with a slight frown.

"I love it, but I also want you in my mouth."

He understood and we repositioned. I lifted one of his heavy thighs, laying it on my shoulder, and buried my face in the dark curls. My cock was now conveniently close to Errol's mouth, and he resumed his earlier efforts. It was no easy task to do a good job while he was wreaking havoc on my body, but Errol's slit was oozing the good stuff and screaming for my attention. I flicked out my tongue, tasting him for the first time. It was sweetly salty, and his musk was nothing like the sickening perfumes a lot of guys used to try to mask nature's scent. Who the hell wanted to be with someone who smelled like jasmine or roses?

Pushing thoughts of others aside, I took him in as far as possible. Errol was large in stature, and perfectly proportioned, so I might have gagged a bit, but I persevered. Soon he was rocking against my mouth and I against his. Our pace grew more frantic, and when I felt the first gush hit the back of my throat, I swallowed convulsively. His moans of pleasure vibrated near my shaft, triggering my own reaction, and I came with a shout.

After a few minutes, we swiveled around, and he gathered me close. His shirt felt a little scratchy against my bare chest, but it also felt good to lie in his arms and listen to his heart thundering in the aftermath. We were bare from the waist down, and the sensation of his soft skin against mine was heavenly as our legs brushed against each other.

"Were you satisfied?"

I was wrung out with multiple emotions but touched that he bothered to ask.

"You know I loved every second, but we'll have to go back to the palace," I said regretfully. "Put aside your scruples and sleep in my bed tonight. My parents will send a small army if we don't return soon."

"Aye, I expect they will," he grumbled. "I need to let Snow out before we go."

"Do you want to bring her along?"

"Not while there's a crowd. She'll miss me, but I can't have her running wild while I'm locked up in your room."

"I can assign someone to take care of her," I suggested. "We have people who care for all the pets roaming around the palace grounds."

"No, that won't do," he said. "Snow is my responsibility and has never been handled by strangers."

"Perhaps you'll reconsider in a day or two when things are settled between us?"

He nodded but didn't respond.

"Is something wrong?" I asked, leaning on my elbow and trying to decipher the look on his face. What if he'd changed his mind? Were we a better fit in my head than his?

"No, I'm processing," he admitted. "Two days ago, I was single, and now I find myself fully invested in our future."

I kissed his cheek gratefully. "It's a lot to digest, but I think we've established a few things in the last few hours."

"Oh?"

"We're well matched physically and Snow likes me."

"Aye, that's more than I knew before I walked out the door earlier this evening."

"And after we spend the night together, we'll know more," I promised. Not that I could divulge Mama's plan, but I was certain several more hours in bed would prove how compatible we were in that regard. The rest would depend on magic.

"Let me take care of Snow," he said, reaching for his kilt.

Before I could pull myself together, Errol was back with Snow padding silently behind him. She woofed at my sleepy form and hopped up on the bed, nuzzling close like she was a long-lost friend.

"Hey, pretty girl," I said in a voice I barely recognized. Obviously, I'd dredged it up from some reserved spot meant for dogs and children.

Snow acknowledged me with sloppy dog kisses.

"Eww," I cried, pushing her big head away. "Where's that tongue been?"

Errol laughed. "I'd say you were too finicky, but I know better."

"She's a dog," I reproached. "And a lady one at that."

"A little ass breath between friends shouldn't be a problem regardless of gender."

"How about you kiss me instead?"

He shoved Snow aside and kissed me long and hard. By the time he pulled back, I was hard and ready for round two. He noticed but shook his head.

"Come on, Bash. Your parents will send out a search party if we're not back soon."

"Okay, but let's take Snow. I'm not comfortable leaving her."

"This wouldn't be the first time I've left her alone overnight. She'll be fine."

"But then you'll have to rush back in the morning to let her out and feed her," I reminded him. "This way we can linger in bed all we want without worrying."

"Are you always this pushy?"

Pouting, I gave him a look I'd perfected when I wanted something and was denied. "No. I thought I was being considerate."

Errol stared, probably digesting my words. Finally, he made a decision. "Is there a back way into the palace? I don't want any drama with your guests."

"Of course," I assured him. "Let me handle everything. Gather whatever you need for the night and leave the rest to me."

He bowed with flourish. "Our lives are in your hands, Your Royal Highness."

Chapter Eight

ERROL

The party was still in full swing when we drove through the palace gates—dance floor crowded with revelers and food tents packed—and Bash directed me toward the end of the long driveway to a private garage, where the royals parked their personal vehicles. I slid my SUV beside a bright red Mini Cooper convertible, which turned out to be one of Bash's favorites. Snow would love the freedom of having the constant wind in her face, but I doubted she'd ever have the opportunity. I couldn't imagine Bash letting her take up the entire back seat, then again, he'd surprised me this evening by insisting she spend the night. If this was his way of proving he was adaptable, then he was succeeding. So far, he'd been one pleasant surprise after another.

We entered the palace through the kitchen, currently a hive of activity. Bash ordered his staff to prepare dinner, and after asking my advice on what Snow could or couldn't eat, added her meal to the menu. I was grateful for his consideration because I was ravenous. The butler was summoned, and raised both eyebrows at the sight of Snow, but he did his best to accommodate Bash's many orders, which included finding some sort of bedding for my pet.

We continued our clandestine route upstairs via the back stairs to avoid bumping into anyone. Snow wasn't leashed, and as properly trained as she was, the excitement of being in a new environment was tempting her to explore. Twice, I had to call her back, and although she obeyed, I could tell the poor thing was on the verge of bolting. Her cute button nose was lifted high as she sniffed out the enticing aromas wafting up from downstairs.

Bash's suite was every bit as luxurious as I'd expected. Upon entering, there was an inviting sitting room decorated in shades of blue, buttercup yellow, and cream. A navy blue sofa with recliners on either end faced a fireplace with a large flat-screened television positioned conveniently above the mantelpiece. The butler drew the heavy drapes across the tall windows to give us privacy and pointed out the features of the kitchenette off to one side. He opened the refrigerator to show an assortment of drinks, snacks, and also gave me instructions on the use of the fancy coffee machine on the counter. Bash didn't say a word, allowing his butler to do his job.

An enormous four-poster bed took up center stage in the master bedroom, and my jaw dropped when I saw the size and luxury of the bathroom. There was a sunken tub, large enough to accommodate two grown men, outfitted with massaging water jets, and a glass-enclosed shower stall also designed for two. Dual sinks and a closed off commode to assure privacy was a nice touch. Everything was done in creamy Carrara marble—a favored medium I used for many of my sculptures—with 24-karat gold fixtures.

Although I came from a humble background, my life had improved exponentially as my fame grew. In recent years, I'd traveled the world, staying at many five-star hotels, but they paled in comparison to these luxurious accommodations.

Seeing the way Bash lived pulled me up short. The reality of becoming his consort, with all the privileges afforded to the position—and the subsequent duties it would entail—was unnerving. Did I really want to do this? What started out as an experiment, trying to find the perfect man to fill the empty space in my heart, was turning into a defining moment. My life would never be the same again, and any decision I made going forward would have to be discussed with my prince.

Bash must have sensed my disquiet, because he was by my side within seconds. "What is it? Is there something you need?"

I shook my head, at a loss for words. How could I explain my feelings without sounding like an ungrateful lout? There was definitely a connection between us. I couldn't deny that we were compatible in bed, and he seemed eager to please, judging by his generosity with Snow, but I was dismayed by the daunting choices I would be facing in the next few days. The doctor's examination alone would be a huge invasion of my privacy. I sat down on the edge of the tub and buried my face in my hands.

Sinking down to his knees, Bash leaned into me. Feeling left out, Snow pawed at my leg with a pitiful whine. When I lifted my head, they were both watching me expectantly.

I ended up shaking with nervous laughter. "For heaven's sake, you two are ridiculous."

Snow woofed and wagged her tail at my reaction while Bash said, "What can I do to help?"

I stood and went to wash my hands and face. "I think some dinner and a few shots of that good whiskey will calm my nerves."

"Why are you nervous?" Bash asked, looking stricken. "Are you having second thoughts?"

"Let's just say I'm a little overwhelmed at the moment."

Bash bit his lower lip.

Putting down the hand towel, I leaned over and kissed his forehead. "I'm not going anywhere, ye ken? I've a mild case of the heebie-jeebies."

"Okay," Bash said, exhaling with relief. "Let me run downstairs to make sure my parents know I'm back. Dinner should be ready by the time I return. In the meantime, I'll have the butler bring you a stiff drink."

"That sounds good. Thank you."

While Bash was off doing his princely duties, the butler reappeared with my drink and an impromptu bed for Snow.

"Where would you like me to lay the dog's bedding, sir?" he asked politely.

"Near the sofa," I pointed. "She likes to be close to me. What is your name?"

"You may call me Charles, sir."

"Very well," I said, reaching for the drink. "Thank you for attending to our needs. You've probably never had a houseguest with so much baggage."

"Prince Sebastian has never invited anyone to share his quarters before, sir."

"How long have you been on staff?"

"Since the prince was a young boy."

"So you know him pretty well?"

"I would say so," Charles replied stiffly. "Is there anything else you require?"

"What's the prince like when he's not being so affable?"

"I beg your pardon?"

"Does he have any particular quirks? One thing that usually puts him in a bad mood?"

Forehead wrinkling, Charles glanced at the door. "I really shouldn't...."

"I'm planning to marry him," I blurted. "It would be nice if I knew what to expect."

Charles cleared his throat and gave me a wry smile. "He's not very good at taking orders."

"There's no need to elaborate," I replied. "I've experienced his bossiness already."

"Only when he thinks he's in the right, mind you," Charles clarified. "He'll stand up to anyone who goes against his core beliefs."

"Can you give me an example?"

"The Royal Highnesses have been pushing Prince Sebastian to marry since he was twenty-one, but he resisted. A love match was more important to him than his duty."

Huh. That was interesting. Would our arranged date grow into love? In truth, I was halfway there, but he had no way of knowing that. Or was I missing something?

"Is there anything else, sir?" Charles asked, interrupting my train of thought.

"Has the prince had many boyfriends?"

"None in an official capacity, sir."

"He's never had a steady guy?"

"No, sir."

"I thought there was a whole slew of men before me?"

"You're mistaken, sir. May I leave?"

"Aye, thank you."

"The dinner tray should be here shortly, sir."

"I think I'll wait for the prince, Charles."

"As you wish, sir. Have him ring the kitchen when you're ready."

I nodded, taking another sip of my drink. Staff was always a good source of information, and none better than a butler who was all-knowing when it came to palace shenanigans. I'd been under the mistaken impression that Bash was an inveterate playboy who tossed men aside like last season's fashion. Learning he was a lot more circumspect was reassuring. I was coming to terms with this new information when Bash returned, beaming happily when he saw me sitting on the sofa with Snow by my feet.

"Oh, good," he said when he walked through the door. "You're still here."

"You were expecting otherwise?"

"I wasn't sure," he admitted. "You looked queasy when I last saw you."

I waved away his concerns. "Is everything all right with your parents?"

"Couldn't be better," Bash replied. "Are you ready for dinner?"

Bobbing my head, I told him to pick up the house phone. "Charles says to call when you're back."

Bash grinned. "We must always do what Charles says or get in trouble."

"Does he rule the roost?"

"Mama can't function without him, and the staff would dissolve into chaos if left on their own."

"I'll bear that in mind."

"I thought we could take a walk after dinner, so Snow could take care of business before we retire for the night."

"That's very thoughtful of you, Bash. I was going to slip out on my own."

"I'd love to tag along," Bash said. "There's a secluded area out back that'll meet her requirements."

Conversation ended when Charles, accompanied by two footmen, wheeled in our dinner. The round table was covered in pristine white linen with a tasteful flower arrangement in the center. When everything was laid out, Charles bade us good night and left. The three-course meal was delicious, as I'd expected, and we ate in companionable silence as the footmen hovered, catering to our every need. Bash was relaxed, accustomed to being waited on, while I was once again reminded that my life, as I knew it, would be forever changed.

Now that our immediate needs were met, there was no need to rush, and we strolled through the private gardens watching Snow mark her new territory while we talked about our possible future. There were a few things I had to clarify before I could put my doubts aside. With that in mind, I sank down on the first available bench and patted the empty space beside me.

"Can we talk?" I asked.

His forehead crinkled with worry. "Is this when you tell me you're bailing?"

"Not at all," I said gently, pulling him down beside me. I put my arm around his shoulders and drew him closer. "This evening has far exceeded my expectations."

"Mine as well," he agreed. "I couldn't be more pleased."

"And since we've been frank from the start, I want to get a few things out there so you're not blindsided."

"All right," he responded warily.

"I've never been married, ye ken?"

"Neither have I," Bash said immediately.

"But I've had a few relationships in the past whereas you haven't."

"Says who?"

"Charles."

"He had no right to divulge that information," Bash said defensively, "What does my past have to do with the present anyway?"

"Blending two lives isn't always easy," I reasoned. "I need your assurance that my role as your consort won't interfere with my career."

"I would never ask you to give up your art for me."

"Can you give me a general idea of your expectations?"

"As the next in line to the throne, I'm obligated to attend daily meetings with my father and his ministers to learn the business of running this country. There's no need for you to be a part of that. There are a few charities I endorse, which I hope you'll support, and I would expect you to escort me to any social events. Likewise, if there's anything you'd like me to do to promote your art, feel free to ask. I'm hoping we can share most of our meals, unless something comes up, but we can discuss our daily schedule at breakfast each morning. Oh, and last but not least," Bash added. "No out-of-town trips without me."

"You'd be willing to travel for my work?"

"Absolutely."

"Good to know," I said, nodding. "What about the child?"

"Once the pregnancy is over, you won't be required for anything else. The nannies will handle all of the unpleasant business of being a dad: diaper changes, midnight feedings, and pram duty."

"What if I want to be a part of the *unpleasantness*? I'm not having my child raised by a third party."

"We can certainly talk about that," Bash said cautiously. "I was raised by my nanny and didn't turn out too bad."

"True enough," I acknowledged, "but I'd like to be more than a father figure."

"I agree in principle," Bash said. "It's the details we'll have to work out, and we can't do that until the child is born."

"But you have no objection to becoming a hands-on dad?"

"I might balk at the diaper changing," he said stiffly.

"It's all or nothing," I insisted, laughing at the look of horror on his face.

"You drive a hard bargain, Errol Maitland."

Chapter Nine

SEBASTIAN

Did he seriously expect me to behave like a regular dad? I tried to recall one moment in time when Mama or Papa had put their royal status aside to tackle my daily needs and came up short. This lack of parental bonding hadn't turned me into a sociopath, so why on earth would Errol choose to get involved in the nitty-gritty of child-rearing? I could only surmise it had to do with his own upbringing and not mine. But that was beside the point. I was prepared to compromise, and if Errol put so much importance on these mundane tasks, I would learn how to change a fucking diaper—and do a damn fine job—come what may.

Errol was calmer after our exchange in the garden. For one scary moment, I was sure he'd grab Snow and tell me this was all a mistake—a cosmic joke initiated by my parents in which I was a willing accomplice—but he'd surprised me with his honesty. He could have kept his misgivings to himself, or simply catered to my every whim, standard behavior more common in my world, but he wasn't going down that path. His genuine lack of artifice and ability to exchange views on a wide assortment of subjects made me fall that much harder.

Now it was time to crush the magic pebble. If Errol spent a miserable night on my hand-knotted, double-sided, outrageously expensive, bespoke mattress, then Mama and Papa would be satisfied, and we'd move on to the last and final phase of this courtship. Errol would be examined by the royal physicians to make sure our blood types were compatible, so his uterus wouldn't reject the implanted embryo.

Having the option to engineer our future family had only been possible in the last half century. For some inexplicable reason—and the debate continued to rage as to the how and why this was happening so frequently—most men were being born intersex. They presented as male—with a functioning scrotum and penis—while also harboring a uterus and one or two dormant ovaries. This phenomenon had allowed scientists to expand their research on human reproduction. Male pregnancies were no longer an anomaly, but they didn't occur naturally. Ovaries had to be kick-started with drugs, and the eggs were harvested laparoscopically since most men didn't have vaginas. Getting pregnant without scientific help was impossible; however, once a few important steps were accomplished in vitro, the rest of it proceeded as normal. A caesarian section was performed at the end of gestation and the dynasty was assured.

When Errol had answered the questionnaire, he'd agreed—pending medical consultations—to carry our child. I would have done it if pressed, since I did have the necessary parts, but my parents reminded me in no uncertain terms that a consort was replaceable while a prince wasn't. They couldn't crank out another heir if I died in childbirth. For once, I agreed. The good news was the mortality rate had dropped as methods improved, but like anything else involving medicine and doctors, there was an element of risk.

Being young and fit was a plus, and Errol was the embodiment of good health. And if that didn't convince him to take on the Herculean task, I wouldn't hesitate to remind him that I was a spoiled brat and used to my creature comforts. Having to curtail anything I loved for nine long months, from food to social activity, was bound to turn me into a raving bitch. Errol would have to sell several sculptures to buy me something worthy of my sacrifice, and there wasn't enough bling in the world to compensate for the inconvenience. Judging by our diaper conversation, Errol was far more pragmatic, and I could envision him taking the whole thing in stride. He wouldn't even need new clothes. All he'd have to do was move the buttons on his kilt, and holding a healthy child in his arms would be the only reward he'd expect. I was so sure of this, I was willing to stake my life on it.

Buoyantly optimistic, we hung onto each other, stopping occasionally to kiss with abandon. Snow trotted obediently behind us as we headed back upstairs. After getting her settled for the night, we decided a long soak in the tub was in order. I picked up the phone to ask for help when I felt a firm hand on my wrist.

"What are you doing?" Errol asked, warm breath ghosting over my face.

"Calling my valet."

"Why?"

"To bring refreshments and start our bath."

"I don't need anyone to turn a tap and neither should you," he admonished.

And damn if his scolding didn't make my dick hard.

"What about food?" I squeaked. "And some booze to wash it down?"

"Fruit and cheese would be a verra nice touch," he replied.

"Drinks? Do you have a preference?"

Errol snorted. "Bash, asking a Scot for preferences is a great waste of time."

"Silly me," I murmured. "Whiskey is all you'll ever require."

He winked, and I picked up the palace phone and dialed the number that connected me directly to my valet. After issuing my request, I followed Errol into the bathroom. Our earlier foray had been hurried, and now I watched him strip with growing excitement. His superb physique was reason enough to make nightly baths a ritual, a pleasant way of connecting, and not just in the physical sense. I'd spent many nights soaking in this very tub after a particularly stressful day. The combination of aromatic bath salts, heat, and pulsating water was a godsend, far more beneficial than a shower.

"Are ye planning on joining or watching?"

Wrenched out of my thoughts by Errol's strangled query, I discarded my shirt and shimmied out of the impossibly tight pants, noting with satisfaction that I was getting a rise out of my guest. He bit down on his lower lip, and we stood three feet apart, checking each other out. Hungry eyes tracked me from head to toe, lingering when he got to my package. We wet our lips at the exact same time and cracked up at our shared reaction.

"Come on then," Errol urged, giving me a hand and helping me down the steps into the churning water.

Errol gasped when he stepped in and felt the temperature. "Jaysus, Bash. I'm not sure this heat is good for my bollocks. We don't want the doctors saying my wee swimmers were boiled to death."

"It's no warmer than a regular bath," I maintained. "Man up and sit down. Eric will be here shortly."

Errol sat and cussed at the same time. "Fuck, that's hot. Who in the hell is Eric?"

"My valet."

"I thought Charles was the guy in charge."

"He's the butler and handles everything palace-related. Eric is in charge of my person."

"Your person?" Errol mocked, trying to stifle his laughter. "What exactly do you mean?"

"For God's sake," I huffed. "Eric takes care of my clothes and other intimate stuff."

"Like lube and condoms?"

"Be quiet," I said, splashing water in his face.

He hooked his fingers behind my neck and dragged me over to his side of the tub. I ended up sprawled on his chest like a fish out of water. His erection pressed against my stomach, and I squirmed, trying to get more friction against my own cock. His thigh felt like a granite slab, and I used it to my advantage, humping against it frantically.

"Whoa," he said, pushing me back. "I was hoping we'd last more than five minutes this time."

"You're being generous," I retorted. "I'm already on the brink."

"Let's at least wait until your man has come and gone with our snacks."

"Good point," I said, reluctantly pushing off him.

And just then, there was a faint knock on the bedroom door, and Snow sprang to life, barking her head off.

"Shit!" Errol exclaimed. "We forgot to warn him about the dog."

The cacophony coming from the bedroom increased as Eric entered the suite and Snow's barking escalated. Before we could get out of the tub to restore order, the bathroom door slammed open, and Eric rushed in with Snow fast on his heels.

Errol bellowed at his dog, but her momentum was too great, and she ended up slipping on the marble and sliding into the bathtub with a horrendous splash. Eric watched in horror as water overflowed, and he tried to get out of the way, but he also slipped and landed on his knees, dropping the tray laden with slices of apples and oranges, and three types of cheese. Snow took one look at the bounty and managed to get out of the tub using my thighs for leverage.

Eric looked like he wanted to die, and I couldn't really blame him, but the humor of the situation surpassed any irritation I might have normally felt. Seeing the big wet dog gobbling up the food without an ounce of remorse made me crack up, and Errol joined in, shoulders shaking with glee.

"Your Highness," Eric began. "I'm so sorry."

I waved away his apology. "I should have warned you about the dog. No harm done. Have them clean up this mess and do something with Snow. She'll need a long walk after all the food she's inhaled."

"Will she come with me?" Eric asked apprehensively.

I turned toward Errol. "What do you think?"

"Aye, she'll go, but put her on a leash, or you'll lose her."

"Yes, sir," Eric replied, getting to his feet and straightening his clothes. "I'll be back in a minute."

Ignoring Snow, who was licking up the last of the soft cheese, I turned to Errol. "Your dog is a menace."

Errol chuckled. "She's so cute, though. It's hard to stay angry when she looks at me with so much trust."

"You're a big softie," I accused. "You'll probably be this lenient with our child."

"I'll let you be the bad guy," he replied. "You're used to issuing orders and being imperial."

"As my consort, you'll speak for me at all times," I reminded him. "I hope and expect you to be firm when it's necessary."

"Don't worry," Errol said, lip quirking. "I'll be firm when it counts."

My gaze dropped to his groin, and I could see he was proving his point most effectively. "What is it about my commanding voice that turns you on?"

"I'm not sure, but I like it."

Sliding over to his side of the tub, I placed my hand over his heart and began twisting his damp chest hair around my fingers. "As soon as they clean this room, we'll pick up where we left off."

"Count on it," he said gruffly.

Eric walked in with two footmen, armed with mops and buckets, bringing up the rear. Snow's red leash and collar dangled from Eric's hand, and when she didn't lunge, he fastened the restraint around her neck, murmuring *good girl* in a shaky voice. Meanwhile, the footmen made short order of the mess.

"Make sure you dry Snow off before taking her outside," Errol said. "I don't want her to catch cold."

"Yes, sir," Eric said, tugging on Snow's leash. She didn't budge, looking in her master's direction instead.

"Go with the nice man." Errol ordered.

She wagged her tail and followed Eric out of the bathroom.

"I don't know about you," Errol commented, "but I'm ready to get out of this tub."

"I think you're right. My bed is nice and comfortable, and more importantly, it's dry."

"Let's go."

Eric had redeemed himself by setting up a new tray of fruit and cheese in the living room, along with bottles of water and the good whiskey that so appealed to Errol. I poured generously and we decided to finish our drinks on the sofa before heading to bed. Both of us had shrugged on thick terrycloth robes and, with drinks in hand, sat back to enjoy the peace and quiet while it lasted.

"I hope Eric wears your dog out so she falls asleep when they return."

"She'll be fine. I expect he'll leave her out here if your bedroom door is closed, right?"

"Yes."

"Good. I'm so done with interruptions."

"Right?"

Swallowing the last of his drink in a few gulps, Errol put down his empty glass and reached for me. "Bed?"

I nodded and got up to follow him to the room. Now that this was finally happening, I was a little nervous. Sex between us had been great so far, and this next round would probably be fantastic, which meant Errol would be sated and worn out. If Mama were to be believed, he'd be uncomfortable and unable to get any rest. Was I going to put my future in the hands of some dumb pebble, or forge ahead regardless of the outcome?

Chapter Ten

ERROL

Weeks of anticipation, interrupted by stretches of confusion were about to end as we stared at each other while getting ready for bed. Everything I'd said and done since receiving Bash's invitation had been leading up to this moment, and now that it was finally here, I was nervous.

We stood at the foot of the four-poster, still in our robes, hesitant to make the first move. Bash's cheeks were flushed in patches—communicating his own level of stress—highlighting the perfection of his pale skin. He slipped off his robe and let it puddle at his feet. The blush spread down to his neck and bloomed over his smooth chest. The outward manifestation of his fears calmed me more than anything else this evening. I was the one who'd been chosen to embark on this wondrous journey, the commoner elevated to royal status, and Bash seemed more apprehensive than me.

Stepping closer, I pushed back the golden strands that tumbled around his face, tucking the silky locks around a reddened ear. When I brushed his moistened lips with my thumb, his mouth parted and his tongue darted out, tasting my skin in a sensual sweep that went straight to my cock. I searched the blue depths to see if there was any trace of doubt, but his pupils were blown, the desire was unmistakable. A light brush of his lips against mine tipped the scale, and our energy shifted from a slow crawl to full throttle.

He wrapped his arms around my neck, never taking his mouth off mine, and as our teeth clicked and tongues probed, I backed onto the bed and fell on a pile of throw pillows. My robe was discarded in short order, and I tucked my hands behind my head and spread my legs, inviting Bash to take charge.

He crawled toward me, pausing to rake my chest hair with his fingernails before he reached for my cock. My breathing stuttered when he cupped my balls with one hand and encircled my shaft with the other.

Playfully brushing my pubes, he tickled under my scrotum while keeping an eye on me to watch my reaction. He slid his forefinger toward my hole, teasing the sensitive furl, and moving away just as quickly. I might have let out a disappointed moan because he bit his lower lip, concentrating on repeating the move that elicited such a fine reaction.

Breathlessly, he asked, "You like ass play, big guy?"

"Aye," was all I could muster as I squirmed beneath his touch.

"Me too," he confided. "I can't wait until you fuck me."

And just like that, I was done letting him drive the cab.

Flipping him onto his back, I fumbled for the packet of lube I saw in the silver bowl by the bed, and diligently prepared him before I positioned my cockhead at his entrance.

Looking him right in the eyes, I growled. "Ready, love?"

"Oh, yeah."

Bash sucked in a sharp breath when I pierced him, but he didn't stop me. Encouraged, I kissed him deeply before continuing, angling for that secret spot deep inside him, the one that would shatter him into a million pieces. We hadn't exchanged stats on the men in our past, and I wasn't particularly interested, but I was determined to make this night memorable and give him the ride of his life. He submitted wordlessly, clutching my biceps and meeting each stroke with an upward thrust. As the momentum increased, words began tumbling out of his mouth—harder, faster, please, deeper—urging me on as I took my pleasure.

Our breathing grew more ragged, our hips moving involuntarily against each other. I grasped his cock and began a long, slow pump. His hand joined mine and we began working his shaft while I continued to rock in and out of his deliciously tight hole. He tensed, and his irises looked like shards of lapis lazuli before he erupted in a pulsating gush between us. Feeling his warm cum smeared on our bellies made me lose my stride, and all good intentions to prolong this session for as long as possible evaporated in a spectacular orgasm. My roar was commensurate with the exhilaration that suffused my entire being.

We must have passed out, because when my eyelids fluttered open, I was lying on my back, and my prince was curled up like a bug on the other side of the mattress. I was prepared to get up and make the short walk to the bathroom for a washcloth when I realized I'd already been wiped down. The image of Bash cleaning our combined mess before falling asleep elevated him in my eyes and bolstered my decision to become his consort.

He might be a demanding royal in the presence of others, but between us, at our most intimate, we were equals. All worries ceasedas I realized Bash would do whatever was necessary to make our union work.

I hoped to catch a few hours of sleep before life intruded by way of doctors and contracts, but something was poking me on my backside. Had I fallen asleep on the tube of lubricant? I rolled over to check and didn't see anything. The bottom sheet was askew, not surprising considering the moves we'd undertaken earlier, so I got out of bed and tucked in the corners as best as possible. My side was completely smooth, and although Bash's wasn't, he didn't seem in the least bit perturbed, so there was no point in disturbing him.

Already up, I decided to check on Snow. She was fast asleep in her makeshift bed but lifted her head and gave out a jaw-cracking yawn before going back to sleep. I was pleased she hadn't paid a price for ingesting all that fruit and cheese earlier. I shut our door gently, went to the bathroom to take a piss, and crawled back into bed.

And was miserable.

The annoying bump on my backside persisted despite all my previous efforts. Huffing in irritation, I got up and inspected the mattress. You could bounce a penny off the perfectly stretched fitted sheet. I was certain it was made of the finest Egyptian cotton, with an outrageously high thread count, a lot better than anything I'd ever owned, and yet...the bloody thing was as comfortable as a sackcloth. I made a mental note to speak with Bash in the morning.

I tried a few more times and finally gave up. Grabbing my pillow, I crept out of the room and headed for the sofa. It felt like a cloud after that lumpy mess and I was asleep within minutes. When I woke up, Bash was sitting cross-legged on the floor with tears trickling down his cheeks. I blinked several times, trying to get my bearings. Was he upset because I wasn't in his arms? I had to set him straight. Sitting up, I scrubbed my face with my hands and shook my head to clear the cobwebs.

"What's wrong?"

"Everything is right," he said, wiping his tears with his sleeve. "Things couldn't be any better. I'm assuming you're here because you hated the bed."

I felt like an ingrate, but I refused to lie. "Aye, I've slept better on the floor in my studio."

He burst out laughing, which confused me even more. And to make matters worse, the door opened and Her Royal Highness, Princess Alexandra, walked in with Prince Emile and his retinue trailing behind her. *Jaysus!* These people had no regard for personal boundaries. How was I supposed to observe protocol, and bow in a courtly fashion, when I was sitting on the sofa with nothing but a sheet covering my morning wood?

"Um, Bash," I whispered, giving him a dirty look. "Ye ken I need a minute to get dressed."

He howled with laughter, and I stared, wondering what I'd missed.

"Please don't get up on our regard," the Princess said in a delighted voice as I stared up at her helplessly.

"I couldn't even if I wanted to."

Everyone in the room was smiling from ear to ear, and I was beginning to think these people had lost their collective minds. Was I marrying into a family of lunatics? I turned to Bash. His tears were gone, and in their place was a lovesick expression usually reserved for the morning after a night of successful lovemaking. This was to be expected, not the tears I'd seen a few minutes ago.

Out of sorts, I snapped, "Are you planning to share the joke, or will you leave me in suspense?"

Bash nodded. Turning to the small group, he commanded, "Please, leave us so Errol can dress."

"I'm hungry and we need to get business out of the way before I can have my breakfast," Prince Emile demanded.

"We'll join you in the dining room shortly."

"See that you do," the Prince ordered on his way out.

"What the hell is going on?" I asked, throwing off the sheet. My cock slapped against my belly and Bash smiled.

"Way more than I realized," he said gleefully.

"Don't get any ideas," I grumbled, heading toward the bathroom. Bash and Snow trailed behind me, and after I finished my business and wrapped a towel around my waist, I demanded answers. "Are you going to tell me what just happened out there?"

"Can it wait?"

"Hell, no. Were they checking to make sure I took your maidenhead? If so, they're barking up the wrong tree. You're no more a virgin than I am."

Bash giggled. "That's not it."

"What then?"

"Mama is a witch."

Flummoxed, I asked for clarification. "Why would you say such a thing about your own mother?"

Bash reached for my hand and gently led me back to the living room. He picked up the phone and asked Eric to bring us some coffee and take Snow outside for a walk. All this while I was sitting on the sofa, still wrapped in a towel, wondering if I'd woken up in some alternate universe. I bit my tongue to keep the tirade from spewing out of my mouth, but by the time Eric and Snow departed, I was ready to explode with unanswered questions.

"It's like this," Bash said, sinking down beside me. "I insisted on a love match."

"Aye," I nodded. "It's what you deserve."

He went on to explain how his wish to choose a partner, rather than settle for an arranged marriage, had germinated into a plan concocted by his mother and seconded by the Prince. I could feel the bile rising up from my gut, accompanied by blinding fury.

"You mean to tell me she used magic to make me fall for you?" I shouted.

"No." Bash paled and scooted back. "Nothing like that, Errol. I was given free rein from start to finish, but there was a small caveat Mama insisted upon to make sure I was making the right choice."

"And what the devil might that be?"

After he explained, I headed straight for the bedroom and lifted the mattress, so I could see the evidence of his mother's chicanery for myself.

"See?" Bash said when I snatched a pebble no bigger than a piece of snot in my hands.

"Aye, all too clearly. What would you have done if I'd slept like a babe in your arms? Discarded me like a piece of garbage and tried again?"

"I would have lied," Bash declared boldly. "There's no way in hell I'm giving you up now that I've found you. I love you, Errol."

Placated, I soaked in the words, and my anger vanished as quickly as it emerged.

"Say that again."

"I love you," Bash said, a little louder this time. "You're the one I want."

"No doubts whatsoever?"

"None."

"Well then...."

"You'll stay?" he asked hopefully.

I nodded, and he rushed forward with a cry of relief.

After we pledged our love and commitment in the filthiest way possible, we showered and made our way downstairs. Arm in arm, we walked into the dining room, and I studied the faces of Bash's family looking at me expectantly.

"Is everything all right?" Princess Alexandra asked.

"Fine, Mama. Errol knows about the pebble and is ready to proceed."

"Excellent," Prince Emile stated.

"Hold on," I said, leaning forward. "I have a few ground rules of my own."

"You're hardly in a position to make demands," Prince Emile stated.

"That's where you're wrong," I countered. "Without me, you've got diddly."

Bash snickered.

"Let's hear them," the Prince said, looking at me askance.

"No. More. Magic."

"You have my assurance," Prince Emile said. "I'm not a proponent of witchcraft."

Princess Alexandra waved him off with a disgusted, "Pish posh."

Clearing my throat, I added, "I rule my household."

The Prince and Princess let out startled gasps.

"What Errol means to say—"

"You don't need to explain," I said, cutting Bash off.

"But we're the royal family," Mama interjected. "You can't tell us what to do."

"No, but I will not be subjected to your demands in my own home. If you wish to visit, you'll need an appointment like anyone else. I won't have you barging in whenever you're in the mood."

"Point taken," the Prince conceded.

"I demand a new mattress."

"That won't be a problem," Princess Alexandra agreed. "Although there's nothing wrong with the one you have."

"It's tainted," I reminded her.

She sighed. "Very well."

"We're going on a three-week honeymoon before starting the in vitro process," Bash added. "That's a deal breaker."

"We've waited long enough for a grandchild," Prince Emile thundered.

"Three more weeks won't kill you," Bash retorted. "We want some private time before the doctors get their hands on us."

"I suppose we can put it off a little longer," Princess Alexandra said. "Where are you planning to honeymoon?"

"As far away from here as possible," I said pointedly.

Epilogue

ERROL

After the medical examination, followed by a speedy engagement, subsequent marriage, and memorable honeymoon on the island of Majorca, life, as we knew it, came to a standstill.

Waiting became our new normal.

First it was the hormone shots. They hurt, made me nauseous, and gave me a mild case of acne. Bash swore it didn't detract from my overall appearance, but it was hard to feel like a sex god when my backside was covered in tiny zits.

Then there were constant blood tests to check my estrogen levels. I felt like a pincushion most days, and the very sight of a nurse holding a needle made me want to run in the opposite direction. Even Snow got a bad case of the yips whenever she saw the lady in a white uniform crossing our threshold. As soon as I'd bellow *not again*, Snow would dive underneath the four-poster and whine until the bloodsucker left our suite, vial in hand.

After that, it was ultrasounds to view my newly awakened ovary close up. As it filled with eggs, it would double in size, and once that was accomplished, I'd be ready for the next phase. Harvesting.

God, the word alone made me ill. It had such a bad connotation. Vampires, zombies, and grave robbers in search of body parts always came to mind. I knew I was overly sensitive to the changes occurring within my body, but no one had warned me of hormone therapy side effects. No matter how hard I tried to stop the mood swings, they were out of my control. I could go from zero to maniacal within minutes, and puking had turned into my favorite pastime. I lived on soda crackers, green apples, and mineral water, which only added to my frustration. I was a carnivore, a steak and potato man from the word go, and having to subsist on rabbit food because my innards were rebelling turned me into an ornery bastard.

There was no reasoning with me once my temper flared or the nausea hit. My respect for the entire female population grew tremendously as I slowly submerged into the uncomfortable realm of hot flashes, cravings, and tender nipples. What a fucking nightmare. And it was only going to get worse.

Bash did his best to keep me on an even keel, employing every sexual trick in his vast arsenal, but no one warned us that my libido would tank. I felt unattractive and too focused on what was happening within my body to think about getting off.

"This is temporary," the doctor assured me. "Your sex drive will return once this first phase of in vitro is over."

I literally rolled my eyes. The thought of anyone touching me anywhere made me want to pick up a chair and hurl it through a closed window.

Poor Bash. He was frustrated on so many levels. After the wonderful time we'd spent basking in the sun and making love whenever the urge hit— at least four or five times a day— he'd become accustomed to a certain level of sensuality, and to go from overload to deprivation was a dirty trick neither of us had expected.

Nevertheless, he was determined to weather the storm and participate in this pregnancy as much as possible. Putting up with my mood swings was part of his job. He stayed out of my way for the most part and crawled back when the coast was clear. My wishes were usually granted no matter how outrageous. Pickles at midnight, handmade fudge from Ireland, and Scottish shortbread were only a few of the things on my list. The irony was once the craving was satisfied I ended up hurling.

Notwithstanding the long list of demands prior to our marriage, there was nothing Bash wouldn't do now that I was his consort. He was everything I'd hoped for in a partner and invariably put my needs before his own.

"Why are you being so nice to me?" I asked one evening when I'd had a particularly rough day.

"Survivor's guilt," he admitted. "Seeing you under the weather makes me feel like the world's biggest slacker. I should be the one jumping through hoops to produce an heir."

"Aye, but we both know that's never going to happen. Don't worry. You'll pay for this when the kid's born."

"How?"

"You can take the night shift for feeding."

"We'll have several nannies, Errol."

"I want you to bond with our child. Daytime isn't ideal because of your royal duties, so you'll have to suck it up, like all the new dads in the world, and get your arse out of bed when you hear your son's angelic voice screaming for his next bottle at three in the morning."

Bash grinned. "If he's anything like you, they'll hear him clear across the Pyrenees."

"Don't make him wait and you'll be fine."

"Let's have the baby before we start to negotiate."

Harvesting day finally arrived, and Bash accompanied me to the hospital, where I underwent the minor procedure. I was in and out of the operating room in less than an hour, and we were back at the palace by the end of the day. Once again, we played the waiting game. Now our future child was in the hands of the mad scientists as I'd started calling the team in charge of making this work.

Under a microscope, they watched as Bash's sperm fertilized my egg, and once that was accomplished, the resulting zygote was left to grow for a few days before it would be implanted in my womb. Assuming it worked. If the egg and sperm failed to fertilize for whatever reason, the procedure would be repeated.

Fortunately, that wasn't the case, so it was back to the operating room for me, and our baby was implanted in my uterus. Aaand...we were back to waiting.

The shocking news that our zygote had split in utero, and I was now carrying identical twins, made me quake with fear.

"How does that even work?" I asked, horrified by this turn of events.

"The same way any other pregnancy works," the doctor said, "only now we have to worry about three people instead of two."

"Sorry?"

"You, the heir, and the spare."

I turned to Bash who'd let out a squeak of triumph. "How dare you look so happy when I'm going to swell up like a fucking toad?"

"I can't help it," Bash said, beaming. "We'll surpass everyone's expectations. I knew you were special."

Okay. Hearing that made me feel a bit better, although the fear didn't dissipate. This was going to be a challenge in more ways than I'd ever dreamed. Was I up to the task?

Frowning in concern, I turned to Bash. "I expect you to be at my beck and call twenty-four hours a day."

"Sweetheart," Bash said, getting down on his knees beside my chair. "You can milk this all you want. My family and I will be eternally grateful for your sacrifice."

"Fuck eternity," I grumbled. "I want something in this life."

"Name your price," Bash said. "What can I get you to make this worth your while?"

"I have nine months to think about it, aye?"

"You do, and I'll be taking notes the entire time."

"Why?"

"You'll probably change your mind as things get more difficult."

"Count on it," I said irritably. "The worst part of this is losing my sex drive."

Bash sighed. "Don't remind me."

The longing in his voice set me on fire, and my cock stirred for the first time in a while. I reached for Bash's hand and let it rest on the growing bulge. The smile on his face was priceless.

"How's that for timing?" I asked, grinning happily.

Eyes sparking with desire, Bash snaked a hand up my thigh. "May I?" he asked hopefully.

"Aye, and quickly, mind you. Timing is everything at this stage."

He beamed with joy, and I basked in the glow of his approval. We would live happily ever after, just like he promised on our wedding night, babies, bottles, and diapers be damned.

Acknowledgements

A huge shout out to my friend and copilot, Jeannie, for editing my early drafts. To my dedicated team of beta readers—Sharon, April, Shaz, and Jason—thank you for watching my back. Your ongoing support is priceless.

About the Author

Mickie B. Ashling is the pseudonym of a multifaceted woman who is a product of her upbringing in multiple cultures, having lived in Japan, the Philippines, Spain, and the Middle East. Fluent in three languages, she's a citizen of the world and an interesting mixture of East and West. A little bit of this and a lot of that have brought a unique touch to her literary voice she could never learn from textbooks.

By the time Mickie discovered her talent for writing, real life got in the way, and the business of raising four sons took priority. With the advent of e-publishing—and the inevitable emptying nest—dreams of becoming a published writer were resurrected and fulfilled in April 2009.

Mickie discovered gay romance in 2002 and continues to draw inspiration from the LGBTQA community and their ongoing struggle to find equality and happiness in this oftentimes skewed and intolerant world. Her award-winning novels have been called "gut-wrenching, daring, and thought provoking." She admits to being an angst queen and making her characters work damn hard for their happy endings.

Email: mickie.ashling @gmail.com

Facebook: www.facebook.com/mickie.ashling

Twitter: @MickieAshling

Website: www.mickieashling.com

Instagram:@mickieashling

Blog: www.mickiebashling.blogspot.com

Other books by this author

Third Son
Through My Own Lens

Also Available from NineStar Press

Connect with NineStar Press

Website: NineStarPress.com

Facebook: NineStarPress

Facebook Reader Group: NineStarNiche

Twitter: @ninestarpress

Tumblr: NineStarPress